The One and True Son

A novel

Laurence Ballengee

Copyright © 2022 by Laurence Ballengee

All rights reserved. No part of this publication may be reproduced, distributed, or transmitted in any form or by any means including photocopying, recording, or other electronic or mechanical methods without the prior written permission of Laurence Ballengee except it the case of brief quotations embedded in articles or reviews and certain other noncommercial uses permitted by copyright law.

This book is a work of fiction, and the characters and events in this book are fictitious. Any similarity to real persons, living or deceased, is purely coincidental and not intended by the author.

ISBN: 9798817154429
Library of Congress Number: 2022918480

First Edition Paperback Edition November 2022
Cover Design by Pierre Luc Beaudry

Printed by Amazon in the USA

DEDICATION

This book is dedicated to Ms. Gerri Troisi-Torres

CONTENTS

ONE
The Farmer..2
The Carpenter 8
The Doctor..11
The Mother 16
The Twins 21
The Vender 24
The Brothers 30

TWO
The Student..34
The Prophet..42
The Adversary 50
The Waiter 60
The Reporter 72
The Healer 87
The Heretic 118

THREE
The Moreh 152
The Dover 175
The Dissenter 194
The Terrorist 213
The Investigator 219
The Mechanism 233
The Cop 238
The Dissenter 245
The Investigator 253
The Dissenter 258
The Denier 265

FOUR
The Dreamer 318
The Investigator 344
The Defender 352
The Mechanism 364
The Dissenter 420

FIVE
The Defender 428
The Witness 466

ACKNOWLEDGEMENTS

Thank you to my wife, Lily, and my daughter, Charli, for their encouragement and love.

Thank you to Steve Rast and Ron Tuchin for your proofreading efforts. You made this a better book.

Thank you to Dr. Sherella Cupid and Ariana Williams for your insights in building female, Black characters when I am neither. I'm so proud of you both.

Thank you to Dr. Erica Deluca for your insights into the early chapters of the novel.

Thank you to my big brother, Scott, for reading my novel and encouraging me. You've never let me down.

Thank you to Diana Myers for taking the time to proofread the rather long manuscript. You may have "old eyes," but they are wise. Thank you for everything you've done for me over the years.

Thank you to Dr. Melissa Dunphy for her lifesaving formatting of this manuscript. You are truly wonderful.

The One and True Son

PREFACE

The novel to follow is just that—a novel. It is not intended as a critique of Christianity, nor, for that matter, an endorsement. It is simply a retelling of the Christ story as it may have been told if it were set in modern times. As is the case with all novels, it is a series of *what ifs*. What if He was born in the Twentieth Century? *What if* He performed what could be only described as miracles? *What if* He was viewed as a threat by the powerful and connected. These questions drove the creation of this novel.

ONE

The Farmer

Dave Hampton had to stop. The tall man with the woolly hair hadn't stuck his thumb out or even looked up at Hampton's clunky Ford F-150 pick-up as it rattled down Ensign Road on the way back from downtown Ennis. The very pregnant woman with him *had* looked up and that was enough for Dave. He pulled to the shoulder, his nearly new tires crunching in the gravel just beyond the couple and the two pieces of luggage at their feet.

"Where you headed?" Dave asked as the tall man approached.

"Not quite sure," the tall man said. "We been traveling a bit, trying to find work."

Dave looked at the big man's hands. They were gnarled, calloused and dry. "What kind of work do you do?"

"I'm a carpenter by training," the man said, "but I'll do anything Yahweh puts in front of me."

Hampton didn't know whether the religious reference was a good thing or a bad one. He'd heard many a scoundrel start- off talking about God only to find the guy's hand in his pocket later. But those big hands and the couple's simple faded clothing told Dave that these people were real. There was no game played here.

The farmer looked back at the woman standing behind the truck. She faced the road, and her profile revealed the lateness of her pregnancy. Her loose dress bulged out in front of her, both at her milk-heavy breasts and where the baby, had to be a 10 pounder, waited to make its entrance into this world.

"How far along is she?" Dave asked.

The carpenter looked to the sky for a moment. "Eight and a half, maybe almost nine months."

"You don't know?" asked Dave. "What's her doctor say?"

"Doctor?" the big man asked.

The One and True Son

* * *

What exactly is going on in my head? the farmer asked himself.

Dave continued on to his farm with the carpenter and pregnant woman bouncing on the truck's bench seat next to him. Now, he knew that he was no sucker. He didn't give his change to people on street corners no matter how pathetic their hand-written signs or dirty their clothes were. He knew those people would just drink or shoot up his money and he worked too hard for it to just give it away like that. So, what was he doing here? The man hadn't asked him for a ride. They hadn't even stuck their thumbs out. And yet, here he was taking them… taking them where? To his farm? That was going to be a problem. He'd open his house to them, but he wasn't sleeping in it himself. About a week back, he was surprised to find a scorpion in his work boot. Luckily, out of habit, he'd shaken the boot before he put it on. He used the sole of the boot to crush the life out of the threatening looking bug. It was a striped bark, the only kind of scorpion in this part of Texas to his knowledge. He'd seen maybe four or five of them in his life and he was an Ennis boy, born and raised. So, he was more than a little surprised when one scampered out of the cabinet where he stored his coffee cups. Later, he drowned one in his claw-foot bathtub before he stepped into it to take his morning shower. And then they seemed to be everywhere.

He called an old exterminator buddy of his to come and take a look. Buck, a childhood friend who carried his baby fat but not most of his teeth into middle age, explained that scorpions like to hide in crooks and cracks in the house. He could spray, but it probably wouldn't help.

"Naw," Buck explained. "Them nasty little buggers can hide from most of the stuff I kin throw at 'em. You got a lot of 'em too. Ain't never seen so many in one house. Naw, I should throw a tent up over your house and gas me'. You gotta take the food out and any fluffy pillows and such. Bring the stuff into yer barn. Naw, I'll gas me'. Get every one of them motherfuckers."

At present, Dave Hampton's house looked like a huge, badly wrapped birthday present. He, his basset, Putter, and all his food goods now resided in his tractor barn, a large almost freshly painted structure about 50 yards from his back door. He'd remodeled it and modernized it, a few years back, putting in an office with air conditioning and a multi-line phone. He'd even strung antenna cable from his house TV aerial to a decent sized color set so he could watch the Cowboys on Sundays. The office walls he put up kept the diesel smell from his tractors to a minimum and held the warm air from the space heaters he used in the winter in a manner that may be described as cozy. He had plenty of room for a cot and his clothes and that was where he was living as he thought about putting up two strangers, one of them bursting with a child.

"A shame a hardworking man can't find steady work nowadays," Dave said, breaking the silence in the cab of the truck. "That damned peanut farmer mucked up everything. Reagan'll fix us up, I expect."

The carpenter said nothing, and the woman just looked out at the road ahead of them.

What were these people?

Dave's thought immediately shamed him. He wasn't raised that way. His daddy taught him that any man, be he black, red, or purple, who was willing to work for his dinner was worthy of his respect. He'd hired many a migrant worker up from the crushing poverty in Mexico or trying to get away from the commies in Nicaragua and they all worked hard, real hard. He always paid more than the other farms around Ennis and Waxahachie. Word spread and he always got the hardest workers.

But what were these people? The man had nappy hair like a black man, but his face was narrow with ropey muscles that flexed on both sides of his jaw when he spoke. His nostrils were small by African standards and hinted at some whiteness in his genes. His skin was more caramel than chocolate.

The woman. Well, the woman was beautiful. Even big and pregnant like that. She was more olive skinned than the man and though she had probably been on the road for days, her hair spilled to her shoulders in perfect, soft, ebony waves. Her cheek bones said Indian, maybe. Her thicker lips were from someplace else. But it was her eyes that made her truly special. Dave found himself seeking those deep black eyes out, trying to get her to look at him...just look. This desire was not sexual, Dave knew, but something much deeper. Somehow, he knew that if she looked at him for more than a moment she would see him entirely, and somehow, he knew that she would smile if she did. He wanted that. He would never say it, but he wanted that.

"I have some work you could do around the farm, if you like. I can't pay an awful lot. The problem is-well I'm living in my barn." Dave laughed at what he said, how it sounded. "I mean I'm getting some work done in the house. I suppose you two could bed down in the office. I could set up something by the tractors for me."

For the first time the woman spoke. "We can sleep by the tractors," she said. "You've been so kind. We're used to sleeping where we can."

Dave looked at the woman who looked back at him.

She smiled.

The One and True Son

Dave Hampton had lived on his farm his entire life. His father had done the same and his father's father too. Farming was his only choice in life, and he'd never questioned it. It was hard work, but Hampton relished it. Farming was the reason he ate well, the reason he was quite fit for his age, and sadly, probably the reason he would be alone the rest of his life. He had been with a few women, a couple for what some might consider long term relationships, but no matter how pretty they were, or how much fun they were to talk to at night after a nice steak and a couple glasses of wine, the farm had always come first. Bedtime was always early, and for sleep. Morning was always before the sun came up.

Dave inherited the farm in 1968. He was only 22 at the time but working the 300 acres of cotton fields and renting the 30 horses they had for horseback lessons was as familiar to him as breathing. It had just been him and his father since he was little, so the work didn't change much after his father's death. It just got lonelier.

As he pulled onto Basinger Road, the last of the turns he had to make before turning on to his property, where, spread out in front of them was his house, his equipment barn, his stables and the land that defined him, he decided he actually welcomed the idea of having guests. It was going to be tough though with a baby in the mix. Hampton had always been healthy. He couldn't remember the last time he'd been down with anything worse than a headache. He didn't have a doctor. He never needed one. What'll he do if she goes into labor?

He looked to the couple as they surveyed his place. "I think we can all be comfortable here," he said.

They got out of the truck. The couple stood staring at the huge red and blue tent that hid his home from view.

"Got some pests in the house I had to get rid of," he said. "It should be just a couple of days."

He steered them to the equipment barn, a large, corrugated aluminum building he had constructed in the '70s. Hampton never noticed before how the smell of diesel fuel and axle grease permeated the air, but he smelled it now. It was better in the office, but not much.

He took them in the office. "As I said, you can bed down in here. I can't have guests sleeping in that stink. Your baby'll think you're sleeping in a gas station."

"We wouldn't think of it, Mr…" the soon to be mother said.

"Call me Dave," Hampton said. "Dave Hampton. Nobody calls me mister. I'd never know you were talking to me." He smiled. "And you are?"

The One and True Son

"I'm Maria," she said, offering her hand to shake. "My husband's name is Joe."

"So now that we're all acquainted," Dave said, "you'll accept the sleeping arrangements?"

"Honestly Dave," the carpenter spoke, "we wouldn't be comfortable in here. I don't mean to sound ungrateful, but I'm not sure that the fumes would be good for Maria or the baby. I saw another barn outside. What you got in there?"

Dave laughed. "You think it stinks in here? That's the horse stables. I've got six horses in there. Wouldn't be a Texas farm without horses. Their hygiene leaves a lot to be desired."

"Is it heated?" Joe asked.

"Well yeah," Dave answered. "But stables? I'd be embarrassed to tell anybody I'd even offered a pregnant woman a place with the horses."

"Oh, but we love horses," the woman said. "We love animals, Mr. Hampton."

"Dave," Hampton corrected her.

"Dave." Maria smiled. "You stopped for us. You've offered all you have. We'd be honored to sleep in your stables. Joe can help you with any work you need done around here. He knows a little bit about everything. He's strong too. We won't be more trouble than we already are. We're just tired. We need a place to lay our heads for a few days. And I'm…" She looked down at her near-bursting belly.

The farmer laughed. "Yes, you are."

The Carpenter

Joe was worried about the stable. It was well heated and well maintained. The horses were boarded at the opposite end of the cavernous wooden structure in clean stalls stocked with sweet, fresh hay. Their end, the end where the farmer had placed a queen-sized mattress on the dirt floor, a simple white bedstand and hissing propane lantern, hadn't seen a four-legged resident in some time. Dave had taken a removable divider out to widen the stall so they would have more room. The floor was as clean as some of the houses they'd stayed in.

But he worried just the same. Maria was going to have her baby any day now. He was sure of that. He was also pretty sure that that birth wouldn't take place in a maternity ward. They didn't have any insurance and he had no idea where the nearest hospital was. But they had done what they had been told to do and so far, it worked out for them. Dave had stopped for them, hadn't he?

But a stable? A stable?

Maria and Joe met at the United Temple of Moses three years prior. He'd been a devoted attendee of the temple, but from the day Maria walked into the old, converted storefront looking to serve Yahweh, he could think of little else. He had only lived in Travis City, the second largest city in southern Texas, known for its beautiful river walk and history of battle in the struggle with Mexico for independence, for about six months and meeting her made his move all the more worth it. Their relationship was strictly platonic at first. They'd go grocery shopping or walk along the river with its Spanish arched bridges and colorful potted flowers. They talked about spiritual matters and today's children. She had an easy laugh. And she feared nothing. "Fear is doubt in Yahweh," she would say. "And I never doubt. He is always there. If he wasn't, we would've been gone a long time ago."

The One and True Son

Her confidence spread to him easily like body heat under a blanket and things he had done since his youth, overindulging in liquor and sleeping with the occasional willing woman faded away and blurred in his memory as if he had dreamed it. She became everything to him.

He certainly didn't expect her to say yes when he proposed to her. They hadn't even kissed yet, although they'd held hands occasionally. The romance, as far as Joe knew, at that point, had only occurred in his mind.

He chose a beautiful spring day to ask her. He took her on one of their walks; he'd found a spot on the river walk without much traffic and invited her to sit next to him. They dangled their legs over the slow-moving water, she with her shoes off, her small feet almost tickling the water, he in his steel-toed work boots, the only shoes he had at the time. She wore a blue poncho that matched the depth and brightness of the sky and as usual, she soothed him just with her presence.

"Maria," he said. "You know I don't have anything, so I hope you don't mind what I'm about to say."

Maria nodded, looking at her feet and the water flowing below them.

"I don't have the right, I know…" Joe trailed off.

Maria playfully kicked her feet. "Were you going to say something or were you going to ask me something?"

"Do you know what I'm thinking?" Joe asked.

"I know it's important. You always get this wrinkle in your brow when you talk about important things. It's very cute."

Joe's face turned hot. He was grateful she didn't look at him, but at her feet as they reached for the cool water below. Did she call him cute? It was the first flirtatious word he'd ever heard her use.

"Well, it is important. And, yes, it's more of a question." He took a breath. "I've been thinking an awful lot about you. About us…You know?"

"Joe. Why do you have such a difficult time talking to me? Don't you trust me?"

"Of course, I trust you," he protested. "That's the thing. You always make me feel good. And that's why… I want to ask you… But I don't have anything. I'm a good carpenter. I work hard. Is that enough?"

"Enough for what?" Maria smiled. She knew the answer.

"My wife…" Joe stammered. "Enough for you to be my wife."

"Is that all?" Maria laughed.

"Is that all?" Joe exclaimed.

The One and True Son

The ceremony was to be performed at the temple, two weeks from the day he'd proposed. But, two days before their scheduled nuptials Joe called Maria as he did every day, from a bank of pay phones not far from the temple. He got no answer. He tried later in the day, in early evening, but still the phone rang, unsatisfied. Normally, Joe wouldn't have been too concerned. She'd missed his calls before. She may have been running errands for the ceremony. But in all the time he'd known her, she never missed his call twice. And their wedding was less than 48 hours away. If anything, he would've thought they'd have spoken more than less. After his third attempt, just after 10pm, Joe was beyond worried and racing towards panic.

The Doctor

Joe wasn't the only one worried about the stable. Dave Hampton ruminated over it as soon as he put the couple in there. The woman was going to deliver any minute. Anyone could see that. And he had no experience with pregnant women or newborn babies. He'd assisted the vet when one of his mares foaled a couple of years back. Dave was up to his shoulders in amniotic fluid by the time it was all over. The colt turned out all right. Got a good price for him when he grew a bit.

But he knew that a little baby coming into the world was much more complicated. The man, Joe, he said his name was, said they had no doctor; they probably had no insurance. Once again, he found himself asking himself just what in the hell he was doing. Could these people sue him if something went wrong? Should he call an ambulance? The police?

No, he couldn't do that. He knew that as strongly as when he knew that he had to pull over and pick them up in the first place. They needed him and for some reason, he needed to help them.

He thought of Robbie King.

The name popped into his head out of nowhere. He hadn't talked to Robbie for months, maybe a year, but he saw him all the time when the weather got bad, especially when it looked like a twister might be forming. Robbie had grown up in Ennis, just as Dave had, but he'd gotten out. He was the class valedictorian at Ennis High School, gone to Princeton, pre-med. Once again, at the top of his class, Robbie got into Johns-Hopkins Medical School and by the time he was 28, he was a full-fledged doctor with a shiny pedigree.

Then, a few years back, in July, disaster came to Ennis. Robbie's family, his two brothers, mom and dad, were farmers, like just about everybody around the area. His family was close but never faulted Robbie for wanting to change up and be a doctor. Maybe they harbored some hope that he'd bring himself back from Baltimore and hang up his doctor's shingle. Hell, Ennis barely had a Band-aid let alone a certified doctor.

They ran about a hundred head of cattle, grew some soybeans and maybe some cotton every other season. Between the two younger boys and their mom and dad, they kept things running well enough so Robbie could do what he was called to do. If it got too much, sometimes they'd hire a hand or two from south of the border and work them through to harvest or slaughter. The family was about as happy as any in Texas.

The day had been oppressively hot. In the morning, the sky was the color of a robin's egg, cloudless and hard, but by close to three o'clock, thunderheads formed in the West. The sick green of a twister took over by 3:05 and the storm sirens blared. Every farm here had a storm cellar; Dave was in his praying to Yahweh that his barn and horses would still be attached to the earth when he emerged from his underground vault. He had good reason for concern, because the tornado that punished Ennis from the heavens that day was a T-5, the top of the destructive scale, and ripped the town up as if it had done something to offend it. The storm flattened most of the buildings on the main drag, some of which had stood as long as the town existed. It picked up a semi tractor-trailer driven by a man foolish enough to sprint down US 45 with the notion that he might outrun the monster and flung it halfway to Waxahachie. The damn fool wasn't killed for his stupidity though. He was scratched and bruised, and his rig was a goner. Sometimes the Creator rewards the ignorant and the foolish.

There were only two people that day with the unfortunate distinction of being classified a fatality. That fell to Robbie's parents.

No one knows exactly why the couple, veterans of many storms, didn't take cover in their shelter. Their two non-doctor sons were in Corsicana picking up some feed for the cattle and some other more trivial supplies. The sky looked a little bruised where they were, but they hadn't been aware of what they were driving back to until they were stopped at police blockade at Ennis's outskirts. When they finally maneuvered through the carnage of the only town they'd ever called home, they found that their place, the house, the barns, cattle, all evidence that they'd ever lived there, erased.

As they surveyed their legacy, the clouds left, and the sun came out again. The sunlight in their eyes seemed to mock them.

When Robbie came home to bury his parents, he had no intention of going back to Baltimore. With all his learning and practice, in the end he could do nothing for the people who'd mattered to him most. He left his practice and started studying. He learned terms like "coherent pulse" and "continuous wave." He bought a new Winnebago and put a strange antenna on the top of it. He learned all about the "Doppler Effect" and its uses in weather radar. Maybe he couldn't bring back his parents, but he could try to save others from experiencing his pain.

Many an evening from early spring to late summer Robbie could be seen parked out on the shoulder of the interstate, just watching. He'd learned everything he could about super cells and updraft, cloud rotation and windshear. He watched and waited with a marine weather radio at his mobile home's kitchen table and a CB tuned to the emergency channel that he knew the cops monitored.

Luckily for Dave and the couple occupying his stable, it was as far from tornado season as it gets in Texas, and he was able to get Robbie on the phone rather than hunting him down on US 45.

"Dave. I gotta ask you. Have you lost your mind?"

"I know, Robbie, I know. It's totally insane what I'm doing. I can't explain it. I just...have to."

Robbie sighed. "I know I'm going to regret asking this, but I might as well get it over with. Uh, why are you calling me?"

"'Cause you're a doctor." Dave answered.

"Was a doctor," Robbie corrected.

"You mean to tell me that after going to all those fancy schools and sticking your fingers in god-knows-what orifices in god-knows-how many different people that you just forgot it all."

"I haven't practiced in years. I haven't kept my license current."

"So you don't have it to lose," Dave offered.

"I have everything else. Dave, you know that practicing medicine without a license is a felony."

"Okay, so don't practice it," Dave said. "Just come over and look at her. Tell me what to do. You don't even have to talk to her if you don't want to. I just need some advice."

Robbie had some advice. Tell them to hit the road. But he and Dave knew that neither one of them could do that.

"I'll be over in a little bit," Robbie said.

"Thanks Robbie," Dave said and hung up. He didn't want to tell him not to take too long, but he hoped to Yahweh that he wouldn't.

* * *

" You've got to get her to hospital right away." Robbie had pulled the man he assumed was the father out of the mother-to-be's earshot. The woman's

The One and True Son

amniotic sac had ruptured all over the mattress Dave had provided for them. He really, really didn't want to be the delivering ex-physician.

"I tried to tell her that maybe that was good idea. I said they probably wouldn't turn us away. She wouldn't hear it."

Robbie knew that was true. He'd heard the conversation. She'd said that everything would be fine. That this was the way it was supposed to be. He hoped Dave hadn't picked up a couple of nuts.

"Robbie. You'd better get over here!" cried Jack, Robbie's brother. Robbie brought him and his other brother Donnie for moral support. There wasn't much on TV, so they agreed. When Robbie walked back over to the mattress, he saw what he really didn't want to see. The woman had drawn her knees up and had hooked her arms behind them, pulling them back. About an inch and half of the top of baby's head was presenting itself to the world. She was crowning.

"Oh crap," Robbie muttered. He knew that for the immediate future he would be Dr. King again. He would've liked to at least wash his hands, but there was no time. This baby was coming, and it didn't care how clean the world was when he got there. He kneeled between the pregnant woman's legs.

"Now, Miss I need you to..."

"Maria," the woman said. "My name is Maria, doctor."

Her words struck Robbie in a way he would never be able to describe. Her face was nearly purple and distorted, sweat ran off her forehead in tiny rivers, yet she was serene in her speech. It was as though she was meeting him at a dinner party or a pleasant get-together.

"I'm ... I'm not a ..." he started to tell her of his license's status but thought better of it. Perhaps he could tell her his life's story after she delivered the placenta. He snickered and that surprised him.

"It's very nice meeting you, Maria. You're almost done here. In a minute, I'm going to need you to push."

"I know what I'm doing, Robert. Jessie will be here in a moment. It'll be a moment that you'll never forget."

The Mother

Robert? Robbie? Why am I always so formal? She didn't mean to be. She had been as long as she could remember. Even back in El Salvador, as a little girl on the coffee plantation where her father worked, where she refused to use children's nicknames: Rafael was never Rafa. Alejandra, never Aleja. The others thought her standoffish. She never meant it that way.

It struck her that these were odd thoughts to have as she was about to give birth to her son, to His son. She felt the pressure on her pelvis, the widening of her cervix to make way for the son of Yahweh, the wetness as her buttocks sloshed around in the soaked sheets in which she lay. But those sensations, the pain, the tactile issues that childbirth provoked, were pushed to the back of her mind, as if they were being experienced by someone else. She knew that God didn't want her to suffer. That was not her role. Not yet anyway.

And like knowing Robert's name without being introduced, she knew many things without being told them. She knew that she would have a special purpose in this world, even though she had very little formal education. She knew that a man was waiting for her somewhere; she knew his face, his voice, his gentle manner, years before she saw him in the flesh at the storefront temple. She had known many things, but some she preferred not to think about.

She didn't know the purpose that Yahweh had intended for her until a week before her wedding to Joseph. She thought that maybe she was fulfilling this just by marrying this kind, gentle man. She was as happy as any bride-to-be, thinking of him moving in with her, them making a home. Perhaps they would move out of her apartment. If Joseph got some steady work, perhaps they could buy a small house somewhere and even start a garden.

It was with those thoughts that she went to bed that night.

The One and True Son

She'd been sleeping for perhaps an hour when she heard a whisper: "Despierta, Maria."

She woke but kept her eyes closed. She listened to the room, trying to remember if she left the window open. The whisper could've come from outside. Could she have heard a car go by or an evening breeze rustling the curtains? She prayed for that to be the case. She wasn't going to open her eyes.

"Despierta, mi hija." the whisper came again. "Open your eyes child. I have great news for you. Don't be afraid. You know you don't have to be afraid."

Maria checked her feelings, and the whisper was right. She needn't fear. She knew that now. Maria opened her eyes, sat up in her bed and scanned the room. At first, she didn't see the tall, slim figure sitting in the corner on the chair, just to the left of the window. The streetlight outside cast his features in shadow. She could make out what appeared to be a thin beard and long hair.

"Are you happy, Maria?" this man asked in a soft voice. "Your big day is coming. You must be excited."

Maria leaned toward the man trying to get a better look. "How do you know so much? Have you been following me?"

The man laughed and the volume startled the sleepy woman. He apologized.

"Yes, I've been following you, mi hija. I've been following you your whole life. I was the one who chose you. You are a special woman. You are a most special woman."

Maria swung her legs around from under the bedclothes and sat on the edge of the bed, facing the stranger.

"You chose me?" she asked. "You chose me for what?"

"You never answered my question. Are you happy, Maria?" the stranger said.

"You've been following me," she said. "What do you think? Do I talk like a happy woman? Do I act like one?"

The man laughed again. "People can conceal their unhappiness. They can smile at everyone, pet the neighbor's dog, help an old lady across the street. And yet they may be miserable, mi hija. Is this true?"

Maria had to admit that it was.

"But you are happy, aren't you Maria?"

Even in the shadow she could see him smile. His teeth were almost luminous. She felt a warmth she had felt before. She'd felt it on the lonely ride in the banana truck, the one her father had placed her in after bribing the driver to take her up through Mexico and eventually past the Rio Grande to Texas. She'd felt it in the orphanage where she had spent most of her teenage years, working out in the garden when most of the other children occupied themselves with basketball or talking about boys they had met at dances.

"Yes, I am happy. I really am."

"I know," the stranger said. "That is why I picked you. That is why you are so very special."

"Joseph makes me very happy. If you've been following me, you must know this too. He is the one I've been waiting for."

"I know this too, mi hija."

"So, to what do I owe this visit?" Maria asked.

The man smiled. "You are so special, Maria. A stranger appears in your bedroom while you're sleeping, and yet you are unafraid. He says he has been following you and knows much about you and you ask, 'To what do I owe this visit?' This is why I chose you, hija. You do not fear. And why is this?"

"Yahweh," Maria answered him, again knowing the answer the stranger wanted. She told the truth.

"Yes, hija! Yahweh! That is exactly right. You never question your life. You put absolute trust in your God. This is essential in my choice!"

The woman shifted on the bed. "You keeping saying you chose me. Am I going to learn what it is I'm to do?

"Of course, hija. Of course. But please understand that what your Father is asking of you is not going to be easy. It will at once be joyful and painful. No other woman, or man for that matter has been asked to do as much. For Him. For the world."

Maria didn't know how to respond to this. After all, was this really happening? Was she sleeping? Was this tall man with the thin beard and the glowing smile actually speaking to her in her room? "Please tell me why you're here."

"Of course," the man said. He looked concerned. He moved from the corner where he'd been sitting and started pacing the room. He was even taller than she had first thought. His shoulders were thin but muscled. His hands were long with slender fingers. "This isn't easy, Maria. So much depends on it. First, let me introduce myself. My name is Gabriel. I am the messenger of the Most High. I come to tell you that you are going to help Yahweh give a great gift to the world. You know your Torah?"

"You know I do," Maria smiled.

Gabriel smiled, acknowledging her acceptance of what he'd told her so far.

"Yes. Yes, I do. Then you are familiar with term meshiach?"

Maria again questioned whether she was awake. Could this be happening? "It is the term for the "Anointed One," Maria said softly.

"Correct!" Gabriel cheered. "I knew you were the right one. This is correct. The Anointed One."

Maria was puzzled. "So why do you come to me? I have no power. I am a woman. I can't be the meshiach. I have nothing here. I have this small bungalow. I will have Joseph. Will he be the Anointed One? He's only a carpenter. That isn't a position of power in this world."

"No child. It isn't Joseph. And don't be so quick to diminish the power of a woman. Women hold power that Yahweh gave to no man. A woman brings new life to the world. And it is in this way that you will help your God."

Gabriel let that sink in.

A moment passed.

"Are you saying that I will be giving birth to the messiah?"

Gabriel smiled. "You are very bright."

"But I am a virgin," Maria protested.

"Another prerequisite that put you at the top of the list." Gabriel replied.

"What about Joseph?"

"I will take care of Joseph. He will understand. You will need him, and he will need you. You will do this for your God, won't you hija?"

Maria turned hot. "But how?" She suddenly became defensive. "You aren't going to do it, are you?"

Gabriel burst out his loudest laugh yet. "I am not Yahweh, child." He walked over to her and placed his long hand on her shoulder. "You will go to sleep. While you sleep it will be done."

"And I will still be a virgin?" she whispered.

"Yes hija. Everything is done in the mind of God. He thinks it and it is done."

In the morning, Maria threw up.

The Twins

"Look," Robbie explained to Donnie and Jack, his brothers, "I need you guys to back me up on this. I'm not a doctor. Not anymore."

"You know how to birth a baby though, right?" asked Donnie

Robbie glanced over at the youngest twin who rode shotgun. "That's not helpful. I have no business performing medical care. It's not legal or ethical. I've got to talk them into going to the hospital. Are you going to help me on this?"

"Yeah, Robbie," Donnie said looking down at his boots. "You know I will. I want to help."

Robbie nodded his thanks.

As soon as they parked in front of Dave Hampton's barn, Robbie leapt out of the truck and ran in through the open barn door. The twins looked at each other and after a few minutes got out and moseyed in behind him. They found their brother huddled up with Dave and a large brown skinned fellow. As they'd always done, they stood outside of the conversation, waiting to be told what to do. The men were talking in hushed tones, so Jack leaned into trying to catch what they discussed. Robbie looked at Jack in that way he had, that *older brother, I'll get to you in minute* look he'd shot at him for most of his life.

"You told us to help," Jack said, looking hurt.

"Go and see if Miss…" Robbie looked to Dave.

"Maria," Dave said.

"Maria. Go and see if Miss Maria needs anything. That would help."

Robbie's the doctor, Jack thought. Well, *was* the doctor. Shouldn't he see if the woman needed anything?

Donnie, Jack's twin brother wasn't nearly as put out as his older-by-seven-minutes brother. Donnie had seen many cows being born but never had he seen a no fooling human baby enter the world. And Donnie felt

The One and True Son

something other than wonder at the scene playing out in front of him. He was always considered the slowest of the King boys, but he knew, and his brothers knew, that he wasn't slow at all. No, he *took things* slow; that was true. He took things slow to think about them, to consider them before he acted. There were always many sides to every situation and Donnie wanted to examine all the angles. And there were many angles at play in that barn that day. This woman was special. This baby was special. He could feel it with every fiber of his being. He had no idea why. He just knew.

Donnie sauntered over to the woman lying on the mattress, placed on the floor of a horse stall. Yahweh, she was a beautiful woman. Maybe not in the fashion magazine way that seemed to sell everything from tires to toothpaste, but at much deeper level. She shined. She did. She shined like a new penny and that shining only intensified as she turned her eyes up to him. Her dark, dark eyes. It was as if she could hear what he was thinking and reflected his admiration back to him. A thin sheet covered body.

"What's your name?" the woman asked Donnie.

"Donald ma'am. Folks call me Donnie. Are you doing okay? Is there anything I can get you?"

"I'm close to having this baby, Donald. Very close." A shudder caught the woman. Later, Donnie would swear he saw the contraction right through the sweaty sheet and he would be right. The woman puffed like a steam locomotive and yet her eyes were calm, as if her body was doing one thing, but her mind, her spirit maybe, was doing something else, feeling something else.

"I'm very close to having Jessie," the woman said, mid-pant. "I need you to lift the sheet and look. Something is happening. Jessie is coming.

Donnie didn't move. It would be one of those moments where an observer might use the word "slow" to describe his reaction to things. He didn't even blink. His expression remained unchanged, his narrow eyes opened as far as his eyelids would go, his mouth slack. One might even think drool was about seep from the corner of his mouth. Again, Donnie's cognitive abilities had nothing to do with his lack of response. Fear had him frozen. On the day of Jessie's birth, Donnie had more in common with the woman lying in the soaked sheets than either of them knew. He too was a virgin, if one didn't count the one time he rolled around in the field behind a barn with Sarah Garrote, a girl two years his junior with far more experience in field rolling than he. His inexperience showed when the encounter abruptly ended with embarrassment for him and frustration for her.

"Aw, he's all locked up again," Jack said, disgusted with his twin. "I'm sorry ma'am. He gets that way sometimes. It's hard for me to believe we're from the same mother, let alone twins."

Another contraction wracked the woman's body, but this time it was Jack who noticed the unearthly stillness in her black eyes.

"I need you to check, Jack," she said, nearly out of breath. "Please look under the sheet. Something is happening. I know it is."

Jack lifted the soaked linen. Something was happening all right.

"Robbie!" He yelled. "You better get over here."

By the time the former doctor had approached Maria's side, the situation had changed drastically. One look under the sheet and Robbie knew that calling for an ambulance was moot. The birth had progressed passed the labor stage to the baby's head was already out stage. He whipped the sheet away knowing the time for modesty had expired and kneeled down between the woman's spread legs to aid in the delivery of the rest of the child.

"All right, Maria," Robbie said like millions of doctors before him. "I need you to push now."

The Vender

By eleven p.m., two days before he was supposed to marry, Joe found himself outside Maria's Beacon Hill home. It was a small white three-bedroom house on West Rosewood Avenue. As simple as it was, Joe loved the little bungalow with its blistered paint and exposed rows of cinderblock basement wall, just above the cooked, brown, Texas dirt. Even the rejas, the steel bars that covered every window and stood guard outside every door, seemed welcoming with their swirled ivy patterns and aging paint, more decoration than threat or fortification. The white shingled roof threw the punishing, nearly year-round sun right back up keeping the tiny rooms underneath cool, at least cool for a house in Travis City with no air conditioning. A fading stone driveway, more a path, ran from the street up to the house. A mountain cedar stood alone in the patchy front yard, its two main limbs spread to the left and right as if welcoming one to come in. Unkempt wax myrtle and Texas mountain laurel separated the driveway from the adjacent property with a wall of shiny leaves and strings of purple blossoms. To Joe, the house seemed almost from a dream.

That night, illuminated with a dim streetlight a half block down, the sight of the house filled him with dread. The bungalow was dark with no sign of Maria. In the semidarkness of the evening, the cedar with the outstretched arms looked alarming, foreboding. He walked the path to front door, stuck his scarred and bruised knuckles through the rejas and knocked, patiently, but forcefully. He placed his ear through the bars and listened for rustling for a moment and knocked again. He listened. Nothing.

Joe wasn't leaving, not without speaking to Maria. If it took all night, he would stand outside and wait. He walked over to the wax myrtles at the end of the driveway and mixed himself in with the edges of the leaves and branches as best he could.

The One and True Son

He repeated to himself, *everything is fine. It has to be. I know it is.* After twenty minutes the mantra became, *please Yahweh. Please make sure everything is fine.* By 11:30 he was making his way back up the driveway to rip the rejas from their anchors and kick down the door. He was halfway there when a light flickered on in the front window. Maria appeared from behind a lace curtain in what appeared to be night clothes. Joe stopped in his tracks. He stared at her not knowing how to feel. Should he be angry? Relieved? She stared back at him with those eyes of hers. Those eyes that no one could look away from. They both stood where they were for what seemed ages.

Finally, she waved him in.

"Why didn't you answer the door when I knocked?" He asked, straining to contain the hysteria in his voice.

"I was praying," Maria answered almost whispering. She sat on a worn secondhand sofa in her tiny living room.

He was not expecting her answer. Worry replaced the hysteria.

Joe took a breath. "Did you know that I was calling you. Did you hear your phone ring?"

Maria nodded.

"Were you praying then too?" He asked.

She nodded again.

The carpenter sighed deeply. Neither spoke for a few moments, she, knowing what she was going to have to say, he, fearing what he might hear.

It was Maria who broke the silence.

"Before I speak, Joseph, I must ask you a question,"

"Please," Joseph replied. He knelt in front of her and took her hand in his. "Ask me anything."

"Do you know that I would never lie to you?" Maria asked looking into his eyes.

Joseph smiled. "Of course. I trust you with my entire being."

Maria returned his smile.

"Do you know that I have never lied?" Maria asked.

Joe's smile slipped. What could he say to that? Surely, she exaggerated. Everyone has lied at least once in their lives. As children, everyone has taken that cookie they weren't supposed to. Or claimed they'd brushed their teeth when it seemed such a heavy burden to do so. Wasn't it the first way children learn to prove to protect themselves? And isn't exaggeration a form of lie in itself?

The One and True Son

"Never?" He said finally.

"Never," Maria replied, her eyes locked on his.

"Not even as a child? Or...or to save someone's feelings?"

Maria shook her head. "If it's not true, I don't say it."

Joe went silent.

Maria spoke. "I have something important to tell you and it is vital that you know that whatever I tell you is the truth. Especially now if we are to be married."

Fear took hold of him again. What did *if* mean? "If you say you've never lied, I believe you. I want you to be my wife. If you tell me something, I'll know it's the truth. I swear."

Maria's turn sighed. "Do not swear so easily, Joseph."

"Please Maria," Joseph begged. "Tell me what you have to tell me."

Maria took a deep breath. "Joseph," she said. "I'm pregnant."

Joe let go of her hand. He shook his head like a dog that'd been sprayed by a garden hose. He stood and paced the room.

"We never..." Rage had crept into his voice. "You..." he sputtered. "You are carrying a child. You're pregnant?!" His hands waved wildly in front of him swatting at the air, as if to injure it. "How Maria? Joe screamed. "How could you do this to me?!"

At tear swam in Maria's eye. "There is more to tell you, Joseph. If you would please listen."

Oh, there's more!" Joe spat. "Are you going to tell me who the father is? Well, please do." He plunked down in the rocking chair across from the sofa and crossed his arms in front of him. "I know it wasn't me. Please tell me Maria. Please tell me who put that baby in you."

Maria opened her eyes wide.

"Yahweh," she said.

* * *

At three a.m. the only sounds Joe heard along the Travis City River Walk were the splashing of water that flowed out of the cluster of springs, bumping together, to make the Travis City River and the distant whispers of the warm night winds through the palm trees that lined the walk. He had no idea how he got there. Did he walk? Did he take a taxi? He had no memory of it. He just knew that he'd walked for hours and would probably be walking for hours more.

Joe's life was over.

He could not marry a crazy woman.

He loved her, at least he thought he did. But obviously he didn't know her. How could he not have seen that she was unbalanced? Were there clues he'd missed? Was he so dazzled by her ethereal eyes and her seemingly assured nature that he failed to notice that something was wrong? He walked past the Palacio Del Rio and scaled up and down the many stone steps that ran along the river, replaying their conversations in his head, everyone he could remember. Did she ever say anything as crazy as, "I have never lied," to him? For the life of him he couldn't think of anything she'd said that would've tipped him off.

Joe came to a stone ramp with handrails on each side, near the new Marriott hotel when he had to stop, halfway up. Ahead of him, up in a corner by the stone wall, a unusually tall man, a street vender, was standing behind his cart. A streetlight was shining above him. Joe looked at his watch. It was after 3 a.m.

"Amigo," the man beckoned him. "Keep coming. Business is very slow."

The man awaited him with outstretched arms, the light above him reflecting off the cleanest hot dog cart Joe had ever seen, lit up his long face and beard. His smile seemed to glow.

"Why are you out here?" Joe asked as he approached. "Do you know how late it is?"

"I might ask you the same question, amigo," the vender replied, his smile never dimming. "Travis City can be a dangerous place this time of night. Come. Have one of my hot dogs. They are the best you've ever had. Guaranteed. And, of course, kosher."

"I don't have any money with me," Joe said.

"Then you will have one on the house, my friend," the vender said. "I don't want this food to spoil. That would be a sin. And you look as if you could use a meal. Have you eaten today?"

Joe shook his head.

The vender flipped open a door on the top of his cart and pulled out a fresh, steamed bun. The scent of the bread filled Joe's nostrils. The strange man closed the door and opened another, grabbed a pair of tongs and he fished out a plump brown sausage, bursting with juices. He opened a bun and lovingly placed the sausage inside, moving it around until it fit perfectly.

The vender moved to the side of the cart where a row of condiments waited in plexiglas-covered chambers.

The One and True Son

"What do you want?" The vender said then raised a long finger. "No, I will choose for you. I am very good at this." He looked deep into Joe's eyes, his long fingers stroking the beard on his chin. It surprised Joe that he didn't think this unpleasant. He was not used to being looked at this way. After a moment the vender spread mustard, onions, hot peppers and added just a couple of drops of hot sauce.

"That is exactly what I would've asked for," Joe said, amazed.

"I know," the man replied, smiling bigger than ever. "I told you I'm good." He handed the hot dog to Joe. "Please, eat."

The vender didn't lie. Joe had never eaten a hot dog so good. Its flavors exploded in his mouth. He wolfed it down quickly.

"You're very hungry, amigo," the vender told Joe. "You must have another."

Joe attempted to protest but before he could say anything the man's long fingers were handing him another delicious sausage. With his hunger a bit more sated he was able to savor this one, breathing the spices in through his nose, enjoying the experience.

"So now that you have eaten, you must tell me my friend, why are you walking the River Walk at this late hour?"

Joe paused between bites. Why not tell this man his troubles? He had no one he could speak to. It might be good to clear his mind. It didn't matter what the hot dog vender thought of him. Surely, he'd see that his fiancée was unwell. Perhaps unstable. Joe related his conversation with Maria the previous evening.

When Joe finished the vender said nothing at first. He raised his thumb and forefinger to his lips brushing the facial hair there to the sides. Finally, he said, "And you think Maria is lying to you?"

Joe dropped his hot dog.

He hadn't said Maria's name. He was sure of it. Fear gripped his gut. He backed away.

"Joseph," the vender said reaching his hand out to him.

"I never told you my name," Joe shrieked. "Or Maria's."

The very tall man smiled. It was a peaceful, glowing, beautiful smile. Joe felt the knot in his belly release, his breathing calmed. The fear in him eased as quickly as it had erupted. He was greatly confused.

"You can call me Gabe, amigo," the man said, almost in a whisper. "I'm the one that chose Maria for The Father. What she told you is true. She has never lied. She is a virgin. She is the perfect woman for the task that He requires of her."

The One and True Son

Joe sat on the stone steps. He opened and closed his hands as if trying to grasp the words he'd just heard. *How could this be possible?* He balled up his fists and brought them to his lips.

Finally, he spoke. "What should I do?"

Gabe tilted his head slightly. "Marry her, Joseph."

Joe jumped to his feet. "Marry her? How can *I* marry *her?*"

"What do you mean?" asked Gabriel.

"She is carrying *Yahweh's child*! She's told me—you just told me—that she's *never* lied! I'm not like her. I'm a sinner. I have done many things I knew I shouldn't do."

Gabriel walked around his cart and wrapped an arm around Joe's shoulders. "As I chose her, I chose you as well. She may seem strong, almost invincible, but in a world of sin she is on foreign ground. She needs help in this world, someone who knows it better than she. You are in favor The Father's eyes."

Tears leaked from Joe's eyes.

"Marry her, Joseph," the angel said. "You've loved her from the moment you met her. She needs you."

The Brothers

The baby was perfect. Robbie had seen babies born before, quite a few when he was in residency. He'd even heard it said that this or that baby was perfect, and to some extent, Robbie had to concede, that all babies are a clean slate, having caused no harm. In many ways, they *were* perfect. But this baby was different. Robbie, his brothers and everyone present were weeping large sloppy tears, uncontrollably, with smiles that would remain on their faces for days and in their hearts, though they didn't know it then, forever. They found, all of them, Robbie, his brothers, Dave Hampton, the child's father, found they couldn't stand. They knelt to the child, unable to look away as the boy lay at his mother's breast. Robbie felt that the air had been pulled from his chest and replaced with a light so pure and warm that if he'd chosen, he could forego food or water for the rest of his life and never suffer a pang of hunger or a dry tongue. In fact, he was nearly sure that breathing had become optional.

"Why do you cry, Robert?" Maria asked him, smiling.

"I was going to ask you the same question," Robbie answered, smiling back through the tears. "Who are you, Maria? Who is he? What is all this?"

Maria weeping as well, said, "I am a woman. All life comes from the Mind of The Father and from a woman." She kissed the top of the baby's head. "Jessie is love. You are crying because he is a gift from The Father, to you, Robert, and to everyone. He is the gift of His love that he has always had for you. For us."

The former doctor could no longer speak. He turned his head and rose to his feet.

"Robert," Maria said.

"Yes, Maria," he answered quietly.

"Will you please clean my baby. He must be wrapped warmly and carefully."

The One and True Son

"Of course," Robbie answered.

He took the child carefully and carried him to a nearby sink where he rinsed him with warm water, swishing away the blood and fluids of birth with his fingertips. Dave brought him clean linens and he swaddled the infant carefully. When he finished, he brought Jessie back to his mother.

Afterward, Robbie bid his brothers to join him outside the barn.

Jack and Donnie still had problems speaking. They both knew they'd witnessed something unbelievably important. Robbie didn't need them to speak.

"I need you two to go back to the house. Go upstairs to my bathroom and get me..." He reached in his breast pocket for the pen he almost always had there. It was. Next, he searched his pockets for something to write on.

"Either one of you have any paper?"

Jack pulled out his wallet and removed a yellow receipt from Blockbuster Video. It was for the movie *Being There* with Peter Sellers. Jack remembered renting it thinking it would be laugh out loud funny like *The Pink Panther* movies. It was kind of funny, he thought, but a little slow. He handed the receipt to his brother.

"Okay," Robbie said as he scribbled on the paper. "I need you to get these two things out of the cabinet. They're labeled. You can't miss them."

"Are they labeled in your handwriting?" The first words since the birth of the child, Robbie thought, and Jack was making doctor's handwriting jokes.

Jack looked at the receipt. "What's this stuff?"

"One is an essential oil to massage Maria and the baby. The other is an aromatic."

"You're a doctor," Jack said. "Can't you do better than that?"

"Does anyone here remember *I'm not a doctor anymore*?" Robbie asked the wind. "I can't prescribe anything. Besides, these have been used for centuries."

Jack started to walk away.

"Wait," Robbie cried.

Jack turned around.

"In my room, go to the east corner. You'll see a floorboard with a knothole at the end of it. Stick your finger in the knothole and pull the board up. Take the cash out of there and bring it here. There's about $1500."

Jack tilted his head at his brother. "Are you sure?"

"Just bring it," Robbie said.

Jack turned and headed away and Robbie went to head back into the barn.

"Wait!" Jack called to him. "Which is the east corner?"

TWO

The Student

"Please say the blessing, Jessie."

Jessie shot his mother a look. Of course, he would say the blessing. He *always* says the blessing. Unlike many families, the Carpenteros thanked the Father before every meal— breakfast, lunch and dinner. Even snacks. Joe did the blessing when Jessie was small and unable to speak well; his mother did the honors in Joe's absence, when he was working. But as soon as Jessie could express his joy for the Father's gifts of food and shelter he took on the role.

That morning they gathered around the small kitchen table that Joe had found discarded in an alley nearby. He'd stabilized a crack in the leg that probably prompted its abandonment and painted it white with some spare paint he was given from a completed job. It fit nicely in the small kitchen that also passed as a living room, family room and sometimes a spare bedroom when one was needed for a guest. His mother placed a large platter of eggs and sausage in the center of the table. Three bowls of steaming hominy grits for each completed the meal.

"Are we ready?" Jessie said, an edge hiding in the words.

The elders nodded.

"Father," Jessie began. "We thank you for providing our food for this day. We thank you for the work you provide for Joe and ask for your guidance in this difficult time. You are the creator of all. We humbly bow to your will." He picked up his fork.

"Amen," Maria and Joe said together.

Jessie picked up his fork. He stirred around the eggs on his plate, but he put the fork down a moment later.

"What's wrong, hijo?"

Jessie looked back to her. He didn't answer.

"The blessing. It was short, wasn't it?" Maria pressed. "And you said, 'this difficult time'. Is the time more difficult than usual?" She put down her own fork. "And you haven't touched your food. Something is wrong, hijo?"

The 14-year-old boy looked up from his plate. He wanted to shout, *leave me alone.* He wanted to get up from the table, perhaps tip it over, perhaps scream at these two people at the top of his lungs, that they had no idea how he felt, that they never *would* or *could know.* He wanted to work through the turmoil he'd awakened to that morning. Jessie knew something was very wrong. He just didn't know what.

Of course, he did none of the things he'd thought of. He neither yelled nor threw anything. He, as everyone, was commanded to honor his parents. To respect them at all times.

"Mother," he said finally. "I don't know what's wrong. There's something…" He shook his head. "I don't know."

His mother looked at him, her eyes filled with sympathy. "You will know, hijo. This I can tell you. You will know. But you have asked blessing on this food. I'm sure the Father wants you to eat it." She looked at his untouched plate. "He has given you this today. He knows you need strength. For whatever it is that's bothering you, you will need strength." She smiled.

Jessie couldn't resist his mother's smile and although he couldn't, at that moment return it, he acknowledged it by picking up his fork and scooping a healthy portion of scrambled eggs into his mouth.

* * *

Jessie and his family had known many places as home. They traveled and Joe worked. When Jessie was four years old, the family settled in Oklahoma City in an area called Deep Deuce. In the 1920s, Deep Deuce was a vibrant Black owned area of Oklahoma City where jazz greats Ma Rainey, Count Basie, Ella Fitzgerald and countless others entertained the lawyers, doctor and well-off merchants of the area along with those whites eager to hear the driving music of the "Roaring 20s". As segregation laws changed and the Great Depression hit everyone, Deep Deuce began to fall apart. By the time Maria and Joe moved their family into a small apartment above one the last remaining storefronts in the area most of the historic buildings had fallen victim to wrecking ball or the bulldozer.

It turned out to be the perfect location for a carpenter, because in early 90s the city decided to rehab an area of abandoned warehouses to an entertainment and restaurant district in an adjacent area called Bricktown.

There was so much work that Jessie traveled with his father and got to work alongside him, learning the skills of a carpenter, taking disparate materials, finding how they might work together, and forming something strong that would last.

Occasionally people asked why Jessie wasn't in school. Joe explained that he was homeschooled, which was the truth. On his own time, Jessie studied the Torah and Talmud, making notes in one of the many binders he kept, noting this admonishment or that interpretation. He also took correspondence courses on the more secular subjects to keep within the laws of the land. Eventually he would get his GED.

Jessie loved working next to Joe. The man he called father patiently explained framing, toenailing, tacking, and drywalling with patience and calmness that most teachers struggle for years to perfect. Joe would model what Jessie needed to do. Jessie would do it.

Whenever they broke for lunch, Joe shushed the other construction workers so Jessie could bless the meal, something the less observant workers looked on with wary eyes initially. As this became part of their routine, however, the leery ones gently set their sandwiches down and listen to the boy's grateful words. Some found peace in what he said. All felt that their tuna salad or salami tasted a bit better.

That day in April, the day Jessie felt ill at ease, he and Joe were installing drywall in a rehab that would eventually be an office building. They'd arrived at the sight early, as usual, and were about to take their first break when a deafening blast shook the building, shook the ground, shook everything. Jessie looked at Joe who stood wide eyed, petrified.

"Was that in the building?" Jessie asked.

Joe looked at the corners of the room. He sniffed the air. "I don't know," he said, finally. "It was close wherever it was."

Jessie bolted for the stairway, ignoring Joe's order to stay put. Jessie bounded down three the flights of stairs, barely touching the steps. In seconds, he stepped out onto NW 8th Street. He looked north and saw nothing. As he scanned the horizon, he backed into the street to get a better look behind the building they'd been working in when he was nearly run over by a yellow Mercury that came screaming down the street and swerved around him, not even honking its horn. Jessie had no time to worry about the car. He took off toward North Broadway, toward a thickening cloud of black smoke.

When Jessie arrived at the source of the cloud his mind couldn't process what he saw. He stood aghast, staring at what remained of the Alfred P. Murrah Federal Building. The building had a giant bite taken out of it. People with pale faces poured from the Journal Record Building in front of it, the Federal Court Building behind it, and the Regency Towers down the street. Store fronts and eateries nearby emptied too, filling the sidewalks. A photographer from the newspaper showed up and shot faces in the crowd. An eerie silence took hold. And then he could hear it. They could all hear it. The screaming.

The sirens wailed. Police cars screeched up in front of crowd. Officers, four to a car, began moving the crowd back, away from the carnage.

This is not of My Father's mind, Jessie thought.

Jessie had never been so confused. Papier-mâché-like strips of building material hung from the edges of each floor. A line of cars parked maybe minutes before by people beginning their workday was engulfed in flame, choking the air with thick black smoke.

Jessie was suddenly seized from behind. It was Joe. He hugged the boy tightly.

"We have to go," Jessie told the big man, tears running from both of their eyes. "We have to take a trip."

* * *

It's tradition for Americans of Yahwehian belief to visit the National Temple in Washington DC at least once every 10 years during Passover and there were three days left in the holiday. Nevertheless, they'd managed to book a midnight flight, crowded as it was, and landed in the capital city in three hours. They arrived at Ronald Reagan National Airport and caught a bus downtown.

The National Mall bustled with tourists, pilgrims and government workers. The last blossoms from the cherry trees, given by Japan as a token of friendship in 1917, clung to their branches filling the early spring air. Many of the blossoms lay crushed on the pavement or stuck to the soles of pedestrian's shoes. Potted Passover bushes decorated at their bases with colorful eggs lined the walkways, symbolizing the burning bush on Mount Horeb. The mall with its faux Greek temple for Lincoln at one end and its homage to the Romans and the Greeks sitting high on Capitol Hill at the other seemed to draw the crowds like opposing magnets, pulling the hoards to them, bumping the people into each other as they sought to touch, to absorb, these images of power and history.

Jessie's family made their way along the crowds. They hadn't had time to find a hotel before leaving so Maria approached one of the many food trucks parked along Constitution Avenue and asked the venders if they might know of a hostel where they might bed down for a few days. The

The One and True Son

proprietor, a Salvadorian, recognized Maria's accent and wrote an address where they could get a room for $20 a night.

"You must have some of my food, Señora," the man told her as he wrapped up three tamales, some pasteles and yuca fritas for them to take with them. When she tried to pay him. He refused.

"A little taste of home," he said and smiled. "Remember me in your prayers, Señora. Please."

She smiled at him. He nearly cried.

When she turned back to her family, Jessie was gone.

* * *

Joe and Maria scrambled up and down Constitution Avenue. They called his name with ever increasing panic in their voices. Maria even turned one boy who looked like Jessie from behind around by the shoulders. The boy's mother wrenched the child back and balled her fists, ready to fight.

"I'm sorry," Maria cried. "My son. I can't find my son."

The woman relaxed her hands and rushed her child away.

Jessie's parents circled the National Mall, around the Lincoln Memorial, around the Tidal Basin. They searched every face in the park around the Washington Monument and combed their way up Independence Avenue to the steps of the Capitol Building. Hours passed and there was no sign of Jessie.

Joe sat heavily on a bench at the bus stop. Maria refused to sit.

"Why would he do this to us?" She asked.

"Why did we come here in the first place?" Joe responded. He thought for moment. He stood suddenly, raised a finger and yelled, "Taxi!"

* * *

The taxi pulled up at the corner of Massachusetts and Wisconsin Avenues. There, about 100 yards back from the curb stood the National Temple, an enormous blocky structure with great square stained glass windows depicting scenes from the Tanach: David killing Goliath, the Exodus, the Flood, Masada. Two huge wooden doors stood open for the pilgrims who lined up outside, waiting in winding, roped off lines for their turn to be admitted. Two imposing bronze pillars flanked the doors.

Joe and Maria sprinted across the large open square to the place where the faithful lined up.

"Jessie!" They shouted, almost in unison.

The One and True Son

Maria shouted, "Has anyone seen a boy. He's 14 years old. He's alone."

Most people looked away. Some shook their heads, looking concerned.

A black man sweeping the pavement away from the line called Maria and Joe to him.

"What did you say the boy's name was?" He asked, his kind, aged face, lined from years of hard work. He held his broom with gnarled hands, knuckles bulging from arthritis.

"Jessie," Maria answered him quickly. She held out a flat hand. "He's about this tall. We think he might be here."

The man looked from Maria to Joe and back to Maria. "I think that's what he said his name was." He smiled. "Asked if I could get him in to speak to the morehs. Said he needed to talk to 'em. Now, I don't usually do nothin' like that, but that boy special. Ain't he special, Missus?"

Maria nodded.

"Come now," the man said. "I'll take you to him."

The man took them through a side door as to not upset the crowd waiting to go enter the temple. They entered a long hallway that ran alongside the main temple. On the outside wall, a series of narrow windows had been built, each throwing different shades of reds and blues across the hallway to corresponding doors, all closed. The man turned to Maria and Joe.

"Name's Enoch," the man said. "Been working here a long time. Know the temple like the back of my hand." Enoch reached behind them, flipped a switch, and florescent lights flickered on. "Now we got to go up two ladders to get to where your boy is. See this place was designed like the original Temple of Solomon in Jerusalem. Well, they didn't have stained glass and all that back then. Had to make it bigger too. National Temple and such. But you get the drift. You two okay to climb?"

The first ladder ran up through the ceiling just feet from where the stood. The hallway seemed identical to the one they'd just left with the same red and blue lights splashed across doors on the opposite side of the hall. Enoch put a hand to his ear. Maria and Joe listened too, unsure of just what they were supposed to hear.

"Yep," Enoch said finally. "Still here. Let's go."

The second ladder ascended from the opposite side of the opening they'd climbed through. Making their way down the stained lit corridor it became apparent that a spirited conversation was taking place between several older, weathered voices and one that scratched from puberty.

The One and True Son

The trio approached the one open door they'd seen since entering the building. There, they saw Jessie seated with three moreh's all in ceremonial robes seated in a circle, leaning into each other as they talked.

"You see, my boy, Yahweh has allowed countless incidents of slaughter," an ancient looking Moreh with a long silver beard said. "In the Great Revolt and Bar-khba Rebellions in Palestine, millions of Jews were wiped out. His chosen people. He has his purposes. We have ours."

Another younger moreh spoke: "Yes. It was this loss of life that brought about the writing down of the Oral Law, which differed from that of the Written Law."

"I understand this, teacher," Jessie said. "In Exodus 21:24 it demands an eye for an eye..." Jessie stopped. He turned and looked to his parents and Enoch standing in the doorway. He turned back to the morehs. "Excuse me for a moment."

Jessie stood and walked to the doorway, stepped out, and closed the door behind him.

He gazed into his mother's eyes. "Woman, why did you look for me? You knew I would be with my Father."

Maria couldn't answer. Of course, he was right. She was just his mother. She had forgotten that. There would be many times in the coming years that she'd wish she could.

The Prophet

The Arcangelo Gabriele River flows north to south from the Arcangelo Gabriele Mountains, through Los Angeles to empty into the Pacific Ocean between the cities of Long Beach and Seal Beach. Its watershed has fed forests of willows, cottonwoods and oaks along with the Tongva and Yuhaviatam native peoples for millenea. With most of the watershed encased in concrete from industrialization, few traces of the forest or the ancient cultures exist.

The "Grandaddy of All Bike Trails" runs 28 miles, parallel to the 605 Freeway to Highway 39 above Azuza. It drew bike enthusiasts from all over California. It also drew the disenfranchised, the addicted, the disenchanted, the homeless. Pieced together campsites of salvaged tents, purloined canvas tarps and pilfered grocery carts sprouted up like dandelions along miles of path from just beyond Seal Beach to Rossmore. Trashbags acted as dressers for the residents of the tent suburbs. Campfires were furnaces on cold nights and cooking stoves in the morning. Old rickety bicycles served as family cars. An occasional transistor radio provided music for ambiance. Once in while a three-string guitar sent sad notes dancing in the air.

The homeless were running from something or someone, be it a dangerous habit, a jealous boyfriend or voices in their heads. They all needed something. The dirty sleeping bags on the discarded mattresses were symptoms of their collective disease, the unturned heads of the bikers chugging north and south, the proof of their invisibility.

It was here that Dzon set up his ministry.

He founded his community through a void in a chain link fence that led to clearing between the rocky edge of the bike trail and the equally rocky slope up to the freeway. A sign forbidding loitering, threatening a $1000 fine or six months in jail, rusted a foot from the opening. Dzon himself scrounged the tents. He begged for the food and money on the streets of

Seal Beach dressed only in a burlap potato sack tied at the waste with hemp rope and a tattered pair of jean shorts that'd had complete legs when he'd obtained them. His African hair, twisted and long, bleached nearly orange from the sun, was pushed back and tied like a strong cable. His bare feet, calloused thickly, could walk on shattered glass and remain uncut.

When Dzon had five tents he went looking for souls. He sought the broken people around him. He told them they could come live with him. He had food. If they only had tarps, he had a tent. If they had a tent, they could combine it with his for a bigger one to share. He would find them medicine, he told them. He would help them rid themselves of the demons of addiction. If they felt unsafe, he and God would protect them. Together, they would all protect each other. This was his job. To bring the poor and forgotten to God.

His community grew behind the rusted sign from five tents to twenty to fifty. The police investigated more than once expecting drug activity or criminal goings on, but finding none of that, and talking to Dzon, always clear eyed and respectful, they'd just check a couple of tents and move along. On a number of occasions officers would show up on their own time to offer food and secondhand clothing to the residents.

Dzon spoke of God often. He didn't call him Yahweh as was the custom of most believers; he called him God, The Father, The Creator of All. And this community, these followers, called Dzon a prophet. The faithful gathered before every meal, giving God praise for their full bellies and their conduit to Him. At meals they would all talk and laugh and sing.

Every Saturday Dzon would lead his people up the bike trail to East Fork. The new residents were asked to walk on the craggy rocks, one by one, and join him in the flowing Arcangelo Gabriele River to repent of their sins. Fully clothed, the sinner joined the prophet, and stepped from the sunbleached rocks to the chilly waist-deep water.

"Do you accept the love of God our father, the creator of all you see hear and feel?" Dzon would ask. With a positive response, Dzon would wrap one arm around the other's shoulder and place a hand on the their forehead. The prophet would lean the other into the rushing water, making sure to cover the entire face and body with the waters rushing down from the mountains, miles away. With unnatural strength, Dzon would pull the other from the water, standing them up.

"Do you believe that He, God our father, watches over us and has a plan for us?" Dzon would further inquire. With another positive response, the immersion would be repeated.

The One and True Son

Finally, the prophet would ask: "Do you believe that God our father, will send a deliverer, a redeemer, to rid this world of our sin and to rule over Heaven and Earth?"

With the final agreement would be a final immersion followed by a tearful hug from Dzon and cheers from those still standing on the rocks. After all were baptized, the prophet and his flock would trek back down the Granddaddy of All Bike trails, back to their canvas patch community and eat and sing and laugh.

* * *

"Where are you from, teacher?" A girl who appeared to be about fifteen asked Don one day at dinner. Dzon cherished dinnertime. It was a time when they filled their mouths with what God had provided them and their hearts with each other's company. Everyone was welcome. They would sit in one large group, out in the open air, with what food and drink they'd managed to procure in front of them. They'd cut the legs off of old tables so they could have their food in front of them, eat, and sit comfortably on the grass. The girl was new to the camp, perhaps a runaway, perhaps not, with straw hair tied in hemp-like dreads, and a scarab tattoo on her right forearm. A gold nose ring dangled from her septum.

"What's your name, child?" Dzon smiled at her.

"Dimple," the girl replied, smiling back.

"If I answer you truthfully, will you do the same?"

Dimple nodded, but her eyes looked down a bit.

"Well then," Dzon said. "I am the son of a moreh who was the son of moreh, who was the son of a moreh. It seems I took up the family business."

The group around him chuckled.

"But that doesn't answer your question. You asked me where I'm from. The truth is, Dimple, that my family traveled quite a bit. We were originally from Zaire. They call it the Congo now. We came as refugees to a temple in Birmingham, Alabama. Soon we moved to another in Utah; then we went to Washington and down to California. There were a lot of little places in between. Most of them, I'm sure you've never heard of. We stayed for a year sometimes. Sometimes it was only a couple of months. It sounds exciting, but it wasn't really. It got tedious after a while."

"It's funny," Dimple said. "You don't seem like a moreh."

Dzon looked serious for a moment. "I suppose if you were to ask my father or my grandfather, they would say I'm nothing of the sort." He held out his hand to the girl.

"There is a change coming, Dimple. There will be a deliverer. A messiah. He *is* coming."

The girl took his hand. "Are you him, teacher? Are you the messiah?"

Dzon tilted his head and smiled. He squeezed her hand gently.

"I'm not," he said. "Now, about you? Where are you from?"

* * *

On a blazing hot Saturday, Dzon stood in the cool water of the Arcangelo Gabriele River. The East Fork looked less like a river and more like a series of pools surrounded by sharp pieces, from pebbles to boulders of limestone and quartz running serpentine through the river valley. His followers sat among the rocks. Some waded in the cool water while others fanned themselves under a canopy they'd brought with them, trying to ignore the punishing heat of the afternoon. There were other groups at the Fork as there always was on the weekends. It was a popular spot for people to cool off; families and young people rode their bikes, the cool water being their reward.

Dzon noticed a man standing among a group of his followers. They were talking and laughing. The man was tall and lanky with wooly black hair and a patchy beard. He appeared to be in his thirties and his arms, though thin, were those of a man who'd done substantial work. He wore simple clothes, jeans and a pale purple t-shirt. Dzon knew this man. He had never seen him before. And yet he knew him. Dzon made his way through the water to the man, who greeted him with a smile.

"You're Dzon," the man said. "My name is Jessie. I would like to be baptized."

For the first time in recent memory, Dzon didn't know what to do. He stared at the man, Jessie. *Is this really happening?* He didn't know what he expected. Well, he did. He expected a warrior, one to wield God's wrath. One to lift up the poor, to avenge the deeds of the wicked. And the poor and the wicked were everywhere. Could this tall, thin man take on all that?

And yet Dzon knew that this was the man he was waiting for. Every cell in his body told him that *this* was *him*.

"I think that you should be the one to baptize me," Dzon said, much to the astonishment of those present.

"No, brother," Jessie said, softly. "I have a long road ahead of me. My Father said it is you who should send me on my way."

* * *

The One and True Son

Jessie chose to sleep on the ground, outside, rather than in the newest tent, needing the least repair, as was offered to him. He liked to be close to the warmth of the fire and could be counted on keeping it going all night, as it seemed to consume none of the kindling and limbs used to build it. Dzon's followers, noting their prophet's reaction to him, gave Jessie a wide berth at first, unsure of who it was that was in their midst. They would sit near their shelters and watch as Dzon and the new man talked in whispers, embraced, and talked some more. Jessie's expertise as a carpenter proved a boon for the camp. With the help of the men and women he was able to construct several temporary structures from scrounged wood and fiberglass that could be raised and taken down quickly if need be. The buildings were small, had windows made from plastic sheets and ventilation from carefully placed ducts. They kept people out of the weather. The community used these places for people with children, or for someone who was sick. When the authorities arrived, worried that the homeless might be constructing a permanent settlement along the bike trail, Jessie would demonstrate how quickly the small buildings could be disassembled.

"See, we used hinges with pins in the corners," Jessie explained. He took a hammer and a screwdriver he had hanging from his belt and walked to one of the hinges. He placed the screwdriver under the head of the pin. "One tap and the pin pops out. This hut is down in less than five minutes. You can go back and tell your bosses that they don't have to worry. People who have nothing will still have nothing out here."

Most of the cops knew Dzon. They liked him. They weren't so sure about this new guy. He spoke with an authority they hadn't seen before in a homeless camp. It was an authority that they couldn't ignore. It made them nervous.

"You know they are only doing their jobs," Dzon admonished Jessie after the police had gone and he'd smoothed things over. "Sometimes they bring supplies to us."

"I wasn't really talking to them," Jessie said. "I was talking to the people who sent them. The people here deserve what all people do. They should feel safe. They should feel loved."

"That's not the world we live in, Jessie," Dzon said.

"That's why I'm here," Jessie replied.

* * *

Dzon's people grew used to seeing Jessie at their prophet's side. The two often worked as a team handing out provisions that they'd gathered. The men spoke, often in low tones, almost constantly. To the people of the community, it seemed that Dzon was asking most of the questions.

Dimple, the dreadlocked girl, often followed them around asking questions of them both. Dzon had determined that although the girl appeared to be in her mid-teens, she was in her mid 20s, and unlike many of the others in the camp was there because she wanted to be. She told no stories of abuse, nor addiction. She'd been drawn to the camp by Dzon. She'd seen him asking for donations on the street a few times and was intrigued by him; this man dressed in the simplest of clothes, was barefooted, and yet people seemed to want to help him. Dimple had seen many beggars. Generally, people couldn't get away fast enough from them. One day she followed Dzon down the bike trail to the collection of tents and shelters behind the no trespassing sign. She stayed from then on.

"Teacher," Dimple asked one day, as she helped them distribute freshwater bottles to the people who wanted it. She threw the question to whichever of them wanted to answer: "Why is God allowing so much suffering?"

Jessie set down the case of water he'd been carrying. He looked to Dzon who nodded to him. Jessie took out one of the bottles from the case and held it up so the light of the midday danced through it.

"You see this water, Dimple?" he said. "It's essential for life. It is from the mind of God. He has covered the world in it, enough for every living creature. Dzon and I have been handing this out to people for the last hour." He turned to Dzon. "How many cases did we start out with?"

"Ten cases," Dzon said.

"Ten cases," Jessie repeated. "Would that be enough to keep everyone from getting thirsty today? It seems a bit warm."

Dzon shook his head. "Probably not. We have a lot of people with us."

Jessie held up the bottle again. "The water is from the mind of God. Which part of what I'm holding is from the mind of people?"

Dimple flicked her nose ring. "Um, the bottle."

"That's right," Jessie said. "The bottle. The bottle is from the mind of people. The bottle limits the water. It helps us carry it and give it out. It's basically good. But it does limit the water. And it labels the water too. It tells people about the water, what kind it is, where it comes from. It's this bottle that becomes the problem. Do you know that some people don't want this water? Some people don't like water at all. They want a Coke, or a beer. How many cases do we have left, Dzon?"

Dzon smiled. "Six and a half."

The One and True Son

Jessie put his hand on Dimple's shoulder. "It is not in the mind of God that we suffer. People have created this situation on their own."

* * *

"How long will you be with us?" Dzon asked at supper one evening. He was looking down at his plate, but those around the table, Dimple, Carl, a tall, slim street artist, Robert, a Vietnam vet and PTSD sufferer, Petra, a boat mechanic and Jessie, knew to whom he was speaking.

"I will be leaving soon," Jessie said placing down his plate. "My father has given me a lot to do. There are things he needs to show me, things I still don't understand."

"You seem a pretty fair carpenter to me," Petra said and laughed.

Jessie laughed too. "Joe, the carpenter, was not my father although he loved me and protected me as if I were his son. He was a good and faithful man to my mother and I will always love him and be grateful for him."

Dzon put his arm around Petra and shook her. "You don't realize who we have here. You will thank God that you were here in this special place with our special guest."

"I already do, Dzon," Petra answered. "And I think I know who Jessie is."

Everyone grew still.

Jessie's eyes, the eyes of his mother, gazed into Petra's.

"And who do you say that I am," Jessie asked.

Petra's eyes flooded with tears.

"You're the one and true son," she said.

Jessie stood and threw open his arms. Petra stood and ran into them.

He hugged her and kissed the top of her head.

"Petra, a moment ago you called me a carpenter. You are the first brick in the foundation of my house."

In the morning, when they woke, Jessie was gone.

The Adversary

The arid breezes that dusted Death Valley seared Jessie's nostrils and throat with every breath. If he'd had a thermometer, he'd have seen it filled with mostly red, topping 120 degrees in the direct sun. Dust coated his hair, eyelashes and beard, as if he'd journeyed through a storm of dirty snow. This was the hottest, lowest point in North America. Tourists rarely entered the Mojave in July. The few cars that passed him slowed down when they saw him; some rolled down their windows prepared, it seemed, to offer him a ride. Did he know where he was going? Was he crazy? He waved them all on, saying nothing. Along the way he saw no joggers, no bicyclists, no hikers. It was the way he wanted it.

It took him three days to get out of the Los Angeles city sprawl, past Brentwood, past Barstow, past Nealey's Corner. He found himself going north on Lytle Creek Road, the houses and small businesses, the gas stations and the Quick Marts getting further apart, the hills off the shoulder, with their greasewood and desert holly taking up more and more of the real estate.

Jessie thought of his Father when he got hungry, and the empty feeling would pass. When he'd left Dzon's camp, he brought a student backpack with him filled with bottled water and a large piece of canvas. He allowed himself a few sips of water every hour, careful not take in too much and cause cramps. His pace was steady and focused.

At night, when the unimpeded sun finally ducked behind the desolate horizon, the temperature dropped to a pleasant springlike cool. To sleep, Jessie rolled out the canvas and spread it out on the smoothest rock he could find and slept until sunrise. He knew it would be easier, in fact recommended, that he walk at night and sleep during the day. But Jessie preferred to travel with the light. The heat would not deter him from reaching where he needed to be. Occasionally the desert animals checked him out, a jack rabbit or an antelope squirrel. One night a mountain lion caught his scent and crept up on her haunches to what seemed to be an easy meal. Jessie hadn't fallen asleep yet and sat up. The lion stopped in her tracks and sniffed the air. Jessie adjusted himself comfortably on the rock and looked back at the predator, locking eyes with the cat. After a moment, the hungry lion lay on the cooling ground and rested its chin on her forepaws. Jessie stretched once again on the rock and slept. When he awoke the next morning, the cat was still lying there, though on its back, her paws dangling over exposed belly.

When Jessie got up and continued his journey, the lion followed for a short while, later to disappear behind the baking hills.

Three days later, he entered Death Valley.

He caught Route 178 just north of Shoshone and headed west. If it weren't for the hardy brush dotting the landscape the scene could have been on Mars. The jagged hills in the distance seemed to move away from him as he walked. The further he walked, the further they appeared to be. By then, Jessie had nearly exhausted his water supply and only allowed himself a few sips every couple of hours. There were no trees under which to dodge the relentless sun, very few crevices deep enough to offer shade. The baked, rocky soil appeared to boil around him, the dust, rising from the hot crust like stream, mixed with the faint breeze and disappeared. He could feel the adversary getting closer.

By sunset the day before he reached his destination, Jessie found himself at the Ashford Mills Ruins, the remnants of a gold processing operation from the early twentieth century and pretty much the only manmade structures he'd seen in days. Jessie felt the seasonal abandonment acutely as the heat kept visitors away, his own footsteps the only disturbances in the dust. A lone picnic table sat near the sign announcing why stone walls with windows that hadn't seen glass existed in the middle of the desert. He walked around the site and found himself in the three remaining walls of what was once the office for a less than successful gold mining operation. The walls of heavy stone reminded him of photos he'd seen taken in Jerusalem, Iraq and Syria. Although these walls were millennia younger, they shared with their ancient cousins the failure of material wealth for those who desperately wanted it, or, once obtaining it, wanted to keep it. The walls, incomplete as they were, will always carry that message.

"This is where you want me, Father," Jessie said to dry sky around him. "I'm ready."

He pulled the canvas out of his backpack and spread it on the picnic table. He was grateful for the uniform flatness of the tabletop having slept the last few nights on uneven rocks with the occasional pebble in uncomfortable places. He sat on the edge of the table and watched the sun dip, with fiery orange and bloody crimson, behind the Black Mountains in the distance.

When a deep obsidian replaced the sun's death-celebration in the desert sky, Jessie lay his head on the canvas and watched the stars of the Milky Way creep across his vision. He tried to close his eyes and drift off, but unease filled his thoughts. Although the light was gone, it seemed the heat had not abated. The welcome cool night breeze, something he'd grown to look forward to in this journey, became more akin to hot breath. A sulfurous wisp drifted in and out from a distance.

When sleep finally came, it was fitful and shallow. Several times he awoke with a start, a high hiss scratching at his ears, like the legs of hundreds of thousands, millions, of insects shuffling and digging in the baked earth around him. When he awoke, the hiss hung in the air for a moment then drifted away like smoke.

In the morning he drank the remainder of his water and headed off for Badwater Basin.

The odor of lit matches permeated the air, growing thicker, the closer he got to his destination. Badwater Road, the last desolate stretch of his journey, was bordered on the east by cracked scabs of earth, raised by the turmoil of centuries of anhydrous sun and capricious floods. The hills appeared agitated, picked at. To the west, salt flats took over; the hills in the distance faded to washed out browns and grays. He knew he had reached the basin when he looked up to the hills and saw a sign 280 feet up: Sea Level.

Jessie walked the plank walkway that led to the salt flats. The skin of the earth here was flaked and fragile and protected with rope lines that kept visitors from stepping off too early. The hissing from the previous night returned, this time sounding more like fat on a hot skillet. As he reached the end of the walkway and stepped onto the battered white salt trail trodden by countless years and visitors, the air before him wrinkled and expanded, distorting everything in his vision. Perhaps a football field away he could make out a shape forming in the furnace-like atmosphere. It was a jet.

He walked closer. The aircraft formed fully, conjured from the ancient dust. It was a large white plane with two engines at the tail. Twelve oval windows evenly dotted the length of the fuselage. Against the dirty landscape, the craft gleamed, its tires showing no dust from landing, as if it had been sitting in a showroom. After a click and a hiss, the hatch near the nose of the jet opened at the top and lowered to just above the basin floor.

The One and True Son

A stairway emerged from a compartment underneath the hatch. A lone figure stood in the hatchway.

"Jessie," the figure spoke with a soft southern accent and a buttery voice. "I'm so glad ya could make it."

"I wouldn't miss it," Jessie replied.

The figure descended the stairway, shoes made of a beautiful and recently dead reptile on his feet. His golden hair, expertly coiffed and poofy, shined in the desert sun, unaffected by any breeze. His suit, a sandy brown, made of the finest silks, lay close to his skin, hanging perfectly; it moved with him as only the best tailor could ensure. His face, free of wrinkles, brown like his suit, belied his age with a certain artificiality. His eyes were ice blue. On his lapel, a preserved scorpion, pinned through its back, appeared ready to sting.

He offered no handshake.

"Young man, I've waited so long to meet ya. We have a lot to chat about, you and me."

Jessie only nodded once.

"So, let's get goin'" the adversary said and gestured toward the plane.

The aircraft cabin was magnificent. The seats, spacious and comfortable, were appointed in soft white leather. The same leather adorned the ceiling and the bulkheads. Lacquered buffed mahogany made up the cabinetry throughout; two mahogany tabletops waited in the cabin each with flatscreens and attached telephones.

"This thing sleeps fourteen. Do ya believe it? The seats fold down and there are two private cabins in the back. If ya want to rest, you're welcome to one."

Jessie smiled. He said nothing.

The adversary put a hand on Jessie's shoulder.

"You sure don't talk much, do ya?"

"I do when I have something to say," Jessie responded.

The other guffawed. "Yeah, I guess you probably do. Have a seat and strap yourself in. We're gonna go for a ride."

Jessie sat at one of the tables and fastened the lap belt around him.

"I'd have a pretty stewardess give you the whole emergency exit speech and all that shit, but you know nothin's gonna happen to this plane. I'll spare you that."

The other snapped his fingers and the rear engines began to hum, winding up to a metallic whine. He sat across from Jessie and clicked on his seatbelt.

The One and True Son

"You never know when you might hit turbulence," he grinned, his teeth pearl white, straight and sharp.

The jet moved across the salt flats, gaining speed. In seconds, they were airborne, cruising over the desert in the direction of Nevada.

The two said nothing for some time. The adversary broke the silence.

"Damn, you look like you been through it. You walk all the way?"

Jessie nodded.

"All you brought with ya was that kids backpack," the other gestured toward Jessie's pack in the seat next to him. "You must have been walkin' for a while from the looks of ya. Can't fit much food in there."

Jessie looked back, neither agreeing or disagreeing.

The other's white teeth gleamed at Jessie.

"Now, I got an idea. You're hungry. I know you are." He reached under the table and brought up what looked to be about a five- pound rock. He placed the rock in front of Jessie.

"Change this rock into bread. You can eat up. I'll even get you some peanut butter for it."

It was Jessie's turn to laugh.

"You brought me up here for a magic show?" He said. "We could land in Las Vegas for that. I hear Penn and Teller have a great show."

The other's icy eyes flickered fury. His smiled remained.

"So, you can't do it," he said. "Maybe I got the wrong guy."

Jessie leaned forward. "You know who I am. My Father provided for me on this trip. I needed no bread. All I needed was to think of Him." He picked up the rock and placed it in front of the adversary.

The other went silent again. He stared at the tabletop in front of him, as if looking at some unseen chessboard.

After what seemed an hour, he spoke again.

"I need you to come with me," he said unbuckling his seatbelt and standing. "I want to show you something."

The adversary led Jessie to the front of the plane and opened the heavy curtain that separated the cockpit from the rest of the cabin. Two pilots sat behind the high-tech controls. All aspects of the flight were monitored on two screens of orange, blue, black and green; ever-changing numbers ticked with new readings on altitude, pitch, windspeed and the like. A center screen showed the topography of the earth below them. The crew, a man and a woman, impeccably dressed in starched shirts and matching ties, took no notice of their visitors, focused completely on the screens in

The One and True Son

front them. The woman, seated at the right of the plane appeared to have the controls as her hand rested on the joystick to her side.

"Isn't this cool," the other asked? "I don't know fuck all what any of this shit does, but *man* is it cool lookin'."

Jessie pursed his lips.

The other was unperturbed. "Ah well, I guess it ain't for everybody." He gestured over to a seat behind the pilots, facing toward the left cockpit windows. "I want you to take the jump seat. I got a proposition for you, and I want you to get a good look."

Jessie sat.

"Buckle up," the other said, smiling.

"Svetlana," he continued, "I want you to dip your left wing so our guest here can see where he is."

The pilot moved her hand on the stick slightly and the plane banked to the left.

"She's a damned good pilot, Svetlana. Used to fly for the Russian Navy. She can land this thing on a cockroach's left nut."

Out the window Jessie could see the Vegas strip stretching out underneath them.

"You ever been to Vegas," the adversary asked?

Jessie shook his head. "I've seen pictures of it."

"Aw, you should go some time. It's so much fun. You got shows and great food. You don't even have to gamble. With a little help from your Dad you could clean up though." The other laughed heartily at his joke.

"I might go sometime," Jessie said, "but not to see the shows."

The other's smile dimmed a bit. "Yeah, I bet not."

"Anyway," he continued. "That's Vegas out there. That's mine. I control it. I built it. I run it. I do as I please there."

"So you think," Jessie responded.

"So I know, sonny boy. So I know. But watch this. Svetlana, dip the right wing, sweetheart."

As she applied pressure to the stick, the adversary snapped his fingers.

"You're gonna have to unbuckle to see this," the other told Jessie.

When the wing dipped, they were no longer cruising over the artificial city in the middle of the Mojave Desert. They were over a greener area with much more water.

They were over the Potomac.

The spokes of Washington DC's streets spread out beneath them. As they circled, the massive US Capital came into view. The cars on

The One and True Son

Pennsylvania Avenue took no notice as the jet cruised over the White House and turned north at the Washington Monument.

"I bet you suspected for a long time that this was mine too," the other smirked. "Now, I've had my battles, you know with that Dr. King fella and such, among others. But that guy, he wasn't like you. He'd fuck anyone I'd throw at him. Not that that helped me much."

"So, why all this?" Jessie asked.

"Patience. Patience," the other admonished. "I'm not finished yet. Where do you want to go?"

He snapped his fingers.

"Moscow?"

The view from the window changed from the green hills of Maryland to the lighted walls of the Kremlin. The Eastern Orthodox Temple with its golden spires, topped with the stars of the Soviets, split the night sky.

He snapped his fingers again.

"Peking? They say to call it Beijing but fuck that shit. I'll call it what I want."

Below them, the endless sprawl of the Chinese capitol unfolded with its new ultramodern skyscrapers surrounded by the mundane uniformity of the old economy.

The other held his hand up to snap again. "Fuck it. You want to go to Fiji? It's gorgeous there."

Jessie was growing weary. "I wish you'd get to the point."

"The point!" He shouted. "The point! I want to give this to you! Every place you've seen, everywhere you go! You'll control it! It'll be yours! I'll give it to you!"

"And all I have to do is…" Jessie said.

The adversary smiled his biggest smile yet, the edges of his perfect teeth gleaming like razors.

"Worship me," he said.

Jessie said nothing for a few moments.

"Remember I told you that my Father gave me what I need for this journey?" He said finally. "All that you've offered me, and I won't even mention that your claim is questionable, is transient. Those buildings will all go away. Someone, sometime, will tear them down. Or blow them up." He sighed. "Those people down there. They'll die. Most knowing nothing of power or who controls this or who controls that. Some will know neither me nor my Father. But *they* are of *my Father's* mind. *You* can't separate them for my Father's mind. And *I* am of *His* mind too. *We* are inseparable."

52

The One and True Son

Back in the galley, seated in his spacious soft white leather seat, the adversary was fuming. It was clear that this trip had not gone as planned, a situation he was not at all used to. He took a sip of the drink he made for himself, a scotch and soda. He offered one to Jessie, but he wasn't surprised when he declined.

"You know," he said, tapping his immaculate fingernails on the edge of his glass, "I been thinking. Maybe you're not who you say you are."

"Really?" Jessie mocked.

"Yeah really," the other attempted to mock back. "I mean, you did show up at the meeting point and all. But look at you. You're covered in dirt. You've got holes in your clothes. And you're kinda disrespectful if you ask me. Kind of a smartass."

"Careful," Jessie said. "You might hurt my feelings."

The other slammed his fist on the table. "That's it! I've got a way to make sure. Come on."

Jessie followed the adversary to the front of the plane, just outside the cockpit. The hatch that they'd entered the aircraft through was on the left. A panel with two buttons, one red and one green, was attached next to hatch, installed into the bulkhead. The adversary pushed the red button and the hatch unsealed. The wind roared outside, the other's scotch glass flew off the table and was quickly sucked out of the cabin. The other grabbed the partition between the main cabin and the cockpit. His strength would hold him where he stood. Jessie grabbed a handle next to the hatch. The hatch swung down.

The other screamed over the howling wind.

"I READ IN ONE OF THOSE GOD BOOKS THAT IF YOU WERE HIS SON THAT HE WOULD SEND HIS ANGELS TO SAVE YOU! NOW THIS SHOULDN'T BE HARD IF YOU ARE WHO YOU SAY YOU ARE!"

The smile the other had shown Jessie through this whole encounter morphed into what it had really been all along. A scowl of hate.

"JUMP!" He shouted.

Jessie didn't move. A smile came to his face, but it was a true smile, a sad smile. It was a smile of pity.

"I HAVE ANOTHER IDEA!" He shouted to the adversary. "I'M NOT GOING TO JUMP! BUT I THINK YOU CAN GET THE SAME RESULTS!"

The other looked puzzled.

"PUSH ME!" Jessie shouted.

"WHAT?!" the adversary shouted back.

The One and True Son

Jessie looked the other dead in the eye. "YOU HEARD WHAT I SAID! PUSH ME!"

A new expression appeared on the adversary's face. It was unmistakable. It was the look of disbelief. It was the look of fear.

The other snapped his fingers one final time.

Jessie found himself standing at the edge of the salt flats. It was night.

The Waiter

Silvio disliked weddings, but they were his bread and butter. He much preferred his weekends on the other end of the serving relationship, ordering beers at The Hole in the Wall, a pub near the University of Texas at Austin where he was a third year Law student. The live music there was more to his liking than the usual wedding bands that played everything from old Tom Petty to old Kool and the Gang and he didn't have to cover his tattooed arms with a tuxedo shirt. Sometimes the women would get just as drunk at the weddings and sometimes he could take advantage of that, but he was working. He couldn't drink. And nothing was worse to Silvio than watching people getting drunk without being able to join in.

This wedding was a bit out of his way, about 20 miles west of the city, down 290, maybe a 45-minute drive, in a small town named Cafracana. It was a new town even for Central Texas, built into the bends of the Pedernales River consisting of more McMansions per capita than any other area in the state. Anytime he could get a gig in Cafracana, he'd jump at it. They always paid well and tipped well. The Hole in the Wall would have to wait.

He drove up the dirt road that led to The River House, the place where the wedding and reception would be taking place. The venue must have been there long before the town, Silvio thought, as the main structure was an old barn, stripped of its siding, leaving only the old studs and what appeared to be a new roof. The grounds were beautiful, with gentle rolling hills and ample shade from the mesquite trees and desert willows. Large rocks on both sides of the entrance walk led the betrothed and guests from the dirt parking lot to the barn. The grass would have made any golf course groundskeeper proud. The kitchen facilities were located adjacent to the barn; the bar sat inside the barn itself on the opposite side. As was his standard practice, Silvio arrived three hours before any guests even thought about showing up. He didn't need to. He just liked to walk around and look at things, to get the feel of the place. He imagined he'd do the same thing in courtrooms after he passed the bar exam.

"Silvio," someone called. "Over here."

It was Anthony, the owner of the catering company he worked for. Silvio liked Anthony and vice/versa. They were both about the same age, both driven, mostly by money, and they both liked to get to business early, to do things right. Anthony was a weightlifter, about six feet tall with jet black hair, close cropped on the sides and back and combed back on the top into a "man bun". He had a thick, wiry beard and intense black eyes set back under thick brows. His biceps strained against his white silk tuxedo jacket. No one mentioned his man bun. Not to his face anyway.

"This one's going to be a pain the ass," he told Silvio. "Lucrative, but still a pain in the ass." He gestured to the cases of wine and beer bottles that lay stacked on the other side of the bar. "See the beer bottles? They don't want any kegs. No draft. Only bottles." He added, "No hard stuff either."

There had to be 50 cases of beer, all imported, all expensive.

"They want these iced and poured in beer flutes. God, I *love* rich people."

"What about the wine?" Silvio asked. For every case of beer there seemed to be a case of wine, French reds, Italian whites, German Rieslings, and California Zinfandels for the peasants. And, of course, there was champagne: five bottles of Mag Perignon for the wedding, the bride and groom of course got their own, and five cases of California sparkling wine for the toast.

"Oh, this is a beauty. They brought in this shelf," Anthony said, gesturing to a large bookcase-looking thing placed inside the large U-shaped bar. It was solid wood, probably oak, with wide shelves and no back. The frame had hand-carved wedding scenes, probably by hand. Each scene was separated by twisting grapevines and toasting wine glasses. "The bride's nutty cousin made this especially for her for her wedding day. They want the bottles all *standing,* that's right, I said *standing* with the labels facing out. I guess that's so the guests can count the Rothschilds bottles from the other side of the barn."

Silvio looked at the shelf doubtfully. "The cousin should've just sent flowers."

Anthony laughed. "Tell me about it. I'm glad you're here early. You get the honor of putting these bottles on the shelf."

"Lucky me," said Silvio.

"Hey," Anthony said. "I give the best jobs to the best."

The One and True Son

"Someday I'll learn to be a slacker."

Anthony put his strong paw on Silvio's shoulder. "Not today."

* * *

Jessie and his followers arrived in Cafracana in two vehicles, an ancient Ford Bronco and a minivan, perhaps a Nissan, that had every identifying word or emblem removed with a screwdriver. Maria asked Jessie to be there. She had known the parents of the groom when they were poor and desperate, going to the same storefront temple where Maria had met Joe in Travis City. Through hard work and belief in their Creator, the couple clawed their way to a prosperous life. They never forgot Maria. At each step out of the pit they were in they'd kept in touch with Maria, asking after Joe and their beautiful son. Jessie was reluctant, at first, to attend the wedding. He explained on the phone that he was traveling with his followers now, that he didn't want to be without them at this point. Maria assured him that they'd all be welcome. It'd been ages since she'd seen her boy and she was eager to see whom he'd chosen to travel with. She knew that each of them would be special.

Jessie and his twelve followers dressed in attire appropriate for a Texas wedding complete with a couple Stetsons and several pairs of fancy stitched boots, bolo ties and snap button shirts. Jessie watched as his disciples piled out of the vehicles and stepped out onto the dusty parking lot. They played and teased each other like children, filled with the joy of a wedding.

"I get the first dance with Dimple," Andrew called, poking Dimple in the ribs.

"You must not like your toes," Dimple answered, giggling. "These cowboy boots aren't exactly ballet slippers."

"Try not to be clowns," Praise said, always the serious one. She'd eschewed cowboy garb, choosing instead a simple yellow sundress and plain leather sandals. Her hair was tied in tight plaits; her scalp glistened with castor oil. "Jessie's mother is here. Don't embarrass him in front of her."

Jessie laid his forearm on her shoulder. "Don't worry, dear one. They're happy. And you should be too." He kissed her on the forehead.

Praise smiled up at him. "I'll try," she said.

Maria greeted them in the barn. She ran to Jessie and grabbed him in a bearhug, wiping away happy tears. The twelve stood close by, waiting to be introduced.

"Mother," Jessie said. "This is my family."

The One and True Son

She pulled herself from Jessie to hug each one of them, whispering "Bless you" as she let go of one and moved onto the next. The hosts made sure that the two tables reserved for Maria and Jessie and his guests were close to the happy couple. The large group circled the tables looking for their names on the miniature old-west wanted posters that the wedding planners had made to go along with the cowboy theme of the event. Jessie found his, next to this mother's. The picture on the card showed a faux antique picture of a scraggly bearded character with an eyepatch and holey ten- gallon hat. Jessie's name was printed under the photo. Jessie knew the cards were meant to be lighthearted, yet they made him uneasy.

A tiny flower girl led the bridal procession, dressed in white silk with a wide blue ribbon at her waist, her head of precious brown curls hanging loose and free. The ceremony, performed by the moreh from the family temple, was full of love and humor, the officiant quick with one-liners. The bride, smiling through a torrent of tears throughout the exchange of vows, dressed in a clinging white silk dress with lace sleeves and a veil pinned to the back of her long, straight black hair and draped forward over her large brown eyes and high cheekbones. The groom, also a tad red-eyed, smiled back at her, wearing white western style tails, the collar of his tux shirt closed with a bolo of white silk cord and a platinum head of a Texas longhorn.

While the wedding party posed for photographs, the guests cooled their heels milling around the venue, making small talk and consuming the excellent wines and beers available to them. Although most of the attendees hadn't met or known of Jessie and his followers, they were a source of great curiosity among the small conversation groups that had formed under the barn roof.

"Who is that man?" one older woman asked her cousin. "The tall one. I swear I've seen him somewhere."

"He does look familiar. Is he a musician?" the cousin answered.

Speculation took hold in almost every corner of the venue.

Is he in the movies?

I think he's on TV or something.

He's that woman's son, I think.

The wedding party finally emerged from the seemingly endless post ceremony photo session, smiling but looking winded. The groom shed his jacket. The bride, her veil no longer needed, cast it aside exposing the excited blush of her new status. Everyone made their way to their assigned tables as the waiters shifted into high gear. Plates of poached salmon and ribeye steaks clinked around the room with grace and precision.

A local band opened the festivities with a rousing Dwight Yoakam number.

Silvio greeted Jessie's group after the proper meals were in place.

"I'm Silvio," the waiter said, making eye contact with everyone at the table. "I'll be your server for this evening. If there's anything you need, please don't hesitate to ask." He looked at Jessie and smiled. "That's what I'm here for."

"Where are you from?" Jessie asked.

"I live in Austin," the waiter replied.

"Where are you from originally?"

"I was born in Portugal, a place called Coimbra."

"Isn't there a university there?" Jessie asked.

"Yes," the waiter answered, surprised that this man would know that. "My father was a professor at the University for a short time. He always wanted to come to the states. He was able to get a position UT. I was five when we moved here."

Silvio was a little weirded out. He was reasonably sure that any trace of an accent he may have had had faded sometime in the third or fourth grade.

"Roman Architecture. Is that your father's area?"

It was. The waiter nodded.

Jessie smiled. "Don't worry. I haven't been following you. The Romans are a particular interest of mine. They were a brilliant, but brutal people. Coimbra has a famous aqueduct. I just put two and two together."

The waiter was silent for a moment.

"Are you a student?" Jessie asked.

"Yes," Silvio replied. His smile returned. "I'm third year Law. I do this on the weekends. Sometimes more in the summers."

"The law is an interesting thing," said Jessie. "The ideas of many people. To some it is a way to protect those with power. To others, it's a way to protect those without power from those who have it. It's a worthy endeavor to study the law. Your parents must be proud."

The waiter's smile dimmed a bit. "They're gone now. But thank you."

"Do you close your eyes and see your mother's smile?" Jessie said. "Do you speak to your father in your dreams? Do you feel his hand on your shoulder when he tries to comfort you?"

Silvio nodded. For the moment, he'd completely forgotten why he was in Cafracana. He'd forgotten about waiting on tables, forgotten about law school. The people under this deconstructed barn seemed to fade. Everyone except this man speaking to him. Silvio never told anyone of his dreams.

He supposed they could be common among people who have lost so much so young, but there was something else. This man *knows* something.

Your mother and father are not gone. They are with my Father. They are never gone.

"Silvio!" A familiar voice snapped him back to the wedding. It was Anthony. "I'm sorry folks. I've got to pull Silvio away for a bit."

As they walked back toward the bar, Anthony laid his toned arm around Silvio's shoulder and shook him. "You okay, dude? You looked a little confused back there."

"Yeah, I mean no...I'm... I'm okay."

"Good, because I need you," Anthony said with another shake to Silvio's shoulders.

"This new bartender is in way over her head. She can barely keep up. We're not even doing mixers."

"What about my tables?" Silvio asked.

"I don't want you to pour. I just need you to restock that stupid bookcase with wine. It's almost empty and if she walks away from the bar for a minute, she's going to get way behind. And this is too sweet a gig for any complaints about the cute but slow bartender."

When they got to the bar, Anthony clapped Silvio on the back. "Fix it for me, buddy."

There was just enough room for Silvio to empty the remaining cases and face the labels out so everyone could see the fancy names and the choice vintages. Miriam. A tiny girl with waist length straight black hair, a gift from her Korean mother, was scrambling with the never-ending requests for glasses of Mouton Cadet Rothschild, 2007 and Bernkasteler Riesling, 2002. Silvio thought Anthony was being a little hard on the girl. Although the line seemed to be never-ending, the petite bartender moved steadily from one guest to another, smiled consistently, and looked neither flustered nor tired. Her tip glass filled appropriately.

"You okay, kid?" Silvio asked after he'd cast aside the last empty box.

"Never stops, but it's cool." Miriam smiled, her black eyes shining below her cat's eye mascara. "And who are you calling 'kid'? What are you, 25?"

Silvio smiled back. "Twenty-six, next month. But I remember when I was your age."

"Go away," Miriam ordered with a chuckle.

She's definitely cute, Silvio thought.

As he made his way back to his tables, Silvio and everyone else jumped from an explosive sound, a sudden crash. It sounded like a thousand bottles breaking. It was actually 142. The bookcase/wine rack had given way. Not a single bottle survived. Rivers of 12-year-old Bordeaux mingled with semi-sweet German Spatlese from vintages that had not been this good since 1945. The heavy oaken shelves, from the ill-thought-out bookcase/wine rack, added their own weight to the demise of the glass containers on display, spraying the expensive pumps, tuxedo shirt and flawless black hair of the unsuspecting bartender nearest to the disaster, Miriam, making her appear more like a mass shooting survivor than a witness to what had to be one of the most expensive wine floods in Texas history.

While Miriam and Silvio scrambled for towels, brooms and mops, Anthony was on his phone to every wine supplier he could think of. The day being a Sunday, in Texas, added to the impossibility of his task. He didn't get so much as voicemail. By law, even the liquor stores were closed.

"Well, I hope you weren't planning to get paid," Anthony told Silvio under his breath as he grabbed a broom.

"What?" Silvio replied, perhaps a bit too loudly. "That stupid shelf was the family's idea. We never would've used it!"

"Shhh. I know. But you know how people get. They're going to say you..." Anthony noticed Silvio's clenched jaw. "They're going to say *we* overloaded it. I haven't talked to them yet..."

"Excuse me." A tall man with a prominently swollen lower abdomen and large beige Stetson interrupted from the end of the bar.

"Until now," Anthony continued. "Father of the bride. Keep cleaning this up. I'll see if I can work something out. Maybe they'll be reasonable."

Silvio looked to Miriam. "Think they'll be reasonable, kid?"

"I don't know, old man. In my very limited experience, people who could afford cases of expensive wine for a wedding didn't get that way from being reasonable."

"You're wise beyond your years," Silvio teased.

"Shut up," replied Miriam.

When Anthony returned, he looked relieved. "He was totally cool. The bride's dad hated that shelf more than we did. He just didn't want to hurt the cousin's feelings. I feel bad though. There's no wine. The bride and groom didn't even get to do the toast."

"They can use beer," Silvio suggested.

Miriam rolled her eyes. "I know this *is* Texas, but a wedding toast with beer?"

"Not romantic?" Silvio asked.

"You're not sure, great sage? No wonder you're waiting on tables and not on a date somewhere."

Silvio clutched his chest. "You cut me to the bone!"

"All right, both of you, knock it off," Anthony cut in. "Miriam, help me clean up this mess. Silvio, go tell the guests there will be no more wine this evening."

"Why me?" Silvio asked.

"You're going to be the lawyer, right? You need to practice your bullshit."

Maria was finally getting the names down. The girl with the ropey hair was Dimple. Maria liked Dimple. She was as open as a window in the spring. Jessie's mother could tell that the girl (woman?) hung and her son's every word. Jessie would need that. He needed people who paid attention.

Levi, tall and skinny, with almost translucent white skin, a balding pate and a fourteen-year-old's mustache, was a former agent for the IRS. He told Maria how he'd heard Jessie speaking outside a temple and called in his resignation on his cell phone, on the spot. Levi would know the ways of the government. Jessie was choosing well.

Joodith, a former social worker, an olive complected Indian-American woman with wispy black hair and heavy black brows, explained how she had seen Maria's son reach out to a man she had been trying to get through to for months. The man was hooked on heroin, she explained and threatened suicide whenever he ran out of the drug. She had tracked him down outside of Dzon's camp after she hadn't seen him for a few days. She'd found him huddled outside the opening in the chain link fence which served as the entrance to the camp. He'd been curled into a fetal position, shivering and sweating in the California heat. "When I said the Jessie 'reached out' to this man, I mean that literally," she said. "I had been trying to coax him into my car, to take him to the hospital. I had my cell phone on my hand. I thought about calling an ambulance. And then Jessie was there."

Joodith sat down in an adjacent chair and set her hands on Maria's. "Jessie knelt next to him. He reached down to the man's shoulders. He kissed his forehead." Joodith took a breath. "The man stopped shivering. He opened his eyes. They were *clear*. Mind you, I'd never seen this man's eyes unclouded." She wiped a tear away from her eye."Do you know how special your son is?"

Maria nodded. She knew.

The One and True Son

All of the twelve made a point of introducing themselves to Jessie's mother. Some approached boldly like Petra, Simone and Justice, with their hands extended, eager to discuss the devotion they held for her son. Others were more reticent, like Jack, Jaime, Bart, and Philip, who approached her cautiously, as if they feared they may be judged unworthy. They spoke to her in near-whispers, curious to discover just how much this seemingly ordinary mother knew of her extraordinary son. These men soon discovered that she was no ordinary woman, and she, more than they, knew exactly how extraordinary Jessie was.

And then there was Praise. The young woman sat opposite from Maria, across the circular tabletop, smiling occasionally, but saying little. She appeared uncomfortable at her place at the table, often scanning the room with her eyes, looking for other places to be. When Maria moved next to her and sat in the empty chair, Praise jumped, as she'd been looking the other way.

"You must be Praise," the mother said. "I've heard a lot about you."

"Yes ma'am," Praise answered.

"You were a police officer?" Maria asked. "That's a tough job. It must have kept your parents up at night with worry."

"I was," Praise said. "My father was an officer as well. We didn't get much sleep in our house."

"Excuse me, folks." It was Silvio. "I'm sure you heard that crash a little while ago. I'm sorry to say that that was the wine. I mean all of it. The staff here would like to apologize. Unfortunately, there won't be any more wine for the remainder of the evening."

"That's such a shame," Maria said. "Everything has been done so beautifully. Is there any way to get more?"

"I'm afraid not, ma'am. Sunday's a dry day in Texas. All the liquor stores are closed from here to Oklahoma. Even the champagne for the toast broke open. We've tried everything we can think of."

Maria looked over at Jessie who had been following the conversation from across the table. She raised an eyebrow.

"What?" Jessie asked with a shrug.

"*You* can do something." Maria said.

"Mother, I don't know anyone in the liquor business," Jessie complained. "This has nothing to do with me."

Maria locked her eyes on her son.

"It's not my time, mother."

Maria, unmoved, turned to the waiter. "Do whatever he tells you to do."

The One and True Son

Silvio turned to Jessie. The odd sensation he'd felt earlier returned. Again, the others in the party seemed to fade into the background. The conversations around him squelched; he heard nothing but a soft hum. Although he was sure the man was speaking, Silvio heard his words in his mind, as if it were a separate conversation strictly between the two of them.

You're part of something special. Bring me pitchers of water, as many as you can carry. What you'll see is a lesson in perception. Water, all water, is of my Father's mind. It is the essence of life itself. Bring me this and I will show you what others have not seen. You will see the thoughts of my Father. Don't forget what you see.

As instructed, Silvio went to the kitchen and gathered seven red plastic water pitchers. He filled each one with water, three inches to the top. He gripped the handles of four pitchers in one hand and three in the other and walked them back to Jessie's table. He repeated this process twice more before Jessie told him: "That's enough."

All conversation at Maria and Jessie's tables ceased. The eyes of the faithful all looked to Jessie.

He spoke.

This occasion is a celebration of love, my Father's greatest gift. I say to you all, that you are never lacking. I tell you that my Father has provided for you in all circumstances and if you perceive his thoughts properly, you will never lack what is needed."

Jessie grabbed the handles of two pitchers in front of him. His eyes locked on the water in the pitcher on the left. He took a deep breath and closed his eyes.

After several minutes, he looked up at the waiter.

"Pour a glass from any of the pitchers. Take the glass to your boss. Come back to us and tell us what he says."

Silvio picked up a wine glass from the table. He chose the pitcher closest to him and filled the glass. Trembling slightly, he went to find Anthony.

When he'd returned the trembling hadn't subsided. If anything, he shook more. He no longer held the wine glass. He'd given that to Anthony. Silvio had seen magicians. He'd watched David Blaine and Chris Angel on TV. He'd even practiced a little sleight of hand as a teenager, although his fingers were more attuned to flipping through books than decks of cards. He knew that there was always a trick involved. He also knew that what he'd just witnessed was no trick. He stood at the table for a moment.

"What did your boss say?" Jessie asked.

Silvio cleared his throat. "He said, 'I thought the Mag bottles were broken.'"

"Excuse me?" Levi, the former taxman, asked.

"Magus Perignon, the champagne. He thought the champagne bottles were broken. They were actually. He thought the glass I brought him was Magus Perignon."

"He drank it?" Jessie inquired.

"He did."

"Does he know good champagne?"

"He knows it better than anyone," the waiter answered.

Jessie stood from the table and laid his hand on the waiter's shoulder.

"What do you think the guests will think when they are served from these pitchers? The waiter looked at the unusual man, maybe the most usual man he'd ever met.

"They'll think whatever your father thinks," he said.

The Reporter

"You're shitting me, right?"

Saul Armour shifted in his chair. He usually didn't get visits from the features editor at his desk or anywhere else really. Email was usually sufficient for story questions or edits he wanted to see. There was a bigger issue. Armour couldn't say the visit was unexpected.

"I wish I was, Jim," Armour shrugged.

"My office," the editor said.

Saul Armour got his start in Chicago, at the Tribune. Educationally edified with a Journalism degree from the University of Illinois at Chicago, Armour burst on the newspaper scene as an unpaid intern in the early '90s. By 1995, he'd worked his way up to gofer for the cantankerous columnist Mike Royko who, on occasion, wrote about his assistant's diminutive size and early thinning hair. When Royko died in 1997, Armour finally made it to the big time, to his dream: reporter. He did a stint at the criminal courts beat, sitting in court for every senseless murder in Chicago, which averaged about two a day. Depression and beer became his off-duty companions.

And then he met Lilian. Lilian knew about violence. She had gone in with the Marines in Baghdad during the Gulf War in the early '90s which made her a minor celebrity in reporter circles. She followed that up with frequent stays at the Sarajevo Holiday Inn where she spent almost two years ducking bullets and eating in the hotel restaurant while the other side of the building absorbed daily shelling. At five feet, zero (her description of her height) she joked that it made her a small target. She complained that the bullet proof vest and hardened helmet she was issued only served to make her a bigger duck in the Bosnian shooting gallery. When she was finally rotated back home to Chicago, she took her back pay and hung up her press badge.

The One and True Son

Saul and Lilian met at The Billy Goat, a landmark bar located just under the Tribune on lower Michigan Avenue where Royko, Terkel and countless other journalists downed lakes of alcohol and consumed pastures of thin, greasy burgers. They took to each other instantly. Unlike people who had never seen carnage, neither Saul nor Lilian wanted to discuss the horrors they'd seen. They certainly didn't want to be asked about it. They both wanted to learn to love music again. They both wanted to listen to the quiet. And they both wanted to leave Chicago.

The Austin American-Statesman made him an offer and they made the move to the capital of Texas.

The Features desk was exactly where Saul needed to be. He no longer had to run to a courtroom, listen to the latest atrocity and break it down to "just the facts". Often, he was given as many inches in the paper he needed to go deep into the headliners at the Austin City Limits music festival, or to follow the fundraising activities for the renovation of an aging theater or to interview the guy who created Beavis and Butthead. It was mostly fun, mostly interesting and no one got killed. Saul was in heaven.

The situation that sent him to Jim Klein's office began with an email from, of all places, a funeral home. He recalled that, as he read it, he chuckled and wondered whether he could do a story about the guy's hallucinogen supplier. Or call in an order. Still, the note piqued his curiosity, and he gave the guy a call.

The funeral home was like many he'd visited in Chicago on the criminal courts beat. The layout seemed universal: paisley easy chairs, toned down, homey; tasteful, solid colored, comfortable sofas; light, earth-toned walls, beige; clean, thin pile carpeting; woodwork, lots of mahogany. And boxes of tissue on every table.

The man who'd contacted him, a short, bald man was Tom Shine. He was a former high school History teacher with just the right balance of patience and sadness for his second profession. He appeared from a thick door and shook the reporter's hand with a surprisingly strong grip.

"Thank you for coming," he said in a baritone that, like his handshake, seemed to defy his stature. "I know you must be thinking that I must be… well, insane, after reading my email. I wonder myself. But I was there."

If Saul Armour was anything, he was professional. As much as he'd wanted to smirk, he wouldn't allow it. This guy was serious and one thing he'd learned in his business was when dealing with serious people, they should be taken seriously. You never knew what story might come out.

"Mr. Shine, I…"

"Please. Call me Tom."

The One and True Son

"Tom, I've covered some crazy things in my time. I'm pretty sure I've never run into this before. But I've learned to keep an open mind."

This seemed to put the director more at ease. "Shall we step into my office?" He gestured toward the door from which he'd emerged.

Saul sat in an overstuffed leather chair across from a wide, neat, antique desk. The room was awash in plants. Potted white lilies, orchids and bonsai trees sat on corner tables, giving the office the air of, say, a greenhouse rather the business office of a funeral home. Behind the funeral director's chair, on mahogany shelves, photos, presumably, of his fairly large family were displayed in matching frames. The director sighed deeply.

"So. Where to begin."

He picked up a photograph that had been laying on the desk and handed it to the reporter.

"This is the girl," he said.

* * *

Saul Armour's first attempts at contacting Dr. Weston were rebuffed without reply. The doctor's staff was highly protective of their boss, at first refusing even to take messages. After perhaps ten phone calls, one of the assistants agreed to take a message to the doctor but gave him no assurance that he would receive a response from either her or her boss. After three days, Saul had resolved to go to the physician's office and ask to speak to the man face to face. He was putting on his jacket to do just that when his cell phone vibrated in his front pocket.

"Saul Armour," the reporter answered.

"This is Dr. Alan Weston. I understand you've been trying to get a hold of me."

"Yes! Dr. Weston. I'm glad you called. I wanted…"

"I know why you're calling. You must know that I can't discuss individual patients and their care. There is confidentiality involved. I've never been sued, and I don't intend to be."

"I understand," the reporter replied. "But to say that this is an unusual case is an understatement. That is, if it's true."

"It's true," the doctor said and went silent.

Saul had been doing this job long enough to know when someone said something they didn't mean to say. They usually did that when they *needed* to say something.

"I know this is a kid, a minor," Saul said. "I won't use her name in the story."

The One and True Son

"You think it's that easy?" Dr. Weston said, raising his voice. "You know some people don't dream of seeing their kid's story in the headlines. Some people *like* their privacy."

"I can contact the mother and ask permission for you to talk to me. I haven't talked to her, but she must be confused about what happened. She may want people to know. I'll give her a call. I've Googled her. I think I've got a good number."

"And after this story comes out, how many more people will Google her?" The doctor sounded tired.

"I told you," the reporter answered. "I'll keep their names out of this."

"And what about people looking me up? I've been a physician for 20 years. Something like this could ruin my practice. People could question my treatment. They could question my competency. They could say the whole thing is made up. That I was part of a hoax."

"Doc, I…"

"Doctor."

"Doctor Weston, I have checked you out. That's my job and I'm good at it. You have five stars on every medical website out there. Your credentials are impeccable. Harvard undergrad. Stanford for medical school…"

"I know where I went to school," the doctor growled.

"And so do I. You're credible. If you weren't I wouldn't bother calling you. I don't work for the Enquirer. Don't you think that people should know about what happened? That is, if it happened."

"It happened," the doctor said, sounding tired again.

"Then I'll call her," the reporter said.

"No," the doctor said. "I will."

Three days later Saul got a call from the doctor. Weston said he wanted to meet at a coffee shop on the east side off of Martin Luther King Boulevard.

"Don't you want to meet in your office? Or here at the paper?" The reporter asked. "It seems a touchy subject to be talking in public."

"I don't want you coming here," the doctor explained. "My staff knows something's going on and I don't really want to discuss it with them. There's a place that has a patio right next to a side street. I know the place and they know me. I called them and they're going to move a table away from people so we can talk."

"Will the mother be there?" Saul asked.

"No. And for the moment, she doesn't want to talk to you or anyone. She doesn't know what she wants to do. Part of her wants the world to know. The other part is scared shitless."

"I get that," the reporter said.

The coffee shop was about an hour from the paper which gave the two men time to get there. The place looked familiar to Saul as the shop had a location near the paper, just two blocks down.

If it can be said that there are people whose appearance is perfectly suited for their professions, it would be said of Dr. Alan Weston. He had big feet and short, slightly bowed legs. His face smiled naturally. His eyes, wide and brown, drooped slightly at the edges of his face. His mustache spread just under his nose to a half inch on each side. In short, he was Charlie Chaplin with a stethoscope. And like the little tramp, according to everyone, kids adored him. The fact that he was a pediatrician shocked no one. At first Saul had trouble reconciling the benign looking man sitting behind a honey cream latte with the abrupt, tough voice on the phone.

"This is kind of far from your office," the reporter said.

"Yours too," the doctor replied. "I live near here. I thought it we be better considering what we're discussing. Besides, there aren't any other reporters around. No one can steal your story."

"I don't know that any would want to."

The doctor smiled.

The reporter took out a narrow spiral notebook. "So, Doctor Weston, what happened?"

"You don't waste any time," the doctor said. "Don't you want any coffee?"

"I've had four cups already," the reporter said. "Much more and I won't be able to read my own scribble."

"You're going to write down what I say?"

"It'll be kinda hard to put in the paper if I don't write it down. And my memory is not that good. Don't you want to be quoted accurately?"

The physician looked at the bushes next to the table. A car went by on the street on the other side. "I'm not sure I want to be quoted at all. I don't know what to believe myself."

Saul let the silence sit for a moment.

"So how long have you known Eliana?"

"All her life." Dr. Weston shrugged. "Well, since about a week into it. Her mother lobbied all her friends for me to take her on as a patient. I wasn't taking anymore. My schedule is pretty tight. But she seemed to know every one of my kids' mothers. About three times a day I would hear about this new mother who wanted the best pediatrician in Austin. They all kept saying that. You know, like they'd been coached. Chelsea is one persistent woman. I found out later she was doing this from some mommy website and most of these women only knew her online. She's a genius at marketing."

"So, you took her daughter on as a patient," the reporter said.

"I felt I had no choice," the doctor replied, a slight grin spread under his mustache.

"The power of the internet," Saul said.

"Tell me about it," Dr. Weston replied.

"Did she seem like a healthy kid?"

"Very. She didn't like vegetables, but what kid does? Her mother gave her these pre-squished vegetable packs with fruit mixed in with them. She was very active. She looked strong, especially for a five-year-old. Her mother showed me a picture that her ballet teacher took of her. She looked like a tiny Misty Copeland."

"I saw that picture," the reporter said.

The doctor looked at Saul suspiciously. "You haven't contacted Chelsea, have you?"

"No." The reporter shook his head. "No, I haven't."

"Then how did you see the picture?"

"The funeral director had it."

The doctor looked at his latte. "Oh."

The two went quiet.

Saul excused himself. He'd need that coffee after all. When he got back the doctor was still staring at his drink. He looked more like Chaplain than ever.

"I know this is rough, Dr. Weston," the reporter said. "Do you need to take a break?"

The doctor sighed and looked up. "I'm fine. I'm just wondering why I'm doing this."

The reporter dumped spoonfuls of sugar into his coffee. "If what you say happened actually did happen, don't you think people should know about it?"

"I'm really not sure," the doctor answered. "People are strange creatures. Take cancer, for instance. Everyone wants to cure it and yet we still have millions of smokers, dangerous pesticides are everywhere, and we can't stop people from tanning no matter how much they might look like a catcher's mitt by the time they're 50. And if we cure it, we'll have more or more people worldwide competing for less and less food and water."

"But this guy at the funeral. Shouldn't they know about him? He might have answers."

"I don't know about him," the doctor said, furrowing his brow.

"But you were there. From the beginning. You were at the funeral."

"I was."

The reporter flipped a page in his notebook and took a sip from his coffee. *Shit, too sweet.*

"Let's get back to the girl, Eliana. What happened that day? When she got sick."

The doctor sat back in his chair.

"She really didn't look that sick. She had a slight fever. She was a little touchy, but most kids are when they're sick. The fever was low grade, just above 100. She wanted to sleep. I told Chelsea to get some children's Tylenol and put her to bed."

"Sounds reasonable," the reporter said.

"I thought so. I'd seen hundreds of kids with these symptoms, and nothing happens. They blow their noses for a couple of weeks and their back to turning cartwheels."

"But Eliana was different."

"A tremendous understatement."

"So, what was it?"

"She had been in contact with a non-polio enterovirus."

The reporter put down his pen.

"English please."

"There are a lot of them. Mumps, measles, Epstein-Barr. Usually, they amount to the kid getting sick. Sometimes very sick. But other times, more rarely, they turn into something else."

"And that happened to this girl. What was the something else?"

"Meningitis."

The reporter whistled. "What happened after her mom took her home?"

"Her mother put her to bed, but before long she started complaining that her neck hurt. Not long after that she started vomiting. Her mom took her temp. It spiked to 104.8."

"Yahweh. What did you do?"

"I told her to take her to the nearest ER. I cancelled my appointments and met her there. We started IV antibiotics as soon as they arrived. We used corticosteroids to fight the swelling in the brain. She didn't respond."

"How long did she last?"

"She was deceased by the morning."

The reporter put down his pen again and looked the doctor in the eye.

"I know this is a stupid question, but I have to ask it. Are you sure she was dead?"

The doctor returned the reporter's gaze.

"She had no blood pressure or pulse. Her breathing had ceased. She'd flatlined on her EKG. Her pupils were fixed and dilated. Except for seeing her soul exiting her body, I had pretty good evidence."

"Sorry Doc," Saul said. "I had to ask."

"I know," the doctor replied. "I ask myself the same question every day."

Later that evening Saul was sitting at his desk working on a draft of the story. It was already the weirdest story he'd ever worked on, but he still needed more for it to run in the news section of the paper and not the comics section in "Ripley's Believe it or Not." He was working on the third draft when his desk phone warbled.

"Armour," the reporter said.

"Yeah, this is Sergeant Fewer at the security desk. There's a lady who says she needs to talk to you. She won't give me her name. Says you're doing a story about her daughter."

"Send her up," the reporter said.

Moments later Chelsea Beni stepped from the elevator into the newsroom. Saul Armour was there to meet her. A tall, slim woman, she was wrapped in light, beige trench coat. Her hair was clipped in a short African style. She had high cheekbones and wet-looking large brown eyes.

"Ms. Beni?" The reporter asked.

The woman nodded.

"I'm Saul Armour. I'm sorry, but I didn't expect you. Dr. Weston wasn't sure that you wanted to speak to me. Would you like to talk?"

The mother nodded again. "I would. Is there somewhere that isn't freezing?"

"That would be the break room," the reporter said, smiling. "The publisher keeps this room at just above arctic temperature year-round, so we don't get too comfortable."

The One and True Son

Saul led the woman through the maze of short cubicles to the break room shared by all departments of the paper.

"Would you like some coffee?" The reporter asked.

"I'm always cold. Who else do you see walking around Austin with a trench coat? I think I'm good."

Saul got himself a cup and sat down with her at one of the many empty tables. Austin is a pretty sleepy city after sunset, and they were virtually alone in the room. Chelsea Beni fidgeted with a saltshaker from the center of the table.

"I must admit, I'm surprised by your visit," said the reporter. "Like I said, I wasn't really sure you wanted to talk about this." He shrugged his shoulders. "Understandably so."

"I wasn't sure either," the mother replied looking straight at the reporter. "I'm not sure what to do. Or if I should do anything. It's all so strange. Dr. Weston said you were a good guy. He thought I could talk to you. He said that if after I talk to you, I decide not to be in the story," she took a breath, "to not have Eliana involved that you would protect our identities. Is that right?"

The reporter nodded. "I can see how this is a big risk. I will not put your names in the piece. I promise. I've got to tell you this is about the strangest story I've ever covered."

"Try living it," the mother said resuming her fidgeting.

"That's where you can help me," Saul said. "I can't imagine…Look, I don't have any kids, but I want to someday. I think one of the things that keeps my wife and I from having them is the fear of losing them. In this job, I've seen some really messed up stuff. My wife has too. I can't imagine dealing with the type of pain I've seen on mothers' faces after they've lost a child."

The mother set the saltshaker down.

"It's like having your insides ripped out and shown to you. I couldn't breathe. I didn't want to. I cried until every muscle in my body ached. I had no tears left, but I cried anyway. I just wanted to be with my baby. Wherever she was."

"And now?" The reporter asked.

The mother sighed. "Now? Now I have my baby back."

The reporter looked Chelsea Beni in the eyes.

"You know how crazy that sounds, right? I'm mean, that just *doesn't* happen. When you're dead, you're dead."

The mother flinched.

"I'm sorry," Saul said. "But this is hard to swallow. You say your daughter caught a fatal case of meningitis, died, and was revived at her funeral. Do you see how people are going to doubt this?"

"I do," the mother said. "I didn't want to come here because it *is* unbelievable. But as I thought about it—I thought—I thought that maybe I'm supposed to tell you about it. That maybe I'm supposed to tell everyone about it. To tell everyone about him."

"Tell everyone about whom?" The reporter asked.

"To tell them about Jessie." Chelsea Beni answered.

* * *

The reporter looked at the photo. She was about the prettiest little girl he'd ever seen. Dressed in a pink tutu, she'd posed like a dancer much older than her years, her arms extended out to her sides, like a soaring flamingo, one leg extended behind her, her calf muscle tensed, the other supporting the whole graceful movement as if she'd done this a million times. Her eyes, dark and wet, like her mother's, smiled into the camera.

The funeral director cleared his throat. "That's the picture we used to prepare her body. We dressed her in that tutu."

Saul Armour teared up. He never did that.

"I can't imagine doing your job."

"The dead deserve to look as beautiful as we can make them," Tom Shine said.

Words caught in the reporter's, in Saul's, throat. When he could speak, he did.

"Can I see where the…where this happened?"

"Of course," Tom said, choking up a bit himself.

* * *

The tabernacle where the funeral of Eliana Beni took place was a light and airy room with pale yellow walls and plenty of large windows allowing the warmth of the Texas sun to pour in. That day, the rows of padded wooden chairs were full. Roses, Lilies and orchids filled the room with color and perfume. In the center of the room was the child's casket, solid poplar, white with pink trim. The little ballerina lay on a pink pillow surrounded by teddy bears, her Barbies, and a photograph of her mother.

The One and True Son

Though subdued in volume, the crying was unceasing. Chelsea Beni sat in the front row, weeping into the shoulder of her uncle, the man who had raised her, his large hand rubbing her back, looking stunned.

A procession of mourners passed the body of the little girl. Some didn't want to look, but many found they had to. She was as beautiful in death as she was in life, as perfect as a child can be. As painful as the scene was, the beauty before them was unmistakable.

As soon as the last viewer passed, Chelsea's moreh took his place at the podium next to the reposing child. He removed some papers from his breast pocket. He looked to the child. He looked to the mother. He looked to the other mourners. Then he spoke:

"Yahweh tells us that death is not a tragedy. That death, even when it has come for the young, the precious, the innocent, is not a time for sadness. It is a natural process. As natural as birth, which we rightfully celebrate.

"No, my friends, it is not *death* that is a tragedy. We do not weep for Eliana today. We weep for ourselves. We weep because we do not get to see that smile, that beautiful," the moreh looked down, smiled, and side-eyed the audience, "sometimes devious smile that lit up any room." Some mourners chuckled through their tears.

A group of people no one recognized, most of whom wore jeans or shorts, entered and stood along the back wall.

"No, we don't weep for Eliana," he continued. "We weep for us. We weep because we do not get to see her grow up. We weep because we won't see that dance recital. We weep because we won't see her off to the prom. We weep because we won't attend her wedding. We weep because we do not get to meet her children. And I tell you, my friends. It's okay."

The moreh took a sip of water from a glass on the podium.

He looked to the mother.

"It's okay to weep for that. It's okay to weep for a voice you won't hear again. It's okay to feel the pain of giving away her clothes, a pain that will make labor feel like a minor belly ache.

"It's okay, Chelsea. It's okay. Weep. The absence in your life will seem as big as the sun. But Chelsea, honey, don't weep for Eliana. Yahweh knows where Eliana is.Eliana's life, short as it was, was virtuous. Eliana's life was pure. Eliana's life was joyful. Yahweh surely has a place for her in the afterlife. Of that, I think you can be certain."

The moreh moved from behind the podium. He hugged Chelsea and her uncle and sat down in back down is his chair. Tom Shine moved to the podium.

The One and True Son

"If anyone would like to say a few words in remembrance of Eliana please come forward," the funeral director said.

At first, no one moved. They were too torn with grief. Then a man from the group that had entered late moved up to the podium. He was tall and slim with wooly hair and beard. His eyes were red and swollen from crying. To many in the room, he looked familiar.

He stood for a moment at the small casket. He wept freely.

He turned to the podium, placed his hands on either side of it and spoke.

"I am so sorry, mother." He looked up to the ceiling choking back his emotion. "I am so sorry for your pain. It was never intended. This pain—" he swept his arms in front of him, "—this pain that you all feel was never intended. Not in the beginning." The Father never wanted this for…for anyone."

A soft murmur rumbled through the mourners.

"Do you remember me, child?" He asked looking directly at Chelsea.

At first the mother looked puzzled, but recognition soon spread across her face.

"You were at the wedding," she said. She turned around and looked at the group that he'd come in with. "You were all there. People said you…" She cut herself off.

"What did they say, child?" the man asked.

"They said you turned the water into wine," the mother said.

The mourners rumbled, this time louder.

"And did you hear the wine bottles break? All of them? Did you see the lake of spilled wine?"

She was silent for a moment.

"I did," she said softly.

Jessie smiled.

"And did you taste what was given to you as wine? Was it indeed what they said it was? Was it wine?"

Tears ran from the mother's face.

"It was champagne," she said, smiling, her eyes glistening.

More murmurs.

"Yes, it was, child," Jessie agreed. "It was champagne."

He walked around the podium and got down on one knee in front of the grieving mother. He brushed a tear away from her face.

"Now child," he said. "I must ask you a question. I need you to search your heart." He closed her eyelids gently with his fingertips.

The One and True Son

"Who do you say I am?"

She sat silently for a moment. Suddenly the tears gushed more urgently than before. She opened her eyes and smiled.

"I know," she whispered.

Jessie placed his palms on both sides of her face.

"Child, who do you say I am?"

"You are Him," she said. "You are the Son of God."

The mourners gasped.

Jessie smiled. He stood and gestured to the moreh who was looking on the whole scene, the horror unmasked on his face.

"The moreh here is correct. God always knows where his people are."

He turned to the body in the casket.

He turned his head as he spoke.

"Awake, little one," he said.

One of the mourners screamed. Others felt their breath catch inside of them. Many ran from the room.

Jessie opened the closed portion of the casket lid.

He smiled and ran his hand along her cheek. The girl in the pretty ballerina dress smiled back at him.

"Come sit with your mother."

He lifted the child from the coffin, his arms supporting her back and legs, turned and placed her on her mother's lap.

"Mother, your faith has made you whole again."

* * *

"That's nuts," Saul said, rubbing his forehead.

"That's what I'd say, if I wasn't there," Tom Shine said, standing at the very podium where Jessie Carpenter stood the day of Eliana Beni's funeral. "I'm a lot of things. I'm kind of cheap. I watch wrestling on TV, even though I know it's staged. Sometimes, I'm grumpy. But I don't cheat people. I treat my customers with respect. And I don't lie."

"I meant no offense, but Tom, are you sure she was really dead?"

The funeral director sniffed. "I've seen the death certificate. I've seen the autopsy report. But I don't need either one of those pieces of paper to know she was dead."

"How so?"

"Really?" the funeral director laughed. "I prepared the child for burial, Mr. Armour. I drained her blood. I put nearly two gallons of dyed embalming fluid through her femoral artery. I sewed her mouth closed and put special ping pong balls in her eyes to fill out her eye sockets. She was definitely deceased."

"Oh my God," Saul Armour said.

"Exactly," Tom Shine agreed.

The Healer

The last place anyone would see Andy Cagle would be a music festival in Tennessee surrounded by people half his age, some fully dressed, others, partially, and think that he was there voluntarily. Certainly, those who'd passed took a second glance at the middle aged, graying man in shorts and a Chicago Cubs t-shirt wearing a cervical collar; withered, useless arms dangling at his sides. The collar held his head up. He was unable to without it. The shirt was because he loved the Cubs.

His son Stevie called him and begged him to join him. The younger man arranged the flight from O'Hare to Nashville Metropolitan Airport. He picked up his father at the gate, his badge getting him through security. As Stevie suspected he would, the older man refused a wheelchair or preferential treatment coming off the aircraft. Stevie's father, the musician, the teacher, refused to see himself as disabled. He rarely used the word "ill". He certainly didn't use the word "dying".

They rode in comfortable silence for most of the 55-mile trip to Manchester, silence only interrupted by the occasional questions about Stevie's dating life or an anecdote involving Stevie's mother. They did not discuss "the illness," the amyotrophic lateral sclerosis that had been killing off the neurons in the father's brain stem. They'd talked about it when Andy had been diagnosed three years prior, over the phone, in very frank tones and decided then that they'd only talk about *life* and not about how it would probably end.

The Bonnaroo Music and Arts Festival, an annual event since 2002 was created to allow music lovers who were born after 1969 to experience the love, togetherness and lack of personal hygiene that their parents and grandparents experienced at Monterey Pop and Woodstock. For a decade, hippy wannabes, ravers, painters, performance artists, and comedians had gathered at Great Stage Park to listen to music and sleep where they park. The music ranged from pop to techno, jazz to hip-hop.

The One and True Son

One might assume that there wouldn't be much to enjoy for a retired, disabled, cellist, but one would be wrong if speaking of Andy Cagle, former first cellist for the Chicago Metropolitan Philharmonic Orchestra. Andy was not only an accomplished cellist, but a talented guitarist and pianist as well. Before he'd lost the use of his hands, Andy liked nothing more than to hop into his ancient Honda Prelude and cruise over to Shelley's on Lawrence Avenue and engage fellow musicians in spirited Irish tunes. He loved tuning his guitar to DADGAB, an alternate to the standard EADGBE, which involved a whole different set of chord shapes. Every new song he'd learned felt like a gift.

Stevie felt the festival would be good for his dad. He knew his father. He knew that Andy would never let on that the loss of his livelihood, the loss of his first love, would be more than a setback. But it wasn't a setback. It was devastation. And even though his father always smiled, the older man's hazel eyes told his son all he needed to know. Andy Cagle was dying. Yes, he had this disease that took down Lou Gehrig. And it forced a genius like Stephen Hawking into a wheelchair and to speak through a computer. *That* kind of death Stevie understood, and in a way, accepted. After the diagnosis, the light in Andy's eyes remained strong. When he was forced to wear the collar, his neck muscles too embattled to continue holding his head up, Andy joked that he'd have to get triple extra-large collars for his tuxedo shirt and elastic bowties. It wasn't until the disease reached his arms, his wrists, his fingertips, that notes he'd played since early childhood eluded him. A cellist of his skill never misses those, and his colleagues knew that his playing days were over. They covered for him as best they could, but when Andy got wind that he was being helped, he retired.

The smile remained, but the eyes dimmed. To Stevie, that was unacceptable.

After settling in their parking spot, setting up a tent behind Stevie's SUV and making sure Andy could sleep in the front seat of the car comfortably with seat slightly tilted back, the two men took to walking the grounds.

"You've been here before, I take it," Andy said.

"A few times," Stevie answered. "Once while I was in college. I didn't tell you guys because mom would worry that I was smoking weed."

"You were though," Andy smiled.

"Of course. I was in college."

Andy laughed. "You know, your mom went to college."

"Yeah, but she didn't smoke."

Andy laughed again. "Um, yeah."

"Get out!" Stevie almost shouted.

"I'm not saying anything." The father said.

"Snitches get stitches," the son replied, smiling.

Aside from the main stage, there were a number of small venues where unheard of acts performed in front of small but enthusiastic audiences. Everywhere Andy and Stevie turned a new flavor of music wafted through the air, from West African rolling rhythms to growling punks. Jugglers meandered through the crowds of standing young people tossing everything from flaming torches to bowling balls. Topless women with stars pasted over their nipples, wearing torn nylons, strolled the grounds as if they were dressed for the mall.

Has anyone here ever figured out you're a police officer?" Andy asked.

"Do I look like one?" Stevie answered.

Andy stopped and turned his whole body so he could look at his son. Stevie's reddish hair was close cropped with almost military precision. His Red Hot Chili Peppers t-shirt was tight over his toned chest and arms. Khaki shorts and Timberlands completed his ensemble.

"Kinda," he said finally.

Stevie shrugged. "It never comes up."

It was a sunny, warm day with low humidity. They strolled into Centeroo, the area where the arts and crafts tents and food venders were located. Music drifted in from the Which Stage, a medium sized venue with the iconic Bonnaroo logo over the stage. Andy was getting tired, but he said nothing to his son. He stopped at almost every vender, not to look at their wares, which were colorful and interesting, but to try to coax his weakening legs to move a little while longer.

"You're getting tired," Stevie said. "This is too much for you, isn't it?"

"No, not at all," Andy lied.

"Bullshit. I don't know what I was thinking. I'm sorry, Dad."

Andy desperately wanted to put his arm around his son.

"No. This is the best thing I've done in years. I am…tired. Maybe if we walk back to the car and I can rest a bit. You can walk around and meet some people. There are a lot of ladies here."

Stevie put his hand on his dad's shoulder. It was all bone.

"Not this year. This trip is for us. Besides, I like my *ladies* with a little more clothes on them. At least initially."

Andy smiled.

Stevie smiled back. He had his mother's eyes. "I'll walk you back to the car. You kick back and I'll get us some food. If you're feeling up to it,

The One and True Son

we'll check out some music later. If not, we'll just sit in our spot and listen from there. I wear ear plugs at the shows anyway. I hate earplugs. They itch my ears."

Andy nodded and they headed toward the car. They were passing by "The Wall," a high wooden fence, one of the traditions of the festival. On it, artists of varying abilities and levels of intoxication were encouraged to express themselves in any way that struck their fancies. Many images were psychedelic in nature, painted in bright greens, whites and blues. "The United States of Bonnaroo" painted over a red background took up several panels. Renditions of another of the festival's traditions, The Fountain, a mushroom shaped fixture, redecorated every year, were plentiful in different trippy forms. Pithy quotes, graffiti style, like "Not sure if I took acid or just ate paper," provided chuckles every few feet. It wasn't until Andy and Stevie were near the exit when Andy had to stop. It wasn't his legs this time. It was the wall. Near the top of the wall, large white block letters read: Before I die, I want to…

Some responses took the statement seriously. "Live on a farm." "Wander." "Be enlightened."

Others sought to lighten the subject. "Teleport." "Meow." "Talk to a girl."

At first, Stevie didn't know why his father stopped. Then he looked at the wall.

"Dad…" was all he could say.

They both knew, that for Andy, this was more than a cute way to liven up the grounds of a festival. But this was a question Andy lived every day. A question Andy could answer. And it was an answer that would never come true.

They stood in silence for a moment.

Finally, Andy spoke. "I'm tired. Let's go to the car. You must be getting hungry."

That night, Andy noted that though the rest of his body was eating itself, his ears worked as well as ever. He thanked Yahweh for that. Though Stevie hadn't planned it, he had managed to park at the perfect angle. With the doors of the Honda CRV opened, the windows closed, the music reflected in along with the cool night air. From his slightly reclined seat Andy listened as Alabama Shakes admonished him to "Hold On." He swam in Kendrick Lamar's "Swimming Pool" and vicariously got high with Danny Brown's "Blunt after Blunt." Andy saw value in all musical expression. It was a celebration of life. To him, it was life.

The next day was much like the first. Stevie and Andy walked as far as the older man's leg could handle. Andy bought some music posters. Stevie

The One and True Son

ignored Andy's whispers of beautiful girls at 9, 10 and 11 o'clock. In short order, Andy's legs sent signals to his brain that they were about to go on strike. The father and son made their way back to the car where Andy told him he wanted to be alone for a while. In truth, he didn't. He wanted his son to have some fun. Go flirt. Go be young. Life is beautiful, he thought, but fleeting. From what he'd heard, this festival could be cursed with some very bad weather from time to time. That wasn't going to happen this year. On a day like this it seemed a sin that Stevie was tied to a deteriorating man while all this life strolled by.

"Go," he told Stevie. "I'll be fine."

He spent the day in the car thinking of his son. Andy and Rose, Stevie's mother, were horrified when he picked criminal justice as a major. They'd hoped it meant that he was thinking of going on to law school. Stevie wanted mountains, so he chose the University of Tennessee at Knoxville. After four years, he didn't want to leave. He applied to the Tennessee Highway Patrol and with his high college grades and enthusiasm for law enforcement, he was a shoe-in. Andy and Rose considered kidnapping him and locking him in his room, but as Stevie grew into his job, they'd noted that it hadn't changed him. He was still considerate. He still loved his music. He still loved to laugh. They still jumped when the phone rang, on occasion, particularly later than 8 o'clock, but they'd come to terms with their son's chosen profession.

From the comfort of his son's SUV, Andy listened to Feist count to four and implore for him to love her more. Annie Clark, under the moniker "St. Vincent" asked, "Bodies, can't you see what everybody wants from you?" Radiohead warned him of the Karma Police. Each song, from each artist had a meaning for Andy that differed from perhaps anyone else listening that night. Each reminded him of his condition, of his limitations, his time remaining. He felt connection with the artists in a way he'd never felt before. They knew his pain. Not directly. But they knew it.

After the lights at the main stage went out for the evening, life in Bonnaroo went on. Some people returned to their tents or cars or just to the bare ground while others continued to party at the other numerous mini events that would last until morning.

Stevie returned about 1AM with a wisp of beer on his breath and, much to his father's delight, the cell number of a girl from the area with whom he'd spent most of the evening. Stevie passed out in the tent he'd set up behind the car, lying on top of his sleeping bag.

Andy didn't sleep right away. One thought ran a loop in his mind: Before I die, I want to…

The One and True Son

The next morning Stevie awakened with a headache. He slowly emerged from the tent, the sun searing into his retinas. Shielding his eyes with his hand, he came around to the front of the car to discuss water, coffee, his new *lady* friend and breakfast options. What he found was an empty car seat.

Perhaps it was the residual alcohol in his blood, but panic shot through him like a bullet. What was his father thinking? Did he need medicine? Did he take any? Was he wandering off to die? "Dad!" he shouted in one direction of the parking/camping area and again in the other. A reply came from the inside of a tent a couple of spaces down."Your daddy's not here. It's too early for this shit. Shut the fuck up!" Stevie took off running

Most of the venders in Centeroo hadn't yet opened for business. Their tents were up, the signs with pricing and product descriptions still displayed, but the tables were empty. Only the food venders were active. Stevie weaved his way through the early risers and the late drunks, sprinting from one vender to another, hoping his father was just hungry. No luck.

Stevie decided to head back to the car and see if Andy had returned. He found his father standing at The Wall, near the exit, his dead arms dangling at his sides. Stevie's first impulse was to admonish his father for scaring the hell out of him. The impulse quickly faded when he realized why his father stood staring at the fence.

Before I die, I want to…

Andy stood close to the fence. His eyes locked on the large block letters. A young woman, her shaved head wrapped in a tie-dye scarf, sat on the ground near Andy's feet. On a cloth next to her sat several small tubs of different colored paints, a smeared palate and an assortment of brushes from narrow to wide. Other groups of people were there, some adding to the mural, others taking it in.

Stevie approached his father slowly. "Are you wishing?" he asked, softly.

Andy didn't turn, his eyes stuck on the letters on the dried wood of the fence.

"I guess," he said after a moment. "I didn't sleep well last night." He sighed. "You know, when I was young, maybe your age, I didn't ask myself what I wanted to do with my life. I knew what I could do. I did it. Now granted, I've never played Carnegie Hall, but I did okay."

"You did great, Dad," Stevie said. "You're a great musician and an even better father."

"Was a musician," Andy corrected. "But with the music and with you, I just followed my heart."

The One and True Son

"It's called faith," said a voice from behind them.

Neither Andy nor Stevie had noticed the group of people standing behind them. There were several men and women, some quite young, some approaching middle age. The voice they heard was from a tall man with a bushy beard and kind eyes.

Andy turned his body so he could see them. Stevie turned as well.

"It's called faith," the man repeated. "You were given many gifts. You recognized them. You put your heart into them. They blossomed. You're truly blessed."

"Blessed?" Stevie shouted. "Can't you see that he's...". He stopped.

The tall man placed a hand on Andy shoulder. He smiled at Stevie and turned his eyes to Andy.

"You are standing close to the wall. I imagine it would be much easier to read from a few steps back. Why are you standing so close?"

Andy blushed.

"Please," the tall man said, his hand still on the musician's shoulder. "Don't be embarrassed. I mean you no harm. Why are you standing so close?"

"I was praying," Andy said finally. "I was praying to Yahweh that I could get my arms back."

Tears leaked down Andy's cheeks.

"I don't want a longer life. He could take me when he wants me. If he wants my legs, he can have them. Many people with my disease have trouble swallowing. I don't. He can take that too. Just give me my arms back. That's all I want."

"You were praying." The tall man nodded. "But why are you standing so close to the wall?"

Andy shook.

"I wanted to write on the wall."

The tall man moved close to Andy and looked him in the eyes. He wiped away a tear from Andy's eye.

"You *expected* to be able to, didn't you?"

Andy looked back. He nodded.

The tall man turned to the woman with the paints, near Andy's feet.

"Child? May I borrow one of your brushes? Please, with a little paint on it."

The woman had been watching the scene before her. Her t-shirt was stained with her own tears. She dipped a wide brush in the tub with red paint and handed it to the man.

The One and True Son

"Your faith is strong," he said to Andy. "I want you to paint how you would finish this." He gestured to the white letters. Then he held the brush out for Andy to take it.

No one moved. Stevie looked at the man as if the man were insane. He was about to tell him that when he saw his father's arm twitch. A small crowd had formed around the group. Andy's arm twitched again. His hands, twisted nearly to hooks two years prior, relaxed their fingers. Slowly the arm raised from the shoulder, the relaxed fingers of a cellist reached up and grasped the paint brushes handle. He took the brush.

"Paint your response," Jessie said.

Andy turned his head in his collar. With his free hand he reached up and released the velcro that held the collar in place and let it fall to the ground. Everyone in crowd gasped. Andy handed the brush back to Jessie.

"I don't need to paint it," he said. He turned and threw his arms around his son.

* * *

A large water drop splashed on Evanna's forehead, just above her eye, waking her. It'd rained earlier and the water had made its way through cracks in the vaulted brick ceilings of the catacombs under Baltimore's Lexington Market. The chambers, built to store meat and other perishables in the days before refrigerators, were first discovered in 1951 when the city was building a parking garage over the area. Soon after, they were forgotten again. It'd been six months since Evanna stumbled, quite literally, into the hidden stairwell in a dimly lit corner of the garage. She'd slammed a surprisingly potent hit of brown sugar moments before and needed a place to chill. When she'd emerged from the initial stupor, she realized she had a new home.

It'd been daylight when Evanna ducked into her vault that day. She guessed that she'd slept through the entire rest of the day and most of the evening as the market was closed and the food stand customers were gone, leaving only junkies like herself the run of Lexington Street. Evanna grew up in Baltimore, in Cherry Hill, in Upton, in Montebello, moving from relative's basement to relative's basement. Her mother had been in and out Patuxent and the Maryland Correctional Facilities for Women most of Evanna's life. Her father? She'd never met him. She wasn't even sure who he was.

By the time she was 13, she'd been raped by four men, two of them family.

Despite all that, Evanna loved to read. Before she'd discovered the Mexican Mud that ran through Baltimore like a plague infested river, she was a regular at whichever Enoch Pratt Library was closest to her. Back then, she could be found curled up in an easy chair, a stack of books at her feet. She liked the way James Baldwin wrote, but avoided most books with stories like hers, choosing instead tales of travel, of adventure, of anything that didn't remind her of the hell she'd known as her life.

She hadn't been in a library for at least two years. Maybe three. She couldn't remember.

It was cool for a summer night, although there was rarely a time when Evanna didn't feel cold. She held her forearms closely over her breasts, not squeezing too hard as the dark brown lesions she'd had for weeks were starting to hurt. She was hoping for a customer as she was down to three dollars, not nearly enough to chase away the sickness when it inevitably hits. She strolled along Paca Street, passing the many brick buildings, and came to a stop under the *World Famous, Lexington Market* sign constructed of green I-beams sprouting out of the sidewalk. There, she leaned her rear end against one of the beams and waited from some night owl to come around for a date. The hit she'd slammed still had legs and she found herself drifting in and out of sleep. At first, Evanna thought the sound of squealing tires was part of a less than relaxing dream, and she squinted her closed eyes trying to wish the shrill noise away.

"There's the bitch!" someone shouted.

Evanna opened her eyes to see, not one, but three cars stopped in front of her, the doors open, emptying passengers in her direction.

She recognized one of the men coming toward her. He was short and lean in a wife beater t-shirt and stylishly ripped jeans. *Laquan. Yeah, Laquan.* Maybe she could make some money.

"Hey Daddy," she slurred. "You wanna date?"

Laquan was on her quickly.

"Shut up!" he yelled and slapped her with all his strength in the jaw, sending her sprawling to the pavement. Blood sprayed from her nose and lip.

Evanna found herself surrounded by people, mostly men, but a couple of women. She tried to sit up but her head was spinning from the blow and the remainder of the drug in her bloodstream. She didn't recognize anybody. She didn't know what she'd done. She barely knew who she was.

Suddenly, Laquan was kneeling in front of her. She could smell the gun oil from the pistol in his hand.

"Show me your fucking arms, bitch."

The One and True Son

"Wha...what?" Evanna managed to say.

Laquan shoved the pistol into Evanna's mouth, chipping her front tooth.

"Show me your fucking arms before I blow your fucking brains out!"

To Evanna, suddenly, everything became clear. This was no dream. This was worse than a nightmare. She was no longer concerned where her next slam would come from. She held out her arms. The two streetlights and the Lexington Market sign were more than enough light to show the lesions on her arms.

"That's the shit," came another voice from behind Laquan. "That's the shit I seen on the internet. It's cancer."

"I know it's cancer. I ain't stupid." Laquan stood and looked down on the shaking woman on the sidewalk. He kept the gun pointing down her throat.

"You know how you get that shit? You fucking ho! It's from AIDS!" He drew back his foot and plunged his new Timberland boot into Evanna's side. Her ribs cracked audibly. She bellowed and writhed back and forth.

The angry man drew back to kick her again.

He was stopped by a voice that came from behind the crowd.

"Don't kick her again," the voice said.

Laquan turned in the direction of the voice.

"Who the fuck said that?" he shouted.

He pointed the pistol where the voice came from.

The crowd scrambled to either side. Another group was behind them. There were women and men, some white, some black, some something else. A tall brown man stood in the center of the group.

Laquan wasn't frightened easily. And if he were he never showed it. He'd looked down the barrel of a gun himself more than once. He learned about his father's left hook in seventh grade when he got caught hooking school. But he swallowed that. He swallowed all his fear, all his pain. He was good at it.

For some reason, at this moment, he was frightened.

He pointed his weapon at the tall man.

"Who the *fuck* is you?" he said.

The tall man appeared unconcerned about the pistol. He was calm. His eyes were locked on Laquan's. The man walked slowly to him.

Laquan kept the pistol pointed between the man's eyes.

"You know, young man, that that gun won't work."

"Oh, it works," Laquan nodded. "You 'bout to find out how good it works."

The One and True Son

The man stopped a few feet away from Laquan. His eyes were serious, fearless. What they were showing him, Laquan wasn't sure. It pulled at him. It knew him. His chest burned.

The man spoke slowly, giving space between each word.

"I'm coming to you. Give me the gun."

One of his crew, a 15-year-old, who hadn't been in school for over a month, didn't like that idea.

"Fuck him, Quan. Light him up."

Laquan said nothing.

The tall man looked to the boy. Again, the man's eye showed no fear. The boy took a step back. He shivered where he stood. He didn't speak again.

The man turned his gaze back to Laquan.

"Give me the gun," he said.

Laquan took a step, then another.

He stopped.

For Laquan, everything went dark. He was warm, comfortable. There was moaning, muffled screaming, just out of his hearing. A small dot of light appeared. Still comfortable, but curious, Laquan watched as the dot became a circle, growing every few seconds.

Light obliterated the darkness. A scream built in Laquan's chest. For the first time, he was cold. His skin, covered in a sticky film, felt everything: cold, wet, pain. Huge hands raised him up as the scream building inside him let loose. His eyelids clamped tightly. A cloth wrapped him. He was placed on something warm, something wet, something moving. Finally, something familiar. A study thump-thump.

And then.

He was two. He was tired. His mother had her friend over again. They were on the couch, wrestling. His mother had no pants on. Her friend had his pulled down to his knees. Laquan was hungry. He was supposed to be watching Sponge Bob in the bedroom. He wanted a peanut butter and jelly. His mother's friend was hurting his mother. She was pushing against the man. She moaned. He wanted to stop the man from hurting her. He pounded on the man's back.

The man swatted Laquan with the back of his hand, hard, sending him sprawling.

"Get the fuck out outta here," the man yelled.

His mother was up off the couch.

The One and True Son

"Get the fuck back in that room!" she shouted. "Come out again and I'll smack the black off of you."

And then.

He was with Mook. Mook handed him a bag full of gel caps.

"There thirty Andrew Jacksons in there. That'll get you moving. Five-O show up you get the fuck outta there. Drop 'em if you have to."

Mook, his big cousin, shook his shoulder. "You in business now, Cuz. Do good and you be in the big time 'fore you know it. Bet." Mook grinned showing his gold fronts.

And then.

He was behind a gun. A 9 Mike-Mike. Mook's brother, Ben, had given it to him. The serial number had been chiseled off. It was time to prove himself. Antonio had started talking to the po-po after he got pinched with his inventory. Laquan had known Antonio since middle school. Didn't like him much. Still, he didn't want to kill him.

About noon, on a bright sunny Monday morning, Laquan followed Antonio to his girl's house, a high school kid with tats and Minnie Mouse hair balls on her head. He watched Antonio go in. He counted to 60 and shouldered in the door. If they'd locked all the locks, they might have had a chance. He could hear Killer Mike blasting from a room upstairs. The door was closed.

He walked as lightly as he could, grateful for the volume of the music.

Outside the door, he stopped and took a breath. He could still turn around. He could still not do this. He'd get the shit kicked out of him. Maybe worse. He cleared his mind. He kicked in the door.

And then.

He was Antonio's girlfriend. He watched as the bedroom door exploded in and this man stood there. A man she didn't know. He felt her rush of adrenaline as she screamed and ran toward Antonio. He watched as dirty white smoked puffed from the weapon, one, two, three times. He heard himself, herself, beg for the man to go. To please, let her live. He heard the gun respond, one, two, three more times. He felt the burning holes in her chest, her abdomen, her arm. He felt her fading away. *He* was fading away.

Laquan was back on Paca Street.

The tall man stood in front of him, his hand resting on the pistol.

Tears streamed from Laquan's face.

The tall man's eyes had changed. Laquan understood them. He hadn't seen that look…he couldn't remember. It was love.

"My Father," Jessie nodded to the weeping young man, "your Father, has always loved you. He sent me for us to be together. For you to remember that you are loved. That you *are love*. The hate, the pain. That is the illusion. You feel Him now, don't you?"

"I'm sorry," Laquan said. "I'm...sorry."

He released his hand from around the pistol.

"Forgive me?" He pleaded to the tall man. "Please. Forgive me."

The man handed the weapon to one of his people. He never took his eyes off Laquan.

"A gun won't work if you can't pull the trigger," the tall man said. "And you can't, child. You can't. Forgive yourself. Your Father already has."

No one spoke for a moment. Not Laquan's crew. Not the tall mans. They were surrounded by something they hadn't felt before.

The tall man turned his gaze to the woman on the pavement. He walked to her and kneeled next to her.

Her eyes opened wide, she didn't know if what she was seeing was from the drug she had shot into her foot earlier that evening or somehow she'd slipped into another reality. It was like she felt when she curled up in the chair in the library. She was safe. She was surrounded by a world that didn't hate her. A world that didn't want to punish her. The man who kneeled next to her seemed to glow. She could see the light come from him and she felt it enter her.

"Child of my father," he said softly, "you've never had a chance, have you?" He smoothed her cheek with his palm. With his thumb, he wiped away the blood from her nose and lip. "You thought your Father in Heaven has forgotten you."

Evanna's eyes filled with tears.

"I'm here to tell you that He loves you. To tell you..." He looked up toward the sky as if searching for words. "To tell you that he never left you." A tear swam in his eye as well.

"Please, let me see your arms."

Evanna sat up slowly, wincing from the pain of the blow she'd received from Laquan.The streetlights shone down on her torn and mottled skin. The brown splotches of Kaposi Sarcoma looked like mold on month old bread. The tall man got on both knees and placed both his hands on the side of her face, leaned down and kissed her forehead.

"Yo! Look!" a woman from Laquan's crew shouted. She pointed to Evanna's arms.

The splotches were fading. The needle holes that ran over long collapsed veins from Evanna's wrists to armpits, like chicken tracks in

The One and True Son

mud, went away, as if they'd never been there. Evanna looked at her assaulter. She looked at the crowd around her.

They would later swear she glowed.

* * *

Foster knew that her father's disease had gotten worse when he started talking to a cat named Waldo.

They'd lived in DC on 7th Street SE Foster's entire life, in a house built in the 1930s. Through her toddler years, her first stumbling steps to kindergarten, her awkward journey through middle school and summer camp, her more confident drive through high school, her persistent march to Georgetown University and Law, she'd begun each day with a step through the white framed threshold, across the covered porch and out to the sidewalk. She'd developed the habit early on of stopping at the tree that watched over her front yard, a tree her mother planted as a sapling and had grown with her, to turn and look back at the yellow house with the dark gray shutters.

Her mother and father bought the house in 1977 when Foster was seven years old for $70,000, a tidy sum in those days, but with gentrification nearby and the influx of lobbyists and lawyers to soak in the nation's coffers, that money might update the kitchen, but wouldn't cover the taxes. It was her mother who chose the butter yellow siding and charcoal shutters and when the years dictated that the paint be replaced, the colors remained the same. Her mother, Della, said she'd dreamt of the colors as a little girl and swore that she would never live in a house painted otherwise. Sadly, a prescient statement.

Foster's father, Paul, was an accountant with little regard for politics, an EPA employee since its inception. Paul understood numbers. He could see them, move them around, make them work. They spoke to him while he worked. They danced in his consciousness. They showed him how to feed his family and scolded him when he ignored their occasional warnings.

Oddly, as a child, he was poor at Math. Addition and multiplication made sense to him, delighting him when he reached the correct conclusion, but division, subtraction, fractions, percentages, swam in his head as if in mirky water, confounding him, embarrassing him, robbing him of speech. That changed when he as 15 when a kind teacher worked with him after school. Mr. Carlson was as patient as he was kind. After six months of after school coaching, numbers hummed to him, sang to him, explained to him the meaning of their existence. This was when the voices started.

The One and True Son

Della, his wife of 34 years, an ample woman with strong shoulders, knew of the conversations her husband had with his work. She found it charming. She found *him* charming like a story book that had much more going on than the words written on its pages. She fell in love with him early and never fell out. She passed that love to their daughter, Foster who adored her father's eccentricities with a passion that matched her mother's. Mother and daughter saw Paul's secret world as a bonus, an added value.

When Foster thought of her childhood, the memories were always infused with the smell of cornbread, made from scratch from a formula in her father's head, one made from comfortable memories of his childhood, baked warm and finished off toasted in a frying pan with lots of butter. Her father smiled through the entire process. He once told her that he heard no voices while baking cornbread.

As he grew older, the sounds in his head became more distinct, sharpened. His coworkers weren't always kind, or so Paul believed. Whispered conversations reached his ears, some from around corners, others from cubicles three or four places down.

he's strange?
he thinks he's so much better at this.
does he do anything right?
he's stupid. everyone says so.
who hired him? must've been an idiot.

Many evenings, he'd arrive home, wounded and quiet. Della picked this up instantly, Foster too. They'd cuddle him and coo to him. Foster would play with his thinning hair. Della made the numbers sing again. Foster quieted the gossip.

One evening, Della was not there to smooth out the voices. Foster was sitting on their overstuffed couch, leaning over the large glass top coffee table, tapping away on her laptop, her textbooks piled everywhere, a pen stuck in her auburn ponytail.

Paul sat next to his daughter and sighed.

"Mom's upstairs," Foster said, looking up from her text. "She said she had a bad headache." She smiled. "You okay?"

"Mmm-mmm," Paul responded, looking out at nothing in front of him.

Foster leaned over and kissed his cheek. "Why don't you go up and see her. I bet that'll make her feel better."

"Mmm."

She placed her hand on his shoulder and gave him a little shake.

"Please?"

Della would not wake.

The One and True Son

The hospital said it was a cranial aneurysm, a bubble in a blood vessel that had had enough. Della had high blood pressure, but often her prescription went unfilled. She'd claimed that she didn't have time. Besides, she hated swallowing tablets.

The voices in Paul's head knew who really was at fault. They told him often, at night, while he dressed in the morning, at his desk at the office. He wanted to argue, to plead his innocence, to tell the invisibles around him, judging him, that he didn't know. That he was the one left to suffer. The voices always won out.

Months later, Waldo showed up in the office.

Paul had been analyzing the costs versus benefits of a clean-up of toxic materials at a former steel mill in Baltimore that had been proposed as a revitalization site, with shops, restaurants, a gym and a day care center. The numbers sang for him that day. The thought had occurred to him that the site might not be the best place for eateries and a day care center, but his bosses asked for numbers and the numbers did their dance for him needing little encouragement. Paul was reaching for his coffee mug when he felt something brush his ankle.

A gray tabby lay at his feet, looking up at him, expectantly.

"Good afternoon, Senator," the cat said. He closed his bright green eyes and turned his attention to cleaning his right forepaw.

Startled at first, Paul remembered the cat, Waldo, a kitten he'd brought home to Foster, years ago after he'd discovered him rummaging through overflowed trash at the Potomac Avenue metro stop.

Paul drew his feet away from the cat.

"I'm not a Senator," he whispered to the tabby. "I'm an accountant. You should remember that."

The cat peered back up at Paul, his eyelids open halfway.

"Oh, they got to you."

Paul sniffed. "What are you talking about?"

Waldo fully opened his eyes.

"You really don't remember, do you? You are Senator Paul Carroll. You've served three full terms for the great state of Illinois. You ran against George H. W. Bush for President in 1988. You...oh."

"What?" Paul hissed.

"Nothing," said Waldo.

Paul scooted back his chair and leaned over the cat.

"You can't just do that," he whispered, unaware of how loudly. "You can't go around saying things like that and stop. It's...it's...impolite."

The One and True Son

Waldo glanced away.

"I'm sorry. I just don't know what to do with this new information. You know Bush was head of the company, right?"

"The company? What are you talking about?"

It was Waldo's turn to whisper.

"The company. The C.I.A. Bush ran the whole show. He was up to his earlobes in the Kennedy hit. Why do you think he beat you so easily in the election? It was his turn. If the thing weren't rigged, he couldn't beat anyone. Let's face it. The guy has the personality of a turnip."

"I don't remember any of this," Paul said, stunned.

"No," the tabby said. "Of course, you don't. That's how they work, don't they? What's important now is that you get the hell out of here."

"Why?" Paul asked, no longer whispering.

The cat sat up.

"Because you're starting to remember. They're going to know that. Now let's get going."

Paul grabbed his lunchbox out of his desk drawer. He shuffled the analysis he'd been doing in his old, battered briefcase. The analysis took on new meaning with this new information. Suddenly he *saw* that this study wasn't about restaurants and day care centers. It was something much bigger, much deeper.

In seconds, he was in the elevator. Delores, the analyst in the next cubicle was on the phone to Foster.

By the time Foster had found her father, he'd made his way to Connecticut Avenue, to Dupont Circle, clutching his briefcase tightly to his chest, eyeing everyone he passed as if they were pointing a weapon. Foster, in her third year at Georgetown Law, had bolted from the lecture on property liability law she was attending and jumped into her aging Prius. She scoured every intersection, every alleyway, from the EPA Headquarters on Pennsylvania Avenue, starting close and fanning out. On Connecticut she caught a glimpse of the hunching figure of her father, his face contorted in fear in the reflection on the tinted windows of Starbucks. He was moving quickly. She rolled down her passenger window.

"Dad!" she shouted over the din of horns as she stopped traffic around her and the underpass to her left and below her. "Dad! Daddy! Please get in the car!"

Paul Carroll turned to her voice. His eyes were wide like a lemur caught out of its tree in broad daylight.

"Dad! Come on! Let's get some help."

The One and True Son

Her father dashed to the car, shut the door and pulled the recline lever on the seat and flattened his body. "Drive!" He screamed.

Foster peeled away.

"What's going on, Dad? What's all this about?"

"You know what it's about," her father shouted. "How did you know how to find me? Do they have a GPS on me? I didn't tell anyone I was leaving!"

Foster pulled to the curb near the National Zoo. Before she did anything else, she pushed the child protection button for the power windows and door locks, trapping him inside.

"Now slow down and tell me what this is all about."

Paul stole a glance out the window and hunched back down.

"I know who I am now," he whispered.

"What?" Foster said.

"I know who I am, who I've been all along. And you know too."

Foster threw an exasperated look out the windshield.

"Yeah, I know who you are. You are Paul Carroll. My father. Husband to Della. Accountant for…"

"Don't fucking lie to me!" Her father shouted. "Don't lie to me anymore! I know! I know it all! Are you even my daughter? I need to see some ID!"

Foster was stunned. Her father never swore. One time, when she was about 10, he was taking her to an Oriole's game. They were coming down 895 in Baltimore when a car cut them off to get over to Martin Luther King Boulevard. Her father shouted, "You son of a bitch!" and turned beet red. That was the one time anything even somewhat profane came out of his mouth. That day, Foster ate more hot dogs and drank more soda than she ever had. With each treat he purchased for her came an apology for the "foul language" he'd used on the drive to the park. Foster thought it silly of her father. They said far worse things on television never mind the movies she'd seen. She assured him that he needn't apologize any further, especially when she'd eaten so much her black jeans were getting uncomfortable.

That was it. That was all the swearing from this man she could remember in her 26 years.

Foster was terrified. She'd never seen her father like this.

"Dad, we need to get some help. We have to go see some people who can help you."

Paul covered his face with his briefcase.

"Are you nuts? There's no one who can help me. We have to leave. We have to get out of here?"

"Leave DC?"

"Leave the country," he hissed. "They'll know that erasing my memory didn't work." He shook the briefcase at her. "They know that I have the evidence. I have their plans."

Foster went silent for a moment.

"Dad, listen. I know a place where they can't get you. I'll take you there right now."

"Where? Where could I possibly be safe?"

"The hospital."

Paul reached for the door handle. It didn't work. He didn't think of unlocking it manually.

"I'm not going to the hospital. You don't believe…"

Foster reached for her father's hand.

"I'm trying to help you be safe. Think about it. Murderers of little kids are put in the hospital. Celebrities are put in the hospital. No one can get to them there even though lots of people would like to. Besides, if the people you say are after you think no one believes you, it's just as good as having your memory erased. We can get you safe. Then we'll plan what to do."

Paul didn't speak. He only nodded.

Foster drove directly to Georgetown University Hospital.

From that day Foster had to learn a new language. Words like schizoaffective disorder, psychosis, and mania crept into her everyday discourse. Words created by the government, generic words, created from short forms of chemical compositions like Olanzapine, Quetiapine, Aripiprazole, Ziprasidone, became as familiar as ibuprofen and acetaminophen. Brand names were added to her lexicon: Solian, Zyprexa, Risperidol, Clozaril. Some meds gave her relief, calmed her father, dimmed his daytime nightmares only to fade in effectiveness. Others went on trial for weeks before failure was the final verdict. And still others sent the delusions into overdrive.

"Foster!" Paul Carroll bellowed into the darkness at 2 AM.

The daughter flew into her father's room to see him sprawled on the floor underneath his window, cowering.

"What is it, Dad?" She asked in the most soothing tone she had after being screamed awake. She lay on the floor next to him and placed her hand on his neck. She softly massaged him. His neck was soaked with sweat.

He hid his face under his left arm. With his other he gestured to the window.

Foster pulled herself to her knees and looked out. She saw the roof of their Victorian covered porch, the walkway through the small front yard, the tines of their wrought iron fence.

"I don't see anything, Dad."

"They're gone?" he asked, his face emerging from under his forearm.

"Who's gone?"

Paul rolled over onto his back.

"The men burying the motorcycle."

"What? Dad, that's crazy." She immediately regretted her word choice. "Dad. No one is out there. And why would anyone bury a motorcycle."

"It's a message," he whispered. "You don't understand. You've never had the clearance."

Foster lay on her father's chest. Her tears stained his pajama shirt.

Lithium was next on the menu. An older drug, when used in combination with other drugs, Lithium had been shown useful for people suffering with schizo-affective disorder in that it had a calming effect on them. And that was true with Paul, for a while. He seemed to be more like his old self, less prone to manic bouts of terror. Foster found that she could have conversations with her father, joke with him; occasionally he'd joke back.

Foster even felt comfortable leaving him alone and taking a position as a junior associate at a law firm specializing in antitrust law. She impressed the partners with her sterling college transcripts and her ability to not only hold a conversation with seasoned lawyers, but to lead one. The work was challenging, but she called her father hourly and had an arrangement with their neighbor, Camille, a woman Foster had known all her life. If Paul failed to pick up the phone, Foster provided her neighbor with a key to check on him. A widow herself, Camille would often go next door on her own. She remembered Paul before his illness presented itself and often strolled over to catch up with her old friend. It was no bother.

Working was the freedom she'd been seeking for as long as Foster could remember. She knew as a child she wanted to be a lawyer. At 12 years old she'd made a list of all the attributes she'd have to have to attain her goal. She had to love to read: check. She'd have to keep her head clear, no drugs or alcohol: check. She'd have to study both sides of every subject she would be confronted with and be able to find the most logically advantageous position: check. She seemed born to do this. She *would* be a lawyer.

The One and True Son

  Every day she'd pack up her father's beat up briefcase with affidavits, signed documents, charts and exhibits and take the Metro to the Metro Central station and walk the two blocks to New York Avenue and the firm's fifth floor office. As much as she loved her father, work was a welcome respite from his illness and the stress it caused. Her office, a closet by the senior associate's standards, had no windows, but she'd made it her own with potted plants and grow lights. On the bookshelves the firm provided she had the prerequisite law tomes, most of which she'd never open, but were part of the clients' vision of what a good lawyer would have in her office. Her most personal touch, one she'd gotten an occasional side eye for was her collection of Spawn action figures she'd placed around her desktop. She'd collected them since childhood and had some rare pieces from the 1990s. She still purchased one once in a while on eBay. Violator, a mutant, demon-looking thing with hooked horns on the top and sides of its evil face, its long, narrow, warped alligator mouth open to devour anything in its path, crept up on her coffee mug filled with pens. The Freak sat in his torn Levis, his emaciated bare chest exposed to her clients, a meat cleaver gripped in his skeletal hand, his scraggly, long gray hair, blowing back in an imaginary wind, making sure there would be no typos in her briefs. Demonic clowns, demented robots, all representative, in Foster's mind, of the evils her office was trying to defend against.

 Her office was a sanctuary. For 13 months it was a sanctuary.

 Then one day, the phone rang. It was Camille. Waldo was back.

  Foster's life returned to the chaos of hospital visits, seemingly endless medication adjustments, and surreal conversations with her father, a man who sometimes didn't recognize her as his daughter, but as a spy for the government seeking to silence him.

 Foster was exhausted. More than once, she considered emptying the bottle of Xanax her doctor gave her into her mouth and washing it down with a tall, cold beer. But one thought stopped her. With her gone, what would happen to her father? She loved the man he'd been before all this. She felt that he was still in there somewhere, in his head, confused, scared, desperate to get out. She wasn't capable of abandoning him. She knew, if the roles were reversed, he'd never leave her.

 After her father was released from the hospital, Foster worked from home. The coffee table that served as her workspace as a schoolgirl, a college student, a law student, took on its role once again, covered in the legal litter of her occupation. But when her work was through for the day the table took on a new, more important task. It became the center of her war room. Foster felt with all her heart that her father was retrievable, that somehow, she was missing something. With all the all the science, all the

The One and True Son

money spent on medical breakthroughs, there must be something she hadn't tried, someone she hadn't called, some chemical she hadn't found. Her nonworking hours were spent on the internet. She perused sites from the Mayo Clinic to Johns Hopkins. She read research studies from as far away as Australia and India. Little hope was to be found.

In desperation, she turned to YouTube. Foster was no stranger to the site. In her law school days, she'd pull her head out of her book to watch music videos or the comedy routines of comics like Robin Williams or Louis Black. She often needed a laugh while studying the darkest parts of the law, the parts that seemed unfair, that were obviously written to keep those in power…in power. She needed laughter. She needed the sound of people enjoying themselves to keep moving. She needed light to get through the dark.

But entertainment was the furthest thing from her mind the day she began searching for help for her father. It seemed like the only place left to find some light for him. Above her past views of old ABBA jingles, George Carlin rants and Alanis Morrissett dirges she found the search box and entered words she never thought she would on this site: Help for schizophrenia.

She watched and listened carefully to each video, most done by psychiatrists or psychologists. Most spoke of treatments she was well aware of, indeed most she'd already tried. Others spoke of talk therapy, which again she tried; regretfully, most professionals she'd worked with who had this approach didn't seem to understand that they couldn't talk her father out of his delusions. Still others proposed using hallucinogens. The very idea sent Foster's head spinning.

She tried other search words:

Hope for schizophrenia

New Treatment for schizophrenia

Cured of schizophrenia

These were anecdotal videos of people suffering from the disease, most living with it, most coping. But none of them seemed to be affected as much as her father who was burning through the options in the *Physicians Desk Reference* at an alarming rate.

Hot tears poured down her face. She couldn't lose her father, the sweet man who took her to the National Zoo and told her stories about all the different animals they'd seen, making them up from enclosure to enclosure. The man who would twirl her in their living room to a scratched and battered record of the Beatles, *Love Me Do,* until they both fell down giggling. The man who told her never to be afraid because he'd always be there for her. And he was. When he was able, he was.

The One and True Son

She stared at the evil search box, with its empty promises and its tiny magnifying glass. Fury took a hold of her. Polite fury, controlled fury, but fury, nevertheless.

Desperately, she pounded into the keyboard:

Please! Cure my father!

Foster had no idea what to expect. Truly, she expected some obscure old country song to pop up, an old country song about a pick-up truck and a dog named Duke. What popped up was quite different from her expectations. Videos of people in parks, on city streets, in hospitals all with the two things in common: the name *Jessie* and the word *cured."* She opened the first entitled, as was close to her request, entitled: *Jessie Cured My Father.* She watched the whole 12 minute and 34 second video of a man who claimed that his father, a gaunt man of 82, according to a photo he held up, had been cured of stage four pancreatic cancer after a man named Jessie came to visit him in a hospital in Charlottesville, Virginia. "I'm telling you people and I hope you all hear. God has sent his son. His name is Jessie Carpentero. He is the one we've be*en* waiting for. The doctors can't believe it. They *don't* believe it. They can't explain it. But I'm telling everyone that he is here." The man wiped tears away from eyes, tears that just kept coming.

The man took a breath. He smiled at the camera. Foster thought to herself that either he was one of the best actors she'd ever seen, or one of the happiest people on the planet.

There were many more videos, maybe 30 or 40. Some with a person who claimed to be cured of cancer, epilepsy, addiction; others were family members, or just witnesses to "a miracle." They had the same glow, the same blissful expressions. With each video Foster felt something lift in her. Something she hadn't been sure she'd ever feel again: hope.

She searched through the videos for a glimpse of this man, Jessie, the miracle worker. He didn't appear in any the clips. Not a single one. Foster clicked from video to video, fast-forwarding. Something caught in her throat. She had to find this man, Jessie.

Foster clicked on the filter, where she could organize the videos according to date of the appearance on the website. She started with "this year." She noticed a progression in locations from west to east, from Tennessee to Florida, South Carolina to Virginia. She switched the filter to "this month". Almost all of the videos came from Virginia. The hope rose up in her again. Finally, she switched the filter to "this week."

Foster sucked in her breath.

She recognized immediately the setting of the first three videos to come up. She'd spent days as a child running around the twenty-two sandstone

The One and True Son

pillars with capitals of stylized acanthus leaves, grouped like an ancient Roman temple destroyed by ghost marauders from long ago, leaving only a skeleton of a holy site. She'd gone there as a student, to read, where the world was quiet and the air fragrant with the subtle lemon-honey scent of magnolias and the hint of peachy sweet osmanthus.

Jessie was at the National Arboretum. He was in DC.

The senior partners were more than understanding when she called and told them that she had to take the week off to find help for her father. Sydney, a woman with her name on the door of a major DC law firm for over 20 years, told her to take as much time as she needs. As a young lawyer, she'd had similar challenges with her grandmother, the woman who had raised her, when early onset of Alzheimer's took hold of the sweet woman's mind. Back then, her bosses weren't so sympathetic, and she swore that if she ever was in a position to help someone through a nightmare like hers, she wouldn't hesitate.

And so, on a cloudy, coolish day, Foster found herself sitting among the pillars that formerly stood guard outside the Capitol Building. They were removed during a renovation in 1958 and placed in the arboretum as a centerpiece for the park. Foster sat on the raised edge of a small pool in the center the display. A stone canal ran from the pool, out past the pillars and downhill between a set of stairs where it emptied into a larger, shallow pool. Foster hadn't known what to expect. Was it going to be like a rock concert out here? Would there be lines of wheelchairs and people with red tipped, white canes waiting for this man, Jessie, waiting for his blessing? It turned out there was none of that. It was quiet and calm. For the first hour she saw, maybe, three or four small groups of people, hugging themselves from the damp chill and relegating their sunglasses to the necks of their shirts.

The second hour was much like the first, except for a moment when a group of twelve, mostly young people approached from the New York Avenue direction. It was a group she'd imagined would be around a man rumored to be the son of Yahweh: many races, many styles, and again, mostly young. Wouldn't youth flock to the Son of God?

But the group discussed the weather. The younger ones hung on the pillars and chased each other around while the others, who Foster saw were much older, once they got closer, watched and talked about the budget deficit. A few of them nodded to Foster, a couple of them, again, the older ones, wondered exactly what this woman was doing sitting out virtually in the open, exposed to the chill, when she could be behind the walls of the Bonsai Garden, taking in the miniature giants of the tree world.

The One and True Son

Halfway through the third hour, Foster was close to falling apart. She wasn't sure she could feel her feet. Her rear end felt wet from the chill of the stone wall of the decorative pool. She thought back to the videos. What had she missed? The weather had looked right for this time of year, still warm and slightly breezy, unlike this day. She supposed that even though the videos had been uploaded recently, they could have been shot at any time. Whoever submitted them may have been sitting on them, waiting to have enough time in their busy days to show them to the world. But did that make sense? If they'd witnessed a miracle, if they'd *received* one, how was it possible to hold that away from the world? Especially in the world today, when miracles are so rare. Who could possibly keep that in? How could they not sing it out to the world? She knew she couldn't hold back.

"Are you cold?"

The voice behind her startled her. She jumped.

Foster twisted around to see a tall man with wooly hair and the kindest eyes she'd ever seen in her life. Her words stuck in her throat.

"I'm sorry," the man said. "I startled you. You've been sitting out here a long time. I was worried you might be cold." He took off the denim jacket he wore and offered it to her.

Words finally came to Foster.

"I didn't hear you. I didn't mean to jump. I'm fine, really."

The man gestured next to her. "May I sit?"

Normally, if a stranger approached her like this, Foster would excuse herself as politely as possible and walk away as quickly as her feet would carry her. Unconsciously, she scooted over on the short wall allowing him to sit.

The man, his head still much higher than hers, put his jacket back on. He wrinkled his brow.

"You're waiting for someone."

This wasn't a question and it made Foster uneasy. She wasn't sure how to answer. To say no would make her vulnerable. And it would be a lie. Somehow, she felt the former would be worse than the latter.

She nodded and looked down the stairs at the larger pool. "It's kind of stupid really."

The tall man looked at the sky and back at her, his eyes burning into her. She had to look at him.

"It couldn't be too trivial to be out here on a day like this. And for so long."

His eyes did it. She knew she could tell him. She sensed that he already knew.

The One and True Son

She started with the death of her mother. Her mom had kept her dad safe and when she died, well, he broke. She told him of the cat, Waldo. The CIA paranoia. The drugs. The hospitalizations. Everything.

The man rubbed his brushy beard.

"You've suffered a lot."

"Me?" said laughed. "My father is the one suffering"

His kind eyes bore down again.

"You have suffered too. When pain comes from love, people suffer. Everyone who loves them suffers."

She grew quiet.

He spoke: "So why are you here?"

"Here?" she sighed. "I'm here because I heard there's man who heals. I tracked him through videos, but I guess I missed something."

She felt his eyes again, more intensely than before. She could feel them inside her, in her chest. She couldn't speak again.

"You believed this man could heal your father from his demons, from his disease. You tried medicines. You felt his pain. You heard about this man who can heal him. You sat in the cold, in solitude, to see this man. You *believed.*"

Foster turned and looked deep in those eyes. There was nothing but love in them.

She nodded. Tears spilled out.

The man stood. He reached out his hand. She took it and stood. His skin was both hard and soft, warm and scratchy. He smiled and wiped the tears from her cheeks.

"Go home, child," he said. "You have suffered enough. Your father is whole again. I promise you this."

Foster was confused. Elated and confused. She knew who this man was. In her heart she knew who this man was.

"Your faith has healed him," Jessie told her. He kissed her on the forehead. "Go home."

The Metro ride home was dreamlike. As she sat on the plastic seats of the subway, she remembered her father and their trips to the zoo. She remembered his silly stories about the elephants and the giraffes and the kangaroos. She remembered her mother's smile when they were both home, her funny husband and her bright daughter. Foster couldn't stop smiling.

She entered the gate into the tiny yard that she'd always known as hers. She stopped at the large tree that had watched over her family. She placed her palm on the rough bark, feeling its ruts, its strength. She opened the door to the smell of cornbread. Camille came out of the kitchen. She'd been watching her father while Foster was away. She had tears in her eyes.

"Something's happened," she said to Foster. "He's back."

Foster hugged her neighbor. "I know."

Foster called into the kitchen. "Dad," she said. "I'm home."

His response came as naturally as the wind.

"I am too, baby."

The Heretic

Before he was the Rabbi Doctor Cletus Quest, he was Bobby Smith, born and raised in Travis City, Texas. Cletus didn't mind hard work. He didn't mind reading. And he *loved* people. After all, as a former acquaintance once told him, "The Shepherd must love his sheep, if he plans to fleece them."

Bobby Smith developed a taste for larceny in high school. A place he loathed but, under the threat of his father's belt, he attended. In Travis City, in the seventies, schools were a loose environment. The educational authorities of the day, stunned by the slap of the federal government on issues of desegregation and busing along with white flight that bolstered white private schools throughout the state, took a hands-off approach to students who occupied the buildings, but rarely attended classes. Although Bobby was well known and, for the most part well liked, by faculty and students alike, he rarely saw the inside of a textbook or classroom.

He spent most school days seated on the raised concrete slab under the flagpole in the front lawn of the school, sometimes reading Jack Kerouac, Williams S. Burrows, Allen Ginsberg, sometimes giggling his way through underground comics like Fritz the Cat and the Fabulous Furry Freak Brothers. He almost always had a cigarette dangling from the corner of his mouth. Sometimes the smoke smelled a bit sweeter.

One day, Joan Alvarez, a square faced, solemn girl from Bobby's grade turned purple, or so Bobby had heard, and fell to the floor at her desk, her eyes rolled up in her head, drool bubbling from her mouth. An ambulance was called immediately. Bobby watched the screaming van's arrival as he sat at his perch, his back leaning on the flagpole. The paramedics, carrying heavy bags and a small oxygen tank rushed into the school. They left the back doors of the ambulance open and the engine running.

Before he knew what he was doing, Bobby Smith found himself at the open doors of the ambulance. He'd never ridden in one before, but he'd

The One and True Son

seen enough episodes of *Emergency* on television to recognize most things in it. He scanned the plexiglas compartments that lined the walls of the vehicle, crammed with gauze, tubes, flashlights, and scissors. He was pretty sure that the drugs were in the bags that the medics carried with them into the school. He cursed his bad luck.

He was just about to return to the flagpole when he heard a voice squack from the stretcher:

Fire Response Unit 2. Please respond to 921 Noland Street. They have an unresponsive female, 94, no vital signs...

Bobby saw the source of the noise sitting on the grey blanket: a fire department walkie talkie. Bobby had no idea why he wanted it, but he climbed into the back of the ambulance, snatched it and ran back to his books and sat down, covering the municipal property with a masterpiece from Robert Crumb. When the paramedics returned for the stretcher, they took no notice of the teenager watching them doing their jobs. They seemed oblivious to the crime they'd left themselves open to. They unfastened their rolling bed contraption from its moorings and rushed back in the building. By the time they'd wheeled poor epileptic Joan through the front doors and carried her down the steps, Bobby Smith was halfway home. The perfect crime.

Except it wasn't so perfect. It turned out about three football fields away from perfect. It seemed Bobby wasn't the only person interested in the vehicle with the flashing lights and wailing noises that took away the sick and injured. There were several people looking down from the school building. One girl, Gabriela, stared down from the Science Lab. Gabriela, a freshman, an undeveloped red headed girl, who by her senior year would break the hearts of countless males and some females by not returning their glances, watched to make sure whoever was ill or injured was no one she knew. Gabriela had wanted to be doctor for as long as she could remember and worried that anything needing the assistance of an ambulance must be quite dire. It'd turned out that she did know Joan from one of her classes, though she hadn't really spoken to her. Gabriela cried when she saw it was her.

Gabriela saw Bobby Smith walk from the ambulance with something under his shirt.

Joey loved ambulances. He also loved firetrucks, police cars, even tow trucks if they had their emergency lights turned on. He imagined he was the first person to hear the sirens as the ambulance, probably when it was a mile away, before it turned onto the circular drive that ran in front of the school. Joey loved how the other cars got out of the way whenever these cars, or trucks, or vans, had to get somewhere in a hurry. Someday, Joey hoped, he'd be able to drive a vehicle like that where everyone looked up and thought, *wow*. Joey was in special classes. People said he didn't read so well. They said he was a few years behind everyone else his age, which confused him. He knew his age: 16. Other people were 16. The way people talked was so confusing.

Joey saw Bobby Smith climb into the back of the ambulance. He saw him take something from it, put it under his shirt and run over and hide it under his books. Joey didn't know a lot of things, but he knew when saw something that was wrong.

Bobby Smith was no stranger to Tim Driggers. As Assistant Principal he'd had many a conversation with the long-haired boy who used the school flagpole as his personal smoking area. He liked the boy. He also worried about him. To Driggers, he seemed adrift. Without a doubt, Bobby was bright, a self-directed reader and a voracious one on top of it, but Driggers didn't see any direction in him, and certainly his reading material pointed away from anything productive for him or society.

The boy could tell a story though. Nearly every time Driggers pulled the boy in to discuss his future, Bobby would spin yarns about people he would meet in bizarre corners of Travis City, places people his age shouldn't know about let alone go. He spoke of shooting pool with large black men and whupping their butts so bad that didn't beat him to a pulp. Instead, respecting his skills, they'd give bonuses in beer and cigarettes.

Another time, after one of his teachers complained she hadn't seen him in class the entire quarter, Driggers had him paged on the PA and, like always, he responded. The boy explained that he had missed so many classes because his parents had both been laid off at work and he was forced to get illegally hired in a machine shop to help with the bills. His description of the shop floor with its oil spots and razor-sharp curls of waste metal were so vivid that Driggers found himself transfixed. Of course, the boy said, he couldn't operate the machines; he had to sweep, moving hundreds of pounds of scrap iron a night. His muscles constantly ached, he claimed.

Tim Driggers knew there was a word for the boy's stories. That word was bullshit. But the bullshit was well developed. The Assistant Principal suggested that Bobby might want to show up in English class and put some of these stories to paper. The boy declined.

As Tim Driggers stood behind the glass doors of the entrance to the school, he saw Bobby Smith go to the ambulance, jump in, and run back to his books. Driggers would have nabbed him right there, but he had to keep the halls clear for Joan Alvarez, a good kid, a kid with direction, a kid with an emergency. The Assistant Principal couldn't deal with Bobby Smith in his office anymore. He'd be in another kind of school soon

Bobby spent his next nine months at the Travis City on Salah Road. As was the case outside, Bobby showed little interest in the classes offered: Math, History, English. And as before, he read voraciously from the lock up's sparsely stocked library, pushing the elderly librarian, a bent over man with tufts of silver hair in his ears, to overlook the facility's policy of three books a week. As was the case in his former life, Bobby was well liked by staff and his fellow inmates. To his colleagues in crime, he was cool, experienced. As with his former Assistant Principal, he would dazzle them with bullshit, with crimes he was never a party, with secret knowledge of murders throughout the city. The bloody detail had to be real, his audience told themselves. No one could come up with that shit in their heads.

Bobby Smith's formal education ended with his release from juvey. His father provided a room and food until he was 18, as he felt was proper and legal, but washed his hands of him that birthday. Bobby's present was to find his belongings boxed and stacked on the front porch.

Bobby Smith became a basement dweller, in that he stayed in friends' basements until he'd worn out his welcome or detectives came knocking, often with both events occurring at the same time. He acquired a 1964 Chrysler Saratoga with a patchy black spray can paint job and a three-on-the-tree transmission. He used the car for his first legitimate job: delivering packages to the airport for a fledgling warehouse catalogue business. A *members-only* outfit, customers would peruse slightly underpriced stereo equipment, watches, portable TVs, guitars and women's "personal" vibrators. They'd fill out an ordering form or call one of the first 1-800 phone numbers to be used for this purpose. At the rear of a huge warehouse, Bobby loaded up his car three to five times daily, his trunk packed with mail order dreams of high fidelity and private bliss and headed down US 281 to Travis City International Airport.

Bobby loved the freedom of the job, especially with the windows down, a cigarette dangling from his lips and as much AC/DC as he could pump through his blown stock speakers. Once at the airport he'd swing around to the freight terminal and hand off his trunk's cargo to a bored and overworked freight handler. He drove the job straight for the first couple of weeks. Bobby knew that being a delivery boy wasn't his destiny, but he always kept his eyes open for clues to what it might be. And while keeping his eyes open, he saw another opportunity. It turned out to be a nearly perfect crime.

The One and True Son

The idea came to Bobby while cruising at nearly 80 miles an hour down the highway, windows open, shades on, and The Pat Travers Band blaring, *Born Under a Bad Sign,* a cover of an Albert Collins song, through the mushy speakers connected to his under-dash tape deck. Bobby loved the energy of the song, the thumping bass drum in the opening, the hissing of a closing high hat, the bass guitar melting in with the drums, a chopping, muted, electric guitar waiting in the background. Finally, Travers attacks with a sneering lead. Bobby loved the song. He played the record in his rented room continuously, careful to give it a thorough cleansing with his disc cleaner before returning the needle to the beginning. He'd air-guitar the song, growling into an invisible mic:

Born under a bad sign.
I've been down since I began to crawl.
If it wasn't for bad luck,
I wouldn't have no luck at all.

A pop or a crackle on a record drove him nuts. In the car that day, hearing the song as if it were being played through a kazoo. He snapped the tape out of the player and threw it in the back seat. "This job sucks!" he shouted to his fellow travelers through his open window.

The Small Freight depot at Travis City International was behind Freight Terminal D. It was a single bay with a roll up, high wind rated steel door, a roller conveyer and a beat up, old, steel desk. The depot was usually manned by perpetually bored forty something man named James, a man who resented his job, unions, foreign food and most women. Bobby Smith struck up a friendship early with James, offering name brand smokes (James smoked generics) and the occasional Hostess fruit pie. Bobby would kill time regaling the older man with tales of battles with dark people and conquests of multiple women at once. James would flap his toothless lower jaw at all the punchlines, and say, "I know, right?" in all the right places, making him the perfect audience for Bobby Smith. He was also the perfect mark.

That first day of the scam, James couldn't have been more helpful. Bobby handed James a Marlboro through his open window as soon he set his parking brake. James, grateful and greedy asked for another which Bobby gladly provided. The attendant tucked the spare behind his ear and ran a hand through his greasy hair. "Open up that trunk, boy," he said, brightly and went to get his clipboard. Bobby hopped out and obliged.

The freight clerk returned with his board and his form and began writing in Bobby's items' names, serial numbers, manufactures, and quantities. Once recorded, he'd take a tracking sticker, place it on each item and toss it on the conveyer. When Bobby's trunk was empty, James

The One and True Son

signed the form on the *received by* line. He then tore off a copy and handed it to Bobby.

Bobby put a Marly to his lips.

"Damn, James. I forgot my zippo. Gotta light?"

James patted all the pockets on his coveralls.

"Shit, Bobby," the clerk said with a tired look. "You know I never got a light, but you always ask me. You really gonna make me go look for one?"

"I got another cig that says you will," Bobby answered smiling, a fresh smoke between his thumb and forefinger.

James shuffled to the dilapidated desk and began struggling with the bent and rusted drawers. While the clerk was working on the bottom drawer, Bobby Smith casually walked to the conveyer, picked up a blue box marked *Jensen Coaxial Speakers,* tossed them in the truck and shut the lid.

James kicked the desk. "Goddamit, Bobby, I can't get this fucking drawer open!"

Bobby pulled out his Zippo. "No problem, buddy. Found the Zippo."

The freight clerk joined Bobby at the car. "You put me through all that, shit. I hope I still get the smoke."

Bobby Smith put his hand on the clerk's shoulder and handed him his reward.

"For you, James, always."

He gave the man's shoulder a friendly shake.

Ironically, it wasn't this scam, one he'd run for months, that cost him his job. He'd run the same scenario on poor James about once a week. One week he copped a six-inch portable TV. Another, a sweet turntable with direct drive and a ceramic cartridge. He was able to complete his home stereo with a pair of speakers that he could practically plug into the wall and not blow them. But once again, Bobby Smith's "perfect crime" fell short. It was the police who put an end to his good thing, but it wasn't for theft.

Bobby Smith knew if he got greedy and threw something in his trunk every drop-off, he'd get caught. On the second run, on a Monday, Bobby decided to take a detour. He pulled off the highway and made his way to the North Star Mall. He thought he'd take a walk around, get an Orange Julius, maybe stop by a music store and pick up the new Loverboy album. He was a half mile from the parking lot when he saw the flashing lights in his rearview mirror. He pulled over, turned off the music and waited for the cop.

The One and True Son

Officer Larry Buckholtz, a fifteen-year veteran of the Travis City Police Force, hated to see two things in his city. Well, truthfully, he hated a lot more than just two things, but a long- haired punk and a beat-up car were two that were up there pretty high. He always made a point of touching the back taillight of a piece of shit like the one in front of him, just a thumbprint, just in case the piece of shit driving the piece of shit had a gun and shot him while he walked up. Fingerprints. Evidence the punk with the girly hair was at the scene. Officer Buckholtz always thought ahead. And he could smell bullshit on a windy day next to a rubber factory.

The driver's window was down and the kid behind the wheel grinned like he was meeting a long lost relative.

"Good afternoon, officer," Bobby chirped.

"It ain't afternoon yet," the cop said. "It's 10:47 in the AM. Now, I need to see a driver's license and a registration."

Bobby made a show of checking his pockets, patting at his chest, looking in the open compartment in the dash.

"Oh man," he sighed. "I must have left my wallet in my other pants."

"Uh-hmm," the officer responded, scratching his eyebrow. "What about the registration?"

Bobby Smith feigned embarrassment. "Same wallet. Sorry?"

The officer stepped back from the car. He looked it up and down and made a clicking noise between his teeth.

"You know why I stopped you?" he asked, finally.

"Honestly, Officer, I have no idea. I don't think I was speeding."

The officer chuckled. "No, you weren't speeding. The reason I stopped you is I couldn't tell if you were going to stop or keep on going forever. You got no brake lights."

Bobby slapped his forehead. "Damn it! I didn't know, officer, I swear. I just got this car a week ago. I work at an auto body shop, but I got into a wreck and the owner of the place sold me this one. It's a piece of shit...excuse me...I mean junk. It'll hold me over until I get another Trans Am."

The officer took off his Smokey the Bear hat and wiped his brow. "No shit," he said, locking his sharp blue eyes on the kid driver. "I need some bodywork on my Challenger. Where's your shop? I might bring it by. It's got a 5.6 liter, V8, a Carter four-barrel, Hurst shifter, Glasspacks. You should hear that fucker. It shakes windows going down the block."

Bobby's smile dimmed.

"Oh, it's not around here."

The officer grinned. "Well, I don't live around here. Where is it? Maybe it's closer to where I live."

"It's in Brady Gardens." Bobby was reaching.

"Bingo!" the cop yelled. "Is it the shop on Cupples Road? Andy's Auto? I pass that all the time."

Bobby grinned. "Yep, that's the one. Yeah, you just bring that hummer in there and I'll make sure you get a good deal." Bobby winked. "A real good deal."

The police officer's smile evaporated. He leaned down so he could aim those blue eyes right at Bobby. His sharp white teeth came together. He spoke through them. "There ain't no Andy's Auto on Cupples Road. Now why don't you get out of that piece of shit, real slow like, and put your hands behind your back."

As far as Bobby Smith knew, his theft of several thousand dollars of stereo equipment, televisions, and all manner of new goods was never discovered. He didn't even get pinched for attempted bribery of a police officer for his offer of discount repairs at a fictional auto shop. But he lost his job, nevertheless. It turned out that Bobby Smith never got a driver's license. Insurance wasn't deemed important by the young thief either, which the judge at his court hearing informed him had become mandatory for all drivers two years before his arrest. Bobby couldn't sell the loot he'd accumulated, or more accurately, he didn't try, to pay the sizable fine he faced, so he turned up his contrition knob to bullshit and informed the judge that he'd been living alone in a small, rented room since the death of his parents in a tragic house fire. He related that the very next day, after his arrest, he had gone to a Navy recruiter. The recruiter told him, Bobby said with a shaky voice, that they would send immediately to Boot Camp if he could be freed from the charges against him. That said, Bobby approached the judge's bench and placed a business card of one Petty Officer Second Class Walter Andrzejewski, Naval Recruiter.

The judge, a short, black haired man with curly hair poking out above the collar of his robe seemed moved by the young man with the fresh haircut and neatly pressed clothes. He looked at Bobby a long time before he issued his ruling. Finally, he spoke to him and to the court:

"Young man. The way you have overcome diversity is admirable. You have suffered a lot and yet you approach this court with dignity and respect." He looked around the court room, stopping his eyes on a longhaired boy, maybe a little younger than Bobby with a hole ridden T-shirt declaring *Disco Sucks* in graffitiesque letters smeared on the front. "Something lacking in some of your contemporaries, I'm sorry to say." The judge smiled down on Bobby. "You have planned well. The United

The One and True Son

States Navy is a noble institution. The military is a noble profession. I was a marine, but don't tell your recruiter. He might not take you."

The judge cleared him of the charges against him. Before releasing him the judge, admonished him with one more bit of wisdom: "How you represent yourself is so important. Never forget that."

Bobby Smith never forgot.

He also never joined the Navy.

* * *

Manic Maury's Motor Works was the most famous car dealership in Travis City, maybe in the entirety of Texas. Famous for Manic Maury, also known as Maury Rosencrantz, a 5 foot, 2 inch, 270 pound whirlwind whose commercials were loved and loathed throughout the state, usually playing late at night or during college football games. They all featured Rosencrantz standing like a lineman in an imaginary football game, his sausage fingers extended out in pudgy stars in front of him. Every week he'd have another explanation for the name of his business.

HOWDY THERE! Manic Maury from Manic Maury's Motor Works here! A lot of people ask me, Maury, why is your dealership called MANIC MAURY'S MOTOR WORKS? Well, I tell 'em (Shuffles his feet, runs a hand through his spiked white hair) we're MANIC MAURY'S MOTOR WORKS because that's what we got: THE WORKS! (Fireworks explode over Maury's head) YEE HAW! We got new cars, used cars. The best service. So y'all come down to MANIC MAURY'S MOTOR WORKS TODAY!

The next ad might've explained exactly what was manic about buying a car from him while twirling a buzzsaw around to sound effects to beguile the senses into believing the saw was actually running. Maury had been the subject of many articles in business magazines on the pros and cons of a business owner doing his own commercials. Mostly, the journalists were against it.

Manic Maury's was the next stop on Bobby Smith's journey to success. He was hired to wash the cars, and as with almost every experience at this point in his life, he'd learned something that he would never forget. Even in the wash bay, with its high-pressure sprayer and its myriad of chemicals designed to make the car appear higher quality that it was, there was something to take with him. The wash bay had sprays to make fake leather that had sat in the searing Texas sun for months look like an equestrian's dream saddle, sprays that covered scratches made by weary truck drivers in the unloading process, sprays that made the car smell *new,* however that

The One and True Son

was supposed to smell. The judge was right: appearance and presentation *was* everything, no matter how superficial that appearance and presentation was.

Bobby Smith had no intention of washing cars for long. It wasn't the work. It was the future it portended, one of sopping coveralls and pickled fingertips, little personal interaction and an empty wallet. He saw the wash bay as a way into where he needed to be, and for that moment, that was at a car dealership.

He began adding small touches to his uniform, royal blue coveralls with his name stitched over his left breast. The first week it was a tie, a different one every day. He'd boosted a handful of them at a Salvation Army store so, in his mind, and it turns out, others', he had a different look every day. Once people stopped commenting on that he took to placing folded paisley handkerchiefs in his right breast pocket. Later he would add a tie clip. On hot days, he forwent the tie and donned a dapper ascot. He became a topic of conversation in the showroom, an innocent novelty, which was exactly what he'd sought to do.

One day, Herb Rollings, the top salesman, came out to see what all the buzz was about. Herb rarely came out to the wash bay. Herb didn't like cars, especially the rolling bombs this dealership sold. He cared for car buyers just a little less. The less time he had to spend around either, the better, so he'd hustle the suckers around, find out if they could pay for a car and hide in his office the rest of the time. The moment he saw Bobby Smith he knew he was seeing a kindred spirit.

He approached Bobby in between an old Pinto sold to a college twit and a new cobalt blue Suzuki Samurai, a boxy, weak attempt at an off roader that sold mostly to girls named Megan for their sweet sixteen presents. Bobby was sitting on a couple of milk crates, smoking a cigarette with his knees crossed as if he were the Prince of Wales.

"You must be Bobby," Herb said, turning on whatever it was that earned him six figures a year.

Bobby sprung from his thrown and thrust his hand out to the salesman. Everyone in the dealership knew who the top salesman was. He was more than the guy with the lazy eye. He was the guy with the plushest demo of all the salesman, second only to Maury's Porsche. Everyone knew Rollings.

"An honor to meet you, Mr. Rollings." Bobby's grin was as wide as Dolly Parton's bust line.

"Call me Herb," the salesman answered. "You got another one of those smokes?"

The One and True Son

Bobby tapped one out his pack, passed it to the big man. He flicked and lit his Zippo in one quick motion. Rollings took a long drag and turned his attention to Bobby.

"You know, you're the talk of the coffee room at the showroom."

Bobby tugged at his ascot. "Well, that's great to hear, Herb. I try to give the cars a little extra shimmer, ya know? I want your customers to come back to you again and again."

"That right?" the salesman chuckled. "Then how come you're taking a smoke break out here when there's one of the Suzuki Tonka trucks waiting to be scrubbed?"

Bobby didn't flinch. "I'm glad you asked me that Herb. Ya see, I figure that most people expect a full day's work when they got their heart set on buying a car. If everything's too smooth, something's wrong. Now, I looked at my watch and it's only 11 in the AM. Now, that can't hardly be two or three hours. Somebody's gonna smell a rat."

The salesman plunked down on Bobby's milk crates and started laughing so hard his neck turned a deep shade of purple. He couldn't speak at first. He just waved his cigarette as if he were flagging a taxi.

"You okay, Herb," Bobby asked, looking as concerned as he could muster.

When Rollings could breathe he finally answered. "Oh, you're good, boy. You are good."

Bobby's smile didn't waver. "Like I said, I shine 'em up good. I throw a little turpentine into the water bucket when I'm wiping the car down. Makes the rain bead up."

The salesman erupted again this time, coughing so hard in between guffaws that Bobby wondered if he'd be calling the paramedics.

"Nah boy," Rollings said when he could breathe. "You're a talker! You're so full of shit, I'm surprised your eyes are blue!"

For the first time Bobby's smile dimmed.

"Don't look like that, kid. You're wasted out here. I'm getting you inside where you can make some money."

Bobby tossed down his butt and stomped it out.

"You can do that?"

"Hell yeah, boy," the salesman assured him. "Maury does what I say. I make enough money around here to keep that boozehound and his trophy wife in Jack Daniel's and cocaine for the rest of their lives."

"I don't know how to thank you," Bobby said, the first sincere thing he'd said all day.

The One and True Son

"You know how I make a shit-ton of money in this sewer of a business?" Rollings asked.

Bobby shook his head.

"It's because I can read people." He snapped his fingers. "Just like that, I can read people. I look at them and I got 'em. Now, I look at you…" he looked at Bobby's ascot, "…I see big money."

Bobby's voice cracked. "Really, how can I thank you?"

"Don't worry about it," the salesman told him. "I was a young bullshitter once."

"This the kid?" Maury said, the next day, looking dubiously at Bobby's silk polka dotted ascot.

"Yeah, it's him, Rollings replied. "Trust me on this. He reminds me a little of someone, but I can't quite put my finger on who."

The famous dealership owner puffed hot breath through his nostrils.

Bobby shot out his hand.

"It's a great honor to meet you, Mr. Rosencrantz. I'm a huge fan of your commercials. Always have been. Ever since I was little."

Manic Maury finally cracked a smile.

"That long, huh?" He left Bobby's hand hanging.

Maury walked out of the management office, talking over his shoulder.

"I hope you're right about this. And tell him to take that fuckin' hanky off his neck."

Herb Rollings put a big paw on Bobby's shoulder. "You're in."

From there Bobby was given a crash course in parting customers with their money. Rollings had already sold twice his target that week, so he didn't mind showing Bobby the ropes. He wasn't lying when he told Maury the kid reminded him of someone. Of course, he was hoping Maury would infer that the kid was like *him*; that idiot son of a bitch had an ego bigger than a rhino's rear end. But, in truth, Bobby reminded the top earner of himself, a younger Herb, a planner, willing to do almost anything to make a buck. And this kid liked the game. Rollings could see that right off the bat.

Rollings sat Bobby in his office. Most of the salespeople were in cubicles, but Rollings had an office. The salesman left him in there while he got a cup of coffee. He wanted him to soak in the atmosphere.

And Bobby did. He gazed in awe at the desk, clean, dusted and organized, big enough to take up half of his own rented room. Framed certificates covered every inch of wall space: Gold Seller, Platinum Seller,

The One and True Son

Diamond Seller, each month, every month, for years. The credenza behind the desk displayed framed photos of Herb Rollings in his natural habitat, out in the open lot handing keys to a Senator, a name brand actor, a Hall of Fame quarterback for the Cowboys.

The leather chair behind the desk made that sound a real, plush, leather chair makes as the salesman sat and settled, the air rushing around beneath the animal skin to make the occupant feel wrapped, supported, cozy. He gave Bobby Smith an amused stare, tapping his fingers on the giant desk to a rhythm the younger man couldn't quite place.

"Let me throw something at you," he finally said. "Tell me about the test drive? Ever taken one."

"Well sir," Bobby said, sitting up straight. "I haven't taken one per se, however…"

"Cut the shit, kid," Rollings interrupted. "This is me, *Herb*. You ever call me *sir* again I'm gonna reach over there and pluck your eye out. Now, a test drive: yes or no?"

"No," Bobby answered.

The big man sat back in his chair.

"Now we're getting somewheres." He smiled at Bobby. "The customer ever comes in here looking for a test drive, you skip all the other shit I'm gonna tell you and get 'em into that car. Sprint if you have to."

Bobby looked puzzled. "Why?"

"Because they've done most of the selling for you. Get them into the car, chances are they're gonna open their checkbook."

"What if they don't want to test drive?" Bobby asked.

The salesman leaned forward. "Make 'em."

"Huh?"

"You heard me," Rollings said, smiling brightly. "Make 'em."

"How the hell do I do that?"

"Your first question and it's a good one. What you do is get the model of the car they're interested in. Now, I don't give a shit if they say they don't want air or fancy wheels, or power anything. You go out there and get them the top of the line."

"Why's that?" asked Bobby.

"'Cause when some asshole wastes your time with the 'We're just looking' bullshit you tell him this. Are you ready?"

Bobby nodded.

"You tell them: Just you wait right here. I've got something exciting to show you."

The One and True Son

Rollings picked up an expensive gold pen from his desk.

Bobby waited for a moment then asked: "What's that?"

Rollings took his eyes off the pen and stared at Bobby. The lazy eye threw the younger man off. He didn't know which eye was looking at him.

"The car, dipshit! "Rollings yelled. "The test drive!"

Bobby shrugged. "But the guy already said he didn't want to take one."

"Tough shit!" The salesman bellowed. "What you do is, you go out to the lot, find the most loaded model you can find. While the guy is in the shop looking at stickers, you pull the car up to the side doors. Hopefully it'll be a hot day. It usually is in this godforsaken state."

"Why?" Bobby asked, enthralled.

"'Cause you blast the shit out of the air conditioning. Get that leather smell going around the car. That and whatever toxic shit they spray in the thing to make it smell good. Leave the driver door open when you go in to get the guy."

Bobby couldn't help but rest his elbows on Dave's desk and plant his chin in his palms.

"As soon as you get the guy out there," Rollings continued, "tell him you want him to sit in the driver's seat. Point out the new instrumentation. Show him all the bells and whistles. Play him the radio, nice and loud, so he can hear the speakers. Then shut the door on him."

"What?" Bobby laughed.

"Shut the door on him. He'll be so shocked he won't know what to do. Then you stroll to the passenger's side and let yourself in. Tell him, *Let's go for a spin!"*

"People fall for that?" Bobby asked, incredulous.

"Ninety-nine percent of the time," Rollings assured him.

"What about the other one percent?"

"Tell them you thought they wanted a test ride. Gaslight 'em."

"What's that?" Bobby asked, almost breathless.

"Act like what they heard with their own ears and saw with their own eyes isn't what happened. Look at them like *they're* crazy."

The salesman sat back in his chair again.

"And that shit actually works?" Bobby asked.

Herb Rollings waved his hand around the room, at the frames.

"I don't know. You tell me."

Rollings's tool kit for extracting people's money was vast and varied. There was the "Sold/Hold" tag. Rollings showed Bobby in rear lot.

The One and True Son

"Make sure you always got pen on you," Rollings said, holding up the gold one he had on his desk. "It'll take a few sales before you'll be able to afford one of these babies. 24 Carat. You got a pen?"

Bobby pulled one out from his breast pocket that he'd pilfered out of Rollings's office. Not gold, but nice.

Rollings grinned. "You keep that one. Don't ever lose it. You *won't* take another one."

The salesman took a red and yellow ticket from his jacket. He held it up like a delicate feather. "This here is a Sold/Hold tag. This is what you do. You be the customer."

Bobby took what he thought would be an appropriate pose, standing rigidly straight, with a slight quiver. He was feeling the part.

"Now Bobby let me ask you," Rollings winked at him, "you don't mind me calling you Bobby, do you?"

Bobby Smith assured him that he didn't.

"Let me ask you, Bobby. Do you like this car? 'Cause if you don't love it, I got a full lot of beauties. But I think we're a lot alike. I think that this car is gonna be great for you and your family."

Bobby nodded in agreement to all that was presented to him.

"Okay, so you *love* this car. Is there anything other than price keeping you from buying *this* car today?"

Bobby thought he'd throw Rollings a curve.

"I'm really not ready to buy a car today, Herb," he said grinning.

Rollings returned his grin and placed his huge paw on Bobby's shoulder.

"That's not what I asked you. This car has everything: the leather package, the sport wheels, the six-speaker audio system, the pin striping, the upgraded wipers, air, power windows and mirrors. Is there anything but price keeping you from buying this car?"

Bobby looked down at his toes. He could feel the pressure.

"I guess not, Herb," Bobby said. "Maybe just not today."

Rollings gave his shoulder a shake.

"Great!" He exclaimed and handed Bobby the Sold/Hold tag and his gold pen.

"Now I really want you to have this car, but I don't want anybody coming out here and selling it out from underneath us. So, what I need you to do is sign that tag where it says *Hold*."

Bobby looks at Rollings, doubtful.

"Why don't *you* sign it?" Bobby Smith asked.

The One and True Son

"Because I'm just another salesman. If someone sees me out here putting hold tags on cars, they're just gonna ignore 'em. They'll think I'm hoggin' all the good cars."

Rollings took a step back.

"If you do it, well, you're a *customer* and there ain't no one more important at *this* dealership than the *customer*. Now I'm not telling you to sign the *Sold* side. No, we ain't that far yet. Just go ahead and hold this hummer so we can talk."

Bobby wrote his signature on the card.

"Great," Rollings said with a hardy slap to Bobby's back. "Now, just put that under the wiper."

"I gotta do that too?" Bobby asked, engrossed.

"Like I said, you're the *customer*!"

Bobby did as instructed.

"Congratulations," Rollings said. "You just bought a new car!"

"What do you mean?" Bobby was really confused. "Is that legal?"

Rollings laughed. "Naw, you didn't really buy the car. But you're going to. You just signed the first of many pieces of paper in buying this automobile. The idea is in your head and it ain't coming out."

Bobby was ecstatic.

There were tricks inside the office too.

"So, again, you're the customer," Rollings said sitting down in his comfy chair.

Bobby nodded.

"So, how much can you afford for a monthly payment? Just a guess." Rollings leaned forward.

Bobby shrugged. "I don't know. Three hundred dollars?"

Rollings pointed his index finger and made an upward motion with it. "Up to?"

"I don't know, five hundred?"

"See that?" Rollings beamed. "You just bumped yourself up $200."

"No shit," said Bobby, astonished.

"Yeah, no shit. But don't forget the finger," Rollings said, repeating the gesture. "It visually pushes 'em."

Herb Rollings showed Bobby how to play with the monthly payment and the interest rate to make it look like the car is more affordable than it was.

"You can tack on thousands of dollars and these shit kickers will walk out of here like they got the deal of the century." Rollings sat back and

The One and True Son

eyed Bobby. He liked what he saw. He could almost see the gears working in the younger man's head."

"Now, aftermarket…"

Bobby Smith was an apt pupil. In six months, he was putting his own Silver Seller certificate up in his cube. Three months later, he was framing a Gold Seller. He moved cars the likes of which hadn't been seen since Herb Rollings was green. Neons and Jeeps that had baked in the Texas sun for months finally gave up their spots in the lot when Bobby could box someone into a test drive.

And Manic Maury was pleased. Whenever he saw the young up-start he'd snap his fingers and point in his direction, often with the patented Manic Maury grin from his commercials to go along with it. He even let him wear his ascot.

By the end of his first year, he'd moved from his rented room to a decent apartment with a pool, a weight room and a fine assortment of single women.

One day, Herb Rollings sat down in the chair at Bobby's cubicle. Bobby had just closed a deal on a Jeep Sahara that had been returned as a lemon two months before. He sold it to a schoolteacher, about 30 years old, looked 50, who said she'd dreamed of off-roading. He hoped that the fixes the service shop did were enough to keep her happy. If not, he felt sure he could sell her another one.

"Let's get a smoke," Rollings told his protege.

Once outside, and after Bobby tapped a Marlboro for each of them, Rollings put a gentle hand on his shoulder.

"Kid, you're doing great," he said. "But we're going to have to let you go."

Bobby's smoke fell from his lip. "Why?"

Rollings took a deep inhale. "You're getting too close. There ain't enough decent cars in here for two Gold Sellers, let alone two Diamonds. I can't keep selling like I have been with you around. Sorry, kid."

"Does Maury know about this?" Bobby asked, his voice cracking.

Rollings looked him in the eyes. Bobby still couldn't find the eye he was talking to.

"Not yet," the older salesman said. "He ain't going to say anything. I've been here too long. I know too much. Besides, he still hates your ascots."

A tear swam in Bobby's eye.

"Why'd you do all this? Why'd you teach me?"

"Bored, I guess," Rollings shrugged. "Don't worry, kid. I taught you good. You'll be okay wherever you end up."

The One and True Son

Rollings stamped out his cigarette.

"I just can't have you on my block," he said and went back into the showroom.

And apparently by *his block* he meant the entirety of Travis City as it seemed that no car dealership within a hundred miles had any interest in hiring him. Bobby arranged interviews with the top dealerships in the area, shined and preened himself, and put away the ascot and pocket square, at least until he could show them what he could do. By all appearances, his interviews went swimmingly and yet no one was calling him back. One day, fed up, he returned to a dealership where he'd really thought he'd clicked with the General Manager, a young guy just a few years older than Bobby, named Ben Franklin. Really. They talked cars and sales techniques. From there they shared their love of loud rock and roll, Mexican food and women with braces. When Bobby left the interview, he'd already picked out his cubicle and had ideas how he'd decorate it.

And yet, after a week, his phone remained mute.

Something was wrong.

He rented a car and drove to the dealership, a good half hour from his apartment. The dealership, for Cadillacs, was in a great location, just outside of Elm Creek with its pillared houses and swimming pools. The showroom was fabulous, with gold trim and shiny El Dorados, Coupe De Villes and Allantés aligned perfectly, illuminated in stunning spotlights. Bobby strolled in like he owned the place and went straight to Ben Franklin's office. Ben was on the phone. Bobby tapped on the doorframe. At first, Ben wrinkled his brow when he looked up and saw Bobby standing there. The annoyed look was replaced by a salesman's grin. The General Manager held up an index finger.

"Yeah, sweetheart. Yeah listen, I've got a customer here. I can't keep him waiting. You know, business. Listen, I'll pick you up at eight. We'll get a real nice dinner. All right, baby? Yeah, love you too."

He hung up and stood behind his desk.

"Billy!" Ben Franklin said. "What's up?"

Bobby entered and shook the manager's hand.

"Actually, it's Bobby."

Franklin looked almost embarrassed.

"Oh yeah, Bobby. That's right. Hey, at least I got the first letter right. What can I do you for?"

Bobby couldn't speak for a moment.

"The interview?" he said finally. "I kinda thought I'd hear from you by now. You know. I thought we were *simpatico*."

The One and True Son

The manager sat back down behind his desk.

"Well, I thought so too. That is until I heard about your problem."

Bobby side-eyed him. "What problem is that?"

A look of pity crossed the other man's face.

"Look. I understand why you didn't tell me about it. You're trying to get a job and all. But we can't have issues like that around here."

"What the fuck are you talking about?" Bobby exploded.

"Whoa! Language!" Ben Franklin said putting up his hand to block further profanity. "I know you're upset but we sell Cadillacs here, not Fords."

Bobby took a deep breath.

"I apologize. Now, could you please explain to me *what my problem is?*"

Franklin lowered his voice.

"I know about the toot," he said.

"Huh?" responded Bobby.

Franklin put his index finger to his nostril and took an exaggerated sniff.

Bobby stepped back.

"You mean coke? I don't do that shit."

Franklin leaned toward Bobby.

"C'mon. I do a line every now and again. But I don't go tradin' my demo for an eight ball."

"What the fuck…"

Franklin put his hand back up again.

"I told you about that. Do it again and I'll call security."

Bobby could barely breathe.

"But…but, I don't know what you're talking about."

Franklin grinned. "Man, every dealership from here to Dallas knows about it. You're famous. Even more than ol' Manic Maury himself."

Bobby Smith spent the next three months swimming in cheap beer and self-pity. He sat among his possessions: his recliner, his big screen TV, his CD player, his new clothes, his custom-made cowboy boots, and asked himself over and over how he would get more. His blackballed status in the auto industry squelched any possibility, as far as he could see, of using his inborn talents. His reading turned dark: Stephen King, Dean Koontz, Christopher Pike, Thomas Harris. He read of monsters, humans and human

The One and True Son

monsters. His dreams became violent. His time outside the confines of his apartment was spent traveling to and from his mailbox, gathering the piles of bills that were becoming increasingly difficult to pay. His television blared nonstop, whether he was reading, using the bathroom or answering the door to collect his delivered dinner or cases of Lone Star. He slept on his recliner to the droning of late-night hucksters, slinging everything from plastic dishes to a magic chamois.

One night, he was shaken from an agitated dream state by a voice he had yet to hear at 2 AM. The voice belonged to a middle aged, tanned, well-toned man with a streaked pompadour and a perfectly tailored suit. In his left hand, spangled with rings of gems and gold, he waved a thick and obviously warn copy of the King James Tanach. He pointed through the screen with his right hand, directly at Bobby Smith.

"There's somebody out there who's disappointed out there. He wasn't really listening before, but he is now! Praise Yahweh! He's tried to become a success. He's talented. (the moreh spoke in a strange unknown language that sounded like jibberish) Oh yes, he's talented! But he hasn't sewn his seed. That's right! He's put in the work on this plane (he ran his free hand along his marble desktop) the earth plane, but he hasn't sewn his seed. He hasn't given to Yahweh... (he looks up to the carefully placed spotlight above him, taking a long pause) ...what is Yahweh's so he can collect his harvest. Jimmy, I need a close up. I need to reach this young man. (The camera frames around the moreh's grinning face.) This is what you need to do young man. You need to go over to that check book and you need to write a check for $1000. That's right, my friend, a thousand dollars! You can write one for fifty. You can. But you want a harvest, not an ear of corn. You send it to this outreach. You do that right now! Hallelujah!"

Bobby sat up, slamming the footrest of the recliner back hard. Bobby had seen the light. Seen it clearer than he'd ever seen anything before. He didn't go to his checkbook. He didn't go to a Tanach, not yet anyway. He didn't own one, but he would by the next afternoon. Instead of going to either of those, he went to the Yellow Pages to find a lawyer. He would have to kill Bobby Smith.

Cletus Quest was born on a yellow legal pad after three cups of coffee and a toaster waffle. He wanted something simple, humble, but memorable. Something inspirational, but short. That first week he unplugged his TV, CD player, gathered most of his new clothes in plastic garbage bags and boxed his cowboy boots. He turned on his salesman charm and sold most of his possessions using ad magazines and by placing handwritten flyers in laundromats. He didn't sell his things cheaply, though the people walking away with it *felt* they were getting a deal.

The One and True Son

Using letterhead he'd finagled out of a doctor's office, he composed a letter for his landlord stating that, due to an undisclosed, but deeply serious illness, he'd need to break his lease. Of course, due to patient confidentiality, the good doctor couldn't disclose the illness, it explained in the letter, but his patient would need near constant care at a "hospice facility". The morning the newly born Cletus Quest delivered the sad news to a pretty secretary at the rental office, he'd quaffed a cocktail of Ipecac Syrup and Castor Oil, and waited for the desired effects of each to kick in. Once in his landlord's office he struggled through the painful story that his life had become. Not only was he relieved of the responsibility for the lease, his security deposit was returned with a note attached from the property manager stating that anything they could do to make his days "more comfortable," he need only ask.

Yahweh was good. Amen?

Cletus Quest put what remained of the late Bobby Smith's life in the back seat of a Ford POS that he'd picked up for $400 and left Travis City forever.

Once relocated in Austin he took up residence in a cockroach infested efficiency apartment in a neighborhood few of his hue would ever consider. He was where he needed to be. He needed the forgotten people, the desperate. He approached his neighbors with a smile they had rarely seen in Texas from someone with blue eyes. He greeted them with what appeared to be genuine glee, which, in reality, it was. A warm handshake was offered to everyone he met, whether they took it or not, followed by a sincere, "Yahweh be with you." He helped his ancient, arthritic, slightly blind neighbor, Mrs. Thigpen, carry her groceries up the three flights of stairs to her apartment, ignoring her trepidation when he approached her to do exactly that. He befriended the teenagers who shot dice in front of his building, offering them neither condemnation or nor advice. He simply offered curiosity in them as individuals, memorizing each kid's name, who was running with whom, who was hooking school, who had a mom, dad, grandma, others who hadn't had anyone. To these kids, Cletus offered a place to go, a safe place, if they needed it, and occasionally, a cigarette. In two months, he was greeted in the neighborhood by all who knew him with a smile and a hug.

Cletus spent his evenings reading. He read until his Tanach was dog-eared and ragged. He read and reread chapter, verse and word from cover to cover, making notes in the margins for future use. Once through the complete volume, convinced that he annotated thoroughly, he perused again, this time looking for passages that pertained to his favorite subject. The holy book was not his only reading material. He also studied psychology textbooks he'd purchased at secondhand bookstores. Cletus

The One and True Son

learned of the subconscious mind and the influence of the group on the individual.

Cletus studied the theater of persuasion. He bought a 10- inch portable color TV from a pawnshop and kept in on it continuously. During actual programming, a talk show, an old *Gilligan's Island,* he kept it mute. He'd jack it up when the commercials came on, blasting his neglected apartment walls with bad acting and corny pitches. He scratched notes in a binder about the lighting and music used: sad, slow music for ads to feed small children in third world countries, framed in dark, dirty backgrounds, shadows; upbeat Top 20 music for cars and food in front of scenery that popped and people who seemingly won in the game of life. There was sunshine, beaches, skiing. Bright yellows, blues and greens lit the screen. Soon Cletus Quest recognized the importance of the angle of every stage light. He knew where reflectors were used, when filters covered lenses. He saw when light had been subdued in the pursuit of persuasion. He recognized it when light filled the eyes. He owned every shadow, every burst and every frequency.

Cletus's first church had been a laundromat, then a beauty parlor, then a Chinese takeout. The landlord was more than happy to have the place occupied. A portly, bald man, about 50, with tattooed arms of black ink that had sunken into his dark skin making the images mostly illegible, he pointed out to the fledgling preacher the hand painted Chinese characters that ran along the bottom edge of the large storefront window. Unknown to the landlord or Cletus they represented love, peace and harmony. "You can scrape that shit off, if you like."

With the money that remained from selling everything in Travis City, Cletus bought an amazing sound system, better than any he'd flipped into his trunk as Bobby Smith. He spared no expense on the microphones and personally tested twelve PA systems until he found the one with the right tone. He bought a lighting system from a defunct community theater and installed it himself. He removed the Chinese calligraphy from the windows using turpentine and a scraper. He put up white vertical blinds that let in the sunlight in beams. He rented a carpet steamer and brought the carpeting back to life after years of neglect. The intricacies of the red and gold floor covering the previous businessman left him pleased Cletus. He painted over the ancient grease that permeated the old paint with a fresh coat of soft white. It looked like an appropriate for a place of worship.

Cletus would need no pulpit. He had no intention of standing behind anything. His last purchase was an older RCA video camera/recorder.

With his temple complete, Cletus endeavored to fill it.

The One and True Son

Cletus spent hours at a copy center a few neighborhoods away, designing and printing fliers to be passed around the neighborhood. Uplifting and powerful, the folded paper promised deliverance from suffering, protection from evil and a fresh relationship with the Creator for anyone who dared proclaim to the world that Yahweh had repaired them. He recruited the boys who shot dice in front of his apartment to slip a flier into every mail slot and under every door they could find. They trusted Cletus and would tell anyone who asked about him that he was legit. The $20 bill he put in each kid's pocket didn't hurt.

Cletus was neither nervous nor unprepared when he emerged from what used to be the Chinese restaurant's kitchen to find every chair taken and people standing along the window waiting to see a miracle. There, his boys stood, his heralds of the block. Gone were the expensive tennis shoes and sagging, unbelted jeans and NBA jerseys, replaced by well-fitting suits of gray and tan, ties closed in half Windsors, and shoes polished to mirrors. Cletus himself wore a tailored suit, the only one he'd kept from his car salesman days. Made from faultless white linen, he'd never worn it at the dealership as he'd been saving it for his debut as a Diamond Seller salesman, which in many ways, this was that day. He wore a matching linen shirt with tuxedo buttons and a soft silk ascot.

Cletus stood by the door as the lighting dimmed. A single spotlight lit a circle at the front of the room. He nodded to the camera, mounted on a tripod and manned by one of his youths, and waited for the music he'd cued in the kitchen. He'd chosen an ethereal Yahwehian chant, charged with a synthesizer and tenor voices. As the music built to a joyful crescendo Cletus slowly strolled down the side aisle, his hands risen in the air, one carrying his Tanach, his smile beatific, peaceful. He crossed to the center of the circle of light, stopped and rocked back and forth on the ebb and flow of the ancient chant. As it faded, Cletus Quest, moreh, lowered his arms. He brought the Tanach up to his lips and kissed it. He spread his arms to his congregation and smiled at all. He nodded to Jerrod, a hulking young man of 16, one of the most feared dice shooters in the neighborhood, who'd moved from his place at the window to the front of the room. Jerrod handed the new moreh a wireless microphone and stepped back, out of the light.

"Brothers and sisters!" Cletus bellowed. "Let us rejoice! Yahweh is here!" He scanned the room, his eyes locking with those of the faithful. "Yes," he said, softer this time. "Yes, Yahweh is in the room."

* * *

The One and True Son

Jessie stood at the gates after he'd announced himself to the security speaker. The gates themselves, wrought iron hammered into the shapes of opposing harps, gave only a glimpse of the opulence that stood beyond them, the easy rolling grass hills, the twisted Corkscrew Willows, the shady American Red Maples and the hardy Canadian Hemlocks. A cobblestone drive rose gently over a hill and disappeared on the other side. Some moments passed before the large lock on the gates clicked and the gates opened with no further noise. Jessie stepped through and the gates closed behind him. He was no more than 10 feet up the drive when he heard the electric whir of a golf cart, its tires thumping on the cobblestones. It soon topped the hill and was headed in his direction. A large black man in an immaculately tailored suit was behind the wheel. He stopped near Jessie.

"Welcome to Rachel Hall," the man said. "I will take you to the moreh."

Jessie stepped into the cart, and they pulled away. On the other side of the hill the true scope of the complex came into view. Straight ahead stood a plantation style mansion of brown brick and layers of angled roofing. The cobblestone drive terminated at a round-about in front of an elaborate pillared entry way. In the distance, to the south, he saw a large private lake complete with a boat house and what appeared to be a substantially powered motorboat. To the north, Jessie saw an airstrip and hangar capable of storing several aircraft. A large private jet sat on dark tarmac, the rising heat disturbing the light above it. A lonely windsock rested in the breezeless Virginia summer air.

Just behind the mansion, Jessie could see the top halves of four large satellite antennas.

A man stood in the entrance under the pillars, away from the intense summer light. He was dressed casually, a blue polo, light brown cotton chinos, a pair of blue canvas deck shoes. A silk ascot covered his throat. His silver hair looked tossed despite the stillness in the air. He waved an easy wave as Jessie and the driver approached and stepped out onto the cobblestone drive.

"Well, it's good to finally meet you, Mr. Carpentero," Cletus Quest said extending his hand to Jessie.

Jessie accepted Quest's hand.

"Jessie," he said giving the other's hand a gentle shake.

"Of course," said Quest "Jessie. You can call me Cletus. Let's get you in, out of this heat. It's like hell on earth this time of year."

Quest placed his hand on Jessie's shoulder and steered him in through the elaborate double doors of Rachel Hall.

"You must be parched," Quest said with his familiar smile. He turned to the cart driver who'd joined them in the foyer.

"Jerrod, can you please fetch me and Mr. Carpetero," he asked and pointed to Jessie, "uh, Jessie," he laughed, "a couple of jasmine lemonades? Put 'em in the office. We'll be there in few minutes. I want to give Jessie here the 50-cent tour."

The tall black man nodded and left the foyer.

Quest stood back and looked Jessie over.

"So, this is what you look like. I never woulda picked you out of crowd in a million years. You know you're all over the internet, right?"

Jessie nodded. "That's what I've heard."

Quest looked surprised. "I looked on YouTube, OurTube and every other Tube and you're all people talk about. They say amazing stuff. Amazing stuff!"

Jessie shrugged.

"Well, let me tell you," Quest said when he gave up on Jessie saying more. "It's brilliant. I don't know why nobody ever thought of it before. C'mon, let me show you around."

Cletus Quest led Jessie through the enormous home and headquarters owned and operated by the Cletus Quest Outreach Network. He showed him the large indoor pool, the spacious meeting rooms, and parlors, each with colonial fireplaces complete with their own unique hand carved mantles and woodwork depicting scenes from the Tanach. He walked him through the cavernous industrial kitchen.

"This isn't where my food comes from," he told Jessie. "We got a private kitchen for our food. This is just for fundraisers and such." He slapped Jessie on the shoulder. "You never know when you might have two hundred of your closest friends drop in. You know?"

Cletus showed Jessie the indoor go-cart track, complete with miniature Formula One replicas for carts, all electric. The track ducked behind and around models of sacred sites in the Ancient World: The Temple of Solomon, Rachel's Tomb, Mount Olivet. Mount Sinai.

"This was the wife's idea," Cletus confided. "If we have a busload of kids, it's the perfect spot to get some footage of the little ankle biters having fun around important sites to Yahweh. Every time we shoot in here, requests for sick kids to come here go through the roof." Cletus winked at Jessie. "So do the donations."

They strolled into the control room of Cletus's TV studio where a team of producers, all men, with headphones draped around their necks, some sipping from travel mugs, others holding onto bottles of artesian spring water, sat in full business attire. Blank flat screens hovered on the on the black wall facing them. Each man had a control console in front of him with slides, knobs and illuminated screens to determine sound, light and contrast levels.

"Jessie, this is my team," Cletus announced. He turned to Jessie. "These are the best people in broadcasting. We reach 233 countries in every time zone where there's land and a TV. These guys make the shows run as smooth as a newborn's butt. I'll tell you more about that later. Boys, this here is Jessie Carpentero."

Someone gasped in the room, although it wasn't clear who it was.

"You've heard of him, I expect." Cletus said, looking at his crew a little sideways.

No one spoke. No one looked up.

"What the hell's wrong with you guys?"Cletus asked. "You *have* heard of him. I know you guys are on that internet box all the time when you're not running a show." Finally, the man closest to Jessie, a short man with dark hair and eyes, set his mug down on his control console and stood.

"Of course, Mr Carpentero…"

"Jessie." Jessie corrected.

"Of course, moreh. We have heard of you." The man shifted on the balls of his feet.He looked up at Jessie as if he were looking at a raging fire, too bright, too hot to look at for long. "I'm sorry." He looked at the rest of the crew who sat with the same look on their faces. "We're all sorry."

"You damned well better be," Cletus admonished. He looked at Jessie. "I don't know what it is with these technician types. They're kinda fickle. Let's head to the office."

As Cletus and Jessie turned to leave, the darkhaired man called.

"Jessie," he said. "I'm re*ally* sorry."

Jessie nodded.

Two tall glasses of sweet jasmine lemonade sat sweating on a small antique pie crust table by a large picture window overlooking the grounds. From there could be seen a crew out working on the large jet in front of a hangar. The windsock that lay limp earlier grew restless, switching direction in the building, changing breeze. Jessie sat in the chair that Quest had pulled out for him. He scanned the large office. There were photographs, framed and mounted, everywhere. They were taken all over the world; some had palm trees and blue skies, others were somewhere in the desert. Still more had majestic mountain backgrounds while others were framed by red barns and farm equipment with wheat fields, corn

The One and True Son

fields, even sugarcane fields off in the blurry distance. Most of the pictures had three things in common: there were all taken on sunny days, they all had at least two or more people posing together, and they all had Cletus Quest in the center, smiling over a decorative ascot.

Behind a large Edwardian Indo-Colonial desk, complete with a green leather writing surface and ball and claw feet hung the important photos, the treasured ones. In three of them the recognizable easy chairs and draperies of the Oval Office were well represented as was the Moreh Cletus Quest, himself. The chairs stayed the same, but the presidents changed, from decades ago to the current one. Everyone smiled. Photos of Quest with powerful senators, business leaders and clergy, all in their own stately offices, rounded out the group.

"You have a beautiful office," Jessie said quietly.

Quest sat in the chair opposite him and took a sip from his lemonade.

"Well, thank you. Yahweh knows we killed a bunch of trees to do this wood panel stuff. I like it though. I love the smell of the wood." As if to demonstrate Quest breathed in through his nostrils, let it out and grinned that grin known the world over.

"What's your's like?"

Jessie smiled. "I don't have one."

Quest slapped his knee. "Man, I shoulda seen that comin'. But I got a say, I like your schtick."

Jessie ran his fingertips through the condensation drops on the side of his glass.

"What exactly is my *schtick*?" he asked.

Quest pushed his chair back from the table in mock surprise.

"Come on, man. Look at you. The beat-up work boots, that denim shirt right off of a Jim Croce album. The blue jeans. Hell, ya need a haircut."

Cletus grabbed Jessies forearm gently.

"Just kiddin'. You don't. It all works. You think I wear this stupid ascot because I like dressing like a damned fairy? Nah! It makes me noticeable. I learned a long time ago that *presentation is everything!*"

Jessie sat silently, looking into the eyes of Cletus Quest. The latter fidgeted.

"Don't you wonder why I invited you here? I tell you, I had to spread a lot of cheese around to find you. I even had to ask for the aid of law enforcement, something, I tell you friend, I don't relish. They're good Yahweh people, but they make me nervous. Ain't you curious why I would go to all this trouble?"

Jessie sat back in his chair. "Truthfully, I am. What's this all about?"

The One and True Son

Quest turned on the grin that had filled his coffers for nearly thirty years. "I want to bring you on board! Jessie Carpentero, this is the gravy train, and you got a ticket! Now, I know you got a good thing going with the internet and all and that's good. As a matter of fact, we need that around here. Something new. Fresh-like. But we've got organization here, son. We've got this shit down to a science and with your ideas, and your, ah, *persona,* we can clean up, the likes of which, have never been seen. I mean, nobody knows what you look like and they're calling you the *Son of Man*, whatever that means. This is *big!*"

Jessie grabbed Quest's gaze and held on to it. "That's not even accurate," Jessie said, softly.

Quest's blue eyes squinted. "Huh?"

"Son of Man, it's not accurate."

Quest leaned back in his chair. His shoulders nearly touched the picture window. "What are you talkin' about?"

"A man had nothing to do with it," Jessie answered quietly. "I was born of a woman. A good woman. A woman of pure heart and body. If anything, it should be the Son of Woman."

Cletus Quest looked at Jessie's glass. He pushed a button under the table. A voice came from a speaker hidden in the ceiling.

"Yes, moreh?" the voice inquired.

Quest turned his head toward the voice.

"Jerrod, get in here!" Quest demanded. Jerrod came into the office from a door hidden in the wood paneling.

"Jerrod, what the hell did you put in this man's drink?" asked Quest.

Jerrod shrugged. "Nothing, he answered, his countenance taking on a less confident look. "It's just lemonade. And jasmine. Why?"

Quest turned his gaze back to Jessie who had never taken his eyes from him.

" 'Cause if you didn't slip some moonshine into this guy's drink, there's little explanation for the crazy shit coming out of his mouth. I think we have a nutter here."

Jessie's gaze held Quest to his chair.

"I've got a few more questions," Jessie said, "and then I'll be on my way."

Quest nodded after a moment. He found he could do little else.

Jessie moved his eyes to the jet being prepared on the airstrip. "How much did that thing cost?"

The One and True Son

Quest swiveled in his chair to look behind him. "That's a Dassault Falcon 7X. It was 54 million."

When Quest looked back, Jessie was leaning over the table. His eyes locked on to Quest's and as much as he wanted to look away, the charlatan couldn't.

Jessie voice was nearly a whisper, but it cut through Cletus Quest like a hot knife through butter.

"How many hungry people could that 54-million dollars feed? Do you know?"

Quest sat, mute.

"How many articles of clothing could that go-cart track buy to clothe the naked children of this world?"

Jessie waved his hand to the walls around them. "How much fresh air could these trees on *your wall* provide to the thirsty?"

Jessie turned his eyes away from the man in front of him.

Quest could speak once again. He turned to Jerrod who stood where he'd been standing like a petrified tree. Quest cleared his throat.

"Jerrod! Do your fucking job and get this nutcase out of my house!"

The large man didn't move.

Jessie stood. "Never mind, Jerrod," he said. "I'll find my own way out."

Jessie strolled toward the door through which he'd entered. Once there, he turned back to Cletus Quest.

"You say on your program that you speak to the Father, that he speaks to you and through you." Jessie smiled. "Well, I speak to the Father too. And he says that, Bobby Smith, until you can carry all this, the jet, the mansion, the go-cart track, on your back, you will not fit through the gates of heaven. He will never let you pass."

Cletus Quest blanched.

Jessie left the room.

THREE

The Moreh

This day was different. For Alisa, from the moment she'd awakened from a quickly dissolving dream, the day seemed, what? Important? Maybe important. She wasn't sure. It was summer semester, a break for her. She hadn't been in classes since mid-May. It was August now. Surely, she'd been used to sleeping late and doing pretty much whatever she wanted, much to the disappointment of her Aunt Delores who felt that Target could always use another cashier. But she'd be a senior next semester and after that, probably going for her Masters Degree in Social Work. The way Alisa saw it, she might not be able to laze around for a long time after this summer.

Admittedly, her aunt had a point about her summer routine, which really wasn't a routine at all. When she'd rolled out of bed was anybody's guess, most mornings. Often, she'd stroll to the kitchen in her aunt's apartment, still wrapped snuggly in her light pajamas and flannel robe, her puffy Baltimore Ravens slippers hugging her feet. The slippers looked like football helmets. She loved them. They used to have a plastic box that fit into a pocket on the top of one of the slippers, which, when turned on, would burst with the sounds of a stadium crowd cheering their team after a touchdown. The box was long gone, but she loved the warm cushy feeling on her feet.

Alisa would dig whatever leftovers she could find in the refrigerator and eat them in whatever container, texting people who'd tried to reach her during her morning slumber.

Once sated, Alisa made her way to the bathroom where she would bask in the warm fingers of her aunt's massage shower head, something she truly loved. She could stay in the shower all day; she'd close her eyes to feel the warmth spread through her short, blonde dreads, down over her closed eyes, down over her chocolate-colored neck and belly, down over her legs and painted toes. At times, she felt so relaxed by the time she

The One and True Son

turned the water off, that she'd dry herself slowly, wrap herself in a warm towel and pop back under the covers and sleep some more.

There was a time, not so long ago, that these simple pleasures, these everyday sensations, were lost on Alisa, swimming hopelessly in whatever alcohol she could drown them in. Aunt Delores pulled her to the dock. She pulled her in, straightened her out, kept her safe. Alisa's father died when she was four. He'd been sick with the same thing her mother had. They'd given it to each other. She didn't remember much about him. She remembered the scratchiness of his beard when he laid with her on the bed, her face tucked into his cheek. She remembered his breathing, warm, forced sometimes. She remembered the cool of the bed when he was gone.

This day, she jumped from her bed, the one she'd slept in since she was thirteen, and went straight to the bathroom. Alisa had no idea what time it was, but she knew it had to be early. The sun lit up the opaque bathroom window glass as if it had come down personally to lighten the room, right behind the glass. She looked at herself in the mirror over the sink and looked at her smiling eyes. That's what her mommy had called them, her crescent shaped brown eyes that seemed to smile even when the rest of her had no interest in joining them. "You got smiling eyes, baby," Mommy used to say. "Yahweh gave you those. Don't let no one take them away from you." Alisa eyes were smiling back her this day.

Alisa quickly showered, brushed her teeth and put on some summer clothes, some cool shorts and her favorite t-shirt, the Pink Floyd one with the pyramid prism and a beam of light breaking in the triangle, refracting all the colors of the rainbow. She took a pair of cute sandals from the shoe rack that hung on the back of her door, but quickly traded them for a comfortable pair of tennis. She would be walking today. She pulled a pair of half socks from her dresser, put her footwear on and headed for the kitchen.

Aunt Delores brought home some spaghetti from an Italian restaurant in Patterson Park a couple of nights before. Alisa pulled the remnants of the meal, encased in aluminum container, from the fridge, grabbed a fork from the drawer and sat at the kitchen table. She flipped open her laptop which had been sitting on the table, unused, for a couple of days. *Ah summer,* she thought, marveling that she hadn't even *wanted* to open her laptop lately. "Well, I guess I don't miss school that much, huh?" she said to herself.

August in Baltimore is usually brutally hot. This day's temperature was almost surely going to be in the 90s judging from the last few days, but she wanted to see if the sun was going to hold out. She went to a local news channel's website to check the weather. Alisa loved to look at the

FutureCast interactive radar they had and do her own weather forecast in her head:

Well, today Baltimore, we've got another hot one in front of us. It's clear skies for your morning commute which may cause a little windshield glare, so be careful out there. Looking into the afternoon we have high clouds coming in from the south. Just the white, puffy kind. Nothing to worry about really. Just more heat and sunshine. Back to you Jane...

Alisa went to close out the site and check her Instagram when her the screen did something odd. The radar map moved to Washington DC. DC being just south of Baltimore it wouldn't have been difficult for her to bump the map image, moving it to the capital city. She may have done that. She wasn't sure exactly how, but computers do strange things from just the slightest touch. She shrugged and clicked on the address window of the browser and typed in Instagram's address. Nothing happened. She tried again. Nothing. The computer appeared to be frozen. For no reason, she clicked on the map and the small dot that ran concurrent with the time of day moved from left to right on the bottom of screen. A few small light green blobs, clouds on the radar, flashed in and out of existence inside the capital beltway.

For those of you in the DC viewing area, you'll be seeing a few scattered clouds. Again, nothing to worry about. It should be a beautiful, sunny day. Beautiful if you like the heat...

She chuckled.

That's where you're going.

The thought came from nowhere. She hadn't thought about going to DC for years. From kindergarten to her senior year of high school she'd been packed into a cheese bus like every other kid from Maryland and driven down 95 to the Air and Space Museum, Ford's Theater, The Smithsonian and a million other places that kind of melded into one after a while.

Alisa was six years old. Alisa hated the cheese bus. Most of the kids took it as a kind of step up from the MTA buses they had to catch as Baltimore City used its mass transit to get its children to its schools. Baltimore County didn't. Just the city. Most of her classmates conversed in a high-pitched shout to be heard above the loud bus engine, the traffic and the other kids shouting so they could be heard. It was Martin Luther King's birthday and they were going to the Kennedy Center for a celebration that included kids from all over Maryland and the idea of getting a day off of classes, even in first grade, and to go to DC, made the kids giddy.

The drab green plastic on the padded seats irritated the back of Alisa legs and wrinkled the pretty dress mommy had bought for her to wear, just for this occasion. The kids in the seat in front of her, a rambunctious boy

The One and True Son

named Robert and quieter, but no less mischievous boy, Tijuan, entertained everyone around them with their prodigious flatulence. Robert bragged that he'd eaten some runny eggs for breakfast and consequently farted sulfurous clouds so offensive that the bus driver turned around at one point asking if she had to stop the bus so someone could go to the restroom. Alisa, feeling motion sick before the malodorous onslaught, stood on her seat and opened the window between them, but as soon as she sat back down, Robert, being closest to the window, stood on his own seat and closed it, all the time grinning at her with a mouth that was two teeth short.

Alisa remembered little about the event to honor the slain civil rights leader. She remembered how excited Mommy was to fix the puffy shoulders on her new dress, how patiently and carefully she weaved white plastic beads into her long hair. "How pretty you are 'Lisa," her mom whispered in her ear. "My baby girl. You so pretty. Dr. King'd be proud to have you there."

Alisa was going to DC. She was sure as soon as the thought entered her mind. She closed her laptop and grabbed her backpack that had been hanging on the back of the chair. She checked for her wallet and her student ID. She'd heard the ID could get her into a few places for free. She went to the refrigerator and pulled out two bottles of water and threw them in the bag along with her sunglasses. Her phone went into the bag last. She scribbled a note to her aunt and left the apartment and locked the door behind her.

Two MTA buses and one 55-minute train ride and Alisa found herself under the cavernous, vaulted ceilings of Washington's Union Station. A tourist attraction unto itself, Union Station was part railroad station, part Metro hub and part shopping mall. Built in 1909 when the railroad was still king of the transportation hill, the station fell on hard times that lasted until the 1980s when Congress passed the Union Station Restoration Act with the intention of keeping the architecturally significant aspects of the station intact while updating its purpose from one of moving people in and out of The District to a place to chat, shop and drink designer coffee. Alisa passed under the scaffolding erected the previous year when a 5.8 Magnitude earthquake shook the Mid-Atlantic region causing cracks in the high gold plated ceilings. This day, the quake's aftermath hadn't kept Alisa from ordering a grande Salted Caramel Frappuccino with an extra shot of espresso and double caramel on the whipped cream.

The One and True Son

She stepped out into the intense August sunlight and put on her sunglasses. She had no idea where she was going. The sense of freedom invigorated her.

No plan, no pressure, she thought.

Alisa loved to walk. Her grandmother instilled in her, when she was very young, that walking was the best way to clear the head, the best way to find Yahweh. Grandma Lily was a Witness. She'd been for decades before Alisa was born and would be until the day she died. She took Alisa on her walks to the store, to the pharmacy, and on her weekly walks door to door to spread Yahweh's love as far as their feet could carry them. Grandma would dress Alisa in tasteful but cheerful dresses and flatiron her coarse hair and rub it through with castor oil. Both of their shoes were plain and shined to mirrors. They'd step out into different neighborhoods clad in their finest overcoats armed with Grandma Lily's Tanach to keep them safe.

Alisa rarely spoke on the rare occasions when someone opened their door after they'd knocked *and* spoke more words than *no thank you* before slamming it in their faces. In truth, Alisa didn't subscribe to her grandmother's beliefs. Back then she believed in Yahweh as most kids do who are raised to believe Him. She wasn't sure about the other stuff that went along with Grandma's particular sect. Alisa's mother wasn't having any of it. Apparently, neither were the people who never opened their doors even though they could be seen sitting in their living rooms when they knocked.

But Alisa loved the walks just the same. She loved being out in the open air, especially on cold clear days, wrapped in her best woolen coat, the navy one with the large lapels, her beautiful grandmother walking next to her as quickly as someone half her age in her thick soled mirror black shoes. She felt closest to her on these walks. She felt so safe.

Alisa was seven. She and her mother lived on Glover Street. She was going to her grandparents' house on Greenmount. She remembered going up and down the hills of Greenmount Avenue, staring out the backseat window of Pop-pop's faded yellow Ford Fairlane, looking at the row houses. She wondered how whoever built them had managed to put up straight houses on such crooked land. The sidewalks were crooked. The curbs were crooked. But the brick walls were straight. The roofs were straight. The white front porches with the peeling white paint. They were all straight. She wanted to ask the people who lived there, black people just like them, walking down the street or sitting on their porch smoking a cigarette, how they got their houses so straight. Pop-pop had pushed the block button on the electric window because he got tired of her lowering the window to speak to strangers. She just didn't know how a house could be built like that.

Alisa was with Grandma Lily and Pop-pop then. Sometimes, her mother wasn't home when she woke in the morning, even though she'd been there to tuck her into bed the night before. This had been maybe the third time that this had happened in the last month. It happened the same way each time. She'd wake up. She'd look for her mother. She'd eat a bowl of Cap'n Crunch. And Pop-pop would let himself in the front door with that rusty old car parked out front.

"Where's Mommy?" she asked one day in the car. It was a simple question. It was like, "Where are the car keys?" or "Where's my other sock?" You know, just a question. Apparently, Pop-pop didn't see it that way.

"You mind your business," he barked at her, his eyes not leaving the road. And then he sighed. A real deep, tired sigh. He pulled the big car to the curb and eased the shift into Park. He didn't turn around at first, but rubbed his thick index finger behind his glasses, rubbing out something that bothered him. He turned the rearview mirror so he could see her. Alisa remembered only seeing his eyes from her low angle, those tired, brown, milky eyes. Those eyes had seen a lot. They'd seen death and carnage in Italy when he was a young man. They'd seen neighborhoods go from quiet, peaceful places where kids play in the street and everybody knew everybody else, to locked-down shooting galleries, where kids not much older than Alisa would tell him to fuck off just for looking at them.

"Honey, I'm sorry for speaking to you like that," he said after a long moment. "A lot of people been asking 'bout your mother. A lot of people who really don't care. Just gives 'em something to talk about at the beauty parlor. I'm really sorry, baby. She's trying to get better is all. She's tryin' real hard."

Grandma Lily is gone. Pop-pop is gone. Mommy is gone and Daddy is with her. And this day it was summer, mid-August, and the sidewalk was hot enough to fry an egg. But Alisa still loves to walk. And she could almost hear Grandma Lily's footsteps next to her as she walked the pavement through Columbus Circle, crossed the street and headed down Louisiana Avenue. The traffic was typical for a Wednesday morning, the cars jostling for position heading to the heart of DC, the sidewalks sparsely used by pedestrians who no doubt chose the cool of the underground Metro to the virtual cooking surface of the sunbaked concrete. Alisa relished the temperature change on her face from the ever more intense sunlight to passing under the shade of the oak and maple trees that lined the sidewalk. She needed this, this day, this walk, For some reason, she felt more alive than she had for a long time.

At Constitution Avenue she stepped to the red brick sidewalks that could take her anywhere she wanted to go in the capital city. Alisa stopped and looked around her. To her left stood the US Capitol Building. She'd been there many times on school field trips and didn't feel a pull to go see it again. There would be no surprises there. The congress was on their summer recess so the chances of catching a glance of any one important was virtual none. No, the way to go was to the right, maybe to the National Mall. As she walked the brief entanglement of Constitution and Pennsylvania Avenue, she passed the National Gallery of Art. She was struck, perhaps for the first time, by the similarities in the older buildings in Washington. The Capitol, The White House, the Jefferson Memorial, the Lincoln Memorial, they all looked like ancient places of worship. But not today's temples. Older places, like Greek altars, the Parthenon, or the Temple of the Olympian Zeus. They had the same pillars, the same use of space. They were built of heavy, imposing granite. Unlike those old temples to faded gods, they just hadn't crumbled. Not yet.

The next building on her left, the National Museum of Natural History seemed to be a mashup of other important buildings: the dome of the Capitol, the portico of the White House and the stony bulk of almost every memorial in the city. Inside were treasures of unimaginable wealth: the Hope Diamond, a stunning blue rock blamed by some for the beheadings of Louis XVI and Marie Antoinette; the Star of Asia, a golfball sized blue-violet star sapphire with one of the clearest stars ever seen. The gem, more impressive than the diamond to Alisa, was like a beautiful night sky with a bright perfect star shining in the East. Alisa remembered staring at it on a sixth grade trip, mesmerized, until her teacher, after calling her name several times, threatened to send her back to the bus.

Alisa was eight. Grandma had gathered some toilet paper rolls, a handful of popsicle sticks, some white glue, and placed them on the miniature table Pop-pop had made for her when she was a toddler. Next to that was pile of mismatched socks and orphaned buttons. Alisa's knees soon wouldn't fit under the table, sitting on one of the scaled down chairs Pop-pop created to go with the table, but this was and would be her favorite place to sit in the world for quite some time. Alisa had been pestering Grandma for some dolls. Other girls her age snuck their dolls to school in their backpacks along tiny hairbrushes and changes of clothing and they would preen them like mother ducks, at recess, giving them names and histories and they would coo and cuddle them. Alisa told Grandma all this, how she'd yearned for her own doll and a doll house and a small bed to tuck the doll into at night.

Grandma Lily listened to her closely. Alisa knew when Grandma Lily was really listening because two deep dark ridges popped up between her eyebrows whenever she was listening and trying to think of a response. She got that way when she was studying the Tanach with her Witness group and she got that way when Mommy was whispering something to her.

"'Lisa," Grandma Lily said, "we ain't got money for that kind a thing." Grandma Lily stroked Alisa's hair and face as she said it. "We ain't never had money for that long as I remember. When I was a little one, we always had one thing less than nothin' —and it hurt. I know it hurts, baby. But we learned to make our own toys. We would sew up socks and stuff 'em full of cotton balls and put buttons on 'em and yarn and sure 'nough, we had our dolls. And we'd put paper on an old milk box and we had our doll house. Alisa looked at the pile of sticks and cardboard tubes, the last of the paper stuck in a fibrous line to the adhesive that held it the roll. She looked up and her grandmother. "There's a doll in there?"

Grandma Lily nodded. "If you want there to be, baby. You just have to want there to be. You can tell your fingers to do the rest. And I got some boxes from the grocery store we can make a dollhouse and a bed. You'll see."

Alisa wanted a doll. Grandma Lily did the best she could.

Alisa kept walking. There was something she had to see here, but she hadn't reached it. At the White House, she paused and gazed through the wrought iron spears that made up the fence around the grounds. She wondered how many sensors had been placed in that perfectly manicured lawn, how many cameras were looking at the fountain that rose up in the August heat, how many lenses were trained at the finely trimmed hedges, at the crabapple trees, at the magnolias, at her. She went up to the bars and put her face through the opening so she could see the grounds without the iron obstructions. She placed her hands on the bars like a convict looking out on a beautiful garden.

Alisa was nine. She lived with her mother in a one-bedroom apartment off Northern Parkway. Grandma Lily had had a brain aneurism about six months before. She'd been in what the doctors called a vegetative state and was hooked up to machines that fed her and, according to those same doctors, kept her comfortable. Pop-pop was at her bedside every day. Alisa didn't see either one of them again until they were dressed in their meeting clothes, laid out for viewing, a month after Grandma Lily took ill. Pop-pop passed three days after his wife.

Alisa never saw the inside of the Greenmount house again, although she'd passed it from time to time on errands with her aunt.

The Northern Parkway apartment had one bed, a beat-up microwave and a refrigerator so old it still had a locking handle on it. A TV that didn't work stood in the corner gathering dust with the last attempts to make it work, two flattened pieces of aluminum foil fastened on the end of the antennas, still reaching out for a signal that wasn't coming. They'd never gotten the thing to pick up digital when the government decided it was time to change.

They ate on paper plates they'd gotten from the dollar Store. The food was usually whatever her mother's boyfriend could afford, be it McDonalds or delivered pizza. Sometimes they'd get a frozen lasagne from Aunt Delores, and they'd feast for a week.

Mommy's boyfriend, Marvin, had known her mother since high school. He'd been released from the correctional facility in Sykesville some months before he'd reunited with her mother. It was a drug charge. He was clean and he was staying clean. Marvin worked the night shift at a printing plant. He insisted with his boss, a man hired by the state to rehabilitate ex-offenders, that he always had the night shift so Alisa and her mother could have the bed to themselves. In the morning, usually about 11, Marvin would carefully take his shoes off and lightly step across the tiled living room to the dingy dark green carpet of the bedroom. He'd quietly take off his work clothes and step into bed with Alisa's mother. Once under the sheets, he'd hold her and listen to her breathe.

Usually, Alisa would've been gone to school for hours by the time Marvin got home.

Mommy always knew when it was time for school. She'd roll over on her side and nudge Alisa, first with her foot, which always seemed cold, and then with her bony hand.

"Get up, baby girl," she'd say to her in a gravelly whisper. "The world is callin'."

One day Alisa woke up late. It was April and the sun was already throwing bright rays into the room from higher in the sky then it should be. She turned to her mother. She was still in bed. Her eyes were closed, just like she had seen them the night before. The white sheets were pulled up to her mother's chin.

"Mommy?" Alisa said.

Alisa watched her mother for a long time. She waited for her nostrils to twitch. She waited for the sheets to rise and fall.

The One and True Son

Alisa knew she was alone.

Alisa looked away from the president's house. She expected to see people posing by the fence, adding themselves to the famous scene as if they were truly part of it. But no one was doing that. No one was stopping. She was the only one looking through the fence. She'd probably stood in the very same spot, at least 10 times on school trips, and there were always people here posing. *Odd,* she thought.

And something else was odd. The automobile traffic was moving in the usual way, cars traveling east on the left and west on the right. But the foot traffic was all going the same way. Groups of tourists, couples walking hand in hand, individuals in suits, they were all walking in the same direction: west. *No one* was going the other way.

Was something happening she didn't know about?

As she walked further, the sidewalks became more crowded. On 14th and 15th Streets, pedestrians moved like red blood cells passing through a network of veins. Alisa and what was beginning to look to be a growing multitude passed the Washington Monument, itself wrapped in scaffolding, as it too had been damaged in the earthquake the year before. Alisa looked around to her fellow walkers. No protest signs. No one screamed slogans.

What do we want? I don't know! When do we want it? Beats me!

Alisa snickered to herself. She turned her eyes to a middle-aged man walking next her. He looked like a teacher. He had thinning salt and pepper hair and a close cropped almost white beard. His thick black sunglass frames on a hipster would've been ironic and cool, but on him looked like a pair he'd worn as a teenager. He had on the obligatory cargo shorts and a t-shirt that read *Life is Crap* with a silkscreen of stick figures at a bar with one bent over a bucket throwing up. His leather sandals slapped the pavement next to her.

"Where are we going?" Alisa asked.

"I'm not sure," the man answered, smiling. "I'm not even sure why I came here. I live in Parkville. I just kind of…I don't know… felt like going to DC. It's weird. I came down Connecticut Avenue and I saw these people walking this way. I thought there was a free concert or something. What about you?"

Alisa wasn't sure how to answer. "Just seeing the sights," she said after a moment.

As they neared the Reflecting Pool the crowds began to thicken and spread with people standing and sitting among the cherry trees to drink in the shade and bask in the tranquillity of the shallow water. The teacher guy broke off, but Alisa kept going. For the first time this day she had direction. She had to see where it was taking her.

She and the throng passed behind the Vietnam War Memorial. Another victim of the earthquake as two of the black granite panels were damaged by the shaking earth. Although the throng passed to the rear of what always felt to Alisa like a giant tombstone, the crowd grew quiet as it passed the monument. The add-ons to the memorial: the Three Soldiers statue, a bronze traditional memorial, that put faces, black and white, to the names of the martyrs; the other, the Vietnam Women's Memorial reminded everyone that women shared in the blood, carnage, and loss.

Alisa was 12. Aunt Delores hosted a family picnic in Leakin Park. Alisa hadn't known she had so many relatives. People calling themselves Auntie this and Uncle that, squeezed her and commented how grown up she'd become. Other than Aunt Delores, whom she'd lived with for the past three years, Alisa couldn't recall meeting a single one of them.

Aunt Delores had made her crab cakes and her potato salad and rounded out the buffet with large foil pans of corn on the cob, string beans, collards, macaroni and cheese, and a fresh salad of mixed greens. Everyone ate heartily, especially some of the larger old folks who piled their plates high and went for seconds later. The day was coolish for late June and Alisa remembered being pleased and comfortable. She smiled when she knew she was supposed to and answered questions about school. But mostly Alisa kept to herself, lying on a bench close to the party, but far enough that the strangers' laughter and conversations about people unknown to her were muffled to background noise.

Alisa listened to the birds talk. She knew they were talking, and she listened hard to try to decipher what it was they were discussing. The sunshine that made it through the leaves of the oak tree that protected the bench, warmed her chest, but left her eyes to enjoy the cool shade. She watched as small birds, sparrows maybe, flitted in a jerky dance with each other in the thin branches above her. She thought of her mother. She would love this, Alisa thought. The cool, the birds, the quiet. Her mother hadn't had enough of this in her life. Alisa thought of how her mother would've worn a dress for this day. No jeans. No t-shirt. A light sundress. And they would have done each other's hair in cornrows and rubbed their scalps with soothing oil. As she lay on the bench, she could feel her mother's presence—and her absence.

"There you are," came an unfamiliar voice, approaching the bench. It was a male voice. She sat up on the bench and looked to where the voice coming from. Standing in the full sunlight was a tall man in what appeared

to be a military uniform, the kind that would blend in with the leaves, the trees and the dirt. There was something familiar in the face, though it wasn't the mustache trimmed to military regulations. He had a strong jaw and a muscular neck, but that wasn't drew Alisa's attention. His eyes, deep brown like rich earth, like Pop-Pop's had been in his younger days, like Aunt Delores's, like Mommy's. Alisa sat up on the bench and made room for the soldier.

"I bet you don't remember me," the man in the soldier's suit said.

Alisa shook her head.

"No, I didn't think you did," he said, smiling brightly. "I knew you wouldn't really. But I used to babysit you. I'm your cousin, Bartlett. We used to watch Blue Clues together. But that was before you could remember. I left home a long time ago."

It was then that Alisa remembered why he looked so familiar. In Aunt Delores's bedroom his pictures took up most of her dresser top: small, faded Polaroids of varying degrees of laughter and sleep, a larger elaborately framed photo of a smiling high school grad with a wispy hint of the mustache that would later take its place, a stern-faced, skinny soldier standing in front of an American flag, trying to squeeze as much toughness into the photo as he could manage.

"I've seen your picture," Alisa said quietly. "Where've you been?"

The soldier nodded his head. "That's fair. That's fair."

"I didn't mean anything by it," Alisa said. "I just mean, where have you been? Why haven't I seen you—before now, I mean?"

"Well, it's hard to explain really," the soldier said, smoothing his mustache with his fingertips. "Mom...your Aunt Delores and I haven't always understood each other. She didn't really want me to join the Army. We just don't see things the same sometimes. We talk on the phone a few times a year.... I don't know. Like I said, it's complicated."

Alisa turned to her cousin and put her calf on the bench. "So...where have you been?"

Bartlett smiled. "You're really stuck on the question, aren't you?"

Alisa nodded.

"Well, let see. I've been to Korea, Japan, Germany, and Mississippi."

"Which did you like best?" Alisa asked.

"That's a good question." Bartlett thought for a moment. "Well, it wasn't Mississippi, I'll tell you that. They've got mosquitoes bigger than German Shepherds down there."

Bartlett told her of his times in Korea as a young black soldier in Korea. How the people were friendly, for the most part, but he mostly

The One and True Son

stayed on post because he was just out of high school and didn't see any relationship between Korean and English. He'd had Kimchee once early on and his mouth hurt so much from the heat that he'd eaten pizza most of the rest of his tour.

Japan was beautiful, he told her, but the people, though exceedingly polite, weren't particularly warm to the US military. He'd been a liaison officer in Okinawa to a marine unit there.

"What's that?" Alisa wondered out loud.

Bartlett pointed to a small gold leaf at the center of his uniform, at heart level. "This is a gold oak leaf. It means I'm a major. That's an officer."

"How'd you get that?" Alisa asked.

"I didn't start out as an officer. I was good at my job. My commanding officer thought I'd make a good officer, so he put me up for OCS."

"OCS?" Alisa asked.

"Officer Candidate School. I'd gotten a degree while I sat around in Korea. The Army sent me to a special school to learn how to boss people around," Bartlett said with a smile.

"So what's a liaison?" Alisa asked.

Bartlett looked at his cousin with a gentle side-eye. "You're not thinking of joining, are you?"

"Aunt Delores would kill me if..."

"No," Bartlett interjected. "She'd kill me."

They were quiet for a moment.

Alisa spoke. "So why did the Japanese not like the soldiers?"

Bartlett thought for a minute. "I guess some people don't know how to act when they're in someone else's backyard. Americans did some pretty stupid stuff over there. Crime and stuff. That and the war, World War II, ended a long time ago. Some people are tired of someone else's military being there."

"Do you blame them?" Alisa asked seriously.

"Now you sound like your Aunt," Bartlett replied, just as seriously.

That was as far as their discussion would take them. An Uncle What's His Name wandered over and drew them back to the main party. Bartlett eased in next to his mother, who put a hand over his, but rarely looked him in the face. Alisa caught a moment when her aunt did look at him and the grief that came to the older woman eyes almost made Alisa cry. Aunt Delores didn't speak. She looked like a woman who would never touch her son again.

The One and True Son

That was the last time Alisa saw her cousin in person. After the party and a brief stay with his mother, Bartlett boarded a military transport to Crete. From there, he flew to Aviano Air Base in Italy where he caught a C5 to Afghanistan. Once there, he traveled by ground to Helmand Province. There he met with Afghani military leaders, one of which turned out to be a double agent. He pulled out a weapon hidden in a corner and executed everyone in the room.

Alisa saw her cousin's photo on the news. It was a similar photo that Aunt Delores displayed on her dresser, but the skinny boy had grown to a strong man. The wisp of mustache was replaced by a man's growth trimmed to military precision.

Alisa was there when the officer came to the door to offer the condolences of a grateful nation.

Her aunt sat quietly as the soldier explained the circumstances of her son's death. Delores's lip quivered. When the young lieutenant finished speaking, she looked at him. A tear spilled from her eye and washed down her cheek.

"I told him not to join. I told him he would die for this."

Aunt Delores didn't explain what "this" was. Alisa knew.

Like ants following a pheromone trail, the crowd turned on Henry Bacon Drive and headed toward the Lincoln Memorial. Alisa could see that people were grouping inside the circular roadway that surrounded the temple of white marble. An eclectic mix of people stood, sat, and lounged on the grass, some chatting with the others around them, some shaking their heads, some laughing, and some wearing serious expressions. Alisa weaved her way to the base of the steps and sat. *This is where I need to be. Finally.*

For half an hour the crowd grew. Little grass or sidewalk could be seen from where Alisa sat. The Washington Monument was blocked by a sea of faces and light clothing. The US Park Police arrived with several cars, lights ablaze, and emptied a small platoon into the park. The officers milled around in the crowd talking to people. Why were they here? What were they waiting for? After several minutes the cops looked confused. Not sure what to do, they took to the stairs and cleared a path up the center of the steps in the belief that there might be sightseers who'd want to pass.

Out of the arriving throng a group of twelve or thirteen approached the aisle the police had cleared. They were men, women, black, brown, asian, one graying and one dreadlocked, a couple blondes and one with natural African hair. They were led by a lean, tall man with wooly hair and the clothes of a working man, a t-shirt, blue jeans and heavy, worn work boots.

The One and True Son

The man climbed the stairs with purpose. The group followed until he reached the top stair where he turned and motioned his companions to sit. They stopped where they were and each sat on the stairs. The man looked over the crowd for a moment. He smiled. Then he too sat, comfortably, on the top stair.

The din of the crowd rose for a moment, then hushed to near silence. A small group of police officers ascended the steps.

"Are you in charge of this?" an officer addressed the tall man.

"In charge of what?" the man said smiling.

One officer, a heavyset sergeant, with deep sweat stains under his arms waved his hand toward the crowd. "Did you call all these people here? You know, you can't just have a demonstration here without a permit. There's a system for this. We work with people who follow the rules. Keep everyone safe. You can't just do this. You've got to tell these people to disperse."

"I didn't tell them to come here," the tall man said. "They came completely on their own." Jessie stood. "Did anyone receive a message on the television or see anything on the internet that told you to come here? Please, if you did, or if you got a phone call, or anything from anyone else telling you to come here, please tell the truth to these officials."

Jessie and the police officers looked over the crowd. There were no hands raised. No one spoke.

"You see?" Jessie said. "They followed their hearts here. They came to listen to something, but they had no idea what it would be."

The sergeant wiped his soaked brow with the hashmarks on his sleeve. He would have to change uniforms after this. The idea of retirement entered his mind.

"Look. You can't assemble like this. You have to get the proper permits."

Jessie sat back on the stair. "Assemble like what? These people all came to the same place at the same time. They have no protest signs. They're not shouting slogans or disturbing anyone. They came to this place..." Jessie looked to the memorial, then looked back. "...to this quiet place, quite on their own, with no intention of assembling. They were drawn here, yes, by curiosity, by intuition, but how exactly does one get a permit for that? Do we need permits now because we all came to the same place at the same time? Do you see any buses? Do you see anyone handing out fliers?"

The officer looked down at his feet. Everything the man said was true. There were no buses. There was no PA system set up, no podium. A couple thousand people just came to the Lincoln Memorial at the same

The One and True Son

time. The sergeant looked back at the man. The man's eyes were locked on him. The sergeant suddenly felt it difficult to breathe. There was peace in those eyes, perhaps a peace he hadn't seen before. Or maybe he had in a cooing or sleeping baby or an old man who'd died in his sleep. But there was something else. There was authority. It wasn't the type of authority that a badge would give. It was inborn. It shook him. He turned to his officers. With a quick shift of his head, he motioned them to retreat to the base of the stairs. There, they stood and waited. Like everyone else, they waited.

After a moment, Jessie spoke.

"Do you know who I am?" he asked.

Many people nodded. Alisa wiggled her finger in her ear. She could hear him clearly as if he were speaking right next to her, to her, and not several feet away and up a flight of stairs. And then she nodded too. This was *Jessie*. She'd seen countless videos on the internet: amazing stories, *unbelievable* stories, about things that he'd done, although he never appeared in any of them. She, like most people who saw them, she imagined, had written them off as hype. She'd seen the shows on the Yahweh channels, while channel surfing, run, obviously by conmen and conwomen. She didn't buy any of it. Alisa rarely went to temple. But still, she watched the videos. The people in them needed hope. They needed to feel that God had not forgotten them. After her mother died, she knew that feeling of abandonment. If it hadn't been for her aunt, Alisa couldn't imagine where she would be.

She'd watched the videos as soon as they were posted. The people in them seemed real. She supposed that actors make things seem real all the time, but there was something about these people that seemed to be touched by something, a glow, an aura, something that came through the screen and left a lump in her throat.

Alisa never had gone all-in though. *The Lion King* had left a lump in her throat too.

But here he was. *Jessie*. And she could hear him.

No one said his name. He *knew* they knew.

Jessie smiled.

"While we're all here, let's talk."

People on the grass, the paths and the stairs all sat where they were. The police were the only ones standing. They looked to the sergeant for what to do. He turned and spoke to the group. Apparently, he told them to move to the bushy trees at the corner of the memorial as they did so almost immediately.

The One and True Son

"We have laws given to us by the Father and presented to us by Moses. We need to add to this, a bit. Maybe explain some things. Where to start?" He looked to the cloudless sky for a moment. "Let's start happy," he said finally. "Because happy you should be."

He looked through the crowd, searching the eyes.

"Be happy for the poor in spirit. My Father's kingdom belongs to them. You need only come to Him. Be happy for those who mourn. It's true! Be happy for them. My Father's hand will comfort them."

He leaned down and placed his hand on the shoulder of one of his followers, a dark woman who gazed up at him.

"Be happy for the gentle and the peaceful among us. This earth is their inheritance. When darkness ceases," he spread his arms, "this will be theirs."

Jessie stood and gazed back at the statue of Abraham Lincoln carved from tons of white granite; the Great Emancipator, gazing solemnly from his ceremonial chair. He turned again to the crowd.

"Be happy for those who hunger for what is right and fear that they may never taste it. I assure you. You will taste your fill. Be happy for the purehearted. You will see the Father. Be happy for those that strive for peace. They're here. They are in many places in this world, and you may not see them all. These are the children of God."

Jessie sat back on the stair and scratched at the sides of his scruffy beard.

"Be happy," he said, "when you are insulted and have evil things said of you when you tell them of me. It will happen. My Father will reward you as he has done with the prophets before."

Alisa's mind whirled. *Be happy? Be happy for her mother, her weak mother, who fought alcohol and heroin, only to be punished by a disease, even after she'd conquered those two demons? Be happy for those who mourn? Be happy for Aunt Delores? Be happy for a woman who lost her only son for a country that only a short time ago considered him a fraction of a person? He was talented. He was an A student. Colleges came after him like flies on a popsicle. But they were no match for Army recruiters. "Those colleges, they said, they're great and all. But you'd just read about flying in a book. You'll wait years before you even touch an aircraft. How would you like fly Apaches?" They told him he could be a Warrant Officer. Of course, he'd have to be enlisted before he could apply for Warrant Officers Flight Training. But with his ASVAB general technical score, he'd be a shoe in for the training.*

The One and True Son

Bartlett enlisted. Aunt Delores told Alisa all of it, how she'd begged him not to join. How she'd marched when she was young, to keep poor black men from dying in rich, white men's wars. How she'd called and threatened the recruiters' office if they didn't leave him alone. He was smart. He loved the idea of flying. He could've been an airline pilot or a teacher. He could have been anything. But the Army made him into what they wanted.

Aunt Delores was a peacemaker. Should she be happy?

Alisa went to college. She didn't party, not anymore. She tried to smile to people, to treat them right. But was she happy? Hadn't she done all those things he said people should be happy for her for? Did being happy bring back her mother? Did it bring back Bartlett?

There were rumbles in the crowd. Alisa tried to understand what this man was saying. It seemed she wasn't alone.

Jessie went on.

"You're puzzled. Let me clarify." He stood at the top of the marble stairs.

"You came here today to hear what your heart was telling you that you need to hear." Jessie opened his arms to the throng. He looked them over. His eyes seemed to meet with everyone individually.

"You are the salt of the earth." He said and smiled. "You are the reason the world has its flavor. But what happens when the salt loses the saltiness, the flavor the Father has given it? I'll tell you. Salt with no flavor is worthless. It might as well be dirt.

"You are the light of this world. But when a candle is lit, do you put a bowl over it? Do you hide it behind a curtain? Do you limit the light so no one can see it? No. That leaves only darkness. Let the light of your good deeds shine to others. Place your light on a stand to shine to all the others to please your Father."

Jessie stood silently for moment. The traffic in the capital city could be heard over the crowd.

"Please, don't think for a moment that I'm here to change the law," Jessie said, finally. "I'm certainly not here to abolish it. I'm here to fulfill it. But honestly, until everything my Father plans is accomplished, until heaven and earth are no more, will one sentence, one word, one … comma, of the Law disappear. It will not be gone until everything He wills is accomplished.

"And let's look at the Law: Do not have any Gods other than Him, the Father. Honor your parents. Keep the sabbath holy. Do not worship graven images. Do not take God, the Father's, name in vain. Do not murder. Do

The One and True Son

not steal. Do not lie. Do not wish for something that your neighbor has. They're simple, right? One might even say they go without saying. But are they simple? Ask yourselves. Is it that simple to keep these laws our Father has given us?"

Simple for some, but not for others, Alisa thought. *For some, murdering and stealing is part of their job description. How many so-called leaders have lied every time they've opened their mouths? How many "good people," historical figures, have slept with their mistresses while, while parading around with their wives to demonstrate their virtue? Is it even possible to take a day off from work and feed a family of limited means?*

"Simple?" Jessie said. "No, the Law is not simple. Have you seen these guys, well, men and women, on TV? You know, the people with $200 hairstyles and designer suits, who teach morality?"

People in the crowd snickered.

Jessie smiled. "Yes, you know them. The TV morehs. They prance around like peacocks and toss the Tanach in the air, shouting hallelujah. They fly in their private jets. They will tell you that the law is easy.

"And you've seen the politicians. 'Yahweh bless America.' You've seen them prattle on about their superior morality, while poverty festers, while they order more tanks, while they fatten their donors' wallets. It's almost a joke.

But I tell you that unless you think on a higher level than them, unless you truly carry the Law in your heart, you are no better than them.

"The laws are not just words carved into some old rock. They are like all laws, with subsections and precedents. And they're from God, the Divine, the Creator. You move closer to him if you strive to do what He *can* do.

"Do not murder, your Father tells you. Seems simple…" Jessie shrugged. "Don't kill anybody. Easy for most of us, isn't it? Ah, but it's not that simple. If you carry anger in your heart, you are carrying the seeds for murder. It's true. Carrying those seeds sets you up for judgment by your Father. You must let your anger, those seeds, those sparks for evil, go. In all cases you must let them go. You cannot carry those seeds into heaven. If a person slaps you across your cheek, offer the other as well.

"If you have a dispute with someone who takes you to court, settle with them before you ever enter the courtroom. There is no dispute worth risking your relationship with your Father. Do not carry the seeds of

The One and True Son

discord. As you carry them in your pocket the gates of heaven grow narrow for you, until those pockets are so full you can't fit through the threshold."

Alisa shook. She felt the weight of her own seeds. Until that moment she'd felt justified at her anger at the world. She didn't let it show often, but she'd carried the seeds in huge sacks on her back. She tried to drink them away, but that didn't work. Aunt Delores's strength pulled her back. Aunt Delores, the peacemaker. Could Alisa be rid of these seeds? This anger?

"Love your neighbor, "Jessie said and sat on the top step. "Hate your enemy. Isn't that the way it's supposed to go? But does that make sense, if you wish to please your Father? Isn't it easy…natural, to love those familiar to you, who share your ways? Where is the effort in that? I tell you, children of God, that loving your neighbor and hating your enemy will never change anything. Isn't the goal, the goal of your Father, to make an enemy a thing of the past? To make it a pointless and meaningless word. There is only one way. It may sound crazy, but the only logical way to eliminate an enemy is to love them. You have nothing to fear from your friend. So make your enemy your friend."

Alisa looked to the crowd, listening to Jessie as she was. There were people from everywhere. There were people who came from other lands, Asians, Africans, Europeans. There were people descended from slaves, people descended from slave owners. Alisa looked for her enemy. She looked for any individual who could be recognized that meant her harm. She even looked to the police, who, she'd always felt, had treated people who looked like her differently than others. She looked at each police officer. The men, the women, she looked at their faces, their hair, their ears, their hands. Could she see an enemy? Could she love them anyway?

Jessie spoke for most of the afternoon. The driving heat of the summer ebbed to a warm comfortable breeze. And as quickly as he came, he stood and descended the stairs. His followers stood also and followed him. The crowd stood as well, but they said nothing.

When Jessie got to the last step he stopped and turned to Alisa.

"You have a question, don't you child?" He said looking her deep into her smiling eyes.

At first, Alisa didn't know what to say. But then it came to her. She looked toward the east, to the marble buildings, the houses of power that controlled so much in the world.

"Moreh," she said finally. "What do you tell a person who has made their life comfortable getting rich off the poor, preaching safety by waging war, refusing the sick if their unable to pay? What do you say to *that* person who wants to follow you?"

"Daughter, you have experienced much. You have seen the world outside the mind of the Father." Jessie wiped a tear that spilled down her cheek. "Here is my answer to the person you speak of. I'd say, if you want to follow me, you have to sell everything you own: your expensive clothes, your fine home, your fast car, your big screen TV. Empty your bank accounts. Give everything to those who have nothing. *This is* the way to the Father. Without this, you will never enter His Kingdom."

With those words, Jessie he kissed Alisa on the forehead. He turned and he and his followers headed up the circular path to Henry Bacon Drive and away from the Lincoln Memorial.

The throng remained seated. No one moved to follow or asked more questions. Even the police stood where they were. Alisa had heard him. They all heard him.

The Dover

The new batch of squeakers arrived. Pierre pulled the four yellow crates off the back of his pickup and moved them to a table he'd set up in front of the pen he used for young birds. Opening the top of the plastic crate he carefully grabbed the birds, one by one. This was a special lot, white doves, columba livia domestica, the bread and butter of his family's operation. Truthfully, the birds weren't doves at all. They were homing pigeons. Pierre got them from a special breeder who bred them for their light, snowy feathers and their ability to home. This batch wasn't for the funerals or the weddings his others were used for; those were fine birds for sure, but not special enough for the temple.

Pierre grabbed each bird with his gloved hands and held it up to his ear, listening for the tell-tale squeak of the immature bird. He didn't really need to hear the squeak to know a young bird. The hump on the beak was enough to age it, more or less. He just liked hearing the sound, kind of like the bird introducing itself. The pen, built and rebuilt over the ages by Pierre's great grandfather, then grandfather, then father, then Pierre himself, was seven feet tall, sloping six feet to the back, 12 feet in length, made with chicken wire. Five-gallon buckets were nailed on their sides to shelves running in three levels. Each bucket had its lid trimmed half open so the birds could mate in a cozy home. The floor was hay and grit covered in chicken wire to keep the snakes and foxes from fetching a nighttime snack.

These were special birds. He bought them in January, long enough before the big event so he could get them used to their feeding regimen and trained properly for holy week. His family had been using the same breeder for generations. Like the Donadieus, they've been established in the dover trade since colonial days, but unlike Pierre's family, they focused on racing pigeons as opposed to the white doves he provides for weddings, funerals and, of course, Passover. Pierre's great, great, great grandfather, Guy, purchased the six-acre parcel of Virginia that'd been his home for his entire life while most of DC was more or less unwanted swampland. Family lore had it that Guy, a dover who'd settled in Quebec, traveled with a moreh to establish a temple in Northern Virginia. There were already French merchants and traders who allied with the Native American tribes in the area. The moreh hoped to convert the natives to Yahweh and set up the largest temple in the New World. And like all temples, they'd need a dover for the holy days' celebrations.

The dover had always been part of the Passover celebration, although the practice had changed since the advent of Yahwehanism. In ancient times, animal sacrifice was part of the celebration. Rich worshippers would bring flock animals, sheep or goats, and sacrifice them, sometimes by the thousands to cover for human sin. For the poor, one goat or lamb was a luxury few could afford. So, what could they sacrifice to atone? That was where the dover came in, selling doves to those who couldn't afford to please God and cleanse them of their sins.

Actual animal sacrifice faded after a few centuries and the other animals were spared their lives, but the dover continued to be in the celebration under Yahwehanism. Like the goats and sheep, the doves of olden times weren't sacrificed anymore either. They were released to symbolize the spirit rising to Yahweh. Of course, until fairly recently, the doves had been, well, doves, which made the profession very loss intensive. Doves didn't have the homing abilities of the pigeon. So, dovers gradually switched over to white homing pigeons. Everyone was pleased with the change. The worshippers got to follow tradition, the doves had a home to go back to and the dovers didn't have to refresh their whole flock after Passover.

Pierre was pleased with his new additions. The birds would pair up early on. These pigeons mated for life, another draw to bring them home. The new pairs would set up nests in the plastic buckets. Soon, during the day, Pierre would leave the hatch door open near the top of the coop. The door was latched at the top and swung down like a shelf for the birds to launch and land easily. He'd let the birds out of the pen so they could fly around his property. They'd circle around and get used to the pines and oaks that surrounded his house, to the barn and ramshackle sheds that'd been there since forever. At night, Pierre would shut the hatch to keep out invading critters, and everyone would sleep soundly 'til morning, Pierre included.

Pierre ran the operation by himself. His pa, Jules, had helped him out after he'd turned the business over to him, but after his ma died in 2011, he didn't have much of a taste for it. The old man moved to a retirement home

The One and True Son

nearby, but he seemed more interested in what human embarrassment would be on Maury that day than whether Pierre had a healthy flock for holy week.

Not that their relationship had ever been a pleasant one. Growing up, Jules spoke only about business, those nigger-lovers in Washington, and his general disappointment in his only offspring. Young Pierre spent most of his childhood huddled in his room with his stash of comic books and CDs of Thompson Twins, Cindy Lauper, Tears for Fears and other musical acts deemed so offensive to his father that he dared to play them only on his knock off Walkman. One afternoon, when he was in high school, during spring break, Pierre came home with a new haircut. Or at least half of one. One side of his head was still covered in the longish, auburn hair he'd left the house with, while the other side was shaved down to the skin. Pierre's pa took one look at him and motioned him over with an aggressive movement of his head. Once Pierre was within the older man's reach, the father snarled his fingers in the child's hair and dragged him to a shed behind the pens. Once there, the older man grabbed a pair of shears they'd used to trim chicken wire and commenced to correct Pierre's haircut, leaving the boy's scalp cleanly shaved on one side and a collection of uneven tufts and small streams of blood on the other. When Jules was done cutting, he kicked the boy into the dirt and pigeon shit.

"You go tell your ma to shave that shit down to look like the rest of your stupid assed head," his pa hissed. "Don't you ever come home looking like a goddamn faggot again."

Pierre went inside the house. His mother cried the whole time she shaved his head, asking him why he would provoke his father like that. "You know how your pa is," she said through her own snot and tears. "You know he overreacts."

Pierre did know how his father was. That was why he got his friend Bernie to cut his hair like that. Pierre wasn't upset that he'd lost his cool haircut. He was furious with himself because he'd failed at his mission. He'd known his father would react violently and for the first time in his life, he was going to stand up to him. Pierre had at least two inches on his father in height now and he'd just started growing. He'd decided about a month before, on his 16th birthday, that he wasn't going to live the rest of his life in fear of a man who was so afraid of the world that he took swats at everything and everyone around him.

The beating didn't stop Pierre in his mission.

A few days later, Pierre took the family pickup truck into Manassas. His father didn't say anything when he asked for the keys as he'd been driving to get feed for the birds and picking up groceries since he was 14.

The One and True Son

"You better not burn up all my fucking gas," warned Jules as he tossed the keys to Pierre.

Bernie had been talking about getting his whole arm tattooed like the Stray Cats bass player. He talked nonstop in the truck about where to start.

"I'm thinkin' a dragon!" he exclaimed, spouting a spray of spit over the windshield. "Or maybe a leopard. Yeah, maybe a leopard. Then I could add animals, like chimps, and ooh, a t-rex! Yeah, a t-rex! Maybe I'll start with that!"

Whenever Bernie got excited, and frankly even when he hadn't, his uneven mop of hair, this week dyed blue, would flop around on his head, landing in his eyes and mouth. Most of the teachers and students kept as much distance from him as possible. Pierre loved him for that. Bernie had parents with views similar to Pierre's father, but they loved their son more than their opinions. When Bernie and Pierre were middle school aged, Pierre spent a lot of time at Bernie's house, mostly in the summer. Bernie would go home to hugs and kisses from his mom and a scruffing up of the hair from his dad. Sure, they'd say things like, "I sure do hope you cut this someday," but it was said with a smile and peck instead of snarl and a threat.

Pierre had never thought of getting a tattoo. That was until his pa had given him a wire shears haircut.

They'd found a shop in the Yellow Pages, called Tattoo Ink, Inc. It was just off Liberia Avenue. On the outside it looked like an ordinary storefront with a wide, curtained shop window and an ancient red neon sign humming out the word "Tattoos". A bell rang from the end of long hallway as the two boys walked in. The lobby looked like and old sailing ship, with faux timber siding lining the walls and two antique copper diving helmets sitting on each end of the front desk. Even the floors looked like they'd been salvaged from an old schooner, with thick, old looking, wooden beams laid next to each other. No one would walk barefoot in there without walking out with a splinter.

The walls were adorned with framed stencils, everything from rearing dragons spewing flames through their nostrils to brightly detailed peonies arranged in almost 3D bunches, suitable for a spring lunch table. The boys were looking at a demonic looking cat when they heard a voice behind them.

"What can I do for you boys?" a man asked.

When Pierre and Bernie turned around, they were looking at a tiny man, maybe five feet tall, with worn down holey jeans, John Lennon glasses and a muscle-T. The man's hair ran long and stringy from under a bandana and flipped back over his shoulders. The voice they heard didn't match the man they saw standing there.

Bernie flicked the hair away from his eyes. "We're looking to get tattoos."

"Cool," the man said and strolled over to them. Pierre noticed that the man was wearing cowboy boots, so he was even shorter than he appeared.

"You see anything you like? Me and Mavis, that's my partner, we can do anything you see here. I'm mean, unless you got a picture or something. We can make a stencil of that. It's real easy. We been doing this a long time. Ain't nothing we can't ink out."

Bernie shivered. "Aw man, this is so cool!" He did a little dance where he stood, a little bit Madonna, a little bit David Lee Roth. He finished it up with a Michael Jackson spin on his heels. The little man seemed unimpressed. "You boys ain't on something, are you? We don't do nobody who's drunk or high. That's just policy. We don't want people coming back here after their booger sugar runs out asking how they got this thing on their arm."

Pierre and Bernie assured the man they were sober. "Bernie just gets excited," Pierre told him.

"Okay then boys," the man said, finally. "All I need is some ID and we'll get started."

"ID?" Bernie said, brushing the hair back out of his eyes.

"Yep," the man nodded. "State law. Can't give no one a tattoo under the age of 18. Unless there's a parent giving consent." Then he added, "In person," probably due to a pile of consent letters from "parents" he'd received over the years. Bernies mouth hung open. An idea suddenly occurred to him. Pierre always knew when his friend had a new idea because of the massive hair flip that occurred whenever he had one. "I was planning on getting a big tattoo. Maybe if I chose one half as big, you know, one that costs less, maybe you could, you know, just keep the rest of the money."

The artist's face lit up. "Damn! That's a great idea!"

"Awesome!" Bernie squealed.

The little man's face turned deadly serious. "But I don't think your daddy will go for that when you bring him in for consent. I ain't about to lose my license 'cause some kid wants a tiger on his butt. Go home, boys. Come back when you're legal."

Bernie turned to the door. It was rare for Bernie to lack some kind of response though none was necessary. All anyone needed to know how

The One and True Son

Bernie felt was which way his hair flopped. As Pierre followed him out, he turned to the tattoo artist.

"Can you wait just a second?" he asked. "I'll be right back."

The artist scowled a little. "Listen kid. I'm busy here…"

"Just one second," Pierre pleaded. "I'll be right back."

The tattoo artist watched as the two boys got into the beat-up pickup parked right outside the window. The lanky kid told the blue haired kid something he didn't like because Blue Hair started shouting at. After a moment, the lanky kid came back into the shop.

"I've got ID," he said when he came back in.

The artist looked dubious. "Why didn't you say nothin'? Your friend looked awful pissed."

Pierre shrugged. "I felt bad that he wouldn't be getting one. But I want one…today. He didn't want to wait. But it's my truck."

The artist sighed, drained from the conversation. He held out his hand.

Pierre took the ID out his wallet and handed it to him. Pierre had an older friend, who had an older friend, who worked at the DMV. For a fee, substantial by Pierre's standards, he went in and had this friend of a friend create a Virginia State Driver's License. Due to a glitch he'd discovered in the software, the friend of the friend was able to photograph Pierre, print out the license, and delete the whole transaction from the state computers. The glitch wouldn't be discovered for another two years. The friend of a friend got a hefty sentence.

The tattoo artist handed back the ID to Pierre.

"Looks legit," he said. "Let's go."

Pierre and the tattoo artist headed down a long, dark hall that led to another smaller room. If there was a hair salon specifically for bikers, Pierre imagined this is how it would look. Harley Davidson posters dominated the walls. There were photos of motorcycles of all sizes, vintages, and modifications filling in the gaps between posters. On one tray lay the tools of the artist trade: paper towels, inks, mixers, soap solutions, needle groupings, a fresh dispenser of Speed Stick deodorant and a rotary tattoo pen.

"What's the deodorant for?" Pierre asked.

"That's to transfer the stencil to your skin," the tattoo artist answered. "You know what you want, right?"

"I do," Pierre answered. "I want one word. You got a pen and paper?"

The artist handed them over.

Pierre wrote the word down and handed the pad and pen back.

The One and True Son

"I want it on the fingers of my right hand. One letter on each finger."

"Just like in the movies, huh?" the artist said. "Well, your friend won't be waiting long. Twenty minutes, tops."

The ride back home was quiet. Bernie spoke when spoken to, but nothing more. When Pierre showed him what he had done, Bernie didn't bother lifting his hair.

"Nice," was all he said.

When Pierre pulled into Bernie's driveway, Bernie got out without saying anything. Pierre rolled down the window.

"Listen, I know you're pissed..."

Bernie interrupted. "Yeah, I'm pissed. When were you going to tell me you got a fake ID?"

"I didn't want you to get in trouble," Pierre said weakly.

"Since when are you my mother?" Bernie said, loudly, almost shouting. "You didn't think I'd be grounded until my 40th birthday for getting a tattoo in the first place? I *knew* I was going to get in trouble. That was the *idea!*"

"Not that kind of trouble," Pierre said. "Getting caught with a fake state ID is a felony. I couldn't imagine you being in *that* kind of trouble. It's just that...I don't think you'd be allowed to be you if you were."

Bernie pushed the hair out of his eyes. "Oh, you're so much more equipped to handle jail time than I am. You're too scared to tell your old man that you even hang out with me."

Pierre had run out of things to say. He couldn't tell him that he didn't want him to get a tattoo of a tiger or a dragon or any of the images his friend had in mind. Pierre didn't want Bernie to permanently alter himself. He feared that Bernie having ink embedded in his skin might change him, might make him feel differently about himself, make him feel differently about *him*. On a certain level, Pierre knew he was being irrational. He didn't really understand himself at all sometimes.

"I'm sorry," Pierre told his friend.

Bernie flipped his hair down over his eyes.

"Whatever," he said and walked to his front door, went in, and didn't look back.

Pierre wore gloves for the next few days. In his room, he'd gently dab vaseline onto each letter with his left pinky and put his gloves back on. He told his parents he had a rash on his hands, and he didn't want to get the birds sick.

The One and True Son

"I don't know what you been doing with those hands," Jules said, "to get that kind of thing, but you're damn right you ain't touching the birds with your hands. Try keeping 'em out of your pants for a while."

Pierre took his meals in his room which suited his pa just fine.

He took his gloves off when school resumed, after getting on the bus, but he kept his hand in his pocket while he walked through the halls. He became adept at opening his locker with his left hand. Unless he really had to use it, Pierre kept his right fist behind his left hand while sitting at his desk in class. Apparently, no one was too interested in his tattoo. No one asked about it. Not a teacher. Not a student.

On the bus back home, he'd put on his gloves.

One afternoon the second week back at school, Pierre stepped off the bus to his father's command that he join him at the pen. Jules was building a new coop for the racing pigeons he had purchased. The older man had been talking about branching off from doving, and getting into the racing bird business, thinking it would be the next big thing. After a particularly good Passover, he finally pulled the trigger.

"Get those squeakers off the truck and put them in the old pen, for now. And take those fucking gloves off. Those pants rabbits must be dead by now."

Pierre set his school pack down on the dirt driveway and headed toward the '67 F- 250 pickup they'd had forever. He grabbed the two top wire crates they'd used back then from the five that were stacked on the rusty tailgate and headed for the old pen. Pierre passed behind his father who was screwing in an aluminum plate that would hold the chicken wire in place, making it harder for predators to push through. Pierre was almost to the old coop when Jules called after him.

"What'd I tell you about those fucking gloves?"

When Pierre turned around Jules was there, right behind him. The boy set the crates down at his feet.

"You're fuckin' hiding something, ain't you?" Jules sneered. "What'd you do this time? Paint your nails?" The father's eyes burned red with hatred. "You little pansy! Take them gloves off so I can see what color you picked."

Pierre went blank for only a moment, but he returned in an instant and with clarity that shocked him. He had one thought: the mission. It's time for the mission.

For the first time he could remember, maybe since he was a toddler, Pierre smiled at the man he called Pa. But this was no kid's smile. This was no, "Did I do good, Pa?" smile. This was no, "Look Pa. I took my

166

The One and True Son

training wheels off. See me ride my bike, Pa?"smile. It was no, "Look at the big fish I caught, Pa," smile. It was a smile that Jules had seen before, but not on his son. It was a smile like he'd seen on his own Pa's face, just before the older man kicked him in the balls for forgetting to feed the birds in the morning. And Pierre was the spitting image of Jule's father. Tall, lanky, slightly haunched at the shoulders. Yep, the spitting image. Had been since the day he was born.

Pierre took off his left glove, never taking his eyes off his father. "You want to see my hands, Pa?" he asked. His voice was steady, determined, and cold. He held up the hand so Jules could get a good look. If Pierre had been able to he'd have seen something he'd never witnessed on his father's face before: wariness, doubt. But Pierre was on a mission, and missions take concentration. And Pierre had a lot of time to build this concentration. He had a cold head and the remnants of caking, clotting blood on his scalp. He had a wound where his best friend used to be, his best friend who hadn't talked to him in a couple weeks. He had a thousand moments to build this concentration. The concentration, for that moment, had brimmed and took over.

"See?" the boy held his hand up so his father could see it and wiggled his fingers. "No polish." Pierre turned his hand and looked at it himself. "But, I don't know. Maybe fuchsia would be nice."

Pierre locked eyes on the man he called Pa.

"Now let's take a look at the other one, shall we?"

Pierre grabbed the fingertips of the remaining glove with his left hand and slowly pulled the glove, easing it from his wrist, over his knuckles. He stopped and his cold smile dropped a couple of degrees.

"Here's the fun part," he sneered, pulled off the glove and held out his fingers so his father could read the ink that a needle embedded in his skin: LOVE

The word snapped Jules from his daze. "You fucking fag..."

That was all Jules got to say that afternoon. In a movement the older man never saw, Pierre closed his right hand into a fist. In another movement, Pierre had thrown a jab, straight from the shoulder, planting his tattoo precisely on the bridge of his father's nose. The younger man could feel the cartilage in his father's nose shift to the left directly under his tattoo, his fourth and fifth knuckle contacting his father's cheekbone making a sound like a soft melon splattering on a sidewalk. The older man fell back, a bundle of old clothes, knocking down half of the coop he'd been working on.

Pierre took a breath himself before checking to see if the older man was breathing.

The One and True Son

Mission completed.

*　*　*

Pierre couldn't be more pleased with the new Passover birds. They were snowy white. On blue and sunny days with puffy white clouds the birds seemed to pop in and out of existence as they circled above their release point, looking for whatever it was that showed them the way home. Some who have studied the birds believe that the pigeon creates a topographical map in its tiny brain, a brain that can recognize individual humans from remarkable distances and show preferences for those they favor and disdain for those bent on cruelty. Others believe that the birds read magnetic signposts in earth's magnetic field. The pigeon's beak is adorned with what looks like a calcified hump that grows with age, much like the nose of a man will keep growing throughout his lifetime, looking almost unrecognizable in his later years when compared to the nose of his youth. It is one of the ways, along with squeaking, that dovers can properly age a new bird. But the hump appears to be more than just an ornament on the bird's beak. It may act as a built-in compass for the bird to read unseen magnetic signals emanating from the earth's crust.

Pierre didn't know how the birds found their way home, but he loved them for it. A perfect day for Pierre was when the birds he'd released to train all returned to the coop back home. The loss of one bird, be it by faulty navigation, or the talons of a hungry redtailed hawk was enough to ruin his supper and perhaps his night's sleep.

Pierre's training regimen seemed to be born in him, something he'd known since he'd first opened his eyes. The first couple of weeks he'd leave the new birds in the coop to couple off and establish their nests in the buckets. He'd leave the hatch door at the top of the coop's door open during the day to allow the birds free rein around the property, get to know the roof tops and pines and oaks. They'd circle around and roost in trees; the air fluttered to the near constant flapping of young wings.

The bird's first road trip was a short one, just a mile or so down the stone road from Pierre's home. With his gloved hands he would pull the crated birds out, one by one, and admonish each one that he'd expect them back before lunch. With that he'd send them to circle, to read the earth, to read the land. With the good birds, and this year's birds were exceptional, most of them would be roosting on the trees and gutters by the time his truck pulled into the driveway.

Each week he took his Passover doves a little further out: two miles, five miles, ten miles. If they all, or mostly all, came back, he'd take them out another notch further. DC was 30 miles away. If he timed it right, and

The One and True Son

for the last twenty odd years he had, they'd be ready for the most important week of the year.

Pierre always took his birds through Alexandria and caught the George Washington Memorial Parkway when he headed to the National Temple. In Arlington, he took the chain bridge to Canal Road, Arizona Avenue and finally Massachusetts Avenue. He preferred to stay on the Virginia side of the Potomac as long as possible, avoiding a lot of the congestion, the effect eighteenth century planning had on twenty-first century traffic. Although, Pierre noticed, with the construction of new shopping centers and hotels in the last few years, it probably made little difference. People, it seemed, never could have enough.

Taking a right on Wisconsin Avenue and another right on Woodley, Pierre headed up the twisting drive to the temple where other venders, some of whom had a longer drive than he, were already moving their wares to the square. Pierre took his assigned parking spot and hung the Passover vender tag he'd been given from his rearview mirror.

The traditional chaos was already in full swing. People carrying tables, signs and boxes of products all moved along the narrowing sidewalk that approached the main entrance of the temple to the open square, bumping into each other, some giving each other hard looks. Pierre took his five crates of birds of birds and joined the melee in the making, being careful to keep his distance from the swinging tables, pieces of shelving, and rattling carts carrying rows of hangered t-shirts, each battling to stay on the pavement as it was frowned on, even by the venders, to trample the temple grass.

Once Pierre got to the square, he was assigned an area on the eastern edge of the pavement. It was the space he'd requested and occupied for years as it looked over a hilly area of lawn, far from the trees that lined the temple grounds, giving his birds a clear area to ascend, circle, and find their bearings. It made the whole white dove experience seem that much more spiritual.

He paid his respects to the familiar venders around him, most of whom sold t-shirts or flowers. Pierre tried to stay away from the radicals, the ones selling holy spring water and cloths that supposedly performed miracles in healing and finance. Just on the finance part, Pierre thought, if they made it so you didn't have to pay your bills, why are you here selling them? He asked Parker, a young t-shirt vender, to keep an eye on his birds while he went and got the rest of his stuff.

Once he had his table set up, the crates of birds safely behind it, he picked up the three by five chalkboard he used for a sign and opened up a box of colorful sidewalk chalk he'd bought fresh for this year. Pierre took great care with his signs, using fancy calligraphy he'd taught himself years ago. He never created the signs at home, even though it would be easier without the gloves. He wanted the sign to be clean, with bright spring colors which might smear if anything were to shift in the truck or if he bumped against it carrying it to the square. He washed the chalkboard with a drop of dish detergent and water. Next, he wiped it down with clean water and finished the preparation by wrapping a lotioned tissue wrapped around a new blackboard eraser. He learned that from one of his teachers when he was a kid. She had the cleanest chalkboards in the whole school.

Pierre made small marks on the edge of the board so he could plan the size of the letters he'd use and their positions. He left the bottom open for the prices. Some of the venders advised him to leave the prices off. They said to give them only verbally, that some folks might think the price was too high for birds they were just going to release. But Pierre didn't want to work that way. His price was actually much less than other dovers: 25 a bird, $40 for two. And he wanted to be straightforward about it. If the price was too rich for them, then it was *too rich for them*. He didn't even want to think about tricking someone into doing business with him. When he'd finished the sign read:

Virginia Sacrificial Doves

Let Your Spirit Soar!

$25, Single Dove, $40, a Pair

Pierre set the sign on a wooden stand he'd made for it and slid it front of the table.

Parker strolled over. He looked to be in his mid- twenties with black framed glasses and one of his favorite t-shirts, silk screened with "Yahwehs The Bomb" running diagonally down the front in mock-graffiti letters. Pierre tried to point out to Parker the incorrect grammar in the message, but Parker shrugged it off saying, "It's one of my best sellers. Most people don't know that grammar shit anyway." His hair was cut almost to his skull on the sides with a carpet of thick prematurely grey covering the top.

"You do the best signs, man," Parker remarked looking at it with a slight tilt of the head. "I don't need a sign, though."

The One and True Son

"Why is that?" Pierre responded, knowing the reason because they'd had the exact conversation the previous year. But he liked to keep up his end of the conversation.

"The products *are* the sign," Parker said, with slight condescension in his voice. "What are people gonna think I'm selling? Shoes? Nah, each shirt is a sign in itself, its own…work of art."

Pierre remembered that last year, even his pause was in the same place.

"They're nice shirts," Pierre said, though he'd never bought one, even when he was offered a "colleagues' price" of three for $15.

They stood looking at the sign for a moment.

"Did you hear the rumor?" Parker asked.

"Which one?" Pierre asked. "These venders here spread rumors like cheese on crackers at a house party."

"They say Jessie might show up here today," Parker said, bringing his voice to a near whisper.

"The moreh?" Pierre asked.

"Yeah," Parker answered. "The one that made all that trouble at the Lincoln Memorial."

Pierre had heard of him. You had to be completely unplugged from the internet to not know his name. That was until recently. Cable news reported that he caused a ruckus on the grounds of the Lincoln Memorial, drawing thousands of people using social media, and when the police came, sicced the crowd on them. There were supposed to be injuries, but the moreh got away before he could be detained.

"You think he's coming here to preach?" Parker asked.

"I don't know," Pierre responded. "I don't know much about him, but if he made that much trouble, it might not be good."

Parker headed back to his shirts. "I hope it's just a rumor. This is my biggest gig of the year."

The misty clouds that seemed threatening in the early morning burned away to reveal a clear bright blue sky. The crowd control stanchions were set up through the middle of the square, weaving maroon ropes in a back-and-forth maze to the door of the temple of Yahweh. This placement couldn't be more perfect for the venders as the crowds of the faithful had nothing to look at during their long wait than the wares of their trade. By 10am, Pierre could no longer see across the square as the line built, filling up the cordoned off area and continued on, untwisted, to the curb on Wisconsin Avenue. Those who wanted to wait to see if the line waned milled around the t-shirts, off-brand jeans, holy spring water, prayer towels, personalized Tanachs and freshly roasted coffee beans. Pierre had a

The One and True Son

good morning sending out three pairs of ring-necked pigeons, two pairs for families with kids and one pair for a couple who, from the looks on their faces, would soon be a family with kids. Pierre lived a solitary life at home and he drank in the activity and different faces like a man in the desert stared at a leaky canteen. The murmur of voices seemed to vibrate within him. He missed people. He told himself every Passover that he should get away from the house, go where other creatures of his species roost. The doves were fine, but they didn't keep up their end in the conversation department.

Parker strolled over.

"Hey, brother," he said, jangling the money belt he'd strapped around his waist. "The shirts are flying off the rack. I gotta let them look for a sec. Man, you know what else? I gotta get one of those things you put on your phone to take credit cards. If had one of those, I'd be sold out already." He looked at the bird crates. "You doin' good?"

Pierre nodded. "Not bad. About what I expected. I figure I'll get more folks after they leave the temple. They'll be all full of Yahweh and ready to watch his creatures take off to freedom."

"You get 'em back, right?" Parker asked. "I mean, they fly back here don't they. I think I read that somewhere."

"Not here," Pierre smiled. "They fly home."

"No shit," Parker said, "Man, that's pure profit! I should look..."

Their conversation was interrupted by a crashing sound, like a warehouse pallet full of goods being dropped from a great height. They both looked in the direction of the sound, across the square on the other side of the entrance line to the temple. It was where the venders of holy items were being sold.

"What the fuck was that?" Parker asked, his eyes like saucers.

"Sounded like a car wreck," Pierre responded, equally alarmed.

"Sounded closer than that."

Another crash.

And another.

Parker sprinted to his shirts, shouting over his shoulder.

"Fuck this! I'm outta here. It's that Jessie guy. Those people are nuts."

Parker and several others started stripping down their displays and shoving their goods haphazardly into the boxes they'd kept for the end of the day. Parker wheeled a a cart of shirts, the hangers jangling, shirts falling at his feet. He didn't stop to pick them up.

Pierre stayed where he was. He wanted to see this Jessie. He was doing nothing wrong, near as he could tell, and he guessed that he'd be hearing police sirens soon. As he stood by his birds the line to enter the temple began to disintegrate, some people running for Wisconsin Avenue, others cutting through the collapsing market, heading for the open grass area. One man tripped near Pierre's table almost spilling into his birds, badly scraping his face. Pierre helped the man to his feet. As soon as he was upright, the man continued fleeing leaving Pierre without a word.

Pierre stood where he was.

A small group of people, different age groups, different races, men and women, formed at what had been the end of the line to enter the temple.

A tall man with wooly hair, his skin bronzed by the sun and heredity, stood at the center of the group.

"This is my father's house!" he shouted. "This is a place of prayer and worship! Conmen and thieves! Leave this house and never return!"

The group then stood and watched as the shelves, signs and boxes were carried from the square. All the venders were leaving. They had no interest in fighting this group or being interviewed for the evening news. They busily wheeled their wares away.

All the venders were leaving. All but Pierre.

It took a moment, but his inaction caught the attention of the group. They walked over to him as a group, the tall man in the center. There was no haste in their step, no one ran ahead to tackle Pierre.

When they were about ten feet from Pierre, the tall man spoke.

"You're not leaving?"

Pierre shook his head.

"Near as I can tell, I haven't done anything wrong."

The tall man locked eyes with Pierre. Suddenly, Pierre found it difficult to breathe. The man looked at Pierre's sign.

"Sacrificial Doves," he said. "Tell me what sacrifice is made here."

"It's symbolic of the old ways," Pierre answered, his voice crackly and dry. "The faithful set the doves free after they've paid. They fly to Yahweh."

The tall man smiled.

"That's not exactly true, is it? They don't fly to God. They fly to you so you can use them again tomorrow. Isn't that true? And these aren't doves. They're pigeons."

Pierre nodded that it was true.

The tall man walked to Pierre and placed a hand on his shoulder. "Tell me," he said, softly. "Why do you wear those gloves?"

An icy shock ran up Pierre's spine.

The One and True Son

"The birds nip sometimes," he offered. "They have strong beaks."

The tall man took his hand from Pierre's shoulder. "Hand me one of the birds."

Even though the tall man nearly whispered, in a gentle voice, Pierre took his words for the command they were. Those deep, dark, black eyes and had not left Pierre's for a moment. Those eyes spoke love. They also spoke authority.

Pierre reached in and grabbed a ringed neck and handed it to the moreh.

Jessie spoke: "Open your cages and let the rest of the birds go."

Pierre did what he was told. Those eyes knew he would. They told him he *must.* He took the pigeons one by one out the cage, not taking his eyes off the man standing with him. When he finished emptying the five cages he looked to the sky. The birds should have been circling, finding their bearings to return to their home roost. But they were gone. There were none in the trees. They were gone.

"Those birds will not return to you," Jessie said. "They are your sacrifice today. You are a good man, but you live in untruths. They will find new homes."

Pierre, struck dumb, shook.

Jessie smiled at Pierre.

"Take off your right glove."

The block on Pierre's speech lifted. "Why?" he asked. "I still have to take my table and my cages back to my truck. My hands hurt easily"

"Oh, I believe your hands have hurt you more than you can say," Jessie answered. "But remove the gloves. You have my Father's name on your fingers."

Pierre couldn't move. *How did he know about the tattoo? What did he mean that his father's name was written on his fingers?*

Jessie took Pierre's hand gently. "Here, son. Let me do it for you."

Jessie eased the glove from Pierre's hand. It was the first time his knuckles had felt daylight since he was a teen.

"Look at your fingers," Jessie instructed.

And there was the word. The word Pierre had injected into his skin. The word that'd broken his father's nose.

LOVE

The One and True Son

"This is my father," Jessie said. "This is who he is. And you've been ashamed. You've been frightened. My father says you should no longer wear those gloves.

Jessie held the ringed neck pigeon in front of him.

"Think of this pigeon as me. He will fly back to his home roost. He will let you live in truth."

He held the bird to the sky and released it. Pierre, Jessie and his followers watched as the bird circled several for several moments and finally, flew south.

The Dissenter

Praise looked around the dilapidated living room. The walls were paneled, probably sometime in the late 70s from the style and quality of the processed wood, a job that must have taken whoever did it an hour at the most. Half the water -stained panels were missing exposing the wooden studs underneath; patches of fiberglass insulation hung moldy and, in some places burned, the only protection from temperatures outside. The floor was littered with spent, faded, cigarette butts, fast food wrappers, an old baseball and rat droppings. Filthy, cracked windows faced those of a nearly identically charming Cape Cod bungalow next door. It too had been boarded up years before. The twelve did find a few pieces of mildewed furniture: a three-cushion sofa, minus one cushion; and old easy chair that *may* have been forest green when new, its feet long ago removed, sitting flat to the floor and various other cushions from furniture long lost to time and the county dump.

After the temple incident and the way it was played on the twenty-four hour news cycle, Jessie and his followers headed north on I 95 to Baltimore. They found shelter in Sandtown, a historically black neighborhood that got its name from the sand that dropped off the back of wagons after visiting the quarry that once operated there. Long neglected by the city, state, and country, Sandtown was once a place of hope and employment. Those days were now just a footnote in a history book.

Had Praise imagined she'd be in this place when she ended her law enforcement career? She didn't know what she'd imagined.

Praise had been a member of the Los Angeles Police Department, a legacy, a daughter and granddaughter of cops. She'd joined the academy after doing almost two years at a local community college, studying Criminal Justice, with the idea of going to a larger university and perhaps on to law school.

The One and True Son

She thought of her father, Mitchel, coming home from a long shift one evening, looking tired. Praise, still in school at the time, was studying on the sofa. She remembered her father's large, wide frame settling into the cloth recliner near the couch where Praise lay reading her sociology text, a chapter on poverty and crime. Mitchel was never what Praise considered to be overly energetic. He was more controlled in his movements and reactions than that, which made him a good cop. Even tempered would be how most who knew him would describe him. Praise noticed that her father seemed to come home more drained than she'd known him to be, slower to get ready for work, and slower to kick off his shoes when he got back.

"Tough day on the streets?" Praise said not taking her eyes off the paragraph she'd read over three times.

"Same shit, different day" Mitchel responded. His usually deep voice was flat and scratchy.

Praise remembered she'd closed her book and placed it on her belly. "Then why keep doing it?" It was a question that she'd never asked, that frankly never occurred to her. Her dad had always been a cop. Her granddad had been a cop. To Praise, a 20-year-old who'd grown up around both of them, *that's just the way it always was.*

She rubbed her eyes. Three hours of reading made them sore. "I mean, you've got enough years to retire now, don't you? I don't think anyone would fault you if you hung up your badge."

Mitchel rubbed the top of his bald head, a habit that told her he was thinking. "Do you really want to know?"

Praise set her book on the coffee table and rolled over, facing her dad. "Yeah," she answered.

"Do you?"

"Daddy. I do."

Mitchel kicked in the footrest on the recliner. "Let me ask you something first. Do you know why your granddad joined the force?"

Praise shook her head.

Mitchel didn't speak at first. He nodded with his lips pursed. Finally, he spoke.

"When my dad, your granddad, was young there were two men who were in the news quite a bit. They were cops. One was Earl Broady, a former mailman. The other was a man named Rocky Washington. They were both lieutenants in the LAPD. They were also both black. See, this was in the 1940s and the department was still segregated back then. They were both in the Newton Street Division, though Washington was there first. When Broady got promoted all a sudden the department had a problem. Suddenly there were *two* black watch commanders at a division that had a lot of white officers. They had to wrestle with the question as whether a black lieutenant could give a white officer orders."

Praise sputtered.

"Fucked up. I know," Mitchel continued. "Well, like white folks tend to do, they formed a commission that decided that the best thing to do was to create an *all-black* watch for Washington and Broady to supervise. Pretty soon they came up with some trumped up "problem" with Broady who eventually quit. He went to law school, and later became a Superior Court judge. A couple of years later Washington became the first black lieutenant to supervise white officers."

Praised squinted. "So why did Granddad join? Why would he want to be treated like that?"

"I think he knew what Rocky Washington knew," Mitchel answered.

"What was that?" his daughter asked.

"He knew that if we didn't join up, if we didn't get *represented*, we were never going to have any say in how the police did their business. That was just a fact."

"Is that why you joined too," Praise asked.

Mitchel nodded. "Something like that."

It wasn't long after this talk with her father that she quit school and applied for the police academy.

At the academy, Praise was a star. Logical like her grandfather, patient like her father, she seemed perfectly suited to be a peace officer. Her graduating class was mixed, about 20 percent black, 13 percent latino, a couple asians, a comforting number of women. The department used military camaraderie, pushing them as a group, teaching them as a group. Individual mistakes were shown to them together, without recrimination, so they could all learn as one. She'd felt comfortable around her fellow recruits, for the most part, but a memory from her childhood always loitered at the back of her mind.

She'd been seven years old. To her memory it was early spring, late April, maybe early May. LA had been on edge since the televised beating of a cab driver, a parolee who had a few drinks while watching basketball with his friends. The California Highway Patrol tried to pull him over and the parolee stepped on the gas initiating a chase that reached speeds of 115 mile per hour. When he finally pulled his car into a gas station, the CHP arrested his friends and put them in the back of their squad car. Then LAPD arrived. With the two friends secured in the CHP squad car, five

The One and True Son

officers, *white* officers surrounded the driver. They tasered him, pounded him repeatedly with batons, stomped on his back, handcuffed him, hogtied his legs and threw him in a squad car.

Normally, this might have gone down as just another *resisting arrest* case. But because of the high-speed chase it had been recorded by a circling news helicopter and was the main feature on every news broadcast in the country. That was in March of 1991.

The trial went on for several weeks. The officers claimed that they believed the driver was on drugs and was showing signs of excessive strength and aggressiveness. The tape showed that every time the officers struck the driver, he wouldn't stay down. He'd bounce back up and swing at the officers until they'd bring him down again.

For seven days, the jury, lacking a single black member, acquitted the officers of all wrong-doing.

A year had gone by since the trial began, but the black people of LA had not forgotten what they saw on that video tape. South Central Los Angeles went up in flames. The National Guard was activated. Federal troops and the FBI came in and, when the embers and the acrimony cooled there were scores dead and almost $1 billion dollars in damage.

Praise's mother had been alive back then. She and her momma had eaten dinner alone every night during the unrest. Praise was forbidden to watch the television, her mother fearing that Mitchel might be reported injured or worse. Her daddy had been sleeping at the station when he wasn't holding the police lines. He'd call when he could, and her mother spoke in smothered tones when he did.

Finally, one night, her father came home. Praise remembered his large body in ways she'd never seen before. His head, usually shiny and clean still bore the marks and dirt from the riot helmet he'd worn while dodging rocks and bottles and breathing acrid smoke from the cremation of a city.

He said nothing. He rubbed his big fingers into Praise's hair, kissed her mother's face and went upstairs and took a long shower. When he came down, the marks on his head, the ones from the straps inside the helmet, were still there. They would take days to fade.

Praise's momma warmed the remainder of the dinner and placed it at the kitchen table for her husband. Praise sat and waited for him. He ate in silence, his characteristic patience still with him. When he finished, he handed his wife his plate. She stood and put it in the sink.

"Want more?" Praise's momma asked over her shoulder. "I can make something else if you want."

Mitchel shook his head. He patted the seat across from him for her to sit.

The One and True Son

"In the past couple of days," he said with a scratchy voice, "I've been called every name in the book. I've blocked all kinds of shit flying through the air. I kind of expected it when I took the job." He took a big breath, filling his whole chest. "There was something I didn't expect, though."

Praise's momma sat and laid her hand on her husbands.

"What's that, baby?" she asked, misting up a bit.

"I never thought I'd want to be on the other team," he said. "I never thought I'd want to be the one throwing the shit."

After Praise's graduation the department wasted no time in putting their star rookie to work. The department assigned Praise to the Harbor Area. On a map, the area looks like an old-fashioned flush toilet with the pipes that raise high off the commode to a water tank above. On paper, it was a hornet's nest of rival gangs, drugs and drive-bys. In reality, it was a struggling mass of people, people who have always struggled, the poor, the displaced, the marginalized.

Praise had a few partners in her seven years with the LAPD, most of them competent, most of them agreeable. Conversation, in the squad car, walking the beat was on the business at hand. Most of her partners knew she was unmarried, but very few knew her family's history in the department.

The year Praise met Jessie her partner was Ed, a short, slightly plump man of 29 who, to Praise, resembled Barney Rubble with a buzzcut. Ed had been on the job for five years. He loved being a police officer. Each day, he'd arrive to work at least 45 minutes early. A lot of cops did that to hit the gym or settle down before their shifts. Ed came to shine his badge and shoes, both to a mirrored finish. Other cops teased him, saying that there wouldn't be much tin left on his shield if he didn't knock it off. Ed, a frequent viewer of conservative news, assured Praise that their partnership was going to be no problem as he knew quite a few African Americans at temple and most of them were highly educated, and, she'd be interested to know, were very articulate. "Just like her."

Praise, her father's daughter, didn't let ignorance get to her. She let his *enlightened* comments fly away on the hot air from which they were born. She would do her job and, hopefully he'd do his.

Oddly it was off topic banter, that set her on the course to Jessie. Ed truly liked Praise. He always smiled brightly when she arrived for her shift. He'd announce, "There's the rookie!" for all to hear. The fact that Praise had two years seniority on him didn't deter this proclamation. She stopped reminding him of it after a while. Something inside Praise told her that there was no malice in this. Ed was a kid from the Valley. Everyone probably had nicknames where he came from. It was obvious to her that

The One and True Son

his limited imagination had trouble finding one that wouldn't hurt her. She appreciated that.

One afternoon they were cruising the Harbor Gateway near Torrence. It was a relatively clear day for LA, the wind coming down out of the mountains, blowing the smog out to sea. They saw the people they usually saw. Like her father, Praise was very patient, but she was also logical, like her granddad. She knew that a lot of kids who'd come over and lean on the car and chat were probably slinging when the squad car turned the corner. They were trying to survive in their world, a world that made Praise ache, that wouldn't let her sleep some nights.

"Did you hear we have a cult sprouting up right near the Arcangelo Gabriele Bike Trail?" Ed inquired. He was looking at license plates and running their numbers through the computer to see if anything of interest popped up. "They kicked down a fence and set up tents all over the place. It's between the bike trail and the 605. A few months ago, there was nothing there. Now, it's like a city. I watched a thing on it last night."

Finally, Praise thought. *He said something interesting.*

"What do you mean cult?" she asked.

"You know that cults have this weird leader who does strange shit and makes people do what they say. Probably drugs them or something." Ed stopped talking for a moment. He thought he had something on the car in front of them waiting to turn left on a red light. Ed slapped his forehead. "Shit! I put the number in wrong." After a moment he sighed. "He's okay. Clean. What a boring day."

"So what about this cult leader guy?" Praise asked as she turned the car on to Normandy Avenue. "Did they show him?"

"Only from a distance," Ed responded. "He wouldn't talk to them. There were people on there, though, that said, all he was trying to do was feed the homeless. They said he was there for the powerless and for God. But they had other people on there too. They said they'd been part of it and it was a really a hippy drug commune."

"A hippy drug commune?" Praise interrupted. "What is this, 1969?"

"That's what they said. They said that the guy running it, some African guy, did strange rituals with them and demanded loyalty from them. And they did show something weird."

"What was that?"

"It was one of those hidden camera things. You know, they put a camera with a telescope on the end of it and film them. They shot them going up the river to East Fork and dunking people in the water. It looked like he was drowning them."

The One and True Son

Praise thought about this. "Did they ask anyone about that? Did the reporters, or whatever, ask what that was about?"

Ed thought about it for a moment. "I don't think so. Why?"

"I don't know," Praise responded. "It seems to me if he was taking people up to a river to drown them, they might want to ask why. And why did they film them with a telescopic lens? I've been up to East Fork. We went there a lot when I was a kid. A lot of people go up there. If you wanted to take a camera there and film, I'm sure you can do it. Especially with the cameras nowadays."

"Why would they use the telescope then?" Ed asked, still entering passing license plates into the computer.

"Because using a long lens and filming from far away adds to the belief that something nefarious is going on."

"Nefarious?" Ed repeated.

"Wicked, criminal." Praise clarified. "It sounds like the people doing the report already had their views on what they were doing there." Praise tapped the steering wheel with her palm. "Let's go."

"Let's go where?" Ed asked, finally giving up on wants and warrants.

"To this camp you're talking about. Let's go check it out."

"Why?" Ed asked. "To tell you the truth I don't like that occult stuff."

"Cult and occult aren't the same thing. You said some of witnesses said they were there to sell drugs. We're the *police*. We look for stuff like that. We're about ten minutes from the bike trail."

Ed looked at his partner. "But we're not going there looking for drugs, are we?"

"Curiosity, Ed," Praise answered. Sometimes he wasn't as dense as he sounded.

As advertised, the camp appeared on the passenger side of the black and white, tucked behind a breached chainlink fence. Tents and tarps of all shapes, colors and configurations were strewn from the large gray rocks that sloped from the bike trail to the equally rocky upslope to the 605 Freeway. Praise pulled the car over near the opening in the fence. A sign dangled from its upper left corner, held there by the one remaining bent wire loop. Praise picked up the right corner and read:

PROPERTY OF LOS ANGELES COUNTY PUBLIC WORKS
TRESPASSING- LOITERING
FORBIDDEN BY LAW

The One and True Son

UP TO $1000 FINE OR SIX MONTHS IMPRISONMENT OR BOTH.
CALIFORNIA PENAL CODE SECTION 555 et. seq.

"Well, that's a deterrent," she said and chuckled. "The Department of Public Works better get out here and round these people up."

Ed put on his wrap-around sunglasses that *really* made him look like Barney Rubble. "They're really making a mess out of this place. We should get some other squads out here and clean these people out."

"And send them where?" Praise shot back, her voice raised a bit more than she'd intended. She could ignore most of her partner's takes on modern life, but with cruelty she had a tougher time squelching herself. "The jails are full already. You think this is a vacation for them? There are kids in there."

"It looks like that old movie of Woodstock to me." Ed mumbled under his breath.

Praise stepped through the breach in the fence.

"Where are you going?" Ed asked.

"Let's find out if this is Woodstock or something else."

It was easy to get a sense of disorder with the patched together shelters, the broken furniture being put to use, the battered and rusted bicycles. But looking past all that, Praise didn't see a single paper on the ground, no soda cans, not even a cigarette butt. The residents, seeing the familiar black uniforms and shiny shield badges, didn't shrink away as one may have expected, but all nodded in recognition of a new face; some smiled along with the nod, and continued with what they were doing. Unlike Woodstock, there was no burning rope smell, no beer cans, no liquor bottles. The people appeared washed and clear-eyed.

The two officers headed to the largest tent, or combination of tents, situated in the middle of the others. Praise figured that if the illusive *cult leader* called anywhere home, this would be the place.

A very young-looking white girl with sandy colored dreads met Praise and Ed as they entered what looked be some sort of square surrounded by a ring of tents. In the center, a tarp on poles blocked the sun over a picnic table with the legs cut short so no chairs or benches were necessary. The girl sat on the table, peeling an orange.

"Hey there," the girl said, taking her eyes off the orange. She continued peeling the fruit. "What brings you around these parts, guys?"

Ed started to speak, but Praise raised her hand, and he stayed quiet. She just knew he was going to say something unnecessarily official, and, at this moment, she wasn't having it. Praise spoke for them. "We heard you folks were out here. My partner said he saw something on TV. We thought we'd take a look."

The girl smiled brightly. The crows' feet at the corners of her eyes caused Praise to reappraise the girl's age. Praise liked the scarab tattoo on her forearm, but the nose ring, like all nose rings made her own septum itch.

"We were on TV?" the girl squealed. "Dude, I haven't seen a TV in ages. What did they say about us?"

"Like, I said," Praise answered, "my partner saw it. I'm not much of a TV watcher."

"Where is your guru?" Ed asked before Praise could shut him up. Praise shot him a look.

"Guru?" the girl asked, her blue eyes turning to the sky. "We don't have a guru here. We're not Hindus. Don't Hindus have gurus? I think they do."

Ed opened his mouth to speak, but Praise shot him a new, deadlier look.

"Look..." Praise said. "Can I ask your name?"

"Sure," the girl said. "It's Dimple."

"*Of course* it is," Ed groaned. "Got any ID?"

This time Ed got *the hand*. Traffic cops use the hand. Oprah used the hand. *No one* used the hand better than Praise. Praise spoke to the girl, but her eyes locked on her partner. "Dimple," she said flatly. "We heard there's a man who started this...community. Is he around?"

Dimple lit up. "You mean Dzon. No, he left a little while ago to get some donations. He does that this time of day. If you wait around, I'm sure he'll be back, but I can't tell you what time. Sometimes he's gone for a couple of hours. Sometimes all day. You can wait right here if you want. The tarp keeps it pretty cool. Want an orange?"

The inside of their black and white was icy the rest of that day, but they weren't using the air conditioning. Ed answered everything on the radio, but anything uttered from Praise was answered with grunts and shrugs. Praise understood his anger. She'd had to hold her tongue many times when anything *sensitive* was discussed with people who might not have had the experiences she's had as a black woman. Part of her, deep inside, wanted to ask this white man, as nice as he was to her, *how does it feel?* The other, more dominant part of her, sympathized with him. Ed was a product of his environment, his upbringing, his experiences, just as she was. She yearned for the day when people's experiences matched, and they were joyful.

The One and True Son

At the end of the shift, when Praise parked the car in the station garage, Ed finally spoke. "You cut my balls off out there."

Praise sighed. "Why is it that whenever a man gets shushed by someone, it involves his genitals?"

"You know what I mean," Ed shot back.

Praise thought for moment. "You know, I do owe you an apology, but I don't think it's for shutting you up. Those people aren't hurting anyone out there and you know it." Her voice was steady. She neither raised it nor lowered it. "Did you see anything *new* out in that field? Any stolen goods? They're living on LA's throwaways. They *are throwaways.*"

"I'm sure they bear no responsibility for where they are," Ed said, looking out the windshield.

"Some of them might," Praise agreed, "but not all of them. And why punish them for what you saw today? My guess is you just don't want to see them."

"Well, thanks for the apology," Ed snarked.

"I haven't gotten there yet. I do apologize for bringing you out there. I wasn't interested in looking for drugs. I just *wanted* to see the place. I can't really explain why. I *needed* to. If I go out there again, I'll go on my own time."

Soon Praise was a regular visitor to the camp between the breached fence and the 605 Freeway. Each time she came she loaded up with blankets, canned food, and bunches of flowers, she was greeted with hugs and cups of warm herbal tea. The silence in the squad car, with her partner, grew more pronounced, deeper as the days went on. Praise wasn't surprised when she was informed that she would be getting a new partner. She was equally unsurprised when the new partner turned out to be a black woman, older, with nearly 20 years on the force. It was assumed, Praise supposed, that she would do better with *one of her own,* which may or may not have been the case. She got along with Sharmaine just fine. Praise felt she could get along with anyone.

She spent virtually every day off at Dzon's camp. She looked forward to the days she could sit in the shade talking with Dimple, who was a lot sharper than her white girl with dreads and hippy name might imply. Dimple was a survivor, a child of abuse and neglect, who survived on the notion that people would underestimate her. Praise certainly had.

"I've been on my own since I was 14," Dimple explained one afternoon over a paper cup of jasmine iced tea. My father and mother were both alcoholics who couldn't keep jobs. My father was the passive one. It was as though he wanted to sleep his life away. I'm mean he'd sleep like 14 hours a day. When he did get up, he'd hunt around whatever apartment we lived in for bottles that might have something left in them. If he found enough, he'd drink it all down and go back to bed.

"My mother, she was the one that, like, brought the money in. God only knows what she did to get it. Whenever she came home, she'd be pissed off, you know, 'cause my dad was in bed all the time, and she'd start kicking him with her shoes on. You know? Hard. In the head. Half the time he was too wasted to know what was happening. I'd try to stop her and she'd start kicking me." Dimple took a sip of her tea. "When I got big enough to kick her back, I left."

"What did you do to survive?" Praise asked.

Dimple gave a tired smile. The crows' feet appeared at the corner of her eyes. The girl looked to be fifteen and forty-five years old simultaneously.

"I'd rather not talk about that, you know?" The smile waned. "I did, you know? I just did."

"I'm sorry..." Praise started to say, but Dimple interrupted her.

"Oooh," her blue eyes suddenly bright. "I learned to tattoo. Yep, I did. This guy I met, he owned a shop and taught me how to use the gun, how to mix the ink. I always liked drawing. He did this." Dimple extended her forearm for Praise to look at the art there. "You see how intricate the work is? The gold and the blues. I love it."

"It is cool," Praise agreed. "But why the beetle?"

"It's a scarab. The ancient Egyptians worshipped them. The scarabs would come out of their burrows right after they were born. They were worshipped as Khepera which meant, like, *he who has come forth.*"

Praise told Dimple about life as the daughter and granddaughter of cops, how her mother died a few years back of breast cancer, how her father tried to fill in the holes. She told her how badly she missed her mother and how she still cried at night sometimes.

"I wish I missed mine," Dimple said, chasing an ant with a blade of grass.

* * *

Praise felt uneasy as she loaded her Prius with groceries for the camp. Did everyone she had contact with that morning have a headache when they woke up? The cashier in the co-op, usually a jovial guy, barely lifted his head as he ran her items over the laser scanner. While bagging, the man, maybe about sixty, looked all around her, seemingly avoiding any eye contact. As she organized her reusable canvas grocery bags in her grocery cart, trying to balance the load out so she could carry the bags to her car and not have to bring the cart back, a woman wearing jeans three sizes too small bumped her hard in the calves with the cart she was pushing. Praise looked up at the woman, expecting that she might apologize. The woman said nothing.

"Excuse *me,*" Praise said.

"You gonna get out of the way?" the woman asked, her eyelids squeezed.

"I'm just putting my cart back," Praise answered. "If you'll wait a second, I'll be out of your way."

"Some of us have places to be," the woman hissed.

Praise's patience ended. "Bump me with that cart again and maybe I'll bust you for assaulting a police officer. You got time for that?"

The woman sniffed and went around Praise with nothing more to say.

Praise hated when her inner cop came out. *What was wrong with people?*

The bike trail had few riders as it was a weekday and all but the hardcore riders had work to do. As had become her practice, she drove her Prius onto the trail; it was as wide as a one lane street with gravel shoulders for riders and walkers to move over and let her pass. Normally she would pull her car over near the opening in the fence and take out whatever provisions she'd brought for the camp, but on this day that space was taken up with four black and whites and a command SUV.

Praise got out, grabbed her canvas bags and walked toward the cars. Ed was there with several officers and a lieutenant she wasn't familiar with. They were standing post by the opening in the fence. The lieutenant, a slim man with a bland, pale face was wearing a tactical uniform complete with a baseball style tactical cap over his closely cropped white hair. He appeared to be in his late fifties and Praise guessed that he probably did 200 push-ups before breakfast.

Praise set her bags down.

"What's going on Ed?" She asked, looking only at the man she knew.

"This is an official investigation, miss," the lieutenant answered for him. "You'll have to leave the area."

Praise waited for Ed to say something. After a moment, he did.

"This is Officer Praise Johnson, Lieutenant," Ed said finally. "She's my former partner."

The lieutenant looked at Praise closely. "Mitch Johnson's daughter?"

"The same," Praise answered.

The One and True Son

The lieutenant smiled; his teeth were dull and small. "Your father and I go way back. He's a good guy. What brings you out here?"

Praise didn't want to answer the question, so she asked her own. "What are you guys doing?"

"These folks are squatting on public land," the lieutenant answered still smiling. "We're looking into what's going on here. Whatever it is, they've got to clear out."

"So, you're investigating?" Praise asked.

The lieutenant looked her right in the eye. "We are."

Praise looked over the camp. She didn't see a single uniform. No one was walking around the tents. Praise could see Dzon and Dimple and a few other people she recognized talking at one end of the camp. It dawned on her what was going on.

"Are you letting anyone in there?" She asked, looking past the lieutenant to Ed.

The lieutenant answered. "No one goes in." He pointed to the sign that was now firmly fixed to the fence with strong looking fasteners at each corner. "We let them out if they want to get out. Anyone who wants to go in, goes for a ride to the station."

"So, you're starving them out," Praise said. "How long have you been doing this?"

"Four days now," the lieutenant answered. "No one has left yet, but they'll be getting pretty damned hungry soon."

Praise picked up her bags and headed for the opening in the fence.

"What do you think you're doing, Officer Johnson?" The lieutenant wasn't smiling anymore.

"Going in through this hole in the fence," she answered over her shoulder. "These people are hungry. I have food."

"Praise, don't do this." It was Ed this time. "Come on. You're a good cop. These people aren't worth it. Don't throw it all away."

Praise stepped gingerly through the ragged breach in the chain link fence.

"What will your father say when you lose your job, Officer Johnson?" the lieutenant shouted.

Praise turned around. "I don't know. You're such good pals, why don't you ask him?" She walked a little further and said, over her shoulder: "Don't be surprised if you don't like the answer."

Dimple and Dzon greeted Praise with hugs and smiles. There were close to three hundred people in the camp. Many saw Praise come in and they gathered around her.

The One and True Son

"When did this start?" Praise asked.

"A car started coming around about a week ago," Dimple said. "They'd hang out a couple of hours, then leave. While they were here the two cops would, like, hang around by the fence. They would stop people going in and out and ask them questions, you know, like, where are you getting your food? How are you getting the money for that? Does DCFS know there are children in there. Stuff like that."

Dzon seemed uninterested in the conversation. He placed an arm around Praise's shoulder. "What have you brought us, daughter?"

Praise looked at the four canvas bags of food at her feet. She heaved a heavy sigh. "Not enough. I brought some tuna, maybe ten cans. Some bread. Some small cakes for the kids. Some bottled water. It might feed ten people for a day."

Dzon smiled a broad smile. "You have done well. Please pick up the bags and follow me."

Dzon led Praise through the canvas town, weaving between multi-colored tents, old furniture and pots of water heating on small campfires. He guided her to the center of the camp, the square, and headed for the largest tent. Once there, he spoke through the zipped entrance.

"Moreh," he said. "We have a friend here I think you might like to meet."

A gentle, steady voice answered. "Please come in, Dzon."

Kneeling in the center of the tent of the empty tent was a man in blue jeans and a clean white t-shirt. The man's bare feet sat flat on the canvas floor. It took a moment for Praise's eyes to adjust from the California sun to the blue shade of the canvas. When she could see the man clearly, she saw he had bushy hair and a nest of a beard surrounding his jaw. He was almost as tall kneeling as Praise was standing up.

"Please, daughter, if you would take off your sandals," he said, "as this is our temple. I was just speaking with the Father."

His smile sucked the breath from Praise. She set her bags down.

The man eased from his kneeling position to cross his legs. He gestured for the two to sit across from him. His smile hadn't waned.

"You know Moreh, that the authorities are trying to close off the camp." Dzon looked toward Praise. "This young woman is a police officer. She came here on her own. She has been coming regularly, to give the camp things that we need. Today she crossed through the hole in the fence. I don't think her colleagues liked that."

The One and True Son

The man drew her eyes to his. She had never seen eyes so black, so deep. Even in the dim shade of the tent an energy exuded from those eyes and, at the same moment, pulled energy in.

She *felt* his words in her mind.

*You are here, daughter. You are finally here. You've known for some time that there was a plan for you. There **is** a plan. The most important plan ever. There is a place for you. You are here now. I am so pleased.*

It may have been seconds or hours, Praise wasn't sure, before audible words came to her ears.

"What did she bring to us Dzon?" this man said, still looking at Praise.

Dzon reached for the canvas bags and emptied them on the tent floor. The cans and loaves of bread looked so small, so insignificant to Praise now.

The man reached over to Praise and held his hand out for her to take it. She leaned over. His hand was a working man's hand, strong and dry.

"Daughter. I tell you that your gift is enough. You have saved the camp. I tell you that this gift will feed everyone here for as long as necessary. Do you believe me?"

Praise's eyes filled with tears. She nodded.

The police left after two weeks. Praise never wore a badge again.

* * *

Praise batted a baseball back and forth between the toes of her worn out Converse All Stars. She was restless, more so than the rest of the group. Each of the Twelve were scattered in the ruined rooms of the bungalow, some together, talking softly to avoid detection from the outside, some reading, one, quietly singing to herself. *This room meant something to someone once,* she thought. Her eyes followed the ornate bannister that led up the creaky stairs to the two upstairs rooms. The wood had been painted many times over the years, layer upon layer, until the intricately cut design on the newel post nearly flattened leaving only a ghost of the creativity put into such a small detail. She walked to the small hallway where there was a tiny bathroom straight ahead, all in dusty pink, the water long since turned off. A deeply embedded rust stain had dug its way from the impotent faucet to the drain in the footed tub. The mirror in the ancient medicine cabinet no longer reflected a realistic image, but one of fractures and bent light and the corrupt air of neglect.

Praise turned to the left and stepped into the front bedroom. Jaime and Bart lay asleep on two old mattresses, the latter with a notebook laying open on his chest, the ballpoint pen he'd been writing with still pinched in his fingers. Praise stood in the doorway and watched the men breathe. She wanted to talk to someone. She hadn't felt this alone, at least not for a long time. But she didn't have the heart to wake them.

She turned and walked toward the other room at the opposite end of the hall, passing the bathroom on the right. The setting afternoon sun that made it through the spaces in the boarded windows burned orange. The room must have been the master bedroom. She pushed open the door.

Praise saw Jessie's back. He was sitting on a chair in the center of the room; the back of the chair had broken off long ago and been discarded. Jessie had removed his shirt. His back was to the door.

Dimple stood behind him. She was applying some sort of oil to Jessie's neck, her hands moving slowly and methodically, her thumbs digging deep into the sinew of the moreh's neck. The smell of jasmine filled the air. Jasmine and almonds. Praise walked behind Dimple and picked up the bottle of oil at Dimple's feet, startling her friend.

"Oh!" Dimple jumped. "I didn't hear you come in."

"What's this stuff?" Praise asked, reading the ingredients on the bottle.

"It's message oil, Dimple answered. "I picked it up in DC a little while ago."

Praise removed the cap and sniffed. "This is expensive stuff."

Dimple smiled, continuing the pressure on Jessie's neck. "About fifty bucks if I remember right."

"Do you think this is appropriate?" Praise asked. Her voice had a edge to it.

Dimple clicked her tongue. "It's only a neck rub."

Praise held the bottle out to Dimple. "Not that. I don't care about that. I care about this. You spent fifty dollars on massage oil. How many people could be fed with fifty dollars?"

Dimple stopped rubbing Jessie's neck. "I'm sorry, Praise. But is it really that much? Fifty dollars? I mean, if you're talking, like, fast food, you could get a couple meals."

"That's not the point…"

Jessie cut Praise off.

"Dimple is taking care of *me*. There will come a time when no one will be able to do that."

"That money should have been saved for those who haven't eaten," Praise shot back. "I think that's more important than your sore neck."

Jessie turned to face Praise. "We can't change the luck of the poor. That's not why I'm here. Life for them can't be changed by one man, or a group like us. The world we live in is designed by humans around rich and poor. I am here to change the human heart."

Praise turned to leave the room.

Jessie called to her. "Listen while you can still hear me, daughter. When I'm gone, *you* will feel it."

Praise walked away.

The Terrorist

The tall man had definitely been chosen for this assignment. There were many people with his skills; he'd worked with truly talented individuals, many who could do exactly what he could do with as much expertise as he, as much meticulousness, as much— instinct. The man didn't question *why* he was chosen. He'd learned long ago in Kuwait, in the oil fields, in Nicaragua, in Afghanistan, in other places that weren't so publicly known, that *the why* was irrelevant. Sometimes it was as irrelevant as the *who*. Still, he wondered, *why him*?

The man prepared the mixtures on the long tables his handlers had placed in the large old barn on the farm where they'd sent him. There were no cows, no chickens, no pigs, no horses. All the farm equipment formerly housed there had been removed and resold weeks ago sometime in the dead of night. The corn that surrounded the barn and the modest house was all maintained by a friendly neighboring farm, close enough to do the tending, far enough to leave him alone. Stacks of reinforced paper bags full of commercial grade ammonium nitrate fertilizer lined the wall on the West side of the barn. The eastern wall was the storage area for fifty five gallon drums, some empty, some filled with ordinary diesel fuel. Soon, they will all be emptied, then refilled.

He worked from early morning until late at night, refining the farming products, getting the mixtures exactly right. The man was careful to eat a solid breakfast and lunch, to take his time eating and watch a little TV on his laptop while he did. Old reruns were the best. He enjoyed *I Love Lucy*. It was light. Lucille Ball was a genius at making a beautiful woman look stupid. The period costumes, the pearls she wore when guests arrived in their tiny apartment, the way Ricky Ricardo wore his straw hat, the brim tilted over one eye, they all made for a good laugh. A good laugh was what he needed. A good laugh and a fine meal. His was no job for a man with shaky hands.

The One and True Son

Fully sated, the tall man worked every day, Saturday and Sunday included. He had to finish the preparations quickly as time was important on this assignment. The longer the preparation, the longer to impact. The longer to impact, the lesser effect.

The preparation took three weeks, well within time frame. With the drums full, the bags from the fertilizer burned and ashes scattered in the fields, the tables broken down and picked up in the middle of the night on his signal, he was ready. Using a block and tackle, he lifted each drum each drum and placed them in the former U-Haul truck provided for him by his late-night suppliers. The tall man had to chuckle when he woke up that morning and saw the vehicle his handlers had delivered. *McVeigh, that simpleton.* He went and rented a Ryder truck that could be traced, touching all the documents needed to rent it. This truck was the same size with the familiar orange and white paint job of U-Haul, but all the logos and letters had been removed, leaving ghostly impressions on the side of the truck. The VINs in the cab and on the engine block were gone too. All McVeigh showed was even an idiotic amateur could blow up a big building.

The man had no idea where the target was until he received an encrypted message from his handlers, a message that would cease to exist three minutes after he read it. It wasn't often that the man was surprised when he discovered the target for his labor, but this one did. It was probably the last place he would think of, though surprise was no reason to doubt his mission, or to hesitate in performing it. The directions were explicit down to the time of the event to the approach to the target. *Someone had unusual motives on this one.*

As instructed, he cleaned out the farmhouse of all his personal effects and wiped down every surface, even in rooms he hadn't entered. He placed his clothes in a military duffle, his laptop in a canvas briefcase, and protective gear, gloves, safety glasses in construction grade garbage bags. All this would be picked up by his handlers team a half hour after he notifies them of his departure. All of this would be disposed of.

With the drums out of the way, he raked the barn's dirt floor with a heavy rake, making sure he'd disturbed the soil significantly. This was probably overkill, the man thought, but he always did what he was told by his handlers, assuming there was an angle of discovery that he may have missed. The man was a team player. He always had been.

With the area cleaned, he waited.

At 0200 the tall man left the farmhouse for the last time. He walked out to the barn and opened the doors wide. He took out the burner phone that

The One and True Son

was sitting on the driver's seat and pressed the number he would only dial once. He sent the message his handlers were waiting for:

I can't sleep. I'm going out for a walk.

That done, he threw the phone in the canvas briefcase with the laptop. He was on his way.

The directions were succinct. As instructed, the man drove the former U-Haul south on I-83 over the Mason-Dixon Line. When the interstate split at I 695, he hopped on it and headed in the direction of BWI airport. Luckily, the heartiest Baltimoreans were still dreaming of their morning coffee as 695 was usually a virtual parking lot beginning around 6am.

At I 95, the man continued south toward Washington.

The tall man had time to think on the quiet drive, something he didn't generally approve of when doing a job. But the question had been nagging at him. *Why me?* He was certainly qualified, but this was an unusual mission for him. For one, it was domestic. He'd been all around the world doing this kind work, but usually there was some connection with his skills other than explosive expertise. But there were many reasons for him being in demand for international services. He spoke four foreign languages: Farsi, Spanish, Arabic and French. And he was a bit of a chameleon; he had the ability to absorb the culture around him, the mannerisms and customs. More than once he'd donned a chadaree, a burqa, and passed himself off as a very tall woman, something his handlers at the time thought to be impossible. There was something about him that sucked the energy around him, something he used to project that energy back out. But this job used none of these skills.

He scratched his scruffy beard and cleared his mind. *The job,* he thought. *The job.*

At Maryland 185 he headed south. Expertly trimmed hedges and trees shielded the well-to-do suburb of Chevy Chase from the noise and pollution from the traffic to and from the center of American power. The mansions of the wealthy and powerful looked sleepy, their high-end shops and bakeries closed up and cute, buttoned up in their safe, green community.

At the DC line Maryland 185 became Connecticut Avenue. Still upscale and charming, signs of the decay of American city life soon appeared. A homeless man, his race unidentifiable due to the accumulated dirt on his face and arms, wobbled on the sidewalk, yelling at an invisible someone who was apparently yelling back. A small woman, probably an addict, shriveled and tattooed slumped against the door of a closed pub, the stacked outdoor chairs and tables waiting for another lunchtime rush. The man saw this decay in other parts of the world and for the most part it was more widespread, more of a shared burden. At one time he may have felt something when he saw the losers in the battle for power and money. That'd been some time ago.

The man drove slowly. There was no need to rush. The speed limit was thirty miles an hour and he was still within timeframe. The speedometer needle never broke twenty-seven. Connecticut Avenue splits into rush hour lanes, giving the way with the most traffic an extra lane to get in and out. He wouldn't be worrying about that on his departure.

At Chevy Chase Parkway he made a right and a minute later, a left at Reno Road NW. For most of Reno Road it seemed like he was driving through an upper middleclass neighborhood in the country, the thick trees guarding the houses, the streetlights shining down on what appeared to be clean streets. There was a change however when Reno Road became 34th Street. The trees thinned out. The houses looked more worn. Trash appeared in the gutters. The streetlights turned from a silvery white light to a ruddy amber.

He was getting close.

At Woodley Road NW he took a right and there it was, the target, sitting high up on the hill.

A half a mile away he stopped the truck in the middle of the road. He checked his mirrors and scanned the windshield and seeing no one out walking their dog or taking an early morning stroll, he opened his door and stepped out. Looking around again and not seeing a soul, he walked over to sawhorse barriers blocking the drive to the target. He dragged one over the side and got back in the truck.

There were cars or trucks parked in the service drive, so he killed his lights and slowly made his way to the unloading circle. As instructed, he parked the van behind some dumpsters. Also as instructed he donned a ski mask that covered everything on his face but his eyes, mouth and wiry beard bunched up at his neck. He exited the truck and moved to the rear where he unlocked the padlock he'd put on the doors in the barn and swung them wide. He stepped in the back just for a moment, just long enough to set the crude timer he'd fashioned from a recipe he knew was on the internet and stepped back out onto the tar drive. He closed the doors and replaced the lock.

The tall man had twenty minutes to get to the car left for him by his handlers on a nearby side street. Before he took off down the winding drive, he had one more thing to do. He had to make it look natural, like something had just occurred to him. It was specified in his orders. He looked up toward the temple walls and found the security camera. He looked at it for over a minute. That done, he turned and sprinted down the service drive. Once he hit Woodley Road, he tucked the ski mask inside his denim shirt.

On Macomb Street the man found a red convertible Mini with black fenders. He'd asked for the car specifically. It certainly wouldn't stand out on the thoroughfares of the nation's capital. And for such a tiny car, he could actually fit in it. With the convertible roof down, he had an infinite amount of headroom. He'd known he'd need some air after the job was delivered. He always needed some air.

He found the key fob in wheel well and started the car. All that was left to do was to sit and listen. He was a professional. He couldn't leave until he knew the job was done.

Exactly twenty minutes after the man had set the timer, everyone in an area of approximately ten miles in diameter awakened to a violent thud, an explosion louder than anything most people had ever heard. The man waited for the shock wave, which came, like always, seconds later, shattering windows on the opposite side of the street, the trees moving like they'd been blown by a sudden wind.

The tall man put the car in gear. *Oh good. A stick shift. I like driving stick.*

The Investigator

There was so much wrong here.

The remains of the National Temple lay strewn as far as the eye could see. Phu Trang had seen this before. He was new to the bureau on April 19th, 1995, working out of the Dallas office when the Murrah Federal Building was bombed. The sight was something his training hadn't prepared him for. He doubted then and now that *any* training could prepare anyone for what he had seen: the torn apart bodies, the corpses of children, the solid looking building sliced open like a half- eaten layer cake. Like here, the devastation spread for blocks. And like here, some of the building still stood, although the temple, mostly a one-story structure, only had one outside wall remaining, the wall furthest from the blast, the rest was tossed like droplets from a giant sneeze across several city blocks.

For a moment as he stood in what used to be the square where the faithful awaited entrance into the sacred area of the temple, he was smelling the burning cars of that horrible spring day in 1995. He could smell the line of cars parked in their allotted spaces that'd been waiting like loyal dogs, blazing funeral pyres of oil, metal and paint, black smoke billowing out, flames fighting furiously with the people trying to put them out. He could hear the screams of the one baby he saw personally, from the day care center on the first floor, blood all over her, the crying fire fighter running, his heavy yellow boots clomping to a waiting ambulance.

Phu poked at pieces of the temple at his feet with the toe of his work boot. He'd almost quit the bureau after that horrible day. Almost ended his career before it got started. The dreams came to him for years. That baby's face. Those clomping boots. They almost did him in.

This bombing, also done with a truck, was at the east side of the temple at the circular drive to the service entrance. A ten-foot crater in the blacktop drive marked the sight where a truck exploded. Parts of the rear axle were found three blocks away, a four am wake-up call through a

The One and True Son

neighbor's bedroom window. The TEDAC folks, the Terrorist Explosive Device Analytical Center, put the device at around 1400 lbs of explosives, probably another fertilizer bomb, slightly larger than Oklahoma City. The bomb was probably in fifty-five gallon drums, rigged in the cargo section of the truck in a tent shaped arrangement so the blast would expand out exponentially. Phu had seen this before.

But in many ways, big and small, this was different. Rather than detonating the device in the early morning when people were showing up for work, *when people were there,* this bomber chose to attack hours before dawn. It was still dark, with no people around, none that the bomber was probably aware of. Three morehs, four security guards, and two on-site maintenance workers were unaccounted for. Their bodies, or pieces of them, will probably be mixed in the concrete and glass being analyzed and gathered.

And the National Temple and the Murrah Federal Building were very different structures. The National Temple had a blocky, stone exterior, the sanctuary inside being the attraction and purpose of the building. The federal building was a modern office building, six floors with elevators and offices, more spaces to trap the energy of the blast, more walls to blow out. The temple was all space except for the three stories on the west side of the structure that were used for small gatherings, meetings and rooms for permanent staff. The force of the explosion could do nothing but expand with nothing to stop it, blowing the famous stained-glass images from the Tanach nearly to sand and the walls all over northwest Washington. This attack was not meant to kill people. It was for something else.

Crowds were forming along Wisconsin Avenue and Woodley Road. The faces there, on the other side of the barriers, from the firetrucks, ambulances and TV news trucks from all over the planet, from the police officers walking in the no man's land between them and their temple, securing the crime scene, were all wounded, frightened and angry. Special Agent Trang saw them from where the temple once stood, across an expanse of crisply cut grass. He didn't have to see their individual faces to know their expressions. He knew them all too well.

Pho Trang was lost in his thoughts. A familiar voice snapped him out of it.

"Phu!" the voice shouted. "Come here and look at this."

The voice belonged to Pat Barrios, a colleague from his office. Trang located where the voice was coming from and trotted over. Agent Barrios was kneeling over his laptop. He was watching a CNN broadcast about the event. There was a photograph on his screen.

Barrios looked up at Trang. "Did you know anything about this?"

The One and True Son

Trang knelt next to Barrios. He could see what looked like a security camera photograph of a man with a ski mask, an unkempt beard poking out under his chin.

"How the hell did CNN get that?" Trang asked.

Barrios shrugged. "Beats the shit out of me. Did you know we found the security camera equipment?"

"I didn't know it still existed." Trang scanned the bombing scene. "I don't see how it could. There's nothing left of this place. Even the concrete is powder. What are they saying?"

"Oh, sorry," Barrios said and handed him one of his earbuds.

...exclusive photo provided to CNN shows the alleged bomber. He is described by an unnamed source at the FBI as approximately six feet, two inches tall, in workmanlike clothes. He appears to have a thick beard. At this time, they can't identify the race of this man...

"Who the hell have they been talking to?" Trang barked, pulling out the earbud. He looked around the scene again. He could see news people down by the police line. The reporters were all facing the growing crowd, using the devastated temple site as a backdrop. No one was interviewing anyone from the FBI. He scanned where the temple once stood. There was no press up here.

There's so much wrong here. Trang thought it again. He didn't say it out loud.

As was his custom the Special Agent cleared his mind when he got to the office. He'd been assigned to the Washington Headquarters for the last five years, something he wasn't all together thrilled about at the time. Trang preferred the field. Investigating crime in the rest of the country meant smaller offices, less people, less brass. But being a veteran agent with over twenty years in, a good one according to his performance reports, he was becoming brass himself. For him, that meant less field work, more managing the scene, more reporting up to bigger fish, more paperwork. Most of what he did now wasn't what he loved about the job.

He closed his office door and settled in the worn leather chair he'd brought with him from his last assignment in St. Louis. The chair supported his back and lack of a butt. He could sit in it for hours and think if he needed to. Trang closed his eyes. He stretched his arms out grabbing the edge of his government issue desk, pulling the tension out of his shoulders and neck. Trang tried to clear out the notions that he had when walked into the office. He'd made notes. He knew what was in them. But he found, once he was in the office, behind his desk, it was always best to

The One and True Son

clear the clutter of his senses and think of what he saw in logical, clear terms. As usual, he asked himself questions:

So, what happened?

The temple in Washington DC has been destroyed.

How? A truck bomb very similar to one used to destroy a government building almost two decades earlier. These were two very effective bombs, relatively easy to make. An amateur? Quite possibly.

So, who did this? According to CNN some guy in overalls and a bushy beard.

Why'd he do it? Maybe he hated Yahwehism. Maybe the government? Maybe both?

Who got hurt? Maybe a dozen people. Certainly, the missing will be found in pieces, if they're ever found at all

Again why? So much destruction, but a low body count. Does that make sense?

No, that didn't make sense. Trang rubbed his temples with the ends of his index fingers. To him, terrorism, as a strategy, never made sense. It almost never works. Certainly not with the most powerful military complex in history itching to test out its new toys. Afghanistan knew that now all too well.

His laptop booped at him. He had an email. It was from Barrios. Attached to it were photos taken at the scene from just about every possible viewpoint. Trang sent the pictures to the printer. He got up from his chair and waited as the printer spat out the photos one by one. He gave each one a cursory look as they came out and stacked them in the order of their printing. Once the last came out he grabbed the tape dispenser on his desk and hung each one on the thin wall of his small office. He stood back and looked at the destruction.

Apparently, TEDAC had found the detonator. The first few photos were of a mangled Reisen chocolates tin, pieces of four 9-volt batteries, a couple of transistors with wires hanging from them, some wire and a burnt filament. It was probably attached to some bundled legal fireworks like M88s to set off the fertilizer/fuel mixture. Anyone could get this recipe for this off the internet. The timer was a small kitchen timer the team found in small white, plastic pieces. Definitely an amateur rig.

The photos of the crater showed what a 1400-pound fertilizer bomb could do to a blacktop. The hole was ten and a half feet in diameter and nearly two feet deep directly under the center of the explosion. The blacktop under the crater would have been in the shade of the temple by this time of day, if the temple still existed.

The One and True Son

More questions:

By definition, terrorism is meant to invoke fear into a populace. The best way to do that would be to kill as many unsuspecting, seemingly innocent people as possible. That's what gets on the news: The death. So why was this done to a nearly empty building? What is the objective? To keep people from going to the temple? We've had mass shootings in temples before this. Did anybody stop going to temples? Not really. For many Americans, that's all the more reason to go to temple. Americans don't like to be scared into anything.

So, is this terrorism? Trang stared at the pictures on his wall. *It sure looked like it.*

The questions followed Trang home. He tried to quiet them with a cold beer. He switched on some streamed music and laid down on his worn sofa, kicking off the steel toed boots he wore to the bombing site. He liked 70s rock and almost never played anything else. AC/DC's Bon Scott screeched out from the small but powerful speakers he'd mounted in the corners of his living room, a sound that would have made many who'd had a day like his bury their heads in a pillow.

Diamonds and dust
Poor man last, rich man first,
Lamborginis, caviar
ry martini's, Shangri-La
I got a burnin' feelin'
deep inside o' me
it's yearnin'
But I'm gonna set it free
I'm going into sin city
I'm gonna win in sin city

The song struck him as outrageously funny even though he'd heard it probably thousands of times since he'd first bought the album as a teenager and then, as he grew, the cassette and finally the MP3. Trang laughed loud and long. It was a tension laugh, a release. This day, after all he'd seen, it struck him that this was what it was all about, wasn't it? The struggle between the rich and the poor. It wasn't the first time Phu Trang had thought of this conflict.

Phu Trang was raised in a strict Yahwehian household, the son of a moreh and his deeply religious wife. He attended private Yahwehian schools and attended temple *at least* three nights a week. Yahweh was the first word out of his mouth in the morning and the last word before bed. He was an aggressive student in all subjects, from Mathematics to English, always interested in the details, but where he really excelled was History. When, in first grade, he was introduced to George Washington, Thomas Jefferson and Christopher Columbus, he would badger his teachers for more information, more stories, more details. His teachers found it a bit tiring at times, though they never wanted to discourage an eager learner. What they didn't understand, what frankly, *he* didn't understand, was that he could visualize these heroes very easily. They were very real, *very present,* in his mind. When he was told, as fact, that Washington had admitted to his father, that for whatever reason, he'd chopped down his prize cherry tree, Phu could hear the shameful words come from the contrite boy's mouth. He could see the astonished father, ready to mete punishment, only to watch his face change, glowing from pride at the boy's unwavering honesty. When he was told, again, as fact, that Thomas Jefferson believed in the freedom of all people, that he was willing to *die* for the freedom of all people, he could see the Virginian, risking everything he owned, struggling with an aching back while writing the Declaration of Independence night and day, so finally *all* Americans could be free. When he was told, again, as *fact,* that Christopher Columbus sailed from Spain, risking life and limb and possibly a steep dive off the edge of the planet, to prove that the world was round, to discover *our* country, America, Phu was on the Santa Maria with the great admiral, dodging sea monsters and calming a restless crew.

No one told him those stories were fiction, that they were planted in the American educational system to instill patriotism, a false sense of destiny, a belief in the almost holy origins of the United States. No one told Phu. He had to find the truth in books, in upper school, that were written to inform rather than beatify. These weren't the texts he'd been assigned by his teachers, the revised editions that read almost exactly as the previous revised editions, with lots of pictures and colorful fonts. These were books he'd found on his own, musty books, sitting lonely and mostly untouched on dust covered shelves, unused, even for History reports, ignored in favor of the Encyclopedia.

By graduation, one might've considered Phu Trang a bit of a cynic, and yet he enrolled at A Yahwehian University with the intent to become a moreh. At least with Yahweh, there was consistency. The notions of Yahwehanism were tested by time, reviewed for millennia, historically powerful and universal. He believed that was true until his second year of divinity training, the year that he, again, dug through the old books that went unread, that were deemed no longer useful.

His professor was an older morah, Rebecca Logue, a sturdy stick figure of a woman, rail thin, but muscular, with silklike gray/white hair and hands

The One and True Son

like a farmer, strong with no fat between the metacarpals, only ropy veins and knobby thick joints. He arranged to see her during her office hours. Phu was having trouble with his research paper that carried major weight for his grade. The class was Yahweh in History. He'd discussed ideas with his classmates, and they were all mostly doing variations of the similar themes: which wars were fought over interpretations of the Tanach; how Yahwehistic law emerged in the American Government; how Yahwehanism overtook Judaism in the Middle East. To Phu all these subjects could be covered in an upper school term paper with help from the good old encyclopedia.

"But those themes are rich in detail that may help us understand where our faith is today," Professor Logue said after Phu expressed his issue. "I would wager that most of our students will learn enlightening details they hadn't known before this project. Even you, Mr. Trang, with your question everything approach, might find something you didn't know previously." There was no venom in the professor's voice. Phu's attack on almost everything deemed as fact was no threat to her. She found this endearing for a student, something she didn't see very often. "You know, Yahweh is eternal. He has always been and will always be. There is much to find if one digs in *established history*." She smiled benevolently. "Even for one who questions everything."

Phu smiled back. He thanked her enthusiastically and excused himself from her office. He had the subject for his paper.

After that, Phu Trang spent nearly every free hour in the university library. He sat at the heavy dark wood tables with stacks of books, the covers of which may not have seen light in the library since it had been illuminated with lightbulbs and not florescent tubes. Though there was no telling how long they'd been on the shelves, untouched, many had spines that crackled like an old man's after sitting too long on the porch. Each day Phu scribbled notes in stacks of legal pads, noting sources, citing relevant quotes from people long dead about people who'd been dead centuries longer. The project energized him. When he found a contradiction, he pounced. As he perused each volume of the stack, he found logical fallacy after logical fallacy. He wrote each down, trying to find the thread he'd been looking for. There was something that Professor Logue said that stayed with him, that drove him, but he couldn't yet put it into words. His professor had said: "There is much to find in established history." Established history? When exactly was history established? Does it become established when reviewing old documents? Does it happen when certain interpretations are agreed upon? And when history becomes *established,* is it unchangeable. Is established history *fact?*

The One and True Son

Phu grabbed the stack of books to his left. He took the book off the top opened it, flipped to random sections and glanced through the text. What he was looking for he wasn't sure. He would know it when he saw it. He worked this way for over two hours, returning to the shelves, bringing back more books, taking back the ones that proved unhelpful. As he expected, he knew when he'd found a piece of the puzzle he'd been looking for. The one he'd found was a large one. It came in a book entitled *Samaria and Judah,* published in 1898, which, according to a short forward, was written to clear up some misunderstandings in the historical record of the land we knew as Israel. Phu knew when he ran his smudged index finger, smeared with the dry ink of forgotten books, that he'd caught his thread.

In this book he'd read of places that he'd heard of before, but only in passing, as if they were a pin stuck in the map of history. Places like Megiddo, Dothan, Succoth, Gilead, Hebron. He'd seen these places written about, in name only, in the Tanach. They were almost like postal codes to Phu. With this new information, new to *him*, he could finally picture the tribal nature of the time of the Tanach, the different languages, the different clothing, and these pictures made the reading all the more satisfying for the young Divinity student.

Other words were added to his vocabulary. Names, some he'd heard before, but had no meaning to him. Ba'al, Asherah, El and Anat, Chemosh and Jehovah.

Phu took his notes back to his dorm room nightly, usually after he'd been forced from the library by a fatigued library assistant and typed furiously. His thoughts were already clear in his mind. He'd found something no one in his class was talking about in their papers. He realized it might be controversial to bring up such things, but what was the use of going to college if all the facts weren't presented?

Soon he was looking into Constantine the Great, the first Roman emperor to bring Yahwehianism into the Roman State. The ties he was making between the ancient Israelites and their religions and Constantine's needs in a fractured Rome made perfect sense to him.

He finished his paper early and asked Professor Logue to review it for him, to help him refine it. In truth, he wanted her to see it, to see the facts he'd dug up. He was pleased when she accepted the paper early, and even more pleased when, days later, she asked him to come to her office during office hours to discuss it.

The morah handed him the paper as soon as he sat down. She'd come out from behind her desk and leaned against it, her arms crossed in front of her.

The One and True Son

"I can see you worked very hard on this paper," she told Phu. She said nothing more for a moment. Phu thought there was strange look in her eye.

"I did," Phu acknowledged. "It took me a while to find exactly what I was looking for, but the information was there. I was very careful to cite my sources accurately."

The professor looked at Phu in a way he hadn't remembered her looking at him before. There was something hesitant in her manner that seemed out of character. He grew cold.

"You did a more than adequate job with your citation, Mr Trang," she said. "The paper was well written. The paper was clear and concise. As long as it was, I read through it rather quickly." She shrugged her shoulders. "That said, I can't accept it."

Phu's chest fell.

"I'm sorry, Mr. Trang. You'll have to do another paper. It's a good thing you handed it in early."

The professor returned to her chair on the other side of her desk.

It took a moment for Phu to be able to speak. "I don't understand. I have to write *another* paper?"

"I'm afraid so." Professor Logue said.

Phu waited for her to continue, but she didn't.

"But why?"

"Because your paper is heresy, Mr. Trang."

Phu hadn't expected that. He waited for her to expound on what she'd said, but she appeared to believe the conversation closed. She's shifted her attention to documents on her desk, picking up a pen to add her signature to one of them.

"I don't understand," Phu said, finally, his voice cracking slightly.

Professor Log placed the pen back on her desk. "Your paper is heresy, Mr Trang and at *this* university and particularly in *my* class, we do not condone, or even, as you seemed to have done, *dabble* in heresy. It is unacceptable. You still have plenty of time to write a *legitimate* paper.

Phu felt the blood enter his face. "What exactly is heretical about my paper? Are you doubting the facts that I've presented?"

The professor sighed. "Mr. Trang, do you even realize the implications of what you wrote? You claimed that Yahweh, *our* Yahweh, had *evolved.*"

"Didn't he?" Phu shot back. "Yahweh wasn't always *the* god of the Israelites. He was a warrior god. El was the benevolent father figure. Israel even has El in its name. After time, Yahweh started taking on attributes of other Canaanite gods. Isn't that evolving?"

The One and True Son

"You are misreading history," Mr. Trang. "Those other gods' names you speak of are just other names for the true god."

"The early Israelites didn't think so," Phu said. "If they had, why did they have separate temples for separate gods? Why did they…"

"Enough!" Professor Logue erupted. Seemingly shocked by her own tone, the morah closed her eyes and took a breath. "Yahweh, the one true *god*, did not evolve. By saying so, are you not saying that Yahweh was *created* and not the creator? Is that correct?"

Phu didn't answer. That *was* what he was saying, though the implications of that had not hit him until that moment.

He rose from his chair.

"You still have time for an *appropriate* paper, Mr Trang," the professor said, her voice softened. "Please search your heart before you decide on what to do."

Phu Trang did as he was told. He searched his heart. He dropped out of the university.

Pre-Law and Law school were a breeze for Phu Trang. He'd found his niche. If something was illegal, there was a document somewhere that said so. If there was nuance, there was a court interpretation somewhere that went over it from both sides. Law firms were hotly competing to "bring him on board" sending him all kinds of goodies: tickets for the big game, where he could "meet the team," invitations to the best restaurants in town, where he could "break bread with the firm." The salaries offered were higher than he'd ever imagined. And he had no interest in them. He had one goal: Special Agent for the FBI.

And the bureau was happy to have him. Again, at Quantico, the bureau's training center, he stood out academically and physically. He received the Director's Leadership Award, the highest award given to a recruit. He was given his firearm and credentials and sent to Dallas.

The bureau tried over the years to promote him out of investigations, but he wasn't having it. Whatever fitness exam they threw at him, he passed it, only losing a quarter step with age. He was an *investigator*. That was all he wanted to do.

And his investigator instincts didn't like this bombing. There was no intelligence, at least none that he'd seen, that the temple might be a target. There were many factions in Yahwehianism, but the temple seemed to be neutral territory for all of them. There were services in many sects, and though they disagreed on what Phu would consider minutia, they weren't shooting each other up over it.

The Islamist groups had been quiet in the last few years, having overplayed their hands in 1999 and 2001. Afghanistan looked like the surface of Mars after their last excursion into the US. And there was usually some chatter from cells, both in Europe and the states, before a major target was hit. It could be supposed that they'd gotten wise to American intelligence, but Phu found that doubtful.

He'd just sat up, grabbed his beer ready to take a good slug, when the phone rang.

"Hey man," the voice on the other end said. "It's Pat."

Somehow Phu knew it would be Barrios.

"What's going on?" Phu said dryly.

"Are you watching CNN?"

Phu grabbed his remote, switched off the music and turned to the cable channel.

One of the talking heads, the older guy with the German name was talking to a "National Security Reporter" on the phone.

... again, this comes directly from the FBI. They have identified a man they are calling a known cult leader, one Jessie Carpentero, a person of interest in the deadly bombing of the National Temple that took place in the early morning hours of Wednesday.

What can you tell me about this man, Carpentero? Is he known for any other acts of violence? Is he preaching violence? What do we know about him, Kris?

Well, according to the FBI, he has made many statements that could be construed as confrontational. As far as Carpentero, we know little, but we're learning.

Kris, thank you for your excellent reporting on this. Keep us updated.

"Sure thing."

Word from the White House has been guarded...

"What the fuck, Pat?" Phu said, rubbing his forehead. "Do you know anything about this?"

"Not a thing. Why do think I'm calling you?"

"Sorry, Pat," Phu said. "I didn't mean that the way it sounded. What do you think is going on? I don't know anything about this guy. We weren't given the security photo. We had to see it on fucking television. What's going on?"

The One and True Son

"Some serious voodoo," said Pat. "I'm keeping me head down."

The next morning, on his way into the bureau parking garage he saw something he'd never seen before. There was a press conference in front the Hoover FBI headquarters, right there on the sidewalk. There were trucks from all the major networks, the cable news, and even foreign news agencies parked along Pennsylvania Avenue, their satellite dishes extended skyward. Phu pulled over. He was approached by a Capitol Police officer, but after Phu flipped his badge at her, she went on her way. He stepped onto the curb to where he could see the focus of the world's press attention, a slim podium, bathed in the lights of the media, several microphones attached to it. A group of FBI brass was conferring a few feet behind it. Phu knew all the brass, at least, he thought he did. These were big guns. There was one man he didn't recognize. He was a short, bald man with an exquisitely tailored suit, FBI blue, and he was doing most of the talking. After a few moments, the Deputy Director took to the podium, expressing his gratitude for the hard work the bureau had put into identifying a suspect so quickly. He stressed that, now the suspect had been identified, it was only a matter of time before he would be brought to justice. He went on to tell the cameras what the American people would not tolerate. Phu had heard this speech before, many times, but never with an investigation that had barely gotten going, and never, ever, on the sidewalk on Pennsylvania Avenue.

And as quickly as the news conference had begun, it had ended, no questions, no follow ups.

Once in the building, Phu looked for Pat Barrios, but he was nowhere to be found. Apparently, his crack about keeping his head down wasn't just a throwaway line. Phu went to his own office only to find the photographs removed from the walls, his notes, removed from his desk. Everything was neat and orderly. His pens were gathered in his unused coffee cup with the witticism on the side that read, "It's coffee! Really!". When he'd gone home the previous night the pens were scattered everywhere. His notes were *locked* in a hardened drawer. He was headed out the door to stage his own explosive event when he was met by the bald man he'd seen at the news conference.

The man smiled, amicably, offering his hand to shake.

"Agent Trang,"the man said, his pearly white teeth fully exposed. He grabbed Phu's hand; his hand was soft and manicured. "I just wanted to come over and thank you for your hard work in identifying the suspect. Your fine work has been duly noted by your superiors."

Phu Trang looked at the man's eyes. They were black, deep, emotionless, like a shark. "And you are?" Phu asked.

"Someone who has taken notice of your fine work." The pearly whites flashed at him again. Without another word the man turned and left his office.

Phu Trang sat down hard in the chair he brought with him from Dallas. He took one of the pens out of the coffee cup and drew a large question mark on the calendar on his desk blotter.

What do I know now?

He really knew nothing.

The Mechanism

Up until ten weeks before Richard Fondlen spent most of his days in his sizable garden outside his Point Loma home, an *established money* area of San Diego. His wife wanted a pool with a large patio area. Being from Canada, it was a dream of hers, so he gave her that, but he knocked out a couple of concrete slabs away from the pool for the only thing he wanted: a garden. Specifically, a grape garden. The soil, though not chalky, was dry and flinty, very nice to grow a tasty wine grape. His wife wanted a Japanese garden with rocks, a running stream, flowering trees and koi swimming under a small wooden footbridge, but he explained that you can't make wine from that kind of garden.

Most people knew him as a plain spoken, though somewhat quiet, semi-retired high end insurance executive for an international insurance conglomerate. If one wanted to discuss sailing (he owned a twenty-two foot sloop) or baseball (he's loved the Padres) he always had exciting stories and advice (especially for Padres coaches) to share with anyone who wanted to listen. He was known to enjoy the pool, though not as much as his wife Erica, and friends and acquaintances noticed the many scars on his chest, abdomen, upper and lower back. To anyone curious enough, and frankly, crass enough, to ask him of their origin, he would explain that unfortunately he'd fallen short in the genetics lottery and was highly susceptible to various skin cancers, which, when removed posed no further danger but left their unsightly markings in their stead. This explained to the curious his seeming obsession with various sun blocking skin creams he applied multiple times a day, rain or shine. Although he worked in his garden for hours at a time, his hands felt like brushed velvet.

If one were so bold as to ask about the wider, longer scar, just above his belt line on his right side, an unruly gash, that curved like a branch from an old dead tree, he would explain that is was from an appendix surgery that had had complications. He would further explain, in exacting detail, how the wound had opened in the healing process and become infected and had to be rinsed with sterile saline and packed daily so the wound could heal from the inside out. Usually *that* explanation would halt any further uncomfortable, prying questions.

To his wife, his friends, his acquaintances, and most who met him at his home, Richard Fondlen seemed an open book.

And they knew nothing about him.

They didn't know, for example, that the international insurance conglomerate that employed him didn't exist. They didn't know that he loved the smell of skin cream, that it was one of the only things on this earth that made him feel remotely human, that the scents could hide the stench of his thoughts. Perhaps, this fetish sprang from childhood, from the smell of a young girl who wouldn't look at him except in derision. Perhaps it was the scent of his mother who carried many scents from heavenly camomile to cheap bourbon.

People didn't know the smaller scars that cover much of his body had nothing to do with cancer and certainly nothing to do with the sun. Most torture takes place in dark, wet places, with fetid air and foreign screams drifting in and out.

They didn't know that the large scar was not the result of a botched appendectomy, but the remnants of a knife attack from an Eastern European operative who caught Fondlen where he wasn't supposed to be, or that said operative caught the worse end of the confrontation and is, as they say, no longer with us. Fondlen had sewn the wound himself, which had indeed dehisced, opened, while he made his escape. The repairs were made later in a safe hospital.

Everyone who thought he was an important semi-retired executive couldn't imagine his true job title. Even people who knew how to contact him and knew his credentials didn't have a name for his job. He was simply The Mechanism.

Ten weeks prior, he's been pressing seeds into his freshly tilled and enriched soil when a phone he carried with him everywhere but seldom utilized hummed in the pocket of his cargo shorts. His wife Erica, who'd been reading by the pool, took notice when he stood, removed his gardening gloves and stepped away from his beloved garden bed. Richard knew Erica wasn't privy to his work, but that she recognized that when he answered this phone, a long absence usually followed. He put the phone to his ear and smiled at his wife with an apologetic tilt of his head.

"Yeah Paul," he spoke into the device. "Give me just a minute to get to my office."

The One and True Son

He mouthed *I'm sorry* to his wife and waved his arm at the pool and the house and raised his eyes to the sunshine to remind her that, once in a while, he had to do things to keep what they had.

He entered through the oversized glass doors, crossed through the elegant living room with plush, stunningly white sofas and chairs, tempered glass tables and crystal chandeliers to the bedroom he'd converted to his office. He'd painted the room a fire engine red, a color that he could think in, and surrounded his large modern desk with maps from around the world and photos of friends and family in different poses of mirth and closeness. He sat down in front of the two computer screens that sat on his desktop.

"Dick, we have a situation," the man said on the other end of call. "I've got the particulars here. This is going to need your immediate attention."

"I'll be right on it, sir," Fondlen responded. "Send the info to me here. I'll review it and draw up some scenarios. I'll be on a plane tonight."

"Normally that'd be okay, but we need you moving now. There's a jet waiting for you at the Marine Air Station at Miramar. You've got about two hours. I'll forward the poop to you. You can review it on the flight."

Fondlen cut off the call and grabbed his laptop and placed it in his carrying bag. He had to get out to the pool and smooth out the wife situation before he moved on to anything bigger.

There was a C21A waiting on the flight line at Miramar. It was the military version of an executive Learjet, minus the bar, the wood panel interior and the sexy personal flight attendant. Manned by Air Force personnel, it had the capability to have the seats removed to transport litters in an emergency. One thing it had better than any corporate jet was an air to ground communications system, encrypted and satellite relayed. Richard Fondlen settled into his seat. It was comfortable enough and he fastened in. Before the jet had rotated becoming airborne, he had the attachments sent to him open on his laptop screen.

He separated each subject's files and looked through them one by one. He scanned through the photos first. He liked to get a look at his subjects before he delved into the particulars. Some of the photos were blurry. They appeared to be taken at exclusively outside events. The main subject was one Jessie Carpentero. The clearest photos appeared to be at the Lincoln Memorial. A couple looked to be taken at other places, again, all outdoors. Fondlen clicked out of the files and went to the net. The C21A had full internet capability including the military and State web, but he wasn't interested in those. Not yet.

The One and True Son

He opened YouTube and entered "Jessie Capentero" in the search box. What he saw fascinated him. Video after video of people claiming to be "healed" by this guy. Most of those posting were in tears, or almost. They practically claimed the guy was growing back amputated limbs. And the guy wasn't in *any* of the videos. *Imagine that. This guy* was the reason he was flying to from San Diego to Andrews with two hours notice? Somebody's got a screw loose, he thought, or there was something he wasn't seeing.

He watched each video. They were all the same. There were either a lot of people in on this grift or he was passing out happy pills at his rallies. Fondlen closed out YouTube and opened a file that was sent on a secure site. This was Jessie Carpentero.

He clicked on the video and listened intently. He had to admit, there was something riveting about the guy. The video was filmed on the stairs of the Lincoln Memorial, a place he'd known well from drops and other clandestine meetings. Carpentero made his way up the stairs like a king, and yet, he was dressed like a plumber. From the looks of it, a cop filmed him because whoever it was seemed to be surrounded by them, standing by a bunch trees. The camera, probably a phone, followed Carpentero up the stairs with a group behind him, obviously the other people in the dossier. This *healer* sat on the top steps and the others sat around him. Fondlen was surprised that when the man started talking, he could hear what he was saying, clearly, as if he were standing right next to the camera. He had to be twenty-five yards away from it—at least.

Richard Fondlen listened intently to this man speak, this man that others claimed could heal with a simple touch, or even a word. As his words began to find their way into his consciousness, he understood exactly why he was on this plane.

He opened the dossiers of the other members of the group. They were a mishmash of characters: a former IRS agent, a runaway, a dock worker, blacks, blondes, Indians, men and women. He looked at the last dossier.

"Shit!" he yelled, startling the young crewman, an Airman First Class, who looked up at him and quickly looked away.

I have to fly all the way to DC just to get on this fucking plane and go back to where I came from.

The Cop

Mitchel rubbed his bald head. He sat on the sofa where Praise used to do her studying, back in college. His recliner, next to sofa, wasn't getting much use these days. That chair was his after-work chair where he sat to do anything *but think*. Since his daughter left the department and joined with this Jessie character, he couldn't do anything else.

When Praise called and told him she was turning in her resignation, he begged her to come home and discuss it. That had been two years ago and it still occupied his every thought.

Let me get this right, he told her. *You're quitting the job because you want to live in a homeless camp and help the poor? Okay, I can see...I can see, baby, that you want to help. I can see. But can't you help and keep your job?*

It's not about the job, Dad, she told him. *I can't explain it. Not now. There's something special happening. I'm not sure you would believe me if I told you. It's something almost ...unbelievable. But I have to do this.*

Okay, I'm listening...Praise...

Daddy, I have to go. I call you. I love you.

That call changed his life. He understood now how parents felt when a child goes missing. An almost physical hole opened up in his center, a part of him that was irreplaceable. He was desperate to fill it up, to bring his daughter back.

Mitchel's days were spent by the phone. Unknown to Praise, he'd claimed his pension soon after the call, turned in his badge. He'd hoped that she would somehow get word. He searched YouTube every day. His daughter never appeared in any videos about the group, nor did their leader. He had deep doubts about what he was seeing. As a cop, he knew how people could be easily influenced and with technology the way it was, anyone with a mind to, could sway huge numbers of people to believe in something that wasn't there at all. He *knew* his daughter though. At least he thought he did. She wasn't one to be easily manipulated.

He was doing his daily Google search on all things Jessie there was a knock at the door. Mitchel assumed it was some guy in a too small red polo shirt asking why he's paying too much for his cable and internet service. He was good at saying no and moving on. No *new special deal* flyer would be passed his way. No discussion on what he's paying now or how many movies he streams per month. Thanks, but no thanks. He'd answer the door and that's all the contact whoever was selling things was going to get.

"Sergeant Johnson?"

The man standing on the other side of the door was no salesman. He was a shorter man with an expensive light grey suit, a bald head and cold black eyes. His teeth were white and sharp. He held out his hand for Mitchel to shake. The feel of his palm made the former police officer cringe slightly.

"Mr. Johnson, really. I'm retired, "Mitchel replied. "Who's asking?"

The man in the suit took a badge case from the breast pocket of his suit jacket. Mitchel noticed the man had no weapon, no holster he could see.

"My name's Richard Fondlen," the man answered. "Can I come in?"

Mitchel took a long look at the ID. He'd seen these from time to time. It was FBI. But there was something missing from this one. It took a moment for him to remember what it was. "Why doesn't it say Special Agent? And that picture looks like it was taken yesterday."

The man at the door smiled. If Mitchel didn't know better, he might've sworn that his teeth sparkled in the sun.

"They said you were good," the man said with a chuckle. "The picture was, in fact, taken yesterday. And yes, the words Special Agent are not on these credentials. But they are authentic. Here." Richard Fondlen handed him a business card. "I'm sure you recognize the name on the card. Please, feel free to give Chuck a call. As a matter of fact, he's waiting for it. I'll wait outside."

Chuck Splonskowski was the head of the FBI office in LA. Mitchel had befriended him years ago when he'd helped them out on a human trafficking investigation. Years ago, Chuck wanted Mitchel to join the FBI, but Mitchel knew the LAPD. He wanted to stay with the familiar. He didn't have to look at the number on the card. He had it memorized. The guy was legit, according to Chuck, but Mitchel could tell he didn't want to say much more. He seemed in a hurry to hang up.

Mitchel opened the door and let the stranger in.

The One and True Son

The two sat across from each other, Mitchel on the sofa and Fondlen on the recliner. The scene may have appeared comical to an outside observer, the large man, his legs almost too tall for his own sofa, and the smaller man who looked like he was sitting in his daddy's chair. Mitchel could tell that this man understood power in all its forms, even in choosing a chair. "Very comfortable," Fondlen said.

"What can I do for you, Mr. Fondlen?" Mitchel said, uninterested in his guest's comfort level.

"I come here out of concern, Sergeant Johnson."

"*Mister* Johnson. I told you. I'm retired. I can't for the life of me guess why the FBI would be concerned about me."

Fondlen scanned the living room. The walls, the furniture, the framed photos on the wall, the clean fresh paint, all said happy family. "Your daughter is a police officer, I understand."

"*Was,*" Mitchel replied. "She left the job. Some things were very important to her. But you know she's not a cop anymore. Is she why you're here?"

Fondlen turned to an end table next to the recliner. On it was a photo of Praise, framed in white. She posed kneeling in a soccer uniform, a soccer ball balancing on her knee. She had to be about 10 years old in the picture. Her smile was bright and geniune. He picked up the photo and spoke to it rather to Mitchel.

"It's so hard to know what your children are doing. You go to their games when they look like this, when a soccer ball is important to them. And then they move on. They grow up. You think you know them. You *hope* you taught them well. But you don't know what they're doing…what they're thinking."

Icy impulses shot up Mitchel's spine.

"Mr. Fondlen, if you're here about Praise, I'd appreciate it if you could get to the point. Is she in trouble?"

Fondlen placed the photo back on the table. "I'm concerned…frankly, we're concerned, about the group she's running with."

"Running with?" Mitchel spit back. "What is she, 15? She's not running with anyone. And from what I can tell from what I can get on the internet, they aren't doing anything illegal." Mitchel paused. "And what did you just say? *We* are concerned? Who's *we?*"

Fondlen grinned. "Sergeant Johnson. I showed you my credentials. You spoke to Chuck. Of course, you know I meant the Bureau."

Mitchel wasn't sure of anything.

"I told you. It's *Mister* Johnson."

The One and True Son

The man rubbed his soft hand over his bald head. "Of course. I apologize. Please understand that I have the utmost respect for anyone who chooses to do law enforcement for a week, let alone for decades. I simply use your title…your former title out of deep, deep respect." Fondlen sighed. "Perhaps I started this all wrong. Will you allow a reset?"

Mitchel leaned back on the sofa. He nodded.

"Thank you for that," Fondlen said. "I confess I may be a bit rusty at this. I'm retired too. Some friends, as a personal favor, asked me to look into this Jessie character. I've forgotten that, for family, this is all very delicate." He smiled.

Mitchel's shoulders eased slightly. He always carried stress in his shoulders.

"Now, *Mister* Johnson," Fondlen continued, "what can you tell me about your daughter that I haven't read in a file somewhere? Paint a picture for me. Maybe there's absolutely no nefarious reason for anything she's doing. Maybe they're just trying to save the world."

Mitchel told Fondlen about his daughter. She was strong, though sometimes quiet. She loved Barbies as a little girl, deeply engrossed in the huge dream house she got for the Holiday of Lights, but she was equally at home on a soccer field or playground. She'd been very close to both he and his wife and he worried about her greatly after the death of her mother. Those worries seemed unfounded though as she cried when she needed to and continued on with what she felt important in her life. She talked warmly about her mother, never seeming to focus on her death, but on her life.

Mitchel was surprised when she joined the LAPD, but not overly concerned that she wouldn't be able to handle the job. In fact, she excelled. She was turning into a great cop.

"And yet, she quit." Fondlen said.

"Like I said before, Praise is driven by what is important to her. People are important to her. *All* people. I guess she felt needed by this group. That they needed her. Maybe she wasn't getting that from the LAPD."

"She didn't discuss it with you, before she left?"

"No. She'd decided. And that was that. She's always been like that."

Fondlen tapped his fingers on the arm of the easy chair.

"Do you know where she is now?"

It was Mitchel's turn to rub his own bald head. "No, I'm afraid I don't. She emails from time to time. They seem to move a lot. Once in a while she'll call."

The One and True Son

Fondlen furrowed his brow. "As you said, Mr. Johnson, it's not clear that this group has broken any laws. But we have some intelligence that makes us worry about Mr. Carpentero; intelligence, I'm sorry to say I can't share right now. We want to be fair."

Mitchel nodded.

"But I think I should share some concerns with you," Fondlen continued. "The woman you described to me sounds like she had a balanced, loving upbringing. She was raised to be responsible and caring. But her willingness to uproot her life as she has is something we see with people who become involved with cults. A very charismatic man or woman can have a dramatic effect on a person's psyche. Even as bright a person as your daughter. Unfortunately, we've seen this all too often."

The tension grew in Mitchel's neck and shoulders.

"Assuming that this guy Jessie is a cult leader, which, at this point, I'm not, is being in a cult illegal?"

"Oh no," Fondlen answered, smiling again. "No, it's not. As long as no drugs or physical restraint or forced imprisonment is involved, no. We still have the First Amendment."

"So why are you investigating them?" Mitchel asked.

Fondlen pursed his lips. "Again, there's some intelligence that is concerning. I wish I could share it with you, but, again, we want to be fair."

The conversation ended there. Mitchel escorted Richard Fondlen to the door.

"Please, take my card," Fondlen said handing a calling card to Mitchel. "If your daughter contacts you, will you please ask her to call me?"

"I'll give her the number. What she does with it, I can't promise."

Fondlen smiled again. He took out a pair of sunglasses and covered those sharklike eyes. "That's all I can ask." He put out his hand for Mitchel to shake.

Mitchel took it and was almost repelled by its unnatural softness.

"Thank you, Sergeant…uh, Mr. Johnson."

Mitchel watched him get into what looked like a rental car and drive away. He looked at the card in his hand. There was the man's name and an out of state phone number. There were no other identifying markings.

That was weeks before what the cable news people and the internet were calling, "The Temple Incident". He saw the reports on the Good Morning Happy News he put on to squelch the silence that had become omnipresent in his life since Praise left. The violence bothered him, the kicking over the

The One and True Son

tables and the tone of the shouting. He went to the internet and found other reports and postings over the incident. There were numerous cell phone videos from different angles and points of view. Mitchel was relieved that Praise didn't appear in any of them. It seemed the guy identified as Jessie was doing most of the destruction. The cameras were mostly on him. Was Praise with him? He had to hope to Yahweh that she wasn't. He went to the desk in his office and dug through the middle drawer until he found the card Fondlen had given him. As soon as she called him, he resolved, he would give her the man's number and beg her to call him. He wasn't really comfortable with that. He didn't like the man. Something instinctively told him that the guy was not what he seemed. But Chuck Splonskowski had vouched for him. As uncomfortable as he was with giving Praise the number, he was infinitely more uncomfortable with his daughter going to jail—or worse.

For the next few weeks Mitchel jumped whenever his phone vibrated. He forwarded all calls on his landline to his cell and kept a charger with him at all times, so he wouldn't miss Praises call. But none came. His emails were all spam. He heard nothing.

And then the bombing.

As soon as Mitchel heard that it was at the National Temple his blood turned to ice. His mind raced. He *knew* his daughter. He *knew* she couldn't have been involved in anything like that. But then a new thought came to him, one that he'd never thought before, one that he'd never thought he *would* think. *Did he know Praise? Did he ever know her?* For the first time since his wife Tanisha's death, he cried. It was a wailing, painful cry, the kind of cry that comes when someone is ripped from a person's soul.

Mitchel didn't have to contact Fondlen. Fondlen called him later, the morning of the bombing.

"Mr. Johnson," he told him, sternly. "We've got to talk to your daughter. We're talking capital crime here."

"I know, Mr. Fondlen, Mitchel said. "I know."

It was all he could say.

The Dissenter

The house on Oakhill sat within a chainlink fenced yard of overgrown weeds and grass in the Gwynn Oak Park area of Baltimore, a lower middleclass area, once a highly sought -after location with a mixture of small bungalows and large family homes. The house itself was in reasonably descent shape, only recently abandoned after a family tragedy tore the young family who owned it apart. The neighbors knew that a young child had died. That's all they knew.

 The house was suggested by a neighbor who supported Jessie. After his outburst at the Temple on Passover, Jessie felt that it was best that they split into different areas as to not endanger the whole group from reprisal. Tom, Petra, Andrew and Jaime took up residence in the nearby suburb of Woodlawn, in an empty apartment provided by another of Jessie's admirers. The rent was paid until the end of the lease, and they were told they could stay there as long as they wished. Joodith, Justice, Bart, Simone, and Levi remained in the bungalow in Sandtown. Dimple, Jessie and Praise moved into the small Cape Cod on Oakhill Avenue. They bought prepaid cell phones and kept each other apprised of their daily situations. All agreed explicitly to use the phones only for that purpose, or, if need be, to warn the others of potential trouble. One person at each location was given the phone to hold for the others. Joodith had one phone; Andrew had one in Woodlawn. The other remained with Praise. She carried the phone everywhere she went in the house in the front pocket of her jeans, careful to leave it on vibrate, not wanting to alert anyone to their presence.

 The events at the temple disturbed her, though she tried not to show it. The table flipping, the shouting; it was all unnerving, and although she hesitated even thinking the word: violent. She'd known, talking with Jessie, that he disapproved of the market that sprang up at Passover every year, but she had no idea he was going to, in effect, tear it down. It seemed so out of character for the man she knew.

The One and True Son

When Praise was a child, particularly when she'd started school, she felt herself an outsider. She went to a predominately middleclass school, with predominately middleclass kids. Predominately middleclass *white* kids. And although they more or less treated her like everyone else, and she didn't have the type of teachers who would treat her differently, she felt like a toy truck in a doll shop. In first grade, there were no other black kids in her class. Praise wasn't exactly sure, looking back on it, but there might not have been any in her grade. There was no one with a nose like hers, no one who had their hair braided in tight rows, like her mother used to do to hers. Praise talked and played and had slumber parties with her classmates and indeed she had people that she would consider friends, even to this day. But in some ways, *important* ways, she felt on the outside. She wasn't just the cop's daughter. She was the *black* cop's daughter. And when she went to the slumber parties, didn't she feel a bit *overly accepted* by the parents? Didn't they fawn over how smart she was, how much they loved her hair, how poised and thoughtful she was? It didn't matter enough to her, then, to look too deeply. Those white parents were trying to be thoughtful, weren't they? Trying to make her feel welcome? They were. At least, Praise thought they were. But she had to ask herself: what was it that they had to accept? What was so different about her that they had to make a big deal about it?

At the police academy, she felt the same way. She *did* excel. There was no question that she completed each step in training at the highest level. But the level of surprise, obvious surprise, of some of her white colleagues and instructors grated on her. She was a cop's daughter. Why were they surprised?

She didn't feel different with Jessie. When she visited Dzon's camp and spoke with Dimple and others there, she felt, maybe for the first time in her life, that she belonged. The eyes of Dzon's followers, and later, Jessie's, never registered surprise that she had joined them. She was a cop. A black cop. And still they took her in with no reservations, no references to her past, no preconceived notions on her race or gender. Indeed, they were a mixed group with a leader of ambiguous racial features. Whether it was by design or accident the group had no dominant profile, no one defining complexion. Praise fit in.

And then the temple incident happened and for the first time, Praise felt walls forming. When they got back to the bungalow in Sandtown, the shock of what had occurred had worn off, and anger took its place.

"Why did we do that?" Praise barked once they entered through a boarded window. "That market has been there for years. Couldn't we have protested? Did we have to destroy it?"

The One and True Son

Jessie, who had said nothing the whole way back, looked at her strangely. He didn't appear angry anymore. In his eyes Praise saw something she hadn't seen before. It seemed a mix sadness and pity.

"My Father's house cannot be abused. It means nothing if it becomes a palace to the dollar. It ceases being of His mind."

"So, we smash it?" Praise shot back. "Is that of your father's mind?"

"It is," Jessie replied. He stood and went up the creaky stairs to one of the bedrooms.

The first wall went up at that moment. Praise was on one side, the rest of the twelve on the other.

The next morning, they discussed scattering the group. Everyone was on edge. Even Dimple. It was decided that Praise and Dimple would go to a big box store and buy the pre-paid phones. Joodith would make contact with friendly people in Baltimore and find places to go.

Jessie left early that morning. He woke Praise from her light, disturbed sleep.

"I have some things to do. Please tell the rest that I'll be back soon. Your plans are good. Have everyone go to the separate houses. I'll come back here when I'm finished."

"But Moreh," Praised asked through the fog of near sleep. "What do we do? What if something happens? How can we reach you?"

Jessie looked down on her. He kneeled near the blanket in which she'd wrapped herself. His eyes showed a tenderness she had not seen in a while.

"All will happen that will happen," he said softly. He smoothed her eyebrow with the tip of his finger. "Wait for me here. I 'll be back."

Jessie was gone for 12 days. When he returned to the Oakhill house, he said nothing about where he'd been and Praise hadn't asked. The troubled look had returned to his eyes. He hugged Praise and Dimple and quickly went upstairs. Dimple went up to talk to him but was sent back down.

"He says he needs to pray," she said, shrugging. "I think he's okay. Don't you?"

Praise said nothing. She went to the small living room and laid down on the blanket she'd spread there. She buried her head in the old pillow she used to sleep at night.

A couple of weeks later, the temple was bombed.

Praise found it difficult to speak to anyone when she saw the news on the group's laptop. Hot tears swam in her eyes and though Dimple tried to comfort her she pushed her away without speaking. When she saw the pictures the media was distributing, she couldn't breathe. The security photo could've been a lot of people. The work shirt, the jeans, the boots.

The One and True Son

Anyone could buy them. And many men can grow a heavy, thick beard. And Jessie was here that night.

Or was he?

The bombing had taken place early in the morning. Praise tried to think back. She'd been sleeping a lot lately, mostly from a lack of anything to do, or that's what she told herself. Had she gone to bed early and slept late? There was a good possibility she had. And Dimple slept like the dead. Could Jessie have gone to the temple and back and neither of them know it? Her police training told her he could.

What was he doing those 12 days he'd been away? Why didn't he speak when he got back? Why had the tenderness fled from his eyes?

She knew who she had to call.

Praise waited until the next day when Dimple had gone to the ShopRite on Gwynn Oak Avenue to do the shopping for the group. Praise watched from the porch as Dimple with her worn leather sandals strolled down the street like any twenty-first century hippy might, with a song seemingly playing in her head, a slight sway in her step that could almost be interpreted as dance moves. There was a time, not so long before, Praise would've instinctively smiled and felt her chest warm watching the woman she'd known for a such short time but gotten to know as a sister. That was before. Praise pulled the cell phone from her pocket and headed in the other direction. As was often the case in Baltimore streets, Oakhill Avenue suddenly became California Boulevard at the next intersection. She passed a dozen Cape Cod style houses, nearly identical to the one Jessie, Dimple and she were holed up in, though the colors were wildly different from house to house with each homeowner trying to separate themselves from the cookie cutter monotony of the postwar housing. There were no rich people in this neighborhood and the cars, some old and worn, some new, polished and shiny, lined every inch of curb. The yards were mown, the porches free of clutter. Praise imagined that she may have liked to live in a neighborhood like this one day. The thought saddened her.

At the end of California Boulevard, the street narrowed, and one side of the road became thick woods lined with poison ivy that came right up to the gravel shoulder. This part of the road looked more like a service road for garbage trucks than an actual thoroughfare. She wondered if anyone would notice her walking, but when she stopped and looked around, she saw no one. The shade from the trees was cool and damp. The fresh air was a welcome change for Praise as she felt she'd breathed nothing but stagnant air since arriving in Baltimore. At the curve in the road, she found what she was looking for.

The One and True Son

The trees on her right cleared to the meticulously groomed grass of a public golf course. Praise saw the colorful polo shirts of golfers far off in the distance, but no one was near her or approaching at the closest hole. She easily scaled the rickety chain-link fence that bordered the course and ran behind a cinderblock maintenance shed. The greenery easily shielded her from anyone who might approach, but she continued peering around the corner while she dug the cell phone from her pocket. Praise entered the number and took a breath. She pushed "Call".

The phone call went through and with every ring Praise almost hoped he wouldn't answer. After six rings, he did.

"Hello?"

"Daddy?" Praise said. To her ear she sounded like a little girl. For the first time in her adult life, she felt like one. She was scared.

"Praise! Honey, where are you?" Her father shouted.

Praise burst out crying. "I can't tell you, Daddy. I'm not in California. I'm not near you. I ..."

"Baby, listen, "Mitchel interrupted. "The FBI has been here. Tell me you didn't have anything to do with that bombing."

Praise sniffed. "Of course I didn't, Dad."

"Of course you didn't?" Mitchel said, his voice straining in the phone. "You take off to God knows where? The FBI is coming to *my* house? What am I supposed to believe? Where the fuck are you?"

Praise stopped crying. "I've got to go..."

"Wait, wait, wait," Mitchel said. "I'm sorry, baby. Wait. I'm sorry. This is all so confusing to me. You called me. You need help. I'm your dad. I'm going to help. I'll always help. Please, please, let me."

Praise took a breath. "I don't know if you can."

Mitchel used his training. Never, in his entire life, did he think he'd be using it with his own daughter. He calmed himself. He'd been a thinking cop for over 30 years.

"You said you had nothing to do with the bombing. That means you knew *nothing* about it. None of the planning. Nothing. Is that right?"

"It's true, Dad. I swear," Praise answered.

"What about the people you're with?"

"I'm pretty sure they didn't know anything either. We were all surprised. They're all pretty honest people."

"What about this Jessie character?"

Praise didn't say anything. She could hear her father sigh.

"You're not sure, are you?" he said.

"Dad, I *don't know.*" She started crying again. "He was gone for a few days when it happened. He won't talk about it. I…just…"

Mitchel used the most soothing voice he could muster. He'd used it to talk people out of putting pistols in their mouths, out of jumping off bridges, out of struggling with officers. "Baby, I have a number for you to call. This man is FBI. He kind of creeps me out, but he's thinking you're in a tough position and probably innocent. You've got to call, baby. You've got to tell your…"

The call went dead.

She looked at the phone. Zero bars.

She couldn't get over the feeling she'd talked too long. She snuck out from behind the shed, hopped the fence and headed back to the house.

Praise went right to the unused front bedroom and locked the door behind her. She wasn't sure that she could face anyone. Jessie, Dimple, anyone. Shame seeped into her thinking, although she wasn't sure which situation had her more ashamed: possibly being an accomplice to a terrorist bombing, or using the cell phone, the phone she'd been trusted with, to make a call in her own interest, violating the trust of the people with who she'd invested so much. She curled into a ball on the floor and laid there the rest of the night.

When Praise emerged from the room, early, at maybe 6am, she was alone. She knew that both Jessie and Dimple had been in the house the previous night. She heard them talking in soft voices, for quite some time. Dimple knew how stressed Praise was with the whole situation. Praise guessed that her friend had filled the moreh in on her mental state, probably telling Jessie that it was just nerves, that Praise was strong and would gather herself together once she had a chance to rest. Praise knew this because she knew Dimple. She could almost hear her saying it. Dimple was nothing if not positive.

The walls of the tiny house were pressing in on Praise. She grabbed some grapes from the small ice chest they had in the tiny kitchenette at the back of the house, threw them in a plastic bag and went outside. She stood outside the rotted cellar door that led to the back yard and took in a big breath. If Dimple had told Jessie she just needed some rest to feel better, Praise thought she might actually be right. She did feel better. Maybe it was because it was a bright sunny day with a few cottony clouds. It was warm, but not hot. Comfortable. Not Humid. She considered going behind the old tin shed, empty now, that used to house yard equipment, and climb the fence and go down the back road. Instead, she passed the side of the house and walked through the rusty gate in front to the bumpy old

The One and True Son

sidewalk on Oakhill Avenue. If she remembered right, there was a school with a playground. She wanted to sit where kids play. That would feel good, she told herself. She patted the phone in her pocket, to make sure she had it and headed in the direction of the school.

Praise walked to corner of Oakhill and Norwood Avenues. She turned left. Her mind was lost in the hedges that lined the yard of the house she was passing. She didn't notice the plain gray Ford pull next to the curb. She jumped when she saw the short, bald man, with the Ray-Bans and the perfect suit, get out and head toward her. He smiled. His teeth, to her, looked like razor blades.

"I'm not running," she told the man, something she'd just decided. She backed up against the bushes.

"I didn't think you would," the man said. "I know your father. Would you please step into the car with me. I think we can talk."

The Investigator

Phu Trang needed a vacation. He hadn't taken one in…he couldn't remember when. And he wasn't the only person who thought so. His supervisor, Scott Stevens, a humorless and frighteningly tall man in his early 60s, suggested one, as he informed him that he was being reassigned off the Temple Bombing case. It wasn't the first time for Phu to have either situation, reassignment or the suggestion to "take some time off," but it was the first time that the two events happened simultaneously. Reassignment was no big deal. Phu had no love of the spotlight. The case only interested him because there were things happening in the bureau that made him uneasy. Usually, his need to know the facts, wherever they may lead, took over and he would fight to stay on the case. But something smelled on this one. And whatever it was, it was rotten. It was the time off that was the tough part.

And so, it was somewhat surprising, when Phu, who'd been lounging on his beat-up sofa, his laptop opened to a travel site with stunning photos of Costa Rica, the beaches, the food, the jungle, answered his apartment door, thinking it must be the cleaning lady, and saw that it was someone from the bureau. And it wasn't just anyone. It was the bald guy from the press conference, the one who came into his office after the bombing.

"Phu Trang." the man said offering his doughy hand across Phu's threshold. "Richard Fondlen. Can I come in?"

Phu stepped back and allowed Fondlen to pass. The man was wearing nearly the identical suit to the one he wore in Phu's office, though, for some reason, Pho knew it wasn't the same one. *He probably has a closet full of nearly identical suits.* He carried a leather satchel that had seen better days.

"Do you mind if I have a seat," Fondlen said, gesturing toward the sofa.

"Make yourself at home," Phu said, his voice somewhat flat.

The One and True Son

Fondlen looked at the laptop that Phu had set on the coffee table in front of the sofa.

"Ah, Costa Rica," he said. His teeth emerged in a grin. His dark eyes showed no emotion. "Beautiful. Great beaches. Beautiful women. I haven't been there in a while, but whenever I go, I love it."

"I'm thinking of going there," Phu said while reaching over and closing the laptop. "I've never been there. Never had the time. I do now."

"Yes, I heard about that. That's why I'm here. Please sit."

Phu did as instructed. He sat in the beat-up easy chair that matched the sofa.

Fondlen placed the satchel on the table, opened it and took out a manila folder.

"I'm here to ask you to forgo your vacation for a bit. I was the one who arranged your time off, but I need you to work with me, how do I put it, off the books."

Phu's brow wrinkled. "On a case? You want me to work on a case, but the bureau won't know about it? Is that right?"

Fondlen nodded. "That's right. But *I* will know about it. And that's enough."

Phu sniffed. "I know this might sound, uh, petty, but what about my vacation time? I've worked hard for that."

The teeth came out again. "Indeed, you have. You have 143 days of accrued leave time. I'm asking that you sacrifice these coming weeks in the name of national security. And after this case is brought to its conclusion, I promise you that you will be well compensated for your service."

Phu took a deep breath. He didn't like this guy. He didn't like him from the moment he'd walked into his office. But there was something up here. Something not many people knew. He shook his head. "Why me? I mean, you've got a whole agency at your disposal. They're all professionals. They're all good. You could have an entire team of the best law enforcement in the country."

"That's true, Phu." Fondlen tilted his head and looked Phu with those flat, blank eyes. "Can I call you Phu? It makes things so much more cohesive."

Phu nodded. He felt chilled.

"And I do have a team. Teams really. But they are highly specialized, and they rarely interact. But you will work with me and me only. You see, I know a lot about you. I know, for example, that you dropped out of Divinity College. I read your paper. It was very good, much better than you were given credit for, or, more accurately, *not* given credit for."

The One and True Son

For Phu, the oxygen sucked from room. "How did you get that paper? *I didn't keep copy of it.*"

Fondlen's mouth went flat. "I told you. I have teams. You know you shook up that professor, Ms…" Fondlen looked up to the left. "Logue, yes, Logue. She only lasted two more years at the university. After that, it's rumored that she'd lost her faith. She is no longer a morah. That much is certain."

Phu was speechless.

"Don't look like that," Fondlen said, holding up his pale hand. "You couldn't have been the only factor in her change. The paper was probably just a piece of the puzzle she was putting together for herself."

Phu remained silent so Fondlen spoke. "But the paper told me something important about you. Something crucial, really. Any idea what it is?"

Phu shook his head.

"It told me that you seek the truth. That the truth is important to you. It's what you live for, really. Am I right?"

Phu didn't move.

"I'm right," Fondlen said, smiling that lethal grin. "I know I am. And so, Phu Trang, I want you working right next to me. I want you to see the truth, with me, right by my side."

Phu needed to step outside for a moment. He felt like he did when he drank too much beer, which had been happening more often lately. He didn't like this guy. Did he work for the bureau? Did he work somewhere else, some place darker? One thing was sure. The guy had taken up residency in his head. Phu didn't like anyone running around in there. But Fondlen had him. The stranger had known it when he came to the door. *How the fuck did he get that essay?*

When Phu returned to his living room, Fondlen had had the contents of the manila folder organized on the coffee table. There were thirteen photographs, 8x10s, color, laid in what Phu had guessed was order of importance, from left to right, in three rows, top to bottom. From the way the photographs faced, Phu assumed that Fondlen wanted him on the sofa, next to him. He obliged.

"So who are these people?" Phu asked dryly

"You really have taken time off," Fondlen responded. "You haven't even turned on the TV in the past day or so, have you?"

Phu looked closely at the pictures. He shook his head. He picked up the first photo on the top left. It showed a large man in work clothes, course curly hair, and a thick beard.

"This must be the guy you like for the temple bombing," he said, looking hard at the photo. "He looks like the surveillance photo." He shrugged. "I guess. With that mask on all you've got is a guilty looking beard."

Fondlen chuckled. "His name is Jessie Carpentero. You must've heard of him. He's all over the internet."

"I haven't had much time to surf the net," Phu said. "That is, until recently. What is he? Some kind of cult leader?"

"I wish it were that simple," Fondlen answered. "It's a little more complicated than that. When I leave, I suggest you do some *surfing*."

Phu waved the photo of Jessie Carpentero over the others on the table. "These are his minions?"

"They are his followers yes," Fondlen answered. "They come from various backgrounds. Dock workers, teachers, drifters, tax accountants." He picked up the photo of a woman, probably a millennial, black, serious looking. "This one was LAPD."

"You're kidding," Phu said. He put down the photo of Jessie and took the other from Fondlen. He looked closely. Even though she was in civies, she looked like a cop. Her stride was determined, sure.

"I took that a few days ago," Fondlen said.

"You saw her?" Phu almost shouted. "How did you find her?"

"We put a tap on her father's phone. He's also a former cop. We knew she'd call eventually. She used a burner phone, but we still got the pings off the cell towers, and the number."

"Did you pick her up?" Phu looked at Fondlen who was grinning slightly. "You were pretty close to get this picture."

"Oh, we talked," Fondlen said, as if he'd been talking about a girl he was thinking of dating. "She's an impressive figure. Strong minded."

Phu couldn't believe what he was hearing. "Did you at least get the phone? You could've gotten the rest of them if you'd checked her calls."

Fondlen shook his head. "She wasn't carrying it. I could see that her pockets were flat. Her jeans were tight enough that she couldn't have been hiding it there. She was wearing sandals, so no socks."

"Did you go door to door? The rest of them must've been close by."

"No," Fondlen said, his eyebrows furrowed. "No. As I said. We talked. It was …enlightening, really."

"I'm confused," Phu sputtered. "You like these people for a terrorist attack on the National Temple. You find one of them. And you have a little chat?"

"Don't worry, Phu," Fondlen adjusted himself on the sofa. "I know what I'm doing. People do things for a *reason*. I like to know what those reasons are. It makes everything stronger. As I said, this group is all over the internet. That is *not* hyperbole. And the content of those videos, those posts, makes this issue more sensitive than it first may appear. I suggest you do some research on YouTube. It's quite informative. But, as you do that, I suggest you look at the views that the videos have accumulated. The numbers are in the *billions*. That's billions with a B."

Phu really wanted to throw Fondlen out. He had a feeling that Fondlen *knew* that. When this creepy man called him "Phu," his skin crawled. But this thing was bigger than that. Phu knew it. Fondlen knew it too.

The Dissenter

Praise stared at the two phones. She'd placed them on the living room floor and sat next to them with her legs crossed. When the man in the Ray-Bans let her out of his car, she walked in the opposite direction of the house, to the playground she'd intended to go to in the first place. She sat on a yellow, scratched and dirty roundabout that squawked from rust when she put her weight on it. It was an off day for kids and the school was closed. There were no kids around. She sat there for at least a half an hour, until she was reasonably sure the odd man had gone.

She found her phone right where she'd stashed it when the man approached her, pinched in the branches of the prickly hedge behind her. The phone was still on. She tried to remember if the pings on a cell tower still registered if the phone was on but not transmitting. She freed the phone from the bush and turned it off, just in case. She nearly sprinted back to the house on Oakhill.

Once safely inside, she placed the phones on the floor and sat down. *How could I have been so stupid?* She should have known they'd have her father's phone tapped. All they had to do was look for the burner's number to ping on a couple of cell towers so they could triangulate her approximate location.

The creepy guy had flashed FBI creds at her, something she'd never really seen up close. Even so, they didn't look right to her, like something was missing. He'd caught her by surprise, so she didn't have time to get set, to think on her feet. She couldn't really give them a good look. He said he *knew* her father. Her father had said that the FBI had been to the house. And didn't he say the guy, creeped him out? This had to be the guy her father was talking about. There was no better way to describe him. And he must be legit too. Her father would never let a phony FBI agent slide.

She replayed in her head the events of the last hour. The inside of the car had been immaculate, maybe a rental. The dash, adorned with gray faux leather, and enough extraneous instrumentation to fool uninitiated drivers into thinking they were driving a luxury car. It carried no communications gear that she could see. If it was an FBI vehicle it would certainly have shown signs of wear from repeated use, scuffs in the carpet, slashes from shoes on the door, no matter how new it was. The man had held the car door open for her, the front passenger door, let her get seated, and went around the front of the car to let himself in the driver's side. Either he was completely incompetent and didn't see the risks he was taking by putting her in the front seat of a running car or he not only didn't think of her as a suspect, but he saw no threat from her whatsoever. He placed the car in drive and drove to a nearby side street where he found a large maple tree that threw its shadow over most of the road next to it. He parked in the shade. The air conditioner pushed new car smell throughout the car.

The man looked at her through his dark shades. "I know what you're thinking," he said after a moment. "You're thinking, this guy lied to me already."

Of all the things the man could say, this threw her the most. It was *exactly* what she'd been thinking. She tried *not* to react. She wasn't sure she'd succeeded. She'd been thinking he'd lied when he said he knew her father. Praise had talked to her father. She knew they'd met. She knew that they had *just* met. But this man implied they were more than just one-time acquaintances.

The man had smiled. His teeth looked like a threat in themselves. "It is my business to know people," the man explained. "You see, I *know* people. I know them instinctually. It's something I was born with. When I saw your father, when he opened the door and allowed me into his living room, allowed me to see the photos around the room, of you, of your mother, I *knew* he was a good man, a family man, a man who'd worked hard all his life. When he'd scrutinized my ID and why I was looking for you, I knew that he was a good cop. He was steady. He thought things through. When I said I *knew* your father, that's what I meant. I hope this will clear up any hint of dishonesty."

Praise wasn't sure at all that it did. She said nothing. She could feel the man probing her with his eyes, even with the sunglasses. His eyes were not only unreadable. They were veiled, hidden from her appraisal.

"Would you like me to tell you what I see with you?" the man asked, his teeth still exposed. "I know you would. You're curious by nature. Much more than your father, I would say. I don't mean that as a critique of the man. It's just that he is much more measured in his curiosity, more cautious. He sees boundaries. He dislikes them, but he sees them. He draws on his experience, and he remains on the safe side, if he can." The man adjusted himself in the driver's seat. He looked out the windshield to the street in front of them. "You're not like that, are you?"

She saw no need to respond. It was obvious from her situation that she was not like her father in that way. There was no great revelation there.

"You are a doer, like your father," the man continued. "You don't have much use for idle time. But, you are much bolder than he is. You chose to be a cop, like your father, but not for the same reasons. You joined for altruistic reasons. Your father became a cop to be on the inside, to be included."

"He told you that?"

The man shook his head. "He didn't need to. You don't need to dive too deep into history books, to understand why a black man, a man like your father, of his age group, to understand his need to have a voice somewhere near power. I understand that myself, and I haven't had nearly the obstacles of any black man has had to get close to it."

"So what about me? This seems to be a lecture on racial inequality and the connection to my father."

"Oh, I'm talking about you. You are similar, but different. You're of a generation that sees oppression everywhere. It may be personal, and it is, like racial oppression, but it's also an overall oppression. For you, it's about *all* people. It's the fact that some people have no place to live, that people are hungry, that some have so much, and others have nothing. This is something you can't tolerate."

Praise's head was swimming. Here she thought she was going to brought in for questioning for a very serious incident that she is connected to. But the car hasn't moved, and she is listening to her own profile.

"What are you? Some kind FBI Profiler?"

The man pursed his lips. He shook his head. He took off his sunglasses and aimed his eyes at hers. "No, I'm just an observer. I'm rather good at it, don't you think?"

Praise immediately looked down.

"I observe many things," the man continued. "I observe many people. And when I look at you, I don't see a bomber. I still see the police officer who joined the LAPD for all the right reasons. And, for that matter, a person who quit, again, for all the right reasons. I don't believe, for a moment that you were involved with any bombing."

Praise put her hand on the door handle. The vibration of a sudden click of the door lock told her she wasn't going anywhere yet.

"So, I'm not free to go?" Praise looked at the man. The sunglasses, again, covered his eyes. "You said I was innocent."

"That's not quite what I said," the man said raising a delicate index finger at her. "I said that I don't believe you were part of the *bombing*. I didn't say you didn't have anything to do with it after the fact." The man smiled again.

Praise had to look away.

"Obviously, you know where Jessie Carpentero is, if not right this moment, where he's been hiding with his group. There are serious consequences for this knowledge, of which I'm sure you're aware."

Praise sighed. "So why aren't we driving? You seem to have evidence that I'm a co-conspirator after the fact. Why are we sitting here? We could easily have this conversation downtown. I've never seen it, but I'm sure the FBI has a field office in Baltimore."

"That's true," the man said. "There are offices. They cover Maryland and Delaware as a matter of fact. But I've never cared for offices much in my work. They're much too confining. And so impersonal. In my line of work, I much prefer the outdoors for conversation, for…negotiation."

"Negotiation?" Praise said, her eyes narrowed.

"Yes, negotiation." the man said. "It's the American way, isn't it? Isn't that what we, as a country, do before every important crisis in front of us? We negotiate. We talk. We shake hands and talk nice. We get our cards on the table. We make sure that we've covered all the bases before we go in and obliterate our adversary. If we can salvage some friendships, we may have something positive to look forward to after the ultimate conflict. Because…" the man looked at Praise through his shades for a moment, "when we go in with guns drawn, we tend to leave little behind when we're finished."

"Tell that to the Native Americans," Praise sniffed.

That smile returned to the man's face.

"Oh, they know it all too well. We know that. But they had frightfully little to negotiate with. We had all the gunpowder. But that's ancient history. I truly believe you and I have something to talk about."

Praise chuckled. "What could we possibly have to talk about?"

The man put a very delicate hand to his chin and rubbed his smooth skin there.

"As I said, I read people. There was something I've read about you that I haven't mentioned yet."

Praise grinned her own grin. "You should get a TV show like John Edward. People love psychics."

"Oh, I hate television. The thought of being on TV with that worthless medium nauseates me. Do you want to hear what I think?"

Praise made a sweeping gesture telling him to proceed.

"I believe this whole God thing isn't for you," he said, this time with no hint of a smile. "I think you joined Jessie's merry band because you thought he could be a force for change in the world. Real change, not a ticket to some Disneyland in the clouds, something we can never know we'll get into until we die. You believe in God. You do. But do you believe that you've been eating and sleeping with him in the same house? I don't think you do."

Praise said nothing.

"And I think you understand that all this heaven talk is actually *hurting* the cause you truly believe in. Where is the food for the hungry that you thought would be trucked into the needy? Where are the shelters you thought would be built?

Where are the open pockets of the rich that you thought Jessie could pry open with a word from his mouth? None of that has happened. I know it. And so do you."

Praise ran her hand back and forth of the door armrest.

"So, you want me to be a snitch," she said finally.

The man laughed, a bark really that startled Praise.

"If you like the term, although I think it sounds a little like TV cop lingo to me. I prefer informant, which is a far more accurate. I want you to tell me where *he* is. I couldn't care less about the other members of your group. It can be worked out that none of you will go down with him. It is Jessie Carpentero I'm interested in. What I'm offering may be able to get you what you want. What you've always wanted."

"And what is that?" Praise asked.

"Haven't I made that clear?" the man answered. "I've told you. I can read you. You can help the poor."

"How does informing on my friend help the poor?"

The man placed his hand on her knee. There was nothing sexually suggestive about the gesture. His soft hand seemed to soak through her. It was as though he was offering her the only comfort he could. He was telling her *you already know the answer to that.* Jessie was hurting the cause. He was forgetting it. His cause and hers had diverged somehow and she wasn't sure what was happening. Had Jessie blown up the temple? She wasn't sure. And the fact that she wasn't shook her entire being.

"So, I tell you where he is," she said. "What happens then?"

The One and True Son

The man looked out the windshield again. The heat of the day was bending and stretching the air just over the hood of the car.

"You should know there's a substantial reward for information that leads to his capture. It hasn't been publicized. Not yet. I was hoping I could get your cooperation before news of it was released."

It was Praise's turn to laugh. "Money? You think I'd give him up for money? I thought you said you could read me."

"I said substantial, and I meant substantial. I'm talking six figures. Even an idealist knows, that in this world, that kind of money can relieve quite a bit of suffering. Isn't that what you want? To relieve the suffering of the poor? It can even be the start of something bigger. Many organizations for the poor have started with less than is being offered."

"I don't want money," Praise said quietly.

"Well, it comes with the cooperation so you can do any damned thing you want with it, "the man said. "I'd like to know how you think you're going to help people without it. Are you just going to join them in their poverty? That'll be useful. I'm sure they'd love the extra mouth to feed."

Praise went still.

The man reached into his jacket and pulled out a cell phone. For a moment, Praise thought he had somehow gotten hers from the hedge, but as she looked closer, she saw subtle differences in the one he was holding and the one she'd ditched.

"Go back to where you're stayng" he said. "Think about what I told you. I will wait a few days. When you feel he is vulnerable, use this phone. It will tell us exactly where you are. All you have to do is turn it on. You don't need to do anything else. My team will be in the area."

He handed the phone out for Praise. She took it.

"If I don't get a signal in say, a week, I'll assume you couldn't bring yourself to help me." He paused and looked her in the eyes through the dark shades. "I will use other methods. I can't promise they'll be pleasant. For you or your friends."

He'd let her out of the car.

Praise picked up the two phones from the floor and stood. She looked at them both closely. The one in her right hand was the phone she'd purchased in the big box store. She put in her pocket. She crossed the neglected living room, the room someone fixed up only to leave it when tragedy struck. She'd noticed a loose piece of molding near the entrance to the kitchenette. She gave the white board a wiggle and pulled it away from the drywall. Praise bent down and slipped the phone behind the molding and replaced it. No one would be able to tell it was there.

The Denier

Petra Banik never saw herself running her life around any man, with the possible exception of her father. Yet she waited in an unfurnished apartment, the only woman in a group of four believers, waiting for word from the man who made all the decisions; not a move was considered until he said so. And she wouldn't be moving today. She would wait with Tom, Andrew and Jaime. The Twelve would be getting together this evening, here, in this whitewashed, silent except for the hum of the fridge and occasional cracks from sore backs and knees, apartment in Woodlawn, Maryland. She'd gotten the call early, 5:58am by the clock on the phone. It was Jessie. His message was terse: "We'll be meeting, all of us, at 8 o'clock tonight. There. All of us." Click.

Petra sat on the kitchen floor running her finger through the ridges of the faux hardwood floor. The apartment complex was called the Gardens at Woodlawn. The closest thing to a garden in the entire area was the grubby green carpet in the living room. She'd taken off her work boots, something she only did for bathing. She took off her socks and stuffed them in the boots. She wanted to feel the coolness of the floor on her calloused soles. It was something she imagined poets do. Petra had always admired poets. She even understood what they were talking about sometimes. She'd never tell anyone this, afraid that they might laugh. She wanted to *feel* the cool on her feet.

Petra was a world away from Hephzibah.

* * *

Hephzibah, West Virginia was a town a railroad track for a spine, and very little meat. Petra was born in 1967 in her parents living room, the closest hospital being in Bridgeport nearly six miles away. Her father's old Chrysler had a bad starter on the morning of her arrival and no matter how

The One and True Son

hard he bashed it with a tire iron it wouldn't turn over. She was the last of six children and the only girl.

Located on Shinnston Pike, next to the West Fork River, Hephzibah had a scattering of houses, a small bar rigged to look like a log cabin and a post office. Petra's father, Stanislaus, mostly known as Stan, used to say that if you farted in your car with the windows down when you'd entered town, the smell wouldn't be gone before you knew you'd left it.

In her toddler years, Petra had been close to her daddy. He'd pick her up when he came home from the mine all showered and freshly cleared of coal dust and throw her as high up as he could. He really got his shoulders into it, those strong and narrow shoulders. He'd pitch her like a fresh melon and catch her on the way down, just before she'd meet the earth and possible calamity. She'd stopped seeing him as often when there was a cutback in hours at the mine and they changed his shift to graveyard. She was still small, maybe in kindergarten, when that happened. As the years passed, she'd see him after his shift. He looked drained. The fresh shower smell was replaced by something more medicinal, more like liquid despair.

And Hephzibah hadn't changed. There were still no schools, no shops. Just old warehouses, trailers and houses, mostly sun bleached white and gray.

As a child, Petra was as agile as her brothers. She played army, played baseball, climbed trees and got into general mischief with them as often as she could get away with. Her mother, Magdalena, a first-generation Slovak like Petra's father, wore long skirts and high-necked wool sweaters regardless of the season or the outside temperature.

Even as a fairly young woman, Petra's mother wore her brown hair twisted atop her head in a matronly bun. Her face was reminiscent of an English bulldog, a look she passed down to her daughter, though in a softened, less canid, presentation. It was Magdalena who wanted one more baby, after, repeatedly, and at her insistence "trying for a girl" and being disappointed five times prior.

Through infancy and toddlerhood, Petra's mother doted on and cuddled her only girl, dressing her in mail order dresses and frilly socks, which, even those early years would be pitched off in favor of nakedness, bare feet and dirt. Eventually, Magdalena stopped ordering the dresses in favor of strong dungarees and t-shirts. The cuddling ended there as well.

Petra and her brothers were closer than most siblings in Hephzibah. Her eldest brother, Lukas, 11 years older than Petra, usually led the way on their adventures on the treeless banks of the West Fork River. The runoff from the coal mines in the county dyed the water to a murky rust color; as much as the children wanted to splash in the waters, they limited forays to the retrieval of an overthrown football or the pursuit of the occasional intrepid frog.

For school, all the Balik children attended a Southern Yahwehian school, a kindergarten through 12 school in Clarksburg, past Bridgeport on Route 50. As there were multiple Baliks in different grades on the bus, young Petra always had protection from potential bullies, so she spent most of the trek to and from sleeping or reading comic books. The school uniform required the girls wear skirts of s scratchy navy-blue material, below the knee, and long sleeve white blouses, while the boys wore long trousers, of the same irritating fabric, white, starched and collared shirts and a matching tie. Petra and Magdalena locked horns daily over the child's wish to wear pants and ties like her brothers, fights that grew nearly to the level of violence on both sides.

"You ain't wearing none of that to school," her mother would say with just as much vehemence as she had the day before and the day before that. "You don't even own no school pants, so just stop it."

"Trevor got some old ones he growed out of," was the daily reply. "I tried 'em on."

"They ain't gonna even let you on the bus dressed so ridiculous. And if you do make it to school, they ain't gonna let you in the door."

"I hate wearing skirts," the child would say, sometimes throwing the skirt in the direction of her mother, sometimes in a corner where it was hard to dig it out. "They make my butt cold."

The end of the argument always ended the same.

"Child, it's time you come to reality," the mother would say. "You're a *girl*! It's time you started acting as such."

Petra never won that argument and after a time, dropped it.

Petra didn't seem to click with anyone at school and spent most of her lunch times chewing on mushy butter and jelly sandwiches and sloshing down warm milk. She'd read comic books. Not Bugs Bunny or Archie or anything like that, but superheroes like Batman and Green Lantern, comics that her older brothers left as they moved onto other things. It was her one escape from the isolation that hung around her whenever she couldn't be with her brothers. She liked characters like Bruce Wayne and Guy Gardner. Their parents were gone from their lives, Bruce's gunned down when he was little and Guy's more absent than physically removed. And the two men flourished in anonymity. They were powerful. They covered who they really were and kicked ass all around them. That's what Petra wanted for herself. To kick ass. She read and reread every issue she could get hands on. She read them for years until the paper became soft to the touch, the folds in the center tearing from wear.

The One and True Son

Petra's father, who had smiled at her when she was little and would ruffle her perpetually knotted brown hair, seemed to fade into the background of her life as she grew older. Her mother, always at the door when Petra headed outside, usually had a critique of some nature: *Your face is a mess, child. Those pants will slide down that flat butt of yours. We won't ever be able to marry you out of here.*

As the years ticked off, the brothers whom she'd counted on for support and companionship started moving up and growing out of their lives in Hephzibah. Lukas joined the army the day after high school graduation. He'd been telling everyone who'd listen and some who didn't want to, for years, that he was getting as far from West Virginia as he could as soon as the ink was dry on his diploma. Abram, the next oldest, didn't wait for graduation. He got an apprenticeship in the same coal mine where her father worked. Once he became a full-fledged miner, he packed his beat-up Aerostar and took off to Pennsylvania where mining paid better.

Moab was next in line, or Moe as everybody called him. Moe loved machines. Before he could walk, he was taking his things apart. The mobile of fat little airplanes that twirled around over his crib, powered by two AA batteries, was in pieces within days of its installation. No one at the time was sure how he got into the battery compartment which required a flat headed screwdriver, or whether the other pieces which were lined up on his fitted sheet were placed there by intention or accident. Regardless, the parts were placed perfectly in line.

As Moe grew, the disassembly and reassembly of nearly everything he owned continued, starting with Tonka trucks, moving to bicycles, minibikes and finally, cars. When he was sixteen, he bought a worn out 1964 MG B, a two-seater with cracked leather seats and more rust than paint. Moe stripped it down to the chassis, scattering parts throughout the front yard and in every cabinet and shelf he could without getting yelled at. He put the smaller parts in baby food jars that took up nearly every square inch of flat surface in the room he once shared with Lukas and Abram. The jars took up the majority of space in the medicine chest in the bathroom. The small car occupied every moment of his time that wasn't already taken up by school. In two months, he had the body reattached to the chassis, Bondoed and primed to a rash of gray.

When Petra thought of him in later years, she'd picture his lanky body, his top half in a sleeveless t-shirt stuck to him by sweat and grease, his loose pants growing spots of perspiration, his straight blond hair dangling in his eyes. She could almost hear the clicks of a ratchet wrench as he tightened things down.

The One and True Son

"Pet! C'mere. I need ya!" Moe shouted to her hot one day in May. He'd been working in the front yard. Petra was watching Gilligan's Island, the one where a telephone cable had washed up on the beach of the lagoon. She'd no doubt seen at least 50 times before. But it was after school in Hephzibah. That's what she and her brothers did when they got home. They did their stuff. Moe's stuff was the MG. Petra's stuff was Gilligan.

Petra went outside, more than curious. She'd been warned time and again to stay away from his coveted car; he once hollered at her for *just looking* into the engine compartment.

She'd let the screen door slam shut. "What do you want?"

"Hold up your hand."

"What for?"

"Just hold up your hand. I wanna see somethin'."

Petra put up her hand.

"Thought so," Moe said.

"What?"

"You got the perfect hands. I need your help."

Petra smiled. "Mine?"

"Yes, yours."

"What do I get for it?"

"So you gotta get something to help me?"

Petra smiled even bigger. She couldn't tell if it was because she was flattered that Moe had asked for *her* help or if she was just enjoying torturing her older brother. Really, it was both.

"Okay," he relented. "You get the first ride when she's running."

"Teach me."

"What?" Moe's eyes narrowed.

"Teach me how to fix the car," Petra said. "And the first ride."

Moe took a deep breath. "All right. But why?"

"Just want to know, I guess," Petra said with a shrug. "And it's somethin' to do."

Moe nodded. He understood. She could tell.

"So, what to do you want me to do?"

"I dropped this little pin." He said and held up a retractable tool with a hinge at its wider end. It was like a pen you could pull out. "This here is a magnet probe. I tried to get it, but my hand is too thick. You got skinny fingers, but they're long and tapered. You can reach down there with this thing to get the pin." He telescoped the tool out and then pushed it back in. He put the tool in her shirt pocket.

The One and True Son

He leaned into the engine compartment of the car. "But first things first. Get your head down here. This here is the carburetor. This car got two of 'em…"

Four months later Moe was traveling on Meadowbrook Road with his best friend Steve, who'd just gotten his license. They had a cool 12 pack of Coors Light in the back seat of Steve's mother's old wagon when Steve misjudged the curve at Jack Run Road, crossed the double yellow line and ran head on into the Volvo cab of an 18-wheeler coming from Bridgeport. The police said they barely had time to gasp before their lives ended. There was no pain involved, they said.

That, of course, couldn't have been further from the truth. The pain never left the remaining Baliks. They'd sold the almost completed MG B for scrap. The house became a mausoleum where little was spoken, and eyes rarely met. Petra could've gone to school in a lion tamer outfit after that and her mother wouldn't have batted an eye. Her father, who'd been working on a case of beer every couple of days for the previous decade enhanced his intake with a fifth of knock off bourbon. He rarely spoke when he left for the mine in the morning and was usually half pickled by the time he got back.

By Petra's senior year, the house that for most of her life seemed perpetually crowded felt cavernous and empty. Petra still voraciously read all things superhero. She devoured *Daredevil* and *Deadpool* and the like. She especially identified with the early Deadpool character; he struggled with his self-worth, self-doubt and emotional scars.

She still ate her lunch in furthest corner of the cafeteria she could manage, clutching her pulpy magazines. More often than not, she'd forgo the eating part of lunch, that is if she'd bothered to bring anything. Most of her classmates got the hint that she wasn't really open to company. She usually had a table to herself.

It was a rainy day in April when someone other than a brother sat to join her for lunch. The girl had dark brunette hair tied in a low ponytail. Her uniform blouse was slightly wrinkled. The girl unpacked her lunch and looked up at Petra who used all her willpower to pretend she wasn't there. The girl had smallish green eyes, set close together. There was a plain prettiness about her. Something kind of girly. Her shoulders slumped slightly. Petra hadn't seen the girl in school before and as she'd been going to the school since kindergarten, she thought she knew every face.

The girl picked up her white bread sandwich and took a bite. "You like those, I guess," she said dryly.

Petra didn't answer. She peered over the comic book, just briefly, then turned her eyes back down to the magazine.

The One and True Son

"Comics. You like 'em, huh?" The girl tried again. When Petra didn't respond she kept talking. "I read 'em once in a while. I like Watchman. My daddy don't like me reading them. Says they evil or something. Who watches the Watchman, you know? That's a good point. Who's watchin' the people who are supposed to be watchin' over us. I got all eleven of 'em. Not the book one they got now in the stores, you know, the one with all of the separate books into one book. I like to read 'em one at a time, you know, like, each one's a story in a story that goes to a bigger story. I like that."

"I haven't read it," Petra said through the latest Deadpool saga.

"Ah, you should, you know. It's dark, I'll give you that. It's dark. But so's what you're reading."

Petra lowered the comic. "You read Deadpool?"

The girl's small eyes opened a bit. "Oh yeah, I read Deadpool. I like Marvel, though. I've been knowed to dig into DC every once in a while."

"How come I never seen you school before? Almost everybody here been here since they was babies."

"My daddy was working a mine in Logan. He got in an argument with the foreman. They kinda fought. They was drinking after work. My daddy's half black. Guess the foreman used the n word or somethin'. We had to pack up and move here. There ain't many mining jobs around no more. This was the closest we could get."

Petra looked closely at the girl. She couldn't see any black in her, but then again her daddy was mulatto. She guessed the black must have washed out of her. It turned out her name was Gloria. She was 17, a year younger than Petra and in the class below her. They soon became daily lunch partners, sharing and trading comics and for the first time that Petra could remember, she'd found someone who she could laugh with who wasn't a brother.

Meeting after school became a regular thing for the two girls. Gloria's home was in Clarksburg. Petra took to skipping the bus after school and walking with her friend to her home, less than a mile from the school. The house was much newer than anything in Hephzibah and Petra liked the clean vinyl siding and the modern, slightly green tint of the windows. The inside was always spotlessly clean, the furniture matching, but not altogether new. To Petra it seemed like a mansion. Gloria's mother, whom Petra had met once, was a nurse at the local hospital and was rarely home. Petra could see where Gloria got her small green eyes; they looked so gentle on her mother.

The two would spend hours talking in Gloria's room, laughing at Petra's the antics she'd had with her brothers. Sometimes they were just

The One and True Son

quiet, lying on their backs on Gloria's thick flokati rug her auntie had sent all the way from Athens, Greece. Her auntie, who was just five years older than Gloria and in the Air Force, sent Gloria a bunch of stuff from there, from gold leaf vases with ancient Greek figures painted on them to small replica statues of goddesses, some missing important limbs.

    Sometimes they'd read comics, mostly Marvel, but Gloria had introduced her to romance novels that she'd snuck from a drawer in her parents' bathroom. Most times Gloria and Petra would read a book each, but other times Gloria would read to Petra in a slow patient voice that didn't sound like her. Well, it was her, but the words sounded different; they sounded like the character had gotten in her somehow, like she was playing the part of the person in the book. Petra loved to hear Gloria read and she would lay back in the thick white wool of the rug and close her eyes.

    One afternoon Gloria read about two strangers who made love in a swimming pool on a tropical island. The strangers, a lonely woman with flowing auburn hair and noticeable beauty, a beauty she failed to believe in, and a man, ten years younger than she, a rebel, an outcast, a criminal with a heart of gold, with strong arms and a thick mane of black hair, who came together at last after a series of near misses. They'd seen each other at every important scene in the book, with one or the other being on the periphery of the scene involving the other, able to observe, but no way to intervene. Through these events they learned valuable lessons about the other. By the time they got together at the pool, no words needed to be spoken. They'd known what they needed to know.

    "You ever kiss anybody?" Gloria asked, closing the book.

    At first, Petra thought this was in the book and didn't respond. Her eyes were closed, and her mind was full of salt air and palm trees. She wasn't even sure what was happening in the story. She'd escaped to the pool, to the island, to a place she'd never been.

    Gloria asked again. This time Petra picked up on the change from Gloria's story voice to her regular speaking voice. Petra didn't know how to answer. Her first instinct was to claim that she had, but that was a lie and Petra was always uncomfortable with lying. She thought for a moment and knew that Gloria wouldn't laugh.

    "No, can't say that I have," Petra said, "'cept my momma and daddy when I was little. I expect that don't count though."

    Gloria didn't say anything for a moment. Petra turned over on the rug and rested her chin in her on back of her hand.

    "Promise not to get mad at me?" Gloria said finally.

    Petra smiled. "Nah, I won't get mad."

More silence.

"What?" Petra said, starting to get nervous.

Gloria rolled over and faced Petra. Gloria's face flamed to the color of a grape.

"I kinda want to kiss you. I done it a couple of times. With some boys and a couple of girls. It's... it's real nice."

Petra looked at Gloria, at those small, kind eyes. Words wouldn't come. She'd never been approached for such a thing, so she rarely gave it much thought. She felt herself shiver, though she wasn't cold. It was hard to move, impossible to speak. She just kept looking at those eyes. Gloria inched closer. She looked at Petra's hair and softly flicked a thin lock with her fingertip that had fallen down over one of her eyes. Petra's breathing got faster; for a moment she wondered if she could catch it. Their lips met. It was so warm, so soft, that Petra no longer thought about breathing.

Petra didn't go home after school anymore after that, at least not directly. The route home always led through Gloria's house, through Gloria's room. People at school took notice of a change in Petra. Her teachers and other students saw the taciturn youth laugh when others laughed, speak more than just the minimum when called on to speak. Many guessed, in conversations she wasn't privy to, that she'd found a boy.

Her parents noticed a change as well. They weren't happy that she'd been arriving sometimes as late as ten o'clock, getting out of a maroon minivan with windows so tinted they couldn't see who was doing the driving. They'd see the headlights sweep across the drawn drapes and by the time they'd get to the door, they'd catch the taillights heading back down the road toward Clarksburg.

Petra explained once that she was studying with her friend Gloria, a junior. That she did it all the time.

"How're you studying with somebody ain't in the same grade as you?" her daddy asked. "You ain't got the same classes."

"School ain't the same as when you went to school, Daddy," she answered quickly, trying to get passed him to get to her room where she knew he wouldn't follow. "We got a lot of the same classes. Gloria's really smart in Math. I don't get it half the time."

"Hold up a second," he said stopping with a hand on her shoulder. "You tellin' me that she's helping you with your math." He grabbed her chin with his fingertips. The light was dim in the entranceway to the house as the fixture above their heads held two bulbs, but one of them had been burned out for as long as anyone could remember. He turned her chin to observe the angry purple mark that seemed to be growing on her neck.

"What the hell is this?" he asked, his eyes narrowed. Petra could smell bourbon on his breath.

"I got hit with a tennis ball," she said, looking him dead in the eye. "Becky Holland served one right at me in PE. It was a kinda bitchy thing to do. She's the captain of the tennis team. She knew I wasn't looking. She don't like me, I think."

Her father said nothing. He let her pass.

In her room she'd nearly wretched. Petra had been good in math. Not the best in the class good, but a solid B. She had no idea what Gloria's grades were like. They'd never discussed it. And the Becky Holland thing was a joke. Petra hadn't been in PE all year. She hated the PE uniforms, a pair of running shorts and a tank top t-shirt with the school's name on it and a rectangle for her to write in her last name with permanent marker. The PE teacher, a woman slightly older than the girls she'd been teaching couldn't put Petra's name with a face, or practically any of the others', so she just marked everybody there and went on with her day. If they'd played sports she'd been interested in like baseball or football, even soccer, she'd have probably slipped in, but the only time Petra had seen her class outside they were playing tennis. Which brought Petra to another lie: Becky Holland probably didn't know she existed, let alone have the animus to fire a tennis ball toward her face. They had one class together. Becky was the Class President, the captain of the tennis team, accepted at one of the top colleges in the country, and, as most people knew, destined to be one of the top doctors in the world one day. Petra's daddy hated people like Becky. Petra knew that.

All lies. In the span of maybe a minute Petra had spewed more lies than she had since she'd told one on her brothers after she went running into the river to retrieve a baseball hit way over her head. When her momma saw her muddy overalls and her caked sneakers, she went off, calling her all kind of names. On defense, Petra claimed her brothers dragged her in. She told her mother that they would throw her in the river after the ball and wouldn't let her out of the water. She said that they said the river water would eat all her skin and muscle off like those fish in the Amazon that can strip a cow to the skeleton in 30 seconds. And it almost worked. Her mother couldn't imagine that a girl could come up with an outlandish and violent story like that. Magdalena had broken a switch off an old dead tree and headed toward the boys who were still playing on the clearing next to the river. It didn't take a minute before Petra ran after her yelling,

The One and True Son

"Momma, I lied! They didn't do nothing! I ran after the ball!" The switch turned out to be for Petra after all.

Petra lay in Gloria's arms on the white wooly rug in Gloria's room. They laid in each other's arms most days, talking about their days, about teachers they didn't like, about the last romance book they'd read together. Petra loved Gloria's room. It was dark, the walls painted deep lavender, but parts of it glowed with life, from the pictures of musicians of the Sixties and Seventies, the Rolling Stones, Janis Joplin, that she'd pointed lamps at from below, to the funny posters taken from memes on the internet. She could relax in this room unlike any place she could think of. She'd not slept well the night before after lying to her father. It annoyed her that she cared. She told Gloria about it and about the distance she felt from her family with her brothers being gone, the silence in the house that made her feel like she was dead-- like Moe.

"Well, you got me," Gloria said. "Maybe if they could see you was happy, it'd shake 'em out of it."

Petra shuttered. "Oh, I couldn't tell 'em about this. About you and me. They're really old fashioned about stuff. Maybe, I can show them I have a friend. They don't have to know…you know."

People didn't think Gloria was too smart. It bothered Gloria sometimes that that was the way people saw her. They'd talked about it some. Petra understood how people might get that impression. Gloria was happy, she smiled a lot and laughed at dumb stuff. Serious people don't like that. People didn't really notice that she could read really well. Even Petra had to admit that there were times that she came off a little, well, not dumb, but not thinking much. But there were other times she came up with something that showed she really was paying attention the whole time. If people were listening, this was one time that she did that.

"Petra, you told me that it bothered you that you lied to your daddy." Gloria stroked her open palm on Petra's cheek. "Isn't that just another lie you're going to tell him. Isn't it gonna be lying to your momma too."

Petra snuggled under Gloria's chin and rested her ear on her lover's collarbone, listening to the easy heartbeat. She closed her eyes. "I don't know." she said. "I don't know."

That night they held hands the whole ride to Petra's home. Petra hadn't said much on the ride. She asked that they not listen to the radio on the ride. She said she wanted to think. They both watched the road ahead through the windshield, lit up like a movie from the headlights.

Petra's daddy's face was at the front window when the pulled into the stone driveway. They were earlier than the night before, so she knew her father had a bug up his butt. Normally, he wouldn't bother about seeing

The One and True Son

what was going on if she came home at what he called a reasonable hour. Gloria came to a stop parallel to the concrete stoop in front of the door. Petra gave Gloria's hand a long, warm squeeze, looking into her eyes.

"See you in the mornin', buddy?" Petra said and sniffed a little laugh.

Gloria smiled back. "You bet, pal."

Petra got out from the passenger's side and made her way around to the front door of her house. Petra's father opened the inside door and stood behind the screen door, staring intently at the deep tinted window, obviously trying to make out from the silhouette, just who it was that had driven his daughter. Petra reached the first stair of the stoop when she turned back suddenly to the van. She made a circular motion with her index finger, telling Gloria to roll her window down and Gloria obliged. The front light was on, and Gloria could be plainly seen from where Petra's father stood. Petra stuck her head in the window and said in a clear voice, "I love you."

Petra kissed Gloria gently on the lips for what seemed like a long time. With that she returned to the front stoop, opened the screen door, and walked by her father. He didn't speak.

Petra sat in her room waiting for the fireworks. She sat on her bed with its plain headboard, the same bed that at least two of her brothers had had and her father had before them when he was young. Her room was nothing like Gloria's. The walls had no celebrations, no clever posters, no photos. The room contained a desk and a chair that she picked up at the Goodwill. It sat by the window with an old gooseneck lamp on it, unused in months. An unmatched nightstand stood sentry to the bed, an old clock/radio glowed orange behind numbers that flipped like an old scoreboard. There was nothing from the world outside of Hephzibah. The room seemed little more than a storage locker.

She waited up half the night for her father, or mother, or both, to come in and rip her up. She was sure that her father had told her mother what he'd seen. She felt she knew her daddy and there was no way he could hold that in. She fell asleep in her clothes that night.

When she woke, she jumped up with a start. The old clock/radio had run way past its alarm time since she hadn't set it. She rubbed her eyes. Doubt crept in over what she'd done the night before. Like a lot of things people do when they act on impulse, the reality of the response doesn't hit until later. She looked at the clock again, letting the time register this time: 9:43. Petra took in a big breath of morning air and tried to clear her mind. If she hurried, she could get to school before lunch. It was a long walk, but she could use it.

The One and True Son

She stepped into the bathroom, peed, and brushed her teeth. Her hair looked like Freddy Mercury's in that old Queen video where he was dressed in a tuxedo, with an ascot and cummerbund, made up like an insane vampire. *I'm going slightly mad....* She ran a brush through her hair and headed for the kitchen.

Stan Banik was sitting at the kitchen table. He'd been waiting.

Petra couldn't remember the last time she'd had a conversation with her father that involved more than a question and answer; usually the question came from her father. She moved around behind him to get the coffee out the cupboard. She dumped out the early morning brew sitting cold and oily in the glass pot and filled it with fresh water. The can of Folgers was almost empty, but she was able to tap the remaining grounds into a filter paper cup, enough for a weak pot. She switched on the coffee machine and sat at the table across from her father. Petra wanted to feel strong, but she looked at her nails as she'd always done as a child, trying dig the dirt out from the nail beds. There was no dirt there, but she dug anyway.

"Guess you want to say something," Petra said, eyes down.

Her father sat, unmoving. He was shaved; his hair was combed. Petra smelled no liquor.

"Your momma and I think it's time you get out of here," he said, his voice gravelly from years of cigarettes and whiskey, something that she should've been used to. But there was something in his voice, probably the way he said it that wasn't like him. It seemed almost doubtful, the anger she thought would be there was absent.

"Where do you think I should go?" she replied. "I ain't got no money. I s'pose I could go up into the hills. People ain't seen any bears lately. I should be able to make it a couple of weeks."

Petra looked up her father. What she saw in her father's eyes surprised her. It wasn't anger.

Stan Balik sighed. He raised his hand like it might help him speak, thought better of it, and put it back on the table. He looked to the ceiling, then back at Petra.

"Don't get me wrong, girl. Don't get us wrong, your momma and me. We think..." His eyebrows twisted with effort. His thin, veiny hands flexed their fingers, in and out. "We think that you'll never be happy 'round here. There's nothing—there's nothing for you *here*. This dead place. I know we ain't been here for you. We ain't been here," he shrugged his shoulders, "for nobody. Not even ourselves. Somehow, we gotta figure that out. But you, we think you figured yourself out. If you stay here in Hephzibah, it'll be for nothing. People won't understand you. Not here. There are places you can go. You gotta get out of here, Petra."

The One and True Son

Petra and her father sat for a long time. Did she know this man? Did she ever? Had he known her better than she ever knew he had?

"I think you're right, Daddy," her voice a whisper. "I have Gloria here. That's the girl from last night. I…I don't know." She shook her head. "I don't know. She's real special. Special to me. But I want to see things. She's got this auntie that's been all over the place. All over the *world*. I never really thought about it 'til I met her. I didn't think it was possible that I could see things. But she did, her auntie. She was from 'round here and she got to see all kinds of places. Gloria's got stuff from all over. You should see it, Daddy." Petra teared up. She hadn't thought about showing her daddy, either of her parents really, anything since before she could remember. She'd forgotten what it felt to be a kid, to tell her parents what she's interested in, to see they might be interested too. How old was she the last time that happened?

"Well, Pet," her father said, his eyes red and swollen. "Let's find this out."

Over the next few weeks, they looked over colleges. She had the grades to make it to a state university, but because she never saw it as a possibility, she never took the placement exams. She could take them in the summer, but that wouldn't be in time for the fall semester. And besides that, she was looking out of state. Her daddy told her to get out of West Virginia. Go someplace like California or New York where she could spread her wings a little bit. But, like everything else, she was far too late to apply for the next year, for financial aid, for scholarships. Neither Petra nor her father wanted anything to do with student loans. Stan Balik kept his cars for well over 20 years and he didn't want his daughter to go into hock for the rest of her life for what would likely turn out to be just four years of it.

Petra spent less time with Gloria. Often, she would take the bus back home after school to sit at the same plain gray Formica kitchen table where she'd been fed mashed up food as a baby, where she'd sat on phone books to feed herself when she could reach. She'd sit with her father, if he was home from work, to go over the latest plan. Her mother busied herself around them as they talked, every few moments sticking a glance in to see a brochure, or if she'd heard a rise of enthusiasm in either of their voices. Petra felt closer to them than she ever remembered.

Gloria often sat quietly on the flokati rug when Petra decided to go home with her. Gloria would sit with her feet tucked under her, her arms crossed across her chest. Petra tried to hug her whenever she could get close enough, something that seemed to annoy Gloria to no end. Petra,

The One and True Son

wanting to be straightforward, worked up the courage, and told her of the plans she'd been formulating with her father.

"It ain't so bad around here," Gloria complained when she told her. "Nobody says nothin' to us. It ain't like it used to be around here."

Petra looked at her lover. "We ain't really tried it, have we? I mean, yeah, we walk home together and spend time at school, but it's not like we hold hands or nothing. We don't kiss at school like a lot of the regular couples do. Why do you think that is?"

Gloria sniffed. "It don't matter."

Petra put a hand on Gloria's shoulder "It does matter, Gloria. It does. It ain't no way to live. But not only that. I don't know about you, but I can't see myself living here, living the same life as everybody else around here. I want to go places, do stuff. I think I might be in something important someday. If I let myself.

"Besides, I graduate this year. What am I gonna do? Work in the mines? They're laying off people every day. This place is gonna be deader in 10 years, if you can believe it."

"Did you think of asking me what I want?" asked Gloria, her voice going up an octave. "Did you? You wasn't talking to nobody. You walked around school like you had your tongue cut out, reading those comics at lunch. Weren't you a little old for that?"

"But you..." Petra tried to object.

"I felt sorry for you!" Gloria shouted. "You had no life! You wouldn't be thinking about anything if it wasn't for me! You wouldn't had even *thought* about leaving here! I showed you something different!" She patted herself hard on the breastbone. "You'd still be sitting on that bench reading Deadpool, with everybody in the whole damned school talking about you, if I didn't come over there and drag you away! And now you wanna go?"

Petra went to speak but the words caught in her throat. *You felt sorry for me? That's why you came and talked to me? That's why you said you read comics too?*

Petra stood and walked to the bedroom door.

Gloria leapt up. "Wait!" She stopped Petra at the door and tried to put her arms around her. Petra wriggled away.

"No, you was right," Petra was finally able to say. "You showed me other things. You did. You showed me your stuff from Italy and Greece." She waved her hand around the room. "The pictures and the hand painted whatevers. You showed me who I am, or who I could be." She glared into Gloria's green, now catlike, eyes. "You also showed me who you are. Just now. How'm I gonna stick around for that? You gonna whack me with some low stuff whenever you get pissed off. Like you been saving it for the right time?"

Gloria's face turned purple as a beet. "You said you loved me!"

Petra released the tension from her narrow shoulders, narrow like her daddy's.

"I do." she said. "I do and I will. But that don't mean I can stay here forever. Can you? If you can then we won't be loving each other too long. That's how people get trapped around here. The first time they fall in love they try to make it last, staying where they are, rottin' on the vine. They end up bitter and drinking and trapped."

"So now you're trapped?" Gloria spit, her arms crossed in front of her.

Petra shook her head. "I ain't doin' this. I ain't going 'round and 'round until we wear each other out and forget what we was fightin' about, until the next time and we go 'round all over again. Besides I ain't leavin' in a while. We still got time. If you want it."

"Hey, why wait? My auntie went into the Air Force. She got college there, right on the base. You can just get your ass outta here as quick as you please."

Petra suddenly didn't know the person standing in front of her. She turned, opened the door and let herself out the front door.

By the time she'd walked home to Hephzibah, she'd decided to take her advice.

Her momma and daddy weren't too keen on the military at first. They'd both pointed out, separately and together, that joining up wasn't the same as it was a couple years ago. Carter almost went to war with Iran after that helicopter crash in the desert. Reagan wanted to put lasers in space and Gorbachev was screaming bloody murder. And yet, in the end, they came around to the idea making sense. Petra could get away. The military didn't take gays, but there was no blood test for that. They'd all seen on TV programs about people, officers, heroes, who were gay and nobody knew it until they were done with their service. If Petra didn't go around with a sign on her back, they were sure she could get through it.

Petra researched all the branches. She knew early on that the Marines was out. She wasn't all that hot on the idea of war and the Marines videos seemed to not only be okay with it, but actively wishing for it. She's seen *Full Metal Jacket* about a hundred times on the VCR and whether that was accurate or not, she really didn't want to know.

The Army seemed like a lighter version of the Marines. According to her brother Lukas the biggest complaint seemed to be the crappy living quarters and a lot of oily jobs that didn't involve shooting people or blowing them up.

Gloria's auntie's branch, the Air Force looked good. You could get stationed in Greece or England or Korea. That prospect tantalized Petra. They had good jobs, high tech ones, and, again, according to Lukas, they had the best quarters and bases. But still it was a crapshoot. She could get Korea or Okinawa or even Germany or England, but she could get Minot, North Dakota or K.I. Sawyer, in upper peninsula Michigan. She'd be trading one nowhere for another.

In the end she went with the Navy. She'd be almost guaranteed to be stationed on some coast or another. She'd never heard of a naval yard in Kansas. Petra had never been on a boat before but going to places she had never been, was kind of the point.

Her mother and father were at her swearing in. Gloria was a no-show.

Petra left the day after her high school graduation for Naval Station Great Lakes in North Chicago, Illinois just shy of 70 miles north of Chicago, for boot camp. Many of the recruits referred to North Chicago as the armpit of Illinois, but to Petra it was fascinating. The buildings were old timey in the center of the town and though it looked rather gray and industrial, there were more roads going somewhere than she'd ever seen. Still as agile and almost as strong as most of the male recruits she breezed through the physical part of the training. In the bookwork she was smarter than most. Petra had long been able to shut out what was going on around her to focus on what was important to her, and what was important to her at that moment in her life was the Navy.

After recruit training, Petra stayed at Great Lakes for Seaman's Apprenticeship Training where she would train to be a boatswain's mate, the first word pronounced bosun. She learned about marlinspikes, monkey fist knots, basic maintenance of the outer and inner structure of a ship, along with operating, repairing and loading with equipment like forklifts and pallet jacks. She learned how to load and unload munitions without blowing herself up and her ship with her. Petra found she had a knack for repair and a talent for moving crates quickly without a scratch to the pallet jacks and ship's cranes. She whizzed through all her trials.

Six weeks later, Petra Balik found herself attached to the USS Samuel Gompers, a destroyer tender, or floating repair ship. Named after an American labor leader from the late 1800s, the Gompers was the first of her class. The ship was squat and unremarkable in appearance, especially when it pulled up to its formidable and grotesquely armed cousins, but it was a welcome sight when one of those behemoths was in trouble. She'd seen most of the ports in the Pacific theater from Australia to Hong Kong

The One and True Son

to Vietnam. It was in Da Nang that she picked up the nickname Fat Sam, not because of her girth, but because she was a Fast Attack Tender. The ship was lightly armed and constantly vulnerable to attack, but she had lady luck and when Saigon fell, she escaped unscathed.

The ship scored a couple of important firsts in the US Navy. In the 1980s it was the first tender to do a major engine swap out while at sea. She performed this on the USS Kinkaid off the coast of Oman allowing the destroyer to stay with the fleet and saving the Navy millions in towing and refitting at a friendly port.

The Gompers also had the distinction of the first American naval vessels to bring women into the regular crew. In that way it was ice breaker as other tenders took on women was well, followed by combat ships and submarines in the 1990s.

Petra screamed when she'd received her orders. The Gompers' home port was San Diego, by all accounts a prime station. Each night before she shipped out, she dreamed of the palm trees, the cloudless skies, the clean white sand beaches that sparkled of microbic, worn down, diamonds, the scenes that movie stars grew bored with, but for her would be like living in a never-ending cinematic masterpiece. She wouldn't get much of a chance to sunbathe, though, not that she'd ever done that. Fat Sam would be shipping out at 0500 the morning after her arrival.

Like everything in her naval career, Petra took to sea life as if she'd been born on a boat. Her rack, the bottom bunk on a stack of three gave her more than enough room to stretch out and relax when she wasn't standing watch or repairing something on the ship, in other words, off duty. She lay atop her government issue wool blankets with US stamped in the center and read tech manuals and old magazines swapped among the crew. Petra quickly grew to love the sounds of Fat Sam at sea, the creaks of the steel as it adjusts to the invisible strength of the ocean, the rubbing sound of the hull as it cut through the water. She was especially fond of the open sea when the hatches would be open to allow air flow through the ship. The flow was magic; the fragrance of air and salt water the moment they became one.

The women's berths, sectioned off from the men's had its own head. Anything considered girly was stashed in "the coffin," a storage compartment under the rack along with personal hygiene items, underwear and anything else that kept the sailors from going crazy after weeks or months at sea. Petra got along well enough with the other female sailors but being the sister of five brothers she felt the strongest connection with the men on board, particularly the bosuns' crew.

Being the boot camp deck ape, the newby, on the crew, Petra had known that she'd be tested, but again, Petra was made of strong stuff. Manual work didn't bother her. Swab a deck? On it. Paint the hull that fabulous haze gray? She was happy to do it. She felt truly free, probably for the first time in her life. It would be nice to say that her nearly perpetual smile was contagious. It wasn't. The ship was full of hardworking, often dirty seaman, most of them used to the sway of the ocean, some barely 18, and all of whom had tremendous responsibility with little time on the water frivolous expression. Her smile was rarely returned, at first, and often reciprocated with a scowl and a hardy, *What the fuck are you smiling about?*

She was swabbing the deck in the machine shop when she met EM2 Rocky Little. When Petra read the name stenciled over his breast-pocket she almost snickered. There was *nothing* little about Rocky. His hands were like hydraulic jacks, his fingers, according to some accounts in the crew, had twisted many a finger out of its joint in beer sodden contests of knuckle wrestling. His large head, black and bald, seemed twice the size of the average; he needed to duck at every threshold he'd crossed, almost having to crouch through the hatches. And yet his size *almost* never hindered him as he bopped around the ship, L.L. Cool J or Public Enemy running through his head as he performed like Superman on most tasks assigned to him and some, others couldn't handle. He discovered Petra one day while working on a persnickety boat engine. He'd dropped a crucial pin in a greasy crevice next to the propane engine where his overstuffed fingers couldn't go no matter how hard he fought the cast aluminum engine case to move out of the way. Rocky looked up to see who was around him. He saw Petra and her mop. He was thirsty.

"Hey Boot Camp," he growled. "Get over here"

"What ya need?" Petra said, nearly out of breath from the scramble"

"Go get me a Pepsi."

Petra side-eyed him. Then she looked at the lift with the big man's hand still stuck in it. "What's wrong? Can't get the pin?" She'd been watching him work. He was *really good.* Petra couldn't help but smile. She knew she wasn't supposed to, but there she was. "I dropped a couple of those suckers. In my brother's MG. We did a total rebuild. A real pain to get out. Usually took me a minute or two. Broke my rhythm, you know?"

"You're really funny, aren't you, Boot Camp?"

"I suppose you could use a magnet probe to get it out. You got one of those? I was lookin' for it your tool chest. Didn't see one."

The One and True Son

Rocky Little released his hand from its jail, the diesel blower from one of the two 12v71 engines of a Mike Boat that had been craned up to the deck the day before. He stood to his full height.

"You're funny as shit, little girl." He placed his huge, grease covered hand on her, so far, clean dungaree utility uniform shirt. "I like you. Now go get my Pepsi before I crush you like a cockroach."

Petra looked up at the giant, smiling even brighter. "You want me to get that pin out first?" She opened her hand in front of him spreading out her slim, tapered fingers.

Nobody called her "Boot Camp" after that.

Petra decided to "strike" as an engine mechanic. To strike, the seaman had to request that the captain allow her to train for a specific job. If the request was granted, she would join the Engine Shop for on-the-job training. She knew about striking, but it was Rocky who encouraged her to join the shop. He helped her fill out the proper document and talked to a few people who had the ear of the captain to smooth it all out.

In due time permission was granted and Petra hung up her mop.

The Machine Shop crew was a tight mixture of people from all over. There was Rocky, raised in the South Shore area of Chicago, on East 73rd street, just south of the University of Chicago, a predominately middle class, predominately black area of the city. His parents, his construction working father and his mother, a paraprofessional education assistant wanted the best for their only child. College was the goal, so they made sure Rocky (the name on his birth certificate was Ronald, though no one *ever* called him anything but Rocky) went to South Shore International College Prep, a school not too far from his house and had what his parents had in mind for their son. But Rocky wasn't having it. Reading for too long made him itchy. Math was cool, but the idea of sitting behind a desk for the rest of his life as an engineer never appealed to him. Rocky loved sports and excelled at the big three: Football, Basketball and Baseball. Colleges fell all over themselves to get him signed up; scholarships were offered; the prettiest coeds met him at every college he toured. But that's not what Rocky wanted. It's not what he *ever* wanted. Rocky wanted to use his hands, to fix things, to make them like new. It didn't really matter what it was. Rocky knew he could fix it. Two weeks after high school graduation he snuck to the Navy Recruiter. If there was a better way he could smash his parents' hearts into smaller pieces, he hadn't found it yet. But they got over it. Mostly.

Ethan Ledford, the LPO, or leading petty officer, was older than most of the crew and technically outranked Rocky, though when decisions needed to be made, everyone, including Ledford himself, deferred to

The One and True Son

Rocky. A former gymnast in high school he still had the arms of someone who could hold himself rigid on the stationary rings, but the growing gut of a budding alcoholic as well. Ethan's sexual hunger preceded his arrival to the Gompers as he was known at A school at Great Lakes to have achieved copulation with several young women, at least two of them officers, and one rendezvous on a high-ranking officer's desk. His dry sense of humor and love of Seagram's Seven and Sevens on off duty time had prompted a visit to Captain's Mast, a punishment imposed by the captain as opposed to a court martial. His record had more color than needed to grow in rank quickly, so nearly 10 years in he remained an E-5.

Petra loved being around her shop. She loved joking with Robin, a tall, bony redhead from Tulsa Oklahoma. The shop called him The Professor because he was always talking about Physics, although he prefaced most of the stuff he'd read by saying, "I really don't understand it, but..." before he tried to explain String Theory, Quarks, Alternate Universe Theory and a hundred others that he'd read in his collection of *Scientific American* that arrived whenever the ship got its mail.

"Why the hell didn't you become a scientist or something?" Ledford asked him once while he tried to explain that there may be endless USS Gompers, with an endless amount of Rockys and Ethans and Petras only Rocky might be white or Petra might be a guy.

"I don't know," Robin shrugged. "I didn't really get this stuff in school. I was good at measuring shit and things like that. Geometry, you know? When they started adding letters and weird symbols, they'd lost me. It was a like a different language. And I sucked when I took French too."

On liberty, these four sailors became inseparable. Their first excursion off the ship after nearly two months at sea was at Naval Station Subic Bay. The station was located in the town of Olongapo, an impoverished town in an impoverished nation. To Petra, it felt like another planet. She was stunned by the beautiful filipino people, the smooth dark hair of the women and the elegant Spanish looking shirts of the men. Her nerves tweaked as she walked by these people in her fancy blue-jeans she'd picked up at the original Marshall Field's store in Chicago on a day trip during A school. Her sleeveless light blue t-shirt felt almost too warm in the South Pacific sun.

"Am I showin' too much?" she asked Rocky when she caught an older Filipino man looking at more than a brief glance.

"Nah," Rocky answered. "They're probably just wondering what you're doing with us. They don't see many female sailors walking around. You know, we were the first ship to have females in the crew." He nudged her with his elbow. "They're probably wondering what's wrong with you."

The One and True Son

"I can't help it if the navy decided it needed improvements." She nudged him back.

"We're getting near Shit River Bridge!" Ledford hooted. "Can you smell it?"

"Aww man, I was trying not to," Rocky said, wrinkling his nose. "I love the PI, " Robin threw in. "The weather's great and all, but hoo-wee, you'd think they'd do something about that."

The Magsaysay Bridge was the gateway to the sailor's playground that sat on the other side of the Olongapo River. The river, Ledford explained, got its American nickname because of the raw sewage from the city's barrios that emptied directly into it. Its swirls were lumpy and muddy; it smelled of disease and death. When the odor hit Petra, she gagged.

"The last time we were here," Ledford informed Petra, "there were a couple of little kids over there." They were halfway across the bridge. Ledford pointed to the bank just at the other end of the bridge. "They asked us to throw pennies into the river and they would jump in there and get them."

Petra shot him a look.

"I'm serious! They'd dunk all the way in and come up with the pennies. We were there for about 15 minutes. Those little suckers came up with every one of them. They must've opened their eyes in that shit."

"How could you do that?" asked Petra.

"What? They're used to it. They probably don't even smell it anymore. Besides, I threw them a couple quarters."

"You're disgusting," Petra observed.

"I know," Ledford acknowledged, smiling.

Magsaysay Street was the main drag through Olongapo. The Street was lined with bars, massage parlors and venders. Older men stood at the entrances in short sleeved Spanish looking shirts with four pockets on the front, two breast pockets and two lower pockets. The shirts had intricate embroidery running in two vertical stripes own the front, over the pockets.

"There are a lot of massage places around here," Petra noted. "You guys think I can get a massage? I've never had one, but I hear they're real relaxin'."

The others stopped where they were and looked at each other. Ledford, Robin and Rocky burst out laughing.

"Yeah, they're really relaxing," Ledford said when he caught his breath. "Although they might not want you as a client." He appeared to think about it. "I don't know. Maybe they would."

The men laughed again. Petra wrinkled her brow at them.

The One and True Son

Rocky leaned into her. "It ain't that kind of massage." He said in a lowered voice.

"That's disgusting," said Petra and popped him on the shoulder.

"That's business in the PI," Ledford cackled. He stopped and turned around to the guys. "Hey! Let's go to Skinny's."

Robin looked concerned. "What about, you know, the last time? You know. The fight?"

"Dude, that was over a year ago," Ledford said. "We haven't been back since. You really think they'll remember us with all the squids coming into Subic? I don't think so."

Robin still looked dubious. "They told us we were barred."

"Come on, pussy," teased Ledford. "You think they have mugshots of us over the bar? They're not going to remember us. Besides, we got a lady with us."

They all looked to Petra.

"I'm not sure I like the sound of this." Petra said.

"Come on!" Ledford begged. "Nothing's going to happen. The bar girls will leave you alone." He shot Rocky a look. "Nobody's going mess with you with my man Rock here sitting next to you. Guaranteed."

Petra looked to Rocky. He nodded.

"I guess." She shrugged.

Skinny's or, Skinny's Saloon was just off Magsaysay Street, sandwiched between a massage place and a tattoo establishment. Garth Brooks thanked Yahweh for unanswered prayers as they passed through the beaded curtained entrance; two bar girls sized them up, seemingly pleased with the potential of their visit. They hadn't noticed Petra immediately. When they did, they stared at her for a long time, their black eyes in the cheap, multicolored bar lighting, were shiny and opened wide, as if they were suddenly worried about something. Petra wondered if they were worried for them or her. The girls were beautiful. Maybe, Petra thought, they were the most beautiful girls she'd ever seen; small, in tight, high cut shorts and t-shirts with American sports team logos. Their hair, long and black as oil, gleamed even in the smoky dim party lights of the bar. She knew why the guys in her shop liked to come here. Petra dropped her eyes first.

The crew made their way to a table in the center of the small room. They ordered San Miguel beers for the table. Petra had never drunk alcohol, mostly because of what happened to Moe, but she went along anyway, vowing to herself to pay her friends back for bottles she didn't drink. The waitress, a slightly chubby girl with a flipped up bob, a mole on her cheek and a wide smile, delivered the beers on a tray, one handed, and as she placed each sweating bottle down she offered a salutation to the person who'd be drinking it: for the big, muscle man (to Rocky), for the pretty lady (to Petra), for the man with the mysterious eyes, (to Ledford) and for the man with the fire in his hair, (to Robin). She ran her freshly lacquered fingernails through Robin's hair.

"I like the color of this hair," she purred. "What is it, the color?"

"He's a ginger," Ledford answered for him. "He's a mutation."

Everyone laughed. The waitress looked confused.

"It's red, ah, what's your name?" Robin said finally.

The girl smiled. "Mindy"

"It's red, Mindy," Robin lowered his voice to a register Petra had never heard from him before, "but it's not really red, but that what we call it."

Mindy fingered through his hair a bit more. "Red? I like it." She seemed to be speaking more to herself than Robin. With that, she shrugged and coquettishly walked away.

The table hummed.

"Uh, I think she likes you, Robbie," Petra teased.

"That's what I'm hoping." Robin smiled.

"Don't be fooled, newbie," Ledford interjected. "She just looked around the table and figured he had the most money in his pockets."

"Don't be jealous," said Robin. He picked up his bottle and held it up to the light. "No floaties. Yeah, she likes me."

Ledford reached over and picked up the bottle in front of Petra and held it up to the light. "No floaties in this one either. She must like Pet just as much."

Petra slugged him in the shoulder.

"Ow! Shit that hurt. You must've had brothers."

"You know it," Petra replied, smiling.

The music playing reminded Petra of home. She wasn't really a country music fan, but it'd been around her all her life. It was almost like a soundtrack from home. It was full of loss and sadness, absence and Yahweh. She still hadn't touched her beer, but her companions were drinking it like lemonade on a hot day.

The bar was getting busier as the day turned to evening. Squids from other ships flowed in and out, some hooted when they heard that there were tears in Hank Williams Jr's beer, whiles others turned around at the curtained door, more attuned to Bad Company or Van Halen than country crooning. Empty bottles filled the table, except the three full ones that sat getting warm in front of Petra. The guys regaled the new crew member of liberties past in Guam, Korea and Hawaii.

"Ooh!" Ledford bellowed over John Denver as he sang his ode to country roads, at high volume. "Remember Halterman in Pearl City?"

Everyone but Petra laughed. Rocky shot beer out his nose.

Ledford turned all his attention to Petra. "We were in Pearl Harbor, you know, where the Japanese sunk the fleet to start World War II. We were told specifically to *stay away from Pearl City*. Especially Hotel Street. Some bad shit went down there over the years."

He turns his attention to the guys again. "SO WHERE DID WE GO!?"

Robin and Rocky answered. "HOTEL STREET!"

Ledford turned back to Petra. "So, we go down the streets, talking to the hookers. They were pretty cool, but the best ones were the drag queens. You know, trannies?"

Petra shook her head.

"Trannies. Transvestites. You know? They're men but they dress as women?"

Petra nodded. She felt herself grow hot. She was sure that if it weren't for the colored lights of the bar, they'd see her very differently.

"So Halterman comes strolling up. He used to be a radio technician, but he got washed out for slugging an officer. We couldn't stand the fucker, but every time we ran into him, he'd buy the rounds, so we let him to go with us. Anyway, he starts talking to this tranny, Veronica. They start flirting. He doesn't know it's a guy! So, while they're talking, we take up a collection. We pull Halterman aside and tell him we want to buy him a memory. Man, he was psyched!"

Rocky and Robin laughed, almost gasping for breath.

Ledford wipes his eyes. "So, Veronica takes him in this shitty hotel. And we stand outside and wait. We start taking bets on how fast he comes running out of the hotel."

"I had three minutes," Robin added, laughing.

"So, we wait and wait. All the bets expire. He's in there for a half an hour!"

The boys all laughed again, for minutes.

"He comes strolling out…" Ledford continues, through gasps of laughter, "he comes strolling out like he'd just lost his virginity!"

Everyone but Petra laughs some more.

"Maybe he did!" Rocky threw in and more laughs erupted.

Petra sat stone faced.

The One and True Son

"Did he ever figure out that Veronica was a man?" She asked.

Ledford took a breath. "Don't know. If he did, he's a *fag*. If he didn't, he must've thought pussy smelled like shit."

Petra didn't laugh. She said she had to hit the head but went outside and stood just outside the beaded entrance. She thought about heading back to the ship, but she wasn't 100 percent sure she knew exactly which direction that was. And the idea of walking through the streets of Olongapo wasn't inviting. She decided to go back in the bar and drop hints that maybe it was time to go back.

Back at the table Petra saw they had a new guest at the table. Mindy, their waitress had established herself on Robin's lap. She was running her lacquered fingertips through his hair, gazing into his eyes.

"I love this color, Fire Head. And it's so soft."

Robin swooned. He was in heaven.

Mindy turned and saw Petra had returned to the table.

"Hello, pretty lady. You don't like beer? We have many other drinks."

"No," Petra answered. "Nothing for me."

"Come on, snipe!" Ledford bellowed. "You gotta drink something. I know! Get her a Frog!"

Petra just looked at him.

"Frog. It's this shit they throw together with gin, vodka, rum, some kinda juice shit and Drain-O. You'll catch up to us real quick!"

Mindy looked to Petra, smiling a perfect smile. "You want Frog?"

Petra shook her head and lowered her eyes.

At that moment another bar girl passed the table. With the tiny stature of these women, it was hard to judge their ages, but from all appearances this waitress looked to be 12 years old, maybe 13. Ledford grabbed her by the wrist and jerked her to him. The girl's eyes flew open, the whites bigger than their dark centers. She tried to pull back, but her tiny arms were no match for the former gymnast's.

"Red can't have all the fun," Ledford hissed. "Get over here and sit on my lap, little sister. We'll talk about the first thing that pops up."

The girl squealed; she shook her head vigorously.

"Let her go," a voice ordered from across the table. It was Rocky.

"Oh no, son. This girl's too pretty. She's gonna keep Daddy company tonight."

Rocky stood from the table to his full height. He was a mountain.

The One and True Son

"Let her go, now," Rocky growled in a low baritone. "Let her go or I'll rip out your liver and feed it to you." The big man tilted his head. "Then I'll call your wife."

Ledford let go of the girl's hand. The girl mouthed *thank you* and rushed away.

"Chill man," Ledford told Rocky. "I was just having a little fun."

Rocky turned to Petra. "Come on, Pet. I'll take you back to the ship."

As they headed for the door, Petra heard Robin ask Ledford: "You've got a wife?"

That was the last liberty Petra spent with the boys.

Petra joined the Navy to see what she hadn't seen in her life up to that point. The Navy did that. While sailing to Guam, Fat Sam became intimate with Typhoon Coleen. The weather wizards foretold that a northerly course was preferred to avoid the worst of the storm, but it seems Coleen heard them and hit them with everything she had. It had never occurred to Petra, nor, no doubt, to most of the crew that a ship as solidly built as the Gompers could be sunk by anything less than a torpedo or cruise missile. Certainly, a storm, many smaller versions of which they'd ridden out before, that could throw the ship so violently, so often, just to make their way from bow to stern involved walking on the interior walls of the ship, made that possibility clear. Petra was introduced to the typhoon when she was nearly thrown from her rack. She dressed quickly, bruising her elbow badly putting on her uniform shirt and made her way two decks up. Gray and pasty faces were all she saw. Some seasoned sailors were vomiting where they stood, holding onto fittings for dear life. Others just looked like they'd puke any second. Petra was ordered up to the bridge.

The bridge air was salty steam; the deck was slick. Officers were hanging on to anything bolted down in order to avoid flying into something or someone as the ship pitched angrily from side to side. The scene outside looked biblical. The sky was dark gray, bruised; waves slammed over the bow and splashed the wing wall of the bridge. Petra hung on to hatch frame to the bridge. She spotted her division officer, a middle-aged man with receding salt and pepper hair and a wine-colored birthmark on his forehead, wrapped around the lee helm. Petra waited for the ship to pitch starboard. When it did, she flopped on her butt and slid to the lee helm and grabbed a hold of what was essentially the gas pedal of the ship. She reported in a nearly supine position, her boss hugging the same fixture, above her.

"DAMAGE CONTROL!", the officer shouted.

The One and True Son

When the ship rocked back to port, Petra slid back, stood and scrambled back below deck.

Like most of the crew, after her duties, Petra ended up tied into her rack.

Toward the end of her first enlistment, Petra went back and forth on whether she would re-up. She had seen places she'd never dreamed, taken in air where most Americans had never breathed. Although she didn't go on liberty with her shop, she still felt like they were her brothers. Even Ledford. When she'd joined, she was looking for something. She had no idea what it was. Yes, she wanted to see the world, go to new places, meet people different from her. But there was something under all this. Something calling to her and even though she went to unbelievable places, the calling didn't get louder. It was always out there, whispering in the back of her mind. She had to find that whisper.

Several months later, the fleet was heading for a reward. They had just come out of a relief effort in the Philippines after the eruption of Mount Pinatubo in the Zambales Mountains where the ash and pumice from the explosion traveled 12 miles into the atmosphere, burying the countryside. Rivers of molten lava filled deep valleys with fresh earth as much as 600 feet thick. Clark Air Force Base, a touchstone in the war in Vietnam, eventually closed, leaving a ghostly presence behind.

The reward was a series of liberty ports that most sailors dream of: Hong Kong, Thailand, Australia. The crew of the USS Samuel Gompers was more than ready for the respite, so it was no mystery that when the chaplain came on the ship's main PA system to announce that they were being rerouted to Bangladesh, his impassioned speech was met with jeers and hoots. It seemed that a cyclone had hit Chittagong, one of the world's most ancient seaports in one of the most impoverished nations and the fleet would be steaming to give relief.

As they approached the devastated seaport Petra could only think of a scene in the film *Apocalypse Now,* where Captain Willard arrives at the camp of the renegade Colonel Kurtz to a scene of unimaginable carnage. Until they dropped anchor in Chittagong Harbor, the only dead body Petra had seen was that of her brother, embalmed and in his only suit. She remembered how peaceful he looked, so quiet, all the problems in his life erased. He could rest. The first two bodies to float by the ship were bloated by the polluted waters of the Bay of Bengal. The corpses, both face-down in the murk, seemed in danger of exploding, their skin distended almost beyond their limits. Small hand paddled boats, crewed by visibly exhausted men, with eyes that had seen too much death in too short a time, crept up on the expired with makeshift hooks made from bamboo fishing poles and stiff aluminum wire. In the center of each boat was a pile of something under dirty gray canvas. Petra didn't want to see what was underneath.

Eventually, the retrievable boats were joined by others, small row boats with families, women and children who looked as though they'd been beaten by a mob. The crew brought up boxes of donated chocolate bars and tossed them to the starving, desperate hands below.

Petra felt she was dying inside. She asked permission and was granted to go below deck.

That night, the crew was informed that if they were bitten by *anything*, day or night, they were to report to sick call immediately.

Of course, there was no shore liberty available, though it was doubtful that anyone would want it. The next morning landing craft were sent, small air cushioned hovercraft that glide over the water and up onto the shore, to access how assistance could be rendered and establish a landing zone for supplies and equipment. The first few crafts were met with a hail of rocks and swinging hammers, shovels and anything that could be used as a weapon. Apparently, the locals feared invasion, but through tense negotiation, their fears abated, and teams were allowed to go ashore and assist.

For reasons unclear to the Engine Shop, Petra's team remained on ship, sitting at desks and chairs, not saying much. The disappointment of their lost liberty was dwarfed by a feeling that no one there could articulate. Perhaps it was just the accumulation of emotions from back-to-back disasters. Or maybe it was the fatigue from their work, nearly nonstop for over a month. Whatever it was, the shop was eerily quiet.

The Beachmasters were a team that controls the flow of landing craft (LCAC) and amphibious vehicles from water to shore and coordinates the movement of sailors, equipment and supplies once a staging area has been set up on the beach. On the second day in port, a junior technician, PO2 Swartley decided to visit the shop to, in his words, "shoot the shit."

Everyone in the shop knew Swartley, with his straight black hair that nearly always skirted violation to NAVPERS 15665 uniform standards and the deep cleft in his chin that made clearing out the crevice entirely of beard nearly impossible. He wore the Navy issue "Clark Kent" heavy black framed glasses that only the sailors who didn't care what they looked like wore. Swartley had been on the first team to the beach after the natives were pacified. He was a known storyteller, sometimes a humorous one, so the Engine Shop welcomed him at his best and tolerated him at his worst.

The One and True Son

"Man, what a shit show," he said as he planted himself in an empty chair. "It looks like a muddy nuke detonated out there. You clowns are lucky."

"Lots of dead folks, I imagine," Robin said without looking at him. "We saw a few floating. I'm glad to be in here, thank you very much."

"No shit," Swartley replied. "And they're starting to get ripe. A couple of places we had to put on respirators to keep from puking. It's the hottest time of the year here. The weather gods say it's supposed to be in the mid 90s today."

"Nice," Rocky said, staring into a corner of room.

Swartley seemed to sense his audience slipping. He looked from Petra, who sat at the desk, her head laying on some unfinished paperwork, to Rocky and Ledford, both slumped uncomfortably in their chairs, to Robin, who seemed intrigued by something embedded in the sole of one of his boon dockers. Swartley shifted to the end of his chair.

"Oh! You got to check this out. We were sitting in the LCAC eating MREs. Me and Williams. You guys know Williams? He's a newbie, but he's a funny motherfucker. I think he's from Chicago." He looked to Rocky. "That's your hood, isn't it?"

Rocky nodded. "South Side, but it ain't the hood."

Swartley laughed. "You know what I mean." He waved Rocky off.

"So, me and Williams are sitting there eating MREs."

"You said that," Rocky said, his voice, tense.

"Whoa, let me tell the story, bro," Swartley complained. "I've got to keep the rhythm."

Rocky went back to staring at the corner.

"So, we're eating these MREs. Not bad. I think I had ham. Williams, I think, had spaghetti. We were eating—wait—I had spaghetti."

"Tell the story for fuck sake." It was Ledford that time.

"Okay!" said Swartley, looking hurt. "We're eating and this older dude comes walking up to us. It's hard to tell with these people how old they are. The guy was covered in dirt. Where his hair was hanging down, there were little rivers of dirt coming down over his face. He must've been swimming with the bow weevils when the cyclone hit, and he's got these two little girls with him. They're huddling back from him, holding each other. Like I said, it's hard to tell how old these people are. They could've been 9, maybe 10." He holds out his hand. "They were about yay big, so again, it was hard to tell.

Petra sat up at the desk.

The One and True Son

"The old guy is looking at the MREs like he was staring at a virgin's pussy. I mean, literally he was drooling. And he's says to us that we can *use* the girls in trade for something to eat." Swartley used finger quotes around the world *use*. Do you believe that shit?"

Rocky stopped staring at the corner and looked to Swartley. "What did you say?"

Swartley leaned back in his chair. "We laughed. And Williams looks at the old dude and says, "We've got a lot of food here. I'm stuffed. But you only got two girls there. We only trade food for three girls, minimum.""

Petra looked hard at Swartley. "GET OUT! GET OUTTA HERE RIGHT NOW!"

"What?" Swartley said, stunned.

"Get OUT!" Petra came out from the desk and put her nose an inch from Swartley's. Her face was purple. "GET OUT OF THIS SHOP! DON'T EVER COME BACK IN HERE UNLESS YOU GOT SOME KIND OF WORK TO DO!"

Swartley looked to Rocky.

"Don't look at him," Petra hissed. "I said get out."

Rocky stood. Petra knew what he wanted to do. She put up her hand.

"I got this Rock," she said.

Rocky sat back down and shrugged, a slight smile on his face.

"Who the hell are you, little lady?" Swartley said, leaning back on his chair. "You ain't got enough juice to throw me out of here. You're the same rank as me."

Petra smiled. "Maybe so. But I got the ear of every female on this ship. Maybe I just let it be known what you think is funny. Or maybe, even better, I just follow you around on every liberty. Every time you talk to a woman, go to a bar, a massage parlor, to get your haircut, which you need by the way, and I tell them your funny little story.Granted, some of those women probably heard worse, but they'll think I'm your jealous girlfriend and won't have anything to do with you. It'll be a long, lonely cruise for you, as long as you and me are on the same ocean."

Swartley turned to the others. "You believe this shit? I knew it'd be bad news to bring pussy onboard ships."

"Well, you are kind of an asshole," Robin said.

"Oh, you got something to say, Red?" Swartley shot back. "Maybe we'll talk later."

"Nah, I don't think so." Robin said, his voice steady, calm. "Just go."

Swartley looked at Rocky, then Ledford.

The One and True Son

"Go." Rocky said.

Swartley stormed from the shop, his hair dangling down over his eyes.

The Navy had shown Petra the world. In 20 years, it showed her tropical paradises that no photos, no matter how gifted the photographer, no book, no matter how eloquent the author or poet, could ever capture in their entirety. The smells of water and salt, jungle and desert, smoke and fresh air could never be depicted on a page in a way that would measure up to her memories. The smiles, toothless and full, the voices, barks and whispers, would never be as vivid on a screen or in a song the way they had been embossed into her soul. And even this life that she'd never, as a child, dreamed of, could erase the whisper in the back of her mind.

After retiring, she got a job at the docks in Long Beach working on all types of engines at a small boat repair place in the marina. She could turn a wrench with best of them and it wasn't long before people with everything from fishing boats to motor yachts were asking for her, personally. The owner of the shop, Boscoe, was an old Navy guy himself, did two tours in Vietnam, but was fascinated by the changes that happened between his discharge and hers. He'd immigrated from Ireland in the 60s and cemented his citizenship by going to war for his adopted country. The day she interviewed they hit it off famously. The old man pulled two precarious looking folding chairs for them to talk, set them facing each other in the center of the work area, and set a picnic cooler between them. The Irishman opened the cooler and pulled out two Miller Lites and offered her one.

"It's piss. I know. If I'd go back to Dublin with it they'd kick the shit out of me on principle. So will ya have one with me," he looked at her application, "er Petra? It's another thing the goddamned Navy ruined for me."

"Thank you, sir, but no. I don't drink. But please, have one for me."

"I like that suggestion, girl, and I'll do exactly that. But not right now. I've still gotta work."

With his first beer, Roscoe regaled her with stories of his youth on a PBR, an armed river boat that patrolled the river waters of the South Vietnam.

"The thing wasn't much more than one of these water skiing rigs around here. It had a 31-foot, fiberglass hull, but that thing could maneuver, let me tell you. Turn on a dime. Reverse course just by looking the other way, or not much more."

He took a long swig.

The One and True Son

"Had twin 50 cals in the in the forward tub and M60s mounted port and starboard. Had a grenade launcher too. And we used them a lot. We were in the Rung Sat zone. Ever heard of it?"

Petra shook her head.

"Nah, nothing shocking about that. It was early on. Mid 60s. People weren't paying much attention to 'Nam then. They called it *The Forest of Assassins,* but really that was a bad translation. Can't say what it really was. You see any action? With that Iraq farce?"

Petra said that she didn't. "I was busy doin' rebuilds." She went on to tell him of some of the relief missions she'd sailed to on Fat Sam.

Boscoe smiled.

"The earth owes us a couple of black eyes, if you ask me. It's good you went to help those people. They couldn't help that they were born on it. We thought we were going to help people too. Turns out we were helping some businessmen make more money. That's about it. The South didn't really want us there. They were no better there with us than without."

Petra was hired. She rented a room in a small house on Hermosa Avenue sandwiched between a blocky, modern looking apartment building and a large Spanish hacienda that looked like, to Petra, like a Riviera palace. Hers was a peaceful, shaded room. The house was owned by a married couple, two women who worked in health care, one a nurse and the other a respiratory therapist. They were looking for someone, like them, quiet, matured past the bar scene, who would be there at night and on weekends when they would be working shifts. Petra didn't have much but the clothes she liked to wear the most, sweats, t-shirts, jeans, shorts for the really warm days, so she fit the room easily. The house was walking distance to the marina, so she didn't need a car. She bought a bike instead.

Petra soon fell into a routine that suited her. She'd wake early. Petra had never been an early eater, so she'd make a cup of coffee on the landladies' Keurig, pour a dab of milk in a travel mug and make her way to the shop. She'd take her work boots and socks off at the edge of the beach and walk along the cool, raked sand, the smoothed surface of which only broken by the footprints of the early risers and the dog walkers. Volleyball nets waited in the cool morning breezes for anyone wanting to take up a game. The palm trees stood sentry along East Ocean Boulevard, the whites and grays of the houses and apartments reflected the morning sun. Petra often asked herself on these walks if she was content. Occasionally, she saw large ships on the blue-on- blue horizon and wondered if Fat Sam was there, sitting, surrounded by water, unable to see her, not knowing that one of her own was looking for her. She knew when she got out, when her hitch was up, that it was time. There was still a whisper in the back of her

272

mind that told her that she was not where she was meant to be, not yet. The beach felt closer to the whisper. Just closer.

Petra's landladies, Betsy and Candace, were the nicest kind of people, Petra thought. In the unusual event that they had time off together, on the weekends or an evening, they encouraged Petra to join them at a local restaurant or a small pub. There were many single women in East Long Beach and her two new friends spent most of their off time trying to fix her up.

"You seem awfully lonely, honey," Besty observed over a plate of shrimp scampi at a kitsch little I Italian place near the beach.

Petra had rigatoni that was full of garlic and pungent tomatoes.

"We think you and Melissa would hit it off," Candace said under her newly bobbed hair. "She's a phlebotomist. She's into biking. She knows all the trails. You guys would be great together."

Petra shrugged. "I don't know what I want right now."

"Oh, come on," Betsy prodded, tapping a freshly varnished fingernail on the red and white checkered tablecloth. "You're what? Forty?"

"Forty-one."

Betsy smiled, brightly, the California sun reflecting in her green eyes. "You know what they say. *Forty is the new thirty?*"

"Who says that?"

Betsy laughed. "Somebody does. You've got a Navy pension. A job that you love with a boss who's super chill. You're attractive. I mean, I like our little room, but you seem to like it a little too much. Let us fix you up. We'll all go."

Betsy turned to Candace who nodded.

It took three false starts for the ride to happen, all of them blocked by all the excuses Petra could come up with. Out of excuses, Petra, Betsy and Candace rode their bikes to meet Melissa in the parking lot of the marina. Melissa had her bike racked on the trunk of her 2007 hybrid Civic; she stood behind her car, waiting for them. Melissa was a short, solid woman with longish red-blonde hair, and taut, trim muscles that showed through her tight black bike shorts and European looking jersey. She wore a matching black helmet with an attached tiny rearview mirror and leather gloves with no tips at the ends of the fingers. Petra felt a bit underdressed in her cut off jean shorts and Beatles t-shirt.

Melissa squared her shoulders.

"Petra," she said, offering a crushing handshake. "I've heard so much about you. A real sailor. Thank you for your service."

The One and True Son

Petra always felt a little awkward when she was thanked for her military career. In many ways she thought that she'd served herself. She never had to defend anyone in a foxhole or anything. The whole hero thing never applied to her. She acknowledged Melissas thanks with a nod and a smile.

"You ever do the Arcangelo Gabriele Trail before?" Melissa asked. "It's a mish-mash of everything LA has to offer; scenic mountains, desert fauna, crushing poverty."

"Way to sell it," Betsy teased.

"Just kidding. It's a great ride. Nearly 30 miles one way, if we do the whole thing. A great workout."

"I just got my bike," Petra admitted. "I walk a lot, but I think I'm gonna have to build up to 30 miles."

"Hey, fine with me." Melissa winked at Petra, a friendly endearing gesture. "I like to bring new riders into the fold. We can start small and work our way up."

That first ride, they got as a far as the split at Coyote Creek. The industrial scenery of the beginning of the trail surprised Petra, and maybe disappointed her a bit. The Arcangelo River to left of the trail seemed abused and neglected by the dusty, huge electrical plant that appeared to go on forever as they headed north. The only green they saw was at the Edison Park Community Gardens with its patchwork of vegetables and trees, sectioned off and divided up among participants. Petra, Betsy and Candace could barely keep up with Melissa, the well-tuned biker, and at the footbridge that crossed over Coyote Creek, the three begged their guide to turn around.

"We haven't gotten out of the city yet," Melissa complained.

Betsy pulled her bike out of the traffic. She lowered the kickstand and walked in a small circle like a cowboy who'd been on his horse for a month. "I know, but I've got to tell you. My ass is killing me. It feels like rug burn.

They all laughed.

Melissa turned to Petra. "Are you hurting too?"

"Yeah," Petra admitted. This thing'll take a bit of gettin' used to."

"All right," said Melissa. "Next week. We do this again. Only next time we go a couple miles more. And we do it again the week after that. Either that or we keep going today. I haven't even warmed up."

"I'm out next week," Candace said.

"Me too," Betsy chimed. "Unlike some people, we don't work a cushy five day a week schedule."

Melissa turned to Petra. "You in?"

Petra shrugged. "Yeah, I guess."

"All right, we turn around. *This time.*"

As promised, Petra met Melissa at the marina the next weekend. She had to admit to herself that she did like Melissa. Her genuine smile and enthusiasm for life were both magnetic and contagious. But Petra was aware of her landladies' intentions, and she didn't know how to feel about that. She'd not been in many romantic relationships since Gloria, and she felt she was stepping blindly with Melissa. *Was she in on this? Did she know what Betsy and Candace had in mind?* Petra was aware that she probably was, and that frightened her a little.

Also, as promised, they rode further up the trail. Petra was thankful for the relative flatness of the trail and the generally well-maintained riding surface. She was able to hold her own with Melissa most of the way, although she suspected that Melissa may have been holding back a tad. Melissa had brought a gift for Petra, a riding helmet of black plastic that fit tight to her head.

"Do I gotta wear this?" Petra protested. "I'm afraid it'll give me a headache."

"You'll have to if you ride with me," Melissa said. "Let me ask you something. Have you ever seen a depressed skull fracture?"

Petra shook her head.

"I *have*. My brother and I used to go mountain trail biking. I mean *mountain*. We didn't like wearing helmets. Thought it was stupid. Then one day we were riding this desert trail. I was out front because I was faster. This was out in the desert, so it was hotter than hell, but we loved it that way. We came to this steep downgrade and this big diamondback was sunning herself right in the middle of the trail. I saw it about fifteen feet before I would've plowed in to and I hit the brakes. I turned to warn Mark, that's my brother, but for some reason the idiot wasn't looking in front of him. He didn't see that I'd stopped at first, and when he did, he hit the brakes hard and flipped the bike. He flew about 10 feet off the side of the trail and smacked his head on a pointed rock. At first, I didn't think he was hurt that bad. He got up and walked around. He cussed me out for stopping. I pointed out the snake, but he kept cussing. I mean really mean stuff. He seemed like a broken record. I finally got him to take a seat. I couldn't see any blood, but he had a weird look in his eye. I looked closer and I saw it wasn't just a weird look. His pupils were different. One was wide open; the other was pinpoint. He kept repeating himself over and over. I guess the snake was tired of it, because she slithered away."

"Holy moly," Petra gasped. "Did he, I mean…"

"Yeah, he made it. There were a couple of riders on another part of the trail that saw him fly and came over and asked if they could help. One of them was a paramedic. His girlfriend rode until she could get signal and called 911. They helicoptered him out. The paramedic found the dent in his head. It was about the size of his fist. He was in surgery for 8 hours."

Melissa smiled sweetly. "So, you want to put on the helmet?"

Petra put it on happily.

Each week the two rode a little further up the trail. At Rynerson Park one day, they hopped off the Arcangelo Gabriele trail and zoomed around the parks own maze of trails. Melissa took to bringing a backpack, an insulated one, which she packed delicious breads, crackers, and assorted cheeses that Petra had never had before, but quickly learned to love. This time, she also brought a bottle of wine.

They sat in a grassy spot. Melissa took out the food that looked like a fancy banquet to Petra. She took out a thin blanket, two plastic wine glasses with stems and filled them both.

"It's merlot. It tastes like butter," Melissa said, handing one to Petra.

"I don't really drink," Petra said, but taking the glass.

"This isn't *drinking,*" Melissa said with that wink of hers. "It's *tasting*. There's a big difference. You see, I believe in experiencing the world. We've got to taste it, to smell it, to feel it. Otherwise, what good is it to be here, right?"

Petra took a sip of the deeply red liquid. She'd never tasted anything like it. Her mouth was bathed in flavors she couldn't place, something earthy, something…"

Melissa smiled, "Good, huh."

Petra could only nod. She took another sip. Her face felt as if she'd been sitting near a campfire on a cold night.

Melissa moved in front of Petra and knelt in front of her. "You don't have to wear this while you're sitting here." She reached and unbuckled the strap under her chin and took off the helmet. "I don't think you're going to be smacking your head on any rocks."

Petra and Melissa looked at each for a long moment.

"You have pretty eyes," Melissa said. "Do you know that?"

Petra didn't know if it was the wine or the moment, but she felt her breathing quicken; her face burned. Melissa moved slowly to her and kissed her lightly, playfully. Petra could taste the merlot on Melissa's breath.

"Did you like that?" Melissa whispered.

The One and True Son

Petra nodded.

Melissa kissed her again, softly, longer this time. Petra responded, pushing gently against her lips, breathing in the scents.

Petra backed away, still looking Melissa in the eyes.

"This is a public park," she said, quietly. "There are little kids around here."

Melissa smiled. She kissed Petra on the tip of her nose.

"You're right," she said and sat back on her calves. "Let's keep riding."

Melissa and Petra found time to spend together throughout the week, but it was still the bike rides they looked forward to the most. Petra, always the athlete, found after a few weeks that not only could she keep up with Melissa, but, at times, could roll right past her. Landmarks like Rynerson Park and Telegraph Road began to seem early in the ride even though they were miles past where they rode in the beginning. The further north they traveled, it seemed to Petra, the more abundant the concrete in the houses and surrounding the riverbed. They rode through underpasses where homeless people had set up shelters; the city put up chainlink fences to keep that kind of homesteading to a minimum. One Saturday, one where Melissa had not slept particularly well, Petra rode out front almost the entire morning. Melissa complained of cramps and had to stop frequently. Petra held back from cruising too far ahead, enjoying her lead tremendously, but not enough to be obvious about it. As they rode through Santa Fe Springs Park, Melissa called out to her.

"Pet, stop for a minute."

They pulled their bikes off to the side.

"I'm going to stop here," said, sounding out of breath. "I've got to rest. My back is killing me. Why don't you ride on a bit. I'll lie down in the grass. Once I get my feet back under me, I'll ride until we meet."

Petra set her kickstand and walked to Melissa and stroked her cheek.

"Are you sure? I can stay with you. We'll ride back when you feel better."

"I'm sure. I know you love this. I can see it in your face."

Petra knew that was true. "Is it safe here? I don't remember riding this far."

Melissa pointed to the grass about ten feet from the trail. "I'm lying down right there. I've got the blanket from lunch. There are people riding by all the time. I'll be fine. Just don't ride to Oregon."

Petra kissed her on the cheek. "I'll probably turn around at the state line."

Petra thought about Melissa a lot. During the day, at the boat repair shop, she found herself daydreaming about her laugh, the small lines at the corner of her eyes, the way she stroked Petra's hair when they talked, nothing planned, completely natural. Was she falling in love? She had no idea. But she liked what she was feeling.

It was a beautiful day with a light breeze at her back; cottony white clouds took up small portions of the sky. The scenery grew arid, desert taking possession of the scene around her, with sparse clusters of trees and parched, tangled weeds weaving in and out of the rusty fence along the side of the trail. The whisper in her mind had been silent lately, an occurrence that Petra took to mean she was closer to where she should be in her life. She thought Melissa might have something to do with it. Or her job with the coolest boss anyone could want. Or maybe it was Long Beach, with a community that accepts her, like her parents had wanted for her. The whisper had almost gone until that day.

It didn't come back as a whisper, more like a roar.

HERE!

Petra jammed her brakes, her rear tire leaving the trail surface. She released them in time to avoid flipping over the handlebars.

"WHAT?" she shouted, to whom or to what she didn't know. She scanned her surroundings. There were people on the other side of the fence, maybe a football field away. No one was close enough to shout to her as loud as she'd heard it. There were makeshift shelters and a patchwork of tents, like a tent—if not city—a tent town. There was an opening in the fence, just feet away from a rusty sign hanging by one screw warning against such a town. Petra leaned her bike against the sign and entered the breach in the fence.

As she walked toward the encampment her thoughts returned to the Bay of Bengal, to Chittagong, to tossing chocolate bars to starving people. She could hear the desperate pleas from a shirtless, dark-skinned man, his hands held up with palms together, as if the ship were Yahweh himself. The yellowed scleras of the man's eyes pleaded in a language everyone could understand. The man wept as he rowed away, chocolate in hand.

Here are people, Petra thought, much better off than the man in the small skiff, and yet there was need here.

A man appeared from behind one of the tents. He was a muscular man, with long twisted African hair bleached by the sun, with a tattered t-shirt and worn-down jean shorts. He was smiling.

"Here you are," the man said beaming. "My name is Dzon."

* * *

The One and True Son

At eight o'clock Jessie called Petra's cellphone. "Please buzz us in and unlock the door."

Dimple and Praise carried in what looked to be supplies for a meal, followed by Jessie. The two women set the plastic bags on the counter and sat on the dull green carpet of the empty living room. A moment later the door buzzed. "We're here," came the response through the speaker on the wall. Through the door came Jack, Joodith, Bart, Justice, Levi and Simone. Jessie told them to have a seat in the living room with the others. He went into the kitchen and started rustling the bags and the opening and closing of the oven.

There was a solemnity hovering in the air. No one spoke after being separated for what seemed weeks. Their eyes dropped and their minds focused on their own thoughts. After fifteen minutes, Jessie called from the kitchen.

"Praise? Could you come in here for a moment. I need some help."

A moment later they emerged from the kitchen. Praise was carrying a box of red wine and a single red plastic cup. Jessie followed her into the room with a paper plate on which looked to be a single matzah.

The moreh spoke: "Please join me in a circle. We will eat together today."

The Twelve formed a circle, leaving a space for the teacher to sit with the sliding glass doors behind him. The sun was down, but the darkness of night had not yet reached into the room. Clouds were beginning to fill the twilight.

Jessie sat with his followers and placed the plate in front of him. He took the box of wine from Praise who was seated next to him and cracked the seal. He poured the cup to nearly full.

The moreh closed his eyes. "My Father. We thank you for what we are about to receive. We praise your creation and ask that you bless all present here."

Jessie was silent after this for some time. He sat with his eyes closed; his breathing was smooth and deep. The Twelve was getting restless. Simone fidgeted. Dimple looked to the others.

"Moreh," she whispered, finally. "Are we having seder? I'm confused. Pesach was months ago. Where are the bitter herbs? The salted water? The egg?"

The moreh considered this, his eyes still closed.

"This is something new, my chosen twelve. These are times of even more suffering, of lack, of despair. This is why I am here. To fulfill my father's covenant with you all."

The One and True Son

He raised the cup and again thanked his Father.

"Drink from this cup, all of you."

He handed the cup to Praise who did as she was instructed and handed it to Tom next to her. They passed the cup until it returned to Jessie.

"This wine is my blood. It will be shed for you and everyone for the forgiveness of human sin."

The others looked to each other. Their shocked eyes met and quickly looked away.

Jessie picked up the unleavened bread from the paper plate. He raised the bread in front of him and thanked and praised his father.

"Take a piece of this bread, all of you. Eat it." He placed the bread on the plate and handed it to Praise who, again, did as she was instructed and handed the plate to her left. When the plate returned to Jessie, he set the plate in front of him.

"This bread you have eaten is my body. When you eat, I want you to think of me."

The room grew deathly silent. The more, again, closed his eyes.

It was Simone who broke the silence.

"Wait. Moreh, you have to explain to us what's going on. If it's bad, we'll protect you."

Jack spoke next. "Is there trouble coming? We *need* to know. If we've got to fight, we will." Eleven of them shook their heads in agreement. Jack tossed a buck knife in front of him. "Whatever it takes, moreh."

Jessie opened his eyes and looked at the knife. A slight smile took hold of his lips.

"That thing can't do anything to stop what is coming. Put it away and never think of it again. What is going to happen is already in motion." He turned and faced Praise.

"Isn't it." This wasn't a question.

Praise turned gray. "Moreh. I..."

"Do you have the phone?" Jessie asked, almost gently. "Did you make the call yet?"

"Moreh. Your thinking is dangerous," Praise burst out. "If you understood..."

"They're waiting for you, Praise." Jessie interrupted. "You can't disappoint them, can you? You'd better dial the number. They won't be patient. You know that from experience, don't you? I don't want to know why you *think* you're doing this. Just do it and get it over with."

Jack dove at Praise, but Jessie stopped him with one large hand. Petra stood.

"Hold on!" she shouted. "You'll turn him in? Well, you ain't goin' anywhere, missy."

The moreh looked at Petra. "Petra, before the sun comes up in the morning, you will deny even knowing me."

Petra's jaw fell. "No! How can you say…"

"I do say it. And not once. Three times."

Jessie turned to the others.

"Let her go," he ordered. He turned to Praise. "Go."

Fifteen minutes later, the door flew in.

Once released, Petra walked to Woodlawn Drive. If anyone had seen her, they may have mistaken her for a junkie or drunk, walking listlessly, a blank expression on her face, her hair tossed and tangled from running her fingers through it, her eyes fixed on something that wasn't in front of her.

The FBI, or whoever they were, battered in the metal door of the apartment with three swings of that metal battering thing they use. In a matter of seconds, everything changed. With the shouting, the automatic weapons, it was as if someone was filming the scene with a camera in slow motion and dropped the camera, blurring all the images. Petra thought she heard something like, *Homeland Security,* but she knew that that could be just about anyone. She saw no badges, no identification. The agents wore blue windbreakers with nothing on them and blue jeans or khakis. That was except for two them: one, an Asian guy wearing a hoody and some sweatpants and a bald man, creepy looking, wearing what had to be a very expensive suit. Petra guessed that these two were running the show.

After the agents secured everyone's hands with plastic ties, they sat them on the living room carpet.

"Good evening, everyone," the creepy man said. He was rubbing some kind of lotion into his hands. "I'm so excited to finally meet you all. My name is Richard Fondlen and I've been following your exploits for some time. You all are really quite impressive. Your commitment is unshakeable. That's so rare, nowadays." The man's smile looked, to Petra, like a rabid chimp.

"I need to bring in someone you know," he said, his eyes moving around the room, taking everyone in. "Officer, can you come in here please?"

Praise entered, not looking at anyone. She stood next to the bald man.

"This is just a formality really. According to Officer Johnson, only one of you was involved in the heinous crime committed in our nation's capital." He shrugged wrinkling his well-tailored jacket around the neck. "Of course, there is harboring a suspect in a terrorism case, but again, Officer Johnson assures me that you weren't aware of his role. We will go with this theory." That vicious smile again. "For now."

He turned to Praise. Officer Johnson, will you…"

Praise shot him a look. "I'm not …"

He silenced her with one well-manicured finger. He pressed it to her lips before anyone saw him move. "Shhhh…Now, please identify the perpetrator of the alleged crime."

Praise walked to Jessie and kneeled in front of him. A fat tear ran down her cheek. "I'm sorry, moreh." She leaned forward and kissed him on the forehead.

Jessie watched her, saying nothing. He seemed to watch the tear as it rolled off her chin.

"Daughter," he said when he finally spoke. "Must you betray the son with a kiss?"

Petra looked as if she'd been slapped. She stood and ran from the apartment.

"Well, that went well," Fondlen said with a clap of his hands. He turned to his people. "Please take the suspect down to the car. Inspector Trang. You can interview the others if you care to. You can let them go if they have no new information. With my blessing."

The Asian man who appeared to be the inspector he was referring to, looked puzzled. He opened his mouth, but no words came out.

Two agents, a man and a woman, came around Jessie and lifted him from the floor. Each grasped an arm and escorted him out the door.

Petra sat on a bench under the trees in a park off Featherbed Road for nearly the entire night. Where she'd go now, she had no idea. The Petra that had left everything, her friends, her job, perhaps the love of her life, was just a ghost to her now. Jessie was gone, taken right in front of her. *How could that be?* She was sure he was the one, the one to fix this broken world. She felt it in every fiber of her being. And now? She didn't know anything.

The agent let them take their belongings, all of which she'd been carrying in a tattered blue school bookbag. They took the phone and Petra never wore a watch, so she didn't have any idea of the time.

The One and True Son

She took stock of where she was and guessed the direction from which she'd come. She headed that way. Maybe Dimple and the others were still around. They could talk about happened, make a plan. Maybe they could raise money for a lawyer. Levi had been a tax accountant. Maybe he could figure it out. She passed by a group of young people. She didn't look at them, hoping they wouldn't notice how out of place she was. They passed by her and the smell of cannabis followed soon after. Petra felt a chill when she heard them stop.

"Hey lady," one of them, a male called out to her. "You was one of those people that brought the Feds to the apartments. What ya do? Rob a bank or somethin'?"

Petra froze. She didn't want to run. That might make things worse.

"No dummy," one of them said. "Didn't you see the guy they put in the car? That's the guy they been looking for. For the temple. The internet guy."

"Shit, nah!" the other responded.

"You know that guy? Was you with him when he blew up the temple?"

"No, that wasn't me," Petra said. "I don't know what you're talking about."

A female voice spoke. "Oh no, I saw you. Me and my sister watched the whole thing. We was in the apartment across the street. We saw you. I know what I saw. Bet she got a big price tag on her head."

Petra looked at the group. There were only three of them, maybe sixteen years old.

"Please, I don't know that guy or what y'all are talking about. I just couldn't sleep. I went for a walk."

"Wait a second," the third said, another male. "Didn't you tear up the joint on Passover? I think I saw your mugshot on the internet. Or a picture of you or something."

Petra's voice cracked. "Please, I don't know that guy you're talkin' about. I don't need no trouble."

The first one spoke again. "We ain't no snitches, but you better get the hell outta here. If you did anything like that Five-Oh gonna get you. Best get going now."

Petra walked away quickly toward the apartments. It hadn't struck her yet that the sun was just peeking over the horizon.

FOUR

The Dreamer

Erica woke from the dream. She could still hear the man screaming. It was the scream of someone losing a limb from a swipe of a rusty saw blade, someone with a kidney stone ripping and tearing its way through a ureter.

She'd have to call Richard. He told her he was out of the country, and that she probably wouldn't be able to reach him. She knew now that he wasn't abroad. He was here. He'd never left the country. He'd lied. She had to reach him before it was too late. She knew how this would end. She'd heard the chant.

Strange dreams, important dreams weren't new to Erica. She'd had them as a child. Her grandmother said they were a family trait, one that had predicted wars, births, and most often, deaths. Gra-mère wasn't trying to scare her. She claimed they were a gift direct from Yahweh himself.

The important dreams, the ones of consequence, didn't come often. In fact, Erica believed she could conjure memories of all of those, close her eyes and nearly relive them. Of course, she had the silly dreams that everyone has. There was the one where she was in a bowling alley at night, the lights dimmed to near darkness in the nonplaying area, the lanes lit from a glow underneath as if the boards of the lanes themselves were emitting it. The players to her sides, faceless and uniformed, rolled their customized, individualized spheres down the lanes with precision, striking the pins with devastating blasts that sent them flying in all directions. Erica didn't feel uncomfortable or out of place. The shadowy light soothed her, strangely enough; the crash of the pins exhilarated her. Something different was coming. She could feel it. Something in the raucous chaos was going to change. She noticed a man strolling to the foul line of the lane nearest to her. Instead of the bowling shirt and the Sansabelt pants the bowlers wore, he was wearing a plaid flannel shirt, its sleeves rolled to mid forearm, and baggy khaki trousers fitted with pockets down the legs. Instead of a bowling ball, the man carried a fishing rod and a bucket, both of which he set down at his feet on either side of him.

The man patted at the breast pockets of his shirt and pulled out a pack of cigarettes and a disposable lighter. He raised the pack to his mouth. A moment later, his head lit in silhouette, a stream of smoke streamed from the man, dissipating yards from him in the other lanes.

The man turned his head, and she could see the features of his face, two dimensional, flat black, the cigarette dangling from his lips, the glowing cherry dipping as he took a drag.

Seemingly ready, he picked up the bucket and took out what looked to be an aluminum soup can and set it at his feet. Next, he tipped the bucket over and sat on it, facing out toward the pins. He picked up the fishing rod and grabbed the hook delicately. He leaned the pole on his hip and reached for the can on his other side. A moment later, he picked up the fishing rod and casted lightly in front of him in a smooth arc. As if it were standard for this type of establishment, the fishhook, a fat earthworm writhing from its recent impalement, plunged through the surface of the bowling lane, which instantly transformed to a fishing pond, still maintaining the shape and lighting of the other lanes. As Erica watched, a large fish, possibly a trout, appeared to catch the vibrations of the tortured worm and moved swiftly to the area of the splash. The fish struck viciously and the man's line flexed, the reel on his pole buzzing in protest.

The man stood from his bucket, prepared for a fight. Erica could see the fish was just as prepared and pulled back from the man trying to reel him in. And just as quickly as the struggle began, it ended, the line went slack and the fish retreated with worm, hook and some line, back under the stacked pins.

Erica woke up laughing.

As an adult, she told no one about her dreams. No one except her husband, Richard, who listened quietly as she spoke (often she was shaken by the important ones, the ones that truly meant something) massaging her hands with his soft fingers, telling her in that calming way he has with her that it was fine, that it was a dream, synapses firing in her head. Coincidences, he'd say. Nothing more. Richard had a way of contradicting her, a way of explaining harsh realities, without condescending to her. He was merely explaining, that's all. She knew that others found this off-putting. But he was a businessman, a good one. Part of being a good businessman, he'd say, was conveying the truth to those who don't want to hear it. And he was a good businessman.

Erica had met Richard Fondlen 15 years prior. He'd been a client. She'd been working in a tiny health spa called *The Human Touch,* located

The One and True Son

on the second floor of a old row house on Harford Road in Baltimore, with three massage rooms, a clean and fresh scented restroom, and a tiny lobby with room for one chair and the desk where the owner, Rachel, sat night and day. Rachel greeted the clients with a cup of warm herbal tea and a cleansing foot wash.

The lobby was bright in the day from the overhead skylight and modern picture window that looked out at the gas station sign across the street. At night, the room glowed warmly from hidden lamps installed at the top of the cream-colored walls drifting down through the leaves of healthy hanging ferns.

Erica was 23, a recent graduate of the Holistic Health Training Institute, where she learned techniques in Swedish massage, Deep Tissue, Reflexology, Shiatsu as well as energy techniques, Reiki and aromatic therapies. Originally from a suburb of Montreal, Plateau Mont-Royal, an artsy and friendly place, Erica enrolled in medical school at the University of Maryland to follow her mother's dream of Erica becoming a doctor. The idea of helping people appealed to her, but she found after a year that she really didn't have the drive to continue on. Her mother, furious with her decision, cut her off.

Her parents divorced when she was 14 and her father, an artist of talent, but little following, offered to take her in at his small loft in Montreal. Erica had taken a liking to Baltimore; its row houses with their cupolas and turrets reminded her of the row homes of her childhood. She'd rented a row home with four of her fellow therapists, in Camden, a trendy area with young professionals and students from the many universities nearby. In the creaky hardwood floors, she'd felt the imprints of those who'd lived there previously, in its 100 -year existence. The imprints weren't ghosts per se, just feelings, wisps of memories. She turned her father down and buckled down on spending. She knew she could make it work.

At 23, Erica wasn't thinking of marriage. She wasn't really thinking of dating. She went out with guys who seemed interesting, but found most of them fell into two categories: the driven undergrad or law school or med school or business school student who had little time for more than coffee or dinner at a small nearby eatery. Often, they had little to talk about other than politics. There were also the rudderless guys, the ones with no plan, no experience, no idea of where they'll be in ten years or even five. It was with the latter group that she usually paid for the coffee or the small eatery, mostly with money she hadn't made yet.

After about three months of coffee shop conversations and blossoming credit card bills, she told her friends and roommates that she'd declared a moratorium on set ups and blind dates. She cancelled her subscriptions to

The One and True Son

dating apps, which truthfully never amounted to anything and took solace from her occasional loneliness in the arms of a comfortably warm sweater, with a cup of hot buttered rum and a good book.

She'd been working at the spa about three months before Richard Fondlen booked her for an hour and a half massage. Massage can be rough on the therapist's own muscles and joints, particularly in the hands, which, according to her training, needed to stay supple and fluid to allow her healing energy pass from her to her client. Erica paced her movements, listening to the signals she received from her hands, and adjusted the tension and relaxation of her knuckles, her forearms, her palms and her fingertips, and by three months, an extended massage seemed no more physically taxing as one of a half hour.

Richard Fondlen had just finished his tea when Erica emerged from her massage room the day they'd met. Fondlen stood when she came to greet him, his feet freshly cleansed in mint and lemon grass water, the cuffs of his khaki pants rolled up nearly to his knees. He was wearing a pair of aviator sunglasses. Erica, unconsciously looked to the skylight. The sky was cloudy, looking somewhat dismal, to her eye.

As if reading her thoughts, he spoke: "I have sensitive eyes from time to time." He smiled.

Erica's breath caught. His smile was frightening, sharp and tight, like that of a carnivorous reptile. The smile was at once, to Erica, both dangerous and fascinating. *What created a smile like that?*

Erica took Richard back to her massage room. She'd prepared it before she'd gone out to greet him, lighting sandalwood incense and aromatic candles, putting on soothing, spiritual music and replacing her previous client's linens with freshly, cleaned white linens and a pre-warmed knit cotton blanket. She had her oils warming in a bath of replenished warm water. She liked to think of her massage room as a luxurious oasis in the middle a harsh and unforgiving desert. Richard sat, looking slightly awkward in his polo shirt and immaculately tailored sport coat. He took off his shades and placed them in a case in his inside jacket pocket. In the dim light of the room his eyes were like ink, flat, drawing the rest of the room into them.

"Please feel free to remove as much clothing as you're comfortable with," Erica said after a moment. I will only uncover the areas, I'm working on. Are there any specific places you want me to pay special attention to? You have an extended session, so we have a lot of time to work on things that may be bothering you."

Richard smiled that smile again. Erica really didn't know how she felt about it.

"I think I need a good overall massage. I have the normal tensions from an abnormal workload. Ninety minutes ought to do just right."

Erica smiled. "Well, I let you change. I'll knock when I come back."

She'd started on his arms. She liked to ease her clients into the message, to establish a feeling of trust, almost, but not quite intimacy. She began the process with the client face up, free to look around if they wished, to know they were in a safe space, that no harm would, or could come to them, in her hands. Richard closed his eyes, which pleased her for a number of reasons. She didn't know how to feel about them either. They were unusual eyes. Disconcerting. And yet she feared she'd want to look at them too much. By closing his eyes, he was showing he trusted her, that he didn't watch what she was up to. She could work and he trusted her to do what was in his best interest. She usually could tell if she'd have a repeat client. They usually closed their eyes.

She ran her hands in sweeps, drenched in fragrant oils, using her thumbs and fingertips to find his energy, where it might be trapped. His skin was nothing like anything she'd felt before. It was supple, pliable. And the scars, five or six of them on each arm, some razor straight while others were like cracks in very moist cheese. She felt for his tendons and found them to be narrow, but hard, like metal, like...cables.

She spoke to him in her softest voice, as she did with all her clients, in soothing soft near-whispers. "How is this pressure? Is it comfortable."

He spoke back to her, mirroring her tone. "It's very comfortable, thank you. You're well trained. Very good hands." He took in a breath in through his nose and let it out slowly. "This is just what I need."

As Erica finished with each arm, she'd place it gently at his side and covered it with the thick blanket and linens. She pressed her hands down his chest, through the blankets, moving down over his pectoralis major muscles, preparing them for the therapy she would provide. Flattening her palms, she pressed gently into his rectus abdominus. Erica could feel that he had diastasis recti, a stretching of the abdominal muscles that often occurred in women during pregnancy, that made them look, well, pregnant. She knew exercises that may help him, but she wouldn't presume to tell them of those yet. And truthfully, she hadn't noted a pot belly when she met him in the lobby. Beyond that, he'd come to her for a message, not diagnosis and treatment. She refreshed the oils on the palms of her hands.

When she pulled the linens back to begin his chest massage, she couldn't hold in the gasp. The scars were everywhere. Most were about six inches long, straight and precise. Others where jagged and angry, healed not by needle and thread but time and luck.

The One and True Son

Richard opened his eyes. His smiled said he was amused. Erica couldn't tell what his eyes were saying.

"Don't worry," he said, keeping their agreed upon tone in his voice. "I have a genetic predisposition to certain kinds of cancers. I've had many treatments, but you can't cause me any pain. I've grown quite used to them really. I'm not sure I'd feel right without them."

When Erica looked hesitant, he said: "Please. We're having such good interaction here. I'm comfortable and I want you to be. People are scarred. n your line of business you must've seen that. Some are scarred in the skin. Some in the body. Some in the mind. One leg shorter than the other. A finger missing. This is the human condition. That's why you do this work, isn't it?"

Erica nodded once and smiled.

"That's why I asked for you," he said, almost in a whisper, closing his eyes. "I knew you would understand."

Richard became a regular and certainly her most consistent client. He'd booked her for every Thursday for a solid month. She couldn't say that the experience of massaging him was pleasant, much in the way a walk through a thick jungle wouldn't be, with the bugs and the heavy air, swinging an old, sharp machete just to move forward a foot; yet the experience was worth it, to see what others will never see. His skin was surprisingly soft; the upper layers, transparent, almost like membrane, while the tissues underneath seemed liquid, almost viscous. Why did she chill when he smiled? Did everyone react that way? No one spoke of him at the spa and Erica felt no need to bring him up. He was written into her schedule as Mr. Thursday.

They began meeting for coffee at The Red Dingy, a small coffeeshop and bookstore just down the road. She'd never met a client outside the spa. She'd never met anyone for coffee who wasn't in her age group. Sometimes they'd go out after his session, others they'd meet on her off days. They'd talk for hours, he sipping double espressos, she, herbal teas. Erica realized that people observing them would notice the contrasts, the seemingly obvious opposites, sitting at a small table in the back speaking in hushed tones, often laughing, often sharing a light touch, a brush of fingers, a sweeping away of a curl from her eye, by this man with unnaturally white hands.

She learned that he was an insurance executive, who currently lived and worked in DC. He'd never been married. He traveled extensively in his job. He did a lot of work with disasters occurring around the world where US interests were involved. He never mentioned money although it was obvious to Erica that it wasn't a problem. He dressed impeccably and expensively. She looked up the watch he wore on the internet, an Omega Speedmaster, the *watch that went to the moon*. It sold for over $5000. The price was impressive to her, as it would be to most people who'd never had that much in their checking account at one time, but it's history that most intrigued her. He'd told her all about the Apollo 11 mission, that Buzz Aldrin wore it in a famous photograph from space, that it was an icon then and to this day. No one her age knew of such things. No one could speak of them as if they knew everyone involved.

She knew something was happening between them, something akin to romance. She'd fought this notion at first, even to the point of claiming she had *an appointment* when he asked if they were on for the Red Dingy. He seemed unconcerned when she told him this. He knew she was lying. She could tell. He told her that when she had time, she could call him on his cell. He gave her his number. He said maybe they could go to dinner, or something a little more interesting than just coffee. And then she didn't call.

He cancelled his appointments for two consecutive weeks. By the end of those weeks, Erica was nearly frantic. She called the number that he'd given her, but it went straight to voicemail. After three calls with no answer, she called and left a message this time. In the message she told him she was sorry for not calling sooner, that she'd been dishonest, that she didn't have an appointment. She said that she was afraid of the feelings she was developing for him, afraid that she and he were too different. She admitted that the age difference was a consideration; he might tire of her. She wasn't very exciting. That she didn't know what he could possibly see in her.

He called her back three long days later.

"I apologize for not calling you," he said to her voicemail. She'd been in the shower.

"I was out of the country. You may have heard there was a bridge collapse in Tel Aviv. It was a pedestrian bridge. Several people were killed including an Australian athlete. They all fell into the Yarkon River which is highly polluted, even toxic. One person died just from exposure to the water." He paused.

"I have to tell you, things have changed. I'm going to be leaving DC. I'm moving back to the West Coast. You know, business. I'd like to take you to dinner before I go. Things are moving rather quickly so it will have to be tonight. If you can make it, say around 7:30, I'll have a car pick you up. I'll be in meetings all day so just call me back and leave a voicemail with your address. I truly hope you can make it."

The One and True Son

Erica called the spa and plead illness. She tried her best to sound congested on the phone, practicing a scratchy voice before she'd dialed. Apparently, Rachel bought it. Her boss told her to drink chamomile tea with lots of lemon and honey. "If that doesn't, work" the older woman advised, "pour in as much bourbon as you can handle."

Erica next went to the Towson Mall and got a dress she really couldn't afford at Nordstrom. It was the little black dress that everyone always said that no woman should be without, which she'd lived without until that day. From there, she got her nails done in salon on the first floor, nearly gagging from the overwhelming stench of acetone. She went home to wash her hair with a fancy shampoo and conditioner she'd bought the last time she had her hair cut. She felt as though she'd been preparing for the prom.

The car arrived, a limousine with a bar and soft music playing, at 7:30 on the dot. She felt a mix of excitement and dread. After all, what was she doing? Why did she get herself all dolled up? What was she expecting? Was she saying goodbye? Was he? She didn't know how she felt about anything. Well, almost anything. She had an inexplicable notion that her life was about to change.

The car took her to the Ivy Hotel, a converted mansion in Mount Vernon, one of the most prestigious neighborhoods in Baltimore. When the car pulled up to the understated canopy over the lobby, Richard was there holding a bouquet of bright, exotic flowers, standing, as usual in a crisp blue suit. The sun was just going down, but he still wore his sunglasses.

Richard waved back the chauffeur and opened the door for Erica and offered his soft, pale hand to guide her out.

The hotel lobby was stunning. It was if someone had taken a Victorian home with the finest of furniture, added the colors of nature, colors rarely seen together inside with sky blues and mellow browns, added ferns and exotic plants and polished everything to a degree that no one imagined to be possible. As they walked, Richard told her of the history of the hotel. "It was originally a mansion, built for the banker and industrialist John Gilman and his wife. They sold it to an inventor, a man who made his money making bottle caps and corks. His name was William Painter. It was next sold to a doctor who made it into a clinic. The depression was hard on the area around here and eventually the doctor, a man named Futcher, donated it to Baltimore Parks and Recreation. William Donald Shaeffer, the mayor in the 80s used to wine and dine dignitaries here."

"It's beautiful. I didn't know this place existed. How do you know so much about it?"

"I've stayed here many times when I've had to go in and out of DC," he said. "This time I'm going out."

The One and True Son

He took off his sunglasses and looked at her for what seemed a long time. His black eyes in the chandeliers' light seemed to be soaking her in. She couldn't look away.

"May I say you look absolutely stunning. I should've gotten you out of the spa more often."

Erica blushed. Her hand nervously played with a curl of her hair at her shoulder.

"I thought it would be a special night," she said, surprised at her own boldness. "With you moving back to the West Coast."

"Yes, but let's not talk about that yet. I'd like a drink and I am a little hungry. The restaurant is holding a special room for us."

The restaurant, called Magdalena, was just as opulent and warm as the rest of the hotel with rich lights provided by hanging art deco lamps with faux antique Edison lightbulbs. They lit the room like a sunset. The seating was unostentatious, comfortable and practical. The waiters, all dressed in crisp white shirts, black vests and linen aprons moved effortlessly from guest to guest, their smiles unwavering. The maître d' recognized Richard and immediately approached them.

"Mr Fondlen. So glad to see you again," he said. "We have your room ready as you specified. Please follow me." The host, clad in a smartly tailored tuxedo, led them to a room of rich mahogany tables and walls; a wine-rack spanned all four walls of the room, stocked fully with wines from all over the world, some bottles on their sides while others leaned down like cannons from an old ship, pointing down at a smaller intruder. The maître d', a tall, slim, black man with tightly cropped hair and narrow handsome features, a man Erica was sure could have a lucrative career as a model or an actor, pulled her chair out for her and gently guided her back under the table. He stood, smiling, as Richard seated himself.

Two waiters quickly filled their water glasses.

"Your wine has been opened and breathing, Mr. Fondlen, as you prefer. Marcus will be here in a moment. Is there anything I can do for you and your guest before he arrives?"

"No, Antonio," Richard said, smoothing his linen napkin in his lap. "Everything is perfect as usual. Thank you for your attention to detail. You *are* the best."

"It's kind of you to say, sir." the maître d' said with a muted smile. "Please don't hesitate to ask for me if you need anything."

Erica smiled across at Richard. The table could easily seat six but there were places just for the two of them at either end. She'd never seen so many forks on a table at one time, all, of varying sizes, most of them at the left in order, smallest to longest and one at above the plate, she assumed for dessert. To the right of the plate was an array of spoons, the teaspoon and soupspoon the only ones familiar to her.

"Do you eat here often, or only when you want to impress someone?" Erica teased.

"I've never eaten here with anyone else," Richard said, his head tilting slightly. "The food is excellent. Some of the best I've ever eaten. This is my room though. They hardly ever use it. When I call to tell them I'm coming, they get it ready for me."

"Must be nice," Erica said, smiling.

"It is," Richard agreed. "Ah here's Marcus."

They were joined by a jovial, youngish looking man with a bulging chef's tunic, double buttoned down the front and an unruly mop of yellow/blond hair. Erica marveled at his hands. His fingers looked like uncooked sausages, strong, but somehow delicate.

"Marcus!" Richard stood and put his arm around the big man. "I'd like to present to you Ms. Erica, a very good friend of mine. Erica, this is our executive chef. He's been to almost as places as I have, learning the secrets to the world's cuisine. He will make you forget the best meals you *think* you've had."

Marcus beamed. "Mr. Fondlen is too kind," he said with a slight South African accent. "I cook best for those who appreciate good food. I have something very special for you tonight. There is no need for menus. If you don't enjoy it, I shall resign my position and reimburse you personally."

Richard chuckled. "He knows he's making a bet he won't have to pay." He patted the man on the back. "Now go and bring us this feast!"

The chef laughed and nodded to Erica. "Ms. Erica. It was a pleasure meeting you."

The wine was poured. Something old, red and mellow with flavors Erica had never tasted in a wine. There was no show of tasting the wine, no display of the label on the bottle. The staff knew what Richard wanted and they brought it to him without delay. It was the most wonderful wine Erica had ever tasted.

They made small talk at first. Again, Erica was reminded of the prom; both of them were nervous, as if they didn't really know each other well, but had been admiring each other for some time. Richard asked about the spa. Had she new clients? What music was she playing for them? Was she working her hands too hard? She asked about his recent work in Tel Aviv. He waved it off.

"I don't want to speak of such things tonight. It was all very sad, really, and I am quite happy at this moment."

"Well, tell me then," Erica said, trying to sound playful. "Do you already have a house on the West Coast. By the way, that's a large area. Are you going to tell me where you're moving, or is that a secret?"

Richard smiled that smile that intrigued her so much.

"Not at all," he answered. "As a matter of fact, that was part of the reason I wanted to speak to you tonight." He looked over her shoulder. "But that will have to wait. The food arrives."

The first course, the appetizer or starter, as Marcus referred to it, was Iranian caviar.

"I must tell you," the executive chef said, as he excused the waiter to serve them both personally, scooping the golden fish eggs delicately onto miniature blinis and placing them in front of Erica and then Richard, "that this is the finest caviar in the world. It is Almas Caviar. It's usually only sold at a restaurant in the UK, but they flew me some as a favor. Don't tell anyone." He winked. "Take a look a look at the tin it's served in. It's very special. Enjoy."

As the chef walked away, Erica took a close look at the "tin".

"Is that…?" she said, her tongue unable to finish.

"It is indeed," Richard said, picking up the container. "Gold. 24 karat gold to be exact. Lucky you. You get to keep it as a souvenir."

The caviar was followed by a soup of abalone, Japanese flower mushroom, sea cucumber, dried scallops and shark fin. Erica had never imagined eating such foods, but she'd always said she'd try anything once. It was heavenly. She wondered if she'd ever be able to have it again.

The entrée was blue fin tuna, a rare and fatty tuna from Japan, usually used in Sushi, but it in this case delicately seared and delicious surrounded by light and flavorful herbs and vegetables. Erica imagined that this is how it feels to be royalty, to have the most wonderful food on the planet at your beck and call, all expected, all delivered.

Erica couldn't help smiling. The evening seemed dreamlike. Dessert arrived, small, light pastries topped with fresh fruits, some she could identify and some she'd never seen before, each a miniature piece of art, so attractive that she'd felt a pang of guilt with everyone she'd placed in her mouth, where they melted in flavors she'd never imagined.

A waiter wheeled a cart up to the table.

"I know you're a tea drinker, but you must try this very special coffee with me," Richard said. "They prepare it I way that I'm sure you've never seen. It puts the perfect cap on a wonderful meal."

The One and True Son

Of course, he was correct. The magic performed involved sugar, whiskey, rare coffee, flame and showmanship. Erica wasn't a coffee drinker, but she could drink this coffee all day. After a meal this exciting, she was exhausted.

With the coffee in front of them they spent many moments just looking at each other. Finally, Richard spoke.

"You know that I've enjoyed our time together. Your talented hands, your laugh, your insights. It has been very special to me."

Erica felt it difficult to breathe. "It's been special to me too, Richard. I can't tell you how much I looked forward to your sessions. The coffee and our talks. They… they meant a lot to me too. You're an unusual man, Richard Fondlen."

Richard smiled that smile that confused her so yet intrigued her more.

"So here is my idea," Richard said and moved to the chair next to her. "I think you should come with me. To San Diego. It's a beautiful city. It has beaches and sun and palm trees. I have a house there. I've been thinking of building another. So, I'm wondering. Will you come?"

Erica teared up. She really didn't know what to say.

"I know. It's asking a lot…"

"Richard," Erica stopped him. "I don't know what to say. We have such a good time together. But I have the spa. There would be so much involved. I'd have to move across the country. And living together. I've never done that. What if you don't like me as much as you think you do?"

Richard put his left hand on her right. "One thing you should know about me is that when I know about something, I act. I know you, better than you know yourself. And strangely enough, I think that you know me too, at least on some level. And I must correct you are about one thing you said. That we would be *living together*. That's not at all what I have in mind."

With his right hand, he slipped his hand into his jacket and withdrew a ring case. It was clad in a soft velvet with a French name embossed in gold.

Erica gasped.

Please open it.

In the case was a ring, stunning with the whitest diamonds she'd ever seen; the first layer of the setting, a circle of six diamond of equal brightness and clarity, inside them, another circle, slightly raised, of six more, smaller diamonds. The top layer, six more, white, bright, clear diamonds cluster, slightly raised in the center of the ring.

"I thought about getting you the crown jewels, but you don't strike me as a crown jewel type of gal."

"Richard," Erica said, her eyes streaming. "What do I say?"

"A simple yes will do," Richard replied.

At that moment they were joined by Marcus, the executive chef. "Do I have to resign my job or was that a wonderful meal?"

Marcus looked at Erica holding the ring case open in her hand.

"Oh, this is marvelous!" Marcus exclaimed. "Well, Ms. Erica which is it? Put it on and meals like this are guaranteed every time you come to visit."

Erica took the ring from the case and slid it on her ring finger. It was a perfect fit.

Erica never went back to the row house she shared with her colleagues. She never returned to the spa either. Richard arranged for movers to retrieve her things. He'd booked a first-class seat to San Diego to accompany him there. That night, when she saw the hotel room, she could only say one thing: *It looks like a dream.*

The first time Erica exhibited the family trait, "the gift from God" as her grandmother described it, she was 6 years old. Her parents were still married. Her grandmother had the attic room, right above Erica's. Erica was sleeping in her lavender colored room, in her four-post princess bed, her comforter decorated with small Eiffel Towers and pink and violet ballerinas. Erica loved Paris, although she'd never been there. Her grandmother regaled Erica with tales of her childhood there, with the smells of freshly made bread, the coffee, the old men sitting outside chatting about the soccer match. The cobblestone streets, the Champs Elysees, the Arche De Triomphe, Place du Tertre, the square so clogged with easels and tourists that its colors never seemed to fade, rainy days or sunny. The air hummed, her grandmother told her, with history from the Romans and beyond.

She'd been sleeping soundly that night, which was something uncommon for young Erica, as she often found herself jammed in between her parents, squished between them while they struggled for bed space, the sheets and comforter. The night was warm for Quebec, early summer, early June. She'd left the window open for mother's spring airing of the house; all windows were open to their fullest apertures, welcoming in the spring air after a particularly harsh winter that brought blizzards, torrential rains and combinations of the two. Erica was asleep in her own bed, the air caressing her face when a dream brought her to a green and beautiful place, with tall deciduous trees. The trees were two weeks into their summer leaves and the grass and shrubs were expertly manicured.

This place was *hers,* the *her* in her dream. Erica couldn't see this *her.* She tried to, in the reflections of nearby ponds. She was with another person. A man, young, with a face she'd seen before; at times familiar, at times a stranger. She was happy with this man, she could tell. She'd been unhappy in the past with other men that she'd known, she could tell that too, as thoughts of those unhappy moments dripped in and out of the scene, faces of other men in her life, faces of her father, not her father, but *her* father, faces that may have seemed right at the time, but, in the end, didn't turn out that way.

They were in a parking lot surrounded by the trees and green. The sun dimmed dark from threatening clouds coming in from the west. The man was wearing a black leather jacket. She wore one too, with zippers on the sleeves. They were going to have to go. They couldn't work on their place anymore this day. The weather was coming. It would be too wet to work. Their vehicle was there, a large, shiny motorcycle. She was afraid of this machine, although he'd told *her* that was silly.

"I've been riding since I was ten years old," he told her. "When I was a kid, they were building houses. Before they poured the foundations, the builders smoothed the ground into hills. It was great for riding."

She put on her helmet, a black, full-face type and strapped it under her chin.

"Hop on, honey," the man said after he started the engine. She could hear him in her helmet through the built-in communication system. "We'd better get going if we want to beat the rain."

She did as instructed. She placed her feet on the foot pegs and shifted her weight to center on the bike. She looked down at her shoes and was struck by the oddest thought: she loved these shoes, light yellow dancing shoes made with sparkly material and tied at the ankle with a delicate white bow. The motorcycle vibrated through the soles of the shoes.

The man kicked the bike into gear and eased it out the of the parking lot. Soon they were speeding down the access road that led to the main highway. The air around them seemed charged with electricity. The clouds that only a moment before seemed miles were suddenly overhead and appeared close to bursting.

"It's going to get wet, honey," the man said through her helmet. "After we get to the highway, I'll duck under the first overpass. We can wait it out there."

As if on cue, the sky opened up throwing sheets of water. The man wiped the face shield of his helmet but that only helped for a few seconds.

They stopped at the stop sign that led them out to the main highway. There appeared to be no one on the road but them. The man revved the bike's engine and once again kicked it in gear. The wheels started to turn when a loud noise shook the world. It could have been a moan of a ship's foghorn or the bellow of a freight train. And then the world slipped on its side. Something moved over them, but it wasn't the clouds. For that moment of eternity, the rain could no longer reach them, the wetness no longer an issue. There was pain, excruciating pain, in her legs, in her arms, in her chest. There was light and then there was dark. Sounds like eggshells cracking vibrated in the air. And then there was nothing.

When Erica awoke in the morning she was covered in bruises. Her legs had angry purple marks, inches wide across her thighs. Her arms were marred similarly with blood pooling at her elbows and wrists. She was having trouble breathing. Her tummy hurt. She lifted her pajama top to reveal purple and red blotches larger than a man's fist, ten or fifteen of them, strewn from her collarbone, over her ribcage and down onto her pelvis. She screamed.

Her mother, father, and grandmother all waited outside the emergency room as she was x-rayed, and lab tested and spoken about. Everyone whispered. The police were called. Each member of her family was interviewed. All seemed distraught, the police, the family, the doctors. And then they were puzzled.

The doctor, an anemic looking man in his forties, invited the family into the exam room. The police didn't join them. After speaking with the doctor, they'd packed up without a word and left.

"Mom, Dad," the doctor said as doctors do, using quaint honorifics when talking to parents about something delicate. "I think I have some good news." He scratched his prematurely gray scalp. "I don't see that the bruises were caused by trauma."

"We told you that," Erica's father growled.

Seemingly unfazed the doctor replied: "Yes, well. I have to say that if the trauma *was caused* by someone in the family, I would expect you to tell me exactly that. I have to say, I've heard it before."

"I don't like your tone," Erica's father said.

"Michel! Enough!" Erica's mother said, sharply. "He said we didn't do anything wrong." She turned to the doctor. "So, what *did* happen?"

The doctor made a face like he'd bit into a lemon. "That's the thing. We don't know. We looked at her X-rays. There're no broken bones. Her lab work is all within normal limits. Her platelet count is as normal as could be. I'd like to keep her a couple of days and see if we can figure this out.

But he didn't figure it out. She was released days later, completely normal, with a few fading bruises on her arms, legs and chest.

And things went back to normal at home. Erica went back to school. Her parents went back to silently hating each other. Erica remembered the dream vividly, every moment and image etched in her memory. The dream did not return, as the other important dreams that would come later tended to do. Most nights she slept soundly snuggled into her Paris comforter, her grandmother reading her a French bedtime story.

Early morning on a Saturday. Erica woke to the phone ringing. Moments later she was jolted out of bed by an anguished cry. It was her grandmother. Erica's mother joined in. Erica flew down the stairs. Her mother and grandmother were holding each other, their faces drenched in tears. Both women shook.

"What happened?" Erica asked, tears sprouting from her eyes as well. "What is it, Mama? Gra-mère? What's wrong?" When the two women noticed Erica, they drew her into their hug and cried some more.

When the weeping subsided, they all went into the kitchen. Erica's grandmother pulled out a chair and placed Erica on her lap. Erica's mother set a kettle on the stove.

"Dear child," her grandmother said softly, almost whispering. "Dear child, dear child, dear child. We have had a loss. Your mother, you, and I have had a loss. You were going to meet her later this summer. You were going to meet her husband too. He was a good man."

The tears started to flow again.

"Who Gra-mère?" Erica asked, feeling the tears well up again. "Who are you talking about? What happened?"

Her grandmother composed herself. She blew her nose into a tissue she'd had stashed up her sleeve.

"Do you remember us talking about your cousin Kayla? You've seen pictures of her. She and her husband run a golf course in New York. They're part owners. They spent every penny they had to buy into it. They worked so hard. It wasn't in the best of shape, but they turned it around. They met in business school."

Erica thought for a moment. Yes, she did remember her mother and grandmother talking about them visiting.

Erica nodded. "I remember."

Her grandmother smoothed her still tossed morning hair.

"Kayla is Tante Evelyn's daughter. She died this morning. She and her husband. They were on a motorcycle and there was a sudden storm. They lost control of the motorcycle and were hit by another car." Her grandmother wiped her eyes.

"Erica!" Her grandmother said, alarmed. "What's wrong?"

The color had drained from Erica's face. Her mouth hung slack. She couldn't speak.

Her grandmother carried her up to her room. Her mother followed. They sat on Erica's bed. Her grandmother rubbed Erica's hands to warm them.

"I know it's shocking when someone dies, especially when they are so young, but you've never met Kayla. Or her husband."

Erica looked at her grandmother. Her eyes searched the room for something to say. Finally, she spoke.

"I was there," she said.

Her grandmother furrowed her brow. "What do you mean? You've never been to New York."

"I know, Gra-mère, but I was there." Erica told her about the dream she'd had two weeks before. She told her of the vivid details. She told her of the yellow ballet slippers.

Her grandmother gasped. Without a word, she left the room. She returned quickly, carrying an old photo album, one that Erica had seen many times in her grandmother's bedroom. Gra-mère sat on the bed next to Erica on her bed and opened the album, which made a crackling sound from age and paged through the plastic covered photographs. She found the one she wanted and showed it to Erica.

This time Erica gasped. In the photograph, the only one on the page, a girl, perhaps Erica's age, maybe a little younger sat on a concrete stoop in front of, what was probably then, a new house. The girl had brown wavy hair and eyes like her own, with sleepy circles under them and a smile that was missing a tooth in the front. She was wearing the fashion of the day, a sky blue, oversized sweatshirt, colorfully swirled leggings and a pair of bright pink leg warmers. On her feet were yellow dancing shoes.

"That was Kayla you saw," her grandmother said. "You have the gift. Others in our family have had it. I never did, but my mother and sister did."

Erica burst into tears. Her grandmother wrapped her arms around her. "Don't be afraid, ma chère. It's a gift. An extra vision Yahweh has given you. Have you had other dreams?"

Erica told her of the dream in the bowling alley that turned into a fishing pond.

Gra-mère smiled, sadly. "Do you know who that was?"

The One and True Son

Erica shook her head.

"That was your Gra-père Jean. It figures he'd be bowling and fishing at the same time. That's all he liked to do."

"Was he trying to tell me something?" Erica asked.

"I think he was just saying hello. You never got to meet him, but I know he would just adore you."

The dreams seemed to be limited to her family or to people she'd known. Erica didn't dream of terrorist attacks or killer tsunamis. Her dreams weren't always negative. She'd dreamt that her friend Suzanne was going to have a child. Suzanne and her husband had been trying for two years, even spending money they barely had on fertility treatments and medications. The doctors had nearly given up hope of her ever holding a pregnancy. During a hot and restless night, Erica saw Suzanne and her husband's baby, a tiny girl with her mother's eyes and her father's hair. Erica could tell when a dream was a message and not just a random firing of synapses, because she'd remember every detail, even months after the dream. The messages weren't disjointed flashes or images. It was like they'd been edited, pieced together specifically so Erica would recognize them. They were as clear as a TV show, or a movie shot by a particularly talented cinematographer.

Erica didn't tell Suzanne of her impending motherhood. She'd doubted she would believe her if she'd told her how she knew. Back then, she'd told no one of her dreams.

And then came Richard. She didn't want to hide such a thing from her husband, but how to explain it? Frankly, she'd doubted that she could hide anything from him at all. He always knew when she was upset, like when she'd dreamt of the death of her beloved Gra- mère, peaceful as deaths go, in her sleep, a goodbye without pain or suffering. Erica tried to hide the pain this knowledge inflicted on her. She'd called her grandmother daily, keeping the conversation light, trying to hold back the torrent of tears building with every phone call. But Richard saw through every forced smile, every witticism that had fallen flat.

He sat her in her favorite chair, upholstered in overstuffed calves' leather cushions, as soft as a cloud.

"What is it you're not telling me?" he asked in this way he had, with his black eyes focused and probing, his mouth relaxed and nonthreatening, the corners turned up in a strangely soothing upward curve.

"If I tell you, you'd divorce me," she said with a forced giggle.

Richard pushed the hair out of her eyes and wiped a tear away with a soft finger. "There is nothing you could tell me that would make me do that. When I make a decision, it's an informed one. I never make any other kind. I decided a long time ago about you. I don't go back on my decisions. So what's wrong?"

Erica took a deep breath and let it out with a whoosh. She smiled and her eyes flooded with tears again. "My grandmother is going to die," she said.

Richard furrowed his brow. "Is she sick? Did she give you some bad news?"

Erica shook her head. "No, she isn't—well I don't know if she's sick or it's just of the end. But she is going to die."

"Wait," Richard said, leaning away from her. "She isn't sick, but she's going to die? She didn't tell you she's sick?"

"Uh-huh," Erica replied, nodding.

"So, she doesn't know she's going to die?"

Erica nodded again.

"But you do?" Richard said.

"Yes," Erica said with a sob. "I do."

Richard appeared to be processing this. His black eyes looked around the room, as if he was searching for something. "Can I ask how?"

Erica looked at her husband for a long moment. "I can't tell you now. When it happens, I'll explain."

Richard kissed her forehead. "Let's hope that will be a long time from now."

Erica smiled her saddest smile.

"It won't be," she said.

Ten days later she got the call from her grandmother's live-in caretaker.

"Your grandmother passed away very peacefully," the nurse said. "I thought she'd just slept a little past her usual breakfast time. When I went into her room to wake her she was tucked in her bedclothes as comfortably as can be. She was nice woman. I will miss her."

Erica cried for days, and Richard let her. She thought she was prepared for this day. She knew it'd been coming. Every time the phone would ring, she'd steel herself, answering every ring whether she recognized the caller ID or not. After the first week, she thought, she'd hoped, that maybe this time she'd been mistaken, that maybe a normal dream had slipped into prophetic format, that it meant nothing. She'd hoped that she'd lost the gift, that maybe it had faded with time. But when the phone rang ten days later, she knew.

Richard said little when she told him. He comforted her, held her to him, let her cry. He didn't bring up the dream. Erica had to.

The One and True Son

"I've had dreams like this since I was a child."

Richard looked puzzled for a moment. Finally, he said: "Oh, yes?"

"You don't believe me," she said, looking him in his eyes.

"It's not that, Erica," he replied. "Of course, I believe you. I just think, that… that life is full of coincidences. Your grandmother was getting up there in age. She had to be on your mind a lot. That happens with our elders. It isn't that unusual for us to be thinking of the older members of our family and soon after, have them pass away."

Erica raised her voice, perhaps for the first time in their relationship. "This isn't a one-time thing, Richard. I've been having these dreams since I was little. They are *always* accurate! They *always* come true."

They sat on their bed. Richard continued to stroke her back.

Erica told Richard of the dream about her cousin. She told him the details she still remembered as if she'd just dreamt them five minutes before and not decades ago. She told him about her grandfather and the other, more prophetic dreams, some seemingly important and some comparatively trivial, but *all* the same kind of dreams, *all* in vivid detail, *all* about someone she knew, usually closely, *all* remembered years after most dreams had faded and *all,* without fail, came true.

Richard held her but said nothing more on the subject. Erica couldn't tell if he was annoyed by what she'd said or just giving the subject more thought. Telling him had eased her mind. Yes, she knew her grandmother was old, and that old people die, no matter how much you love them. She was relieved he didn't ridicule her for what she'd told him, although, truly, she'd never seen him ridicule anyone. It seemed beneath him.

As Erica's mourning eased, their lives returned to normal. Erica gave massages in a room built especially for that purpose, with filtered air, lots of windows and enough space for her to work around her clients. Since they'd been in San Diego she'd worked when she wanted to. She only took referrals from people she knew and would limit the amount of clients she'd take on. They didn't need the money. She just wanted to feel connected to people, to her home, to San Diego, which she loved. For the first time in her life, Erica knew what it meant to be content.

Richard had worked very little as well, at least, for a while. He'd putter in his wine garden and sometimes even join her in the pool, although he'd cover himself from fingertips to toenails with lotion and wear an old t-shirt in the water. They were comfortable in his semi-retirement.

It wasn't until he had to leave for an earthquake or tsunami or some disaster that the dreams came to her as they never had before: they repeated. The scenes were different. But the people in the dreams kept coming back. And these were people, except for one, she was pretty sure she'd never met. There was a black woman, maybe a police officer. There was a woman, older, strong, who knew everything about ships. There was a large man, in worn boots. She was not allowed to see his face. Electricity flowed around him. These people all had one thing in common. They were being pursued. And there, for no reason she could determine, was Richard.

The dreams didn't come every night. Sometimes they were weeks apart. Richard called while he was away almost nightly. After she'd had a dream with the police officer or the ship woman or the mysterious man, she expected to be able to pick up some clue as to their connection with her, with Richard. But on the evenings he'd call her, he was his calm, dry humored self. He'd sounded tired, but other than that, no different.

"Oh, the bureaucracy of this stuff just wears me down," he'd say or "I'm not as young as I used to be, I guess. Maybe I'll just pull the trigger and retire for good with this one." He had a way of reassuring her that made her forget the dreams. And then she'd have another.

* * *

They brought the tall man brought into a small brightly lit room. She couldn't see his eyes. They were nearly swollen shut. His orange jumpsuit, soaked, clung to his lanky frame. His thick tightly curled hair hung, also soaked, on the sides of his face. Mucous ran from his nose in a steady stream down to his lips over to the side of his mouth and onto his jumpsuit. His collar was torn at the neck. His shackled ankles and wrists showed no resistance.

A voice from an unseen speaker came from the corner of the room. It was a voice she recognized, but then again, didn't.

"Are you who they say you are?" the voice inquired. The voice was rational, calm, almost soothing.

The tall man said something she couldn't make out. He was weak, in pain.

"I'm so sorry. I didn't hear you clearly. I'm sure you tried to answer. Right? Let me ask again. Are you who they say you are?"

The tall man took in some air. He could barely lift his head.

"Who do you think I am?"

There was a buzzing noise. It seemed to buzz for minutes. A door opened in the featureless wall. A man came in wearing what looked like military fatigues.

The voice spoke again. "It seems the son here is not yet clear in his thoughts. He's already a bit wet. May I suggest the battery this time?"

The One and True Son

And then she saw the smile. It was a smile she recognized. And it was a smile she didn't. It was a confident smile, not one that'd been entertained. It was the smile of a shark.

Her vision faded. She heard the tall man scream. A chant filled Erica's head. A chant of tens, then thousands, then millions of people.

"Fondlen has killed the Son."

"Fondlen has killed the Son."

"Fondlen has killed the Son."

* * *

Richard finally answered his phone.

"Hi, Sweetheart," he said, sounding sleepy. "What time is it there? It' four AM here. Did something happen?"

"Don't do it, Richard," Erica said, her voice flat.

There was a pause.

"Erica? Are you alright?"

"No Richard. I'm not all right. I'm not all right at all."

"What's going on?" Richard asked. "You're not making any sense. Perhaps I should come home."

"Don't do it, Richard. I've seen everything."

"Yes, I should come home." Richard said. "It's a nine-hour flight. I'll arrange it right away."

There's something in Richard's voice, Erica thought. Something she'd never heard before. *What was it? Panic?*

"It shouldn't take you that long," Erica said. "You're not where you say you are."

"I…What are you…Sweetheart, I don't know what you're talking about," Richard said.

Richard stumbled with words. Richard never stumbles with words.

"I think you're having some kind of breakdown. I'm coming home."

Erica didn't speak for a moment. When she did, she was surprised how she sounded.

"Let the man go, Richard," she said. "I've seen it all. I've seen *them* all. It will not end well for you."

Richard tried to say something, but Erica had already hung up.

The Investigator

Phu Trang walked the halls of the dungeon. He'd rumors of its existence, jokes about placing unruly suspects here. He'd been assigned to the Washington Bureau for over a decade and yet he had no idea that the hallway where he walked, or the elevator that took him down to it, probably ten floors below the so-called basement of the headquarters building, really existed at all. Phu had been requesting to speak with the suspect since his arrest, but Fondlen brushed him off, until, of course, that morning. He learned that it was real. It made Phu more curious than ever.

Fondlen said that he was bringing him on the case because he, Phu, wanted the truth. And yet, the man that directed the most unorthodox investigation he'd ever been a part of, kept him at arms-length from nearly all of it. Phu hinted that maybe he should be dropped from the investigation, but Fondlen wouldn't hear of it. As he listened to the sound his shoes made, an almost sticky sound as they made contact with the concrete of the hallway floor, one question stuck in his mind: what is this all about? Phu knew they had this guy on the destruction of the temple, at least, he thought they did. But why all this? We still have Gitmo, although the CIA and bureau have been winding down sending people there. What was with this 10-floor dungeon?

"Why do you want to speak to Carpentero?" Fondlen asked him when he requested an interview.

"Because I've been doing this job for a long time," Phu answered. "You brought me into this, partly for that reason. Since then, I've been doing background stuff. I've never even talked to the guy, and we've had him for weeks. That's not the way I do things."

Fondlen sat behind Phu's desk but remained silent.

"You said that I would learn the truth," Phu said. Well, the truth is sitting in this building, or under it, and I haven't spoken with him. I've got questions. Good questions. I came in on this thing in good faith. For all I

The One and True Son

know this might be the last case I ever work. I've been waiting on the bench long enough. I want in the game."

Phu had noticed that Fondlen hadn't seemed himself for the last couple of weeks. He seemed distracted, if not indecisive. Phu wondered what could do that to a guy like Fondlen.

Fondlen ran his pasty hands over his bald head.

"This is a delicate case, as I'm sure you're aware. But it's true, I brought you into this. I wanted you to find the truth with me. I..." Fondlen stopped, as if another thought had occurred to him. "It wasn't until this moment that I know exactly why I brought you into this. Are you curious?"

Phu nodded.

Fondlen stood from the desk and looked out the office door window. "It's this man, this Jessie character. He looks so ordinary. Yes, he's quite tall. He has a presence for a carpenter, that's also true. But a lot of tall people have presence. What he has is something—intangible. Something that makes people believe he can do impossible things. And not just that. He has billions of followers on the web. This *carpenter* has billions of people following what he says. They don't even see him. He isn't in a single video. They don't for a minute believe that he blew up the temple. How do we deal with a character like that?"

"So why me?" Phu asked.

"Because you aren't swayed by presence. You're an investigator who only follows the facts and you will dig into a subject and cut through the unreliable. Look what you did to that poor professor in college."

"That was not my intention," Phu protested.

"Exactly!" Fondlen exclaimed. "Your intention was to cut through the bullshit and get to the truth. And the truth can be frightening to some."

"So why have I been sitting on the bench?"

Fondlen turned around and looked directly at Phu. Those dead eyes showed nothing, but the rest of his face did. *He* was frightened. Of what, Phu couldn't imagine.

"You're in the game now," Fondlen said.

Phu found the room, or perhaps cell was a better word, by following lit green lights embedded in the floor. There was no guard. Phu knew that the hallways and perhaps the room itself were wired and video surveilled, but there seemed to be a complete lack of human presence anywhere in the halls. He could practically hear his own breathing. His theories of close surveillance were verified as he stepped up to the steel door and the latch opened with a heavy metallic snap. Phu slid the door open and stepped into the room. The door closed behind him.

The room was austere. No television, no radio, no computer, no books, no newspapers. A toilet and sink combination took up one corner of the room. A cot, bolted to the wall. The only comfort provided was a woolen army blanket and two gray hard metal chairs, one of which was occupied by the suspect. The man did not look up. He appeared deep in thought.

"I'm Special Agent Phu Trang," Phu said. "Do you mind if I take a seat?"

"Please," the man they called Jessie said. He didn't look up.

Phu pulled the chair around so they could face each other. He looked the man over. He appeared to be in reasonably good condition. There were no scratches or bruising.

"How are you holding up in here?" Phu asked. "Pretty sad accommodations."

"They're not that bad," Jessie said, finally looking up. "I have all I need here. This room suits its purposes."

"What do you mean?" Phu asked. "Is this a political move? Are you seeking sympathy? I don't know if you know it or not but blowing up the temple is not the best way to garner sympathy. There are some people, many I would say, who are calling for your head."

Jessie said nothing. Phu had interviewed many people who later were convicted of their crimes. He could usually tell even in the first interview if he'd be able to prove them by the way they reacted to being confronted with the charges against them. Most had a *tell*, a nervous twitch or an involuntary look to the side. This man didn't. He looked at him with eyes that almost screamed innocence. Phu was careful not to buy it.

The Special Agent opened the briefcase he'd brought with him. He hadn't carried a briefcase in forever, not since everything ever stored on paper could be carried around in a laptop. But Fondlen insisted no laptops. Phu had no idea why, but he agreed. He took out several thick folders and a yellow legal pad. He set the folders at his feet. He took a pen from the case and clicked it in front of him.

"That's a lot of paper," Jessie said.

"It's all about you," Phu said.

"Is it?" Jessie asked.

Phu looked at the man closely. "It seems to be. There's a picture that looks an awful lot like you at a place you shouldn't be at a very early hour. There are more of you tearing up that very same place not long before it blew up. There's testimony from a Los Angeles police officer who said you were away from the group, and no one knew where you were for an extended period. There are a lot of other pictures too. Would you like to see them?"

Jessie shook his head. "Ex police officer. Praise had quit the police force."

"Are you sure?" Phu asked, smiling. "Police officers *do* go under cover."

"Praise quit." Jessie said.

"You're sure?" Phu pushed.

"I know. I know many things. I know what's in your folders. I know where I am and who I am. I know what I did and what I didn't do."

Phu sat up in his chair. "Then why don't you enlighten me."

Jessie looked him square in the eye. "Because none of that, matters."

Phu, unnerved by the man's gaze, had to look away. He got up and walked around the room. "I'd say it matters very much. It does to the faithful who worshipped at the temple."

"Do you pray, Agent Trang?"

Phu stopped walking and looked back at Jessie. "I don't see where that's relevant."

Jessie turned in his chair so he could face Phu fully. "I'd just like to know. Do you pray to the Father?"

Phu's answer didn't come out immediately, although he knew what it was. He wasn't going to lie. But there was a hesitation. A hesitation that came from within Phu. A hesitation he didn't quite understand.

"No, I don't," Phu said, finally.

"Can I ask why not?" Jessie inquired. "I don't think that was always the case."

Phu nodded. "You're right. It wasn't. I was going to be a moreh."

"So why don't you speak to the Father now?"

"For the same reason I don't say abracadabra before opening a package. I know that doing that won't have anything to do with what's in the box."

"So magic is the problem," Jessie said. "Is that all?"

"Does this have to do with the temple case?" Phu asked, smiling.

Jessie smiled too. "I think it might. You think you see me in some pictures. The man in the pictures looks like me, from certain angles. You don't see the face clearly, but the height and build are right. So are the clothes and the beard."

"Oh, the photos of you flipping over tables are *very* clear," Phu interjected. "It didn't matter what the angle was. That was you."

The One and True Son

Jessie shrugged. "I'll grant you that. I was righting a blatant wrong."

"But who made that your job?" Phu said, half joking.

Jessie's smile waned. "Do you mind if I ask a personal question?"

"I think you already have, but shoot. I'm curious."

"True again," Jessie admitted. "It's kind of a follow-up on the earlier one. Why did you leave your studies? I know that you don't believe in magic, but you were going to dedicate your life to the Father. You had to know that miracles were a part of that before you started studying to be a moreh. What was it that made you fall away from your faith?"

"Do you really want to know the answer to that?" Phu asked.

"I do." Jessie responded.

"Okay. Osiris," said Phu.

"Osiris?" asked Jessie looking confused.

"That's right. Osiris. But not just him. There was also Krishna and Zeus and Baal and Odin. There was The Great Spirit and Buddha Shakyamuni. They've all had their day. People believed in them with all their hearts. People died for them, started wars for them, killed for them. Depending on the so-called deity, people still do. There have been thousands of characters that people have regarded as all-powerful beings, running the universe, creating disasters on a whim. Accepting thanks for all the good in the world and no culpability for the bad. So today it's Yahweh. But Yahweh is different in Islam, Judaism and Yahwehanism. We can't even agree on who *He* is."

Jessie sat quietly for a moment. Finally, he said: "What you say is empirically true. I can't argue with anything you've said. I have thoughts on this. Would you like to hear them?"

Phu looked at his watch. He didn't really come down to the dungeon to discuss theological theory. But he couldn't help himself. After all, people thought this was the son of God.

"I'm all ears."

It was Jessie's turn to stand. He paced to the corner of the windowless room.

"All these deities, as you call them, are manifestations of the Father. The Father is all- knowing. The Creator. The reason we love, we share, we create, we…exist. These manifestations arise because the Father's mind is so beyond human understanding that they have difficulty interpreting His purpose. Imagine that you've been taking a foreign language, say French, and you go to Paris with the expectation that you will communicate with the locals like a native. Will it work? Probably not. The natives have been creating nuances, idioms, cultural connotations, over their entire lifetimes. You can't possibly get all that from a French class.

"But he's *God,* Pho interrupted. "He's the all-powerful, the creator of all we see, think and feel. But he can't get us to understand what he really wants?"

Jessie turned to Phu. "He is God, but he endowed humans with the means to think for themselves. To *construct* for themselves. All these different religions are *human* constructs.

"So, it's *our* fault that Yahweh is unclear?" Phu asked.

"It's not about fault," Jessie said, softening his voice.

Phu shook his head and sat back in his chair. "If you're trying to convince me, you haven't done it."

"Are there any *words* that could convince you?" Jessie asked.

"Not likely," Phu answered. "How could they? We're in my country now, speaking my language with my idea of reality. How do you change that?"

Jessie sat back down. "Pray."

Phu chuckled. "You know, after I left the university, I looked into Buddhism. I have some ancestral roots in that. Even though I didn't buy anymore what I thought I believed for my whole life, I thought there might be a different path. Maybe that path would fill the hole that I was feeling. So, I started going to a Buddhist temple. I read books, old books. I meditated, something I did find some value in. I still do. But then, in a meditation book, written by someone that people believe is a Buddha himself I read something that bothered me. The book told me that during my meditation I should meditate on the truth of the Buddha. Not about truth itself, mind you, but the truth of the Buddha. The author spoke very plainly. He said: 'As you repeat this to yourself, the repetition itself will reveal the truth to you.'"

"Did it?" Jessie asked.

Phu laughed again. "It revealed to me a truth about meditation. Think of it this way. If I meditate daily, in the morning and at night, and whenever my mind wanders, that I'm an aardvark, after months or years of that I will convince myself that I am indeed, an aardvark."

Jessie smiled but there was sadness there.

"I see why you were chosen for this. You are impervious to the metaphysical. It makes sense that my case would be yours to investigate. Your people couldn't have chosen better."

"Well, I don't know about that," Phu said. "I have to admit, there is something special about you. I came in here to talk about a bombing that you *allegedly* did. And you got me talking about Buddha and Odin like we are at Saturday dinner after temple. Do you think we can get back to why I came in here?"

Jessie relaxed in his chair. "There's no need. Everything is in place. There's nothing you can ask me that will change the ultimate result. Truly, Special Agent Phu Trang, this has all been decided. You have no power over it."

Phu gathered up his folders and put them back in his briefcase. "Okay," Phu said, putting on his best *if that's what you want* face. "It's your funeral."

Phu turned toward the door and the bolt slapped open.

"One more thing, Mr. Trang," Jessie said before he turned to the door. "Tell your boss that he needs to go ahead with this, regardless of who tells him that he shouldn't. Please tell him that word for word.

Phu turned to the door and walked out.

The Defender

Sylvio de Graca's hands shook on the steering wheel of his Prius. The electric motor was moving the car; the quiet of the motor almost led Sylvio to forget where he was, dodging traffic in Adams Morgan trying to make his way to the FBI building through traffic circles and diagonal intersections so foreign to him that he may as well have been driving on Mars. He hadn't slept well. He never slept well when he was away from home, away from Miriam, away from their two Labrador retrievers, Bob and Mike.

Two weeks prior he had no way of knowing that he'd be staying in a federally owned row home, preparing to represent a defendant that had been in the news constantly for the past several months. Two weeks prior he was working in his Austin office on the defense of a single mother as the IRS pressed tax fraud charges for bags of clothes she'd claimed she'd given to a local Goodwill, the clothes giving her a nearly $1200 cushion on her tax return. It pissed Sylvio off that the tax goons always went after the little guy, or little woman in this case, and let the big fish cheat and steal to their hearts content. Yeah, she didn't have the required receipts to make the deductions in her return but *fine* her. For some reason the IRS got its butt hurt on this one and wanted jail time.

That case was put in the rearview mirror when the office got the call that he was to go to Washington to represent Jessie Carpentero.

"I guess it makes sense," his supervisor Jenny Ruiz said when he asked the inevitable, *why me* after she got the call. "You're both from Texas. Your name sounds Spanish. Never underestimate the vacuum they call brainpower in Washington DC."

"Must be it," Jessie agreed. "Couldn't be that I'm a good attorney."

Ruiz smiled briefly, just a flash. "You're all right. I'd probably be a better choice. But someone up there likes you." *Up there* was Washington DC.

And so, here he was trying to get to Pennsylvania Avenue via every cockeyed intersection in the district.

Miriam stayed with the dogs. He hadn't told her who he was defending. Sylvio didn't want anyone catching on as to who his client was. People were upset about the bombing, especially in Texas, and weren't above showing up on his front lawn with the very undemocratic, but deeply held belief that someone accused of such a heinous crime wasn't entitled to a defense.

About a half hour later than he'd expected, he pulled into the FBI garage. He'd been told to see an agent in charge of the investigation, an agent named Phu Trang. He would be briefed on the strict security protocols for this particular suspect, even, or maybe, especially, for his lawyer.

As a teenager Sylvio had visited the FBI building on a high school trip to DC as part of the Future Lawyers Club, he'd been active in from his freshman year. They toured all the important buildings that everyone knows: the White House, the Capitol, the Supreme Court. They were all impressive to young Sylvio, but the FBI building had the greatest *gee whiz* factor. He remembered entering the front portico, *J. Edgar Hoover FBI Building* displayed above the doors in brushed metal letters. The staff steered the students to the tour area where young and old would begin the tour. Lit flatscreens were everywhere, next to exhibits, mounted an brackets from the ceiling, even standing alone on austere, blocky pedestals. The displays were all impressive and frightening. Glass cases took up entire walls with the tools people have used to kill and maim for the last hundred years. There were handguns, assault weapons, defused bombs and grenades, packets of artificial anthrax, cans of ricin, delivery systems for biological weapons and attempts at nuclear "dirty bombs". Sylvio couldn't help but feel halfway through the tour that our world was constantly under threat, that evil people hid in every nook, waiting for the opportunity to wipe the generous and the god-fearing out of existence.

The tour guide was a plump, pleasant, and seemingly serious women. She told them she was a retired teacher. She wore a meticulous tour guide uniform complete with wide, blunt, black, walking shoes. She expertly rounded the students into a cohesive group at a corded off the entry point.

The tour guide smiled. "Today's tour will provide you with an overview of the internal workings of the most powerful law enforcement agency in the world: The Federal Bureau of Investigation. In this building there are over 1,400 employees including analysts, laboratory professionals and of course, Special Agents. These employees come from all fifty states

and a variety of socio-economic backgrounds. Investigations include…"
The tour guide stopped. "The young man in the back."

Most of the Future Attorneys Club turned to the questioner, but no one was surprised who it was. His name was Zach Weiner. He was a senior and editor of the school newspaper. Dressed proudly in his unfashionable attire, Zach stood out as one of the most out of step members, fashion-wise, of his generation. Small, almost brittle looking, with slicked down black hair, Zach feared no one. That couldn't be said of the members of the faculty or players on the school sports teams who might've decided to play up stereotypes and attempt to make his life unpleasant. Cross Zach and he'd get you. He'd dig into your life, find out things you didn't know anyone could. Then he'd write about it.

"Isn't it true that the FBI is the defendant in a lawsuit brought by African-American agents who claim that the bureau doesn't hire many minorities? And if the bureau does hires them, it passes them over for promotion, even with equally stellar performance reports and comparable seniority?"

The tour guide huffed. "What is the name of your club?"

"The Future Attorneys Club, ma'am." Zach Answered.

"Lord, we're in trouble," the guide said under her breath, but audible. She gathered herself. "My presentation is about the tour you're about to experience. It's about the history of this agency, which I might add has solved a multitude of crimes of an unbelievably heinous nature. Its job, as the former director and founder Mr. J. Edgar Hoover, the man for whom this building is named, said so succinctly, is to bring justice to the guilty and clear the innocent."

"Is this the same J. Edgar Hoover who is rumored to have worn women's underwear under his suit and was buried next to his secretary, a man who he lived with and was virtually inseparable from, while actively hunting homosexuals in government, ruining their lives and drumming them out of government service?"

The tour guide stared at the boy for a moment. "What is your name?"

"Zach, ma'am."

"Zach what? What is your full name?"

"May I ask why?" Zach asked.

"Your club is for future lawyers. Is that right?"

"Yes, ma'am," Zach answered.

"And that's what you want to be?"

"I do."

The tour guide smiled. "I need your full name in case I get in trouble."

The One and True Son

Everyone laughed.

Where was Zach Weiner now, Sylvio thought as he walked past the tour ropes and headed up the escalator to the *real* FBI, the less flashy but no less intimidating agency than the one he saw on the tour. He'd almost been embarrassed for Zach then. He was almost embarrassed for himself now.

Sylvio found Special Agent Trang standing at a corner coffee maker staring over his coffee mug out the window at the buildings below on Pennsylvania Avenue.

"Agent Trang?" Sylvio said as he approached him offering his hand. "I tried your office, but they said you'd be over here. I'm Sylvio de Graca. I'm Jessie Capentero's attorney."

Trang looked at Sylvio a moment before offering his hand. "Does he know that?"

Sylvio shrugged. "I'm not sure. I'm from the PD office in Austin. Somebody asked for me. I'm not sure who. Does he have counsel?"

Trang shook his head. "Not that I'm aware of. A slew of lawyers have volunteered. From what I hear, he turned them all down. Anyway, let's go back to my office." Trang looked at coffee pot. "You want a cup? It was fresh brewed yesterday."

Sylvio looked at the coffee pot. The coffee had the consistency and color of roof tar.

"Pass," Sylvio said.

They went back to Trang's office. The small room was crammed with file boxes labeled "Temple". Trang shut the door.

"Does Carpentero know you?" Trang said as he sat back in his chair.

Sylvio looked around for a place to sit.

Trang gestured with an opened hand "Oh, make yourself at home."

Sylvio took a stack of file boxes off a chair in front of the desk and sat. "I don't think he knows me. We met… I think we met a couple years ago, but I doubt he remembers it. The Washington office brought me here."

Trang raised his eyebrows. "Have you read the case notes?"

"Yeah, most of them anyway. Sylvio said. "He definitely trashed the place before the bombing. I find the case for the bombing less than compelling. Do you think he did it?"

"Mr. de Graca," Phu said, sounding tired. "I really can't get into that with you. I'm on the other side, remember? Suffice it to say he's still locked up in the dungeon. You can take it from there."

"The dungeon?" Sylvio said.

The One and True Son

"Just a little joke around here," Phu said without smiling. "It's a lockup for high security cases. Stuff like terrorism. It's really not that bad."

"So, you think he's a terrorist? Is that what he's charged with?"

"He hasn't been formally charged yet. But what would you call a guy who blew up a national landmark and a symbol of Yahweh to seventy percent of the country?"

"Allegedly blew up," Sylvio corrected.

"Yeah. Whatever. I told you I can't really discuss the case at length with you. Not at this point.

"So, what can we talk about?" Sylvio asked.

"Well, I guess that's why you were sent to me. I'm going to tell you about the rules."

"I did go to law school."

"No doubt," said Trang, obviously unimpressed. "But this is a special situation. People are dead here. A national landmark has been destroyed. A lot of people are angry here, Mr. de Graca. From both sides. There are people who think this guy is God. There are people on the other side of this that think he's a communist. Both sides are volatile. You're going to be searched going in and out of the high security lockup. You'll also be recorded while you're down there."

"Wait," Sylvio interrupted. "What about attorney-client privilege? How am I supposed to have a candid conversation with my client if it's being recorded?"

Trang shifted in his chair. "Well, that's the thing. He isn't your client. Not yet. You said it yourself. The Federal Public Defenders Office sent you here. He hasn't acknowledged anyone as his attorney. Until that happens, counselor, you're just another guy in a suit going to chat."

"You know that's not right," Sylvio complained.

"How long have you been a PD?" Trang asked.

"Three years," Sylvio replied, his eyes looking down. He knew how that sounded. He was almost a rookie.

"Well, at three years in, somebody thought you were worth it," Trang offered. "But this is the big leagues here. The highest stakes in the justice game. It doesn't matter if it *sounds* right. It frankly doesn't matter if it *is* right. The rules are set by the rulers. And this guy is accused of blowing up something *very* important to the rulers. Those people don't like their toes stepped on. You have to figure out how to use those rules to benefit your client."

Sylvio followed the directions Trang had given him. The agent wasn't kidding when he said he'd be searched before he was allowed to the elevator bank with access to the high security lock up. He had to remove his suit jacket which was searched in every pocket by hand. The security officer pressed on all areas of the fabric, up and down the sleeves and the back. He not only had to turn out his trouser pockets; the officer checked thoroughly, again with his hands, from his groin to his ankle, over his buttocks and pressed over his pubic bone. His belt and shoes, removed, were scanned by some sort of X-ray that saw through everything but the belt buckle. The guard emptied his briefcase and went over it in same manner as the rest of him.

"I hope you send me some flowers later," Sylvio quipped to the officer who nearly cracked a smile.

The elevator trip down seemed to take hours. The elevator made no sound as it slipped into the bowels of what Sylvio guessed was still the FBI building. There were no indictors of floors to which he was descending. After what seemed like minutes, the elevator stopped, and the doors slid open, quiet as a whisper. As instructed, he followed the green lights embedded in the concrete floor. When he approached the door where the lights led him, he heard a heavy bolt thrown. He slid the door to the side and stepped in.

The man he'd seen years before was sitting peacefully in a chair in the corner of the room. He looked the same, perhaps a little older, but his hair had acquired no gray, his eyes no lines from lack of sleep. His hair was the same bushy length it had been back then, his beard full and wiry.

"Mr. Carpentero," Sylvio said, "My name is Sylvio de Graca. I'm from the Federal Public Defenders Office. It's assumed that you have not obtained counsel yet for your upcoming trial. We think that it's a bad idea for anyone to go to court on such serious charges without proper representation. I'd like to represent you if you'd allow me."

"Please, Sylvio," Jessie replied. "Call me Jessie. I've been waiting for you."

Jessie Carpentero gestured to the other chair in the room, already set in front of him.

Did he recognize me? Sylvio thought. They'd spoken briefly several years back, he, Sylvio was only a paid servant, Jessie a guest. There was that brief strangeness when they'd spoken of his parents, but would Jessie remember that? He wiped the thought from his mind.

"So you see the need for representation," Sylvia asked.

Jessie smiled. "I think I understand the concept of representation very well."

Sylvio opened his briefcase. "I have some papers I need you to sign. It will make it all official. Right now, I'm not sure that you're aware, but the

The One and True Son

FBI is listening in on this conversation. As soon as you sign these forms, we'll get that to stop." Sylvio pulled out the forms and dug for a pen. He pulled the papers aside and checked all the pockets in the briefcase. No pen.

"They must have taken it at security," Sylvio said. "You might've gouged my eyes out with it." Sylvio hoped that Jessie picked up on his confidence that Jessie didn't have that capability in him. Jessie gave no indication one way or the other.

"I'll have to go get one upstairs. Or bring you to it. Whatever, we've got to get these signed so we can talk." He stood to go.

"Let's talk anyway," Jessie said, easing Sylvio back in his chair with a raised hand.

"Mr. Carpentero," Sylvio warned. "I can tell you with great certainty that the room is monitored, recorded both visually and audibly. Anything we say can be used against you. We won't have privacy of counsel."

Jessie turned in his chair. "If you look carefully at that corner, you'll see it. It looks like a solid wall. It looks like there are no cracks, no holes. Just solid concrete. But if you spend enough time looking, you can see the difference in the surfaces. There are three lenses there, one large one and two smaller. You have to concentrate, to look, to search to find them." Jessie smiled. "I've had some time to do that."

Sylvio looked where Jessie indicated. "I don't see them."

"Trust me," Jessie said. "They're there. But never mind them. Let's talk. We'll keep it light. Like a reunion."

"You remember me then," Sylvio sat back in his chair.

"Yes, Sylvio," Jessie laughed. "I remember. It was a bad day for the wine industry that day."

Sylvio twitched. *How did he mean that?* "Yeah, I had a lot of mopping up to do that day. I ruined a perfectly good tuxedo shirt."

"Yes, I saw you cleaning that up with that very pretty bartender. How is she doing?"

Sylvio twitched again. He couldn't help it. *Did he know about Miriam?* "Yes, Miriam," he stuttered. "She's fine. Uh, we're married. But shouldn't we be talking about your case? I can just go upstairs and get a pen. Or maybe they can send one down." He looked up at the corner that Jessie said had cameras. "Can you bring one down guys? Are you listening?"

Of course, there was no response.

Sylvio stood to leave.

"I haven't said that I'd accept representation yet," Jessie said, holding up a big hand. "I think we should chat. Get reacquainted."

The One and True Son

Sylvio sank back down in the chair. "We hadn't really gotten acquainted before."

"Ah," Jessie smiled slightly. "Then let's make up for lost time." He folded his hands in his lap. "Tell me, how did the rest of law school go? Obviously, you did well. You couldn't have passed the bar too long ago. But you're a public defender for the federal government. Pretty impressive."

"We really shouldn't be talking about me," Sylvio said. "There are very serious charges you…"

"I know, I know." Jessie assured him. "But shouldn't I make sure that you're the right person to defend me? As you say. These charges are very serious."

Sylvio let out an acquiescent sigh.

"I did well in law school. I was third in my class. I clerked for a federal judge. A US Magistrate judge, Ronald Tuchin. You probably never heard of him, but it was a big boost. Helped me get into the public defenders' office."

"A Public Defender," Jessie said. "That's very impressive. It's funny though. You didn't seem to be the public defender type when you were passing out food at our table. Don't get me wrong. You were very nice. Courteous almost to a fault. But there was something, I don't know, well, *posh* about you. You were wearing top of the line clothes. Gucci shoes, if I remember right. Maybe I'm making unfair assumptions, but someone going to law school and wearing Gucci shoes to wait on tables must have certain expectations on income for when they pass the bar. Am I right about that?"

Sylvio sat stunned for a moment. Yes, he'd been wearing Gucci shoes the day of the wedding. They were Gucci Jordaan Horsebit loafers. He'd polished them for three hours before the wedding. He'd never worn them to a gig before, or since for that matter. Not a waiter gig anyway. They'd cost almost as much as his car. He remembered being worried during the wine spill that he might slosh some wine on them as he was cleaning it up. He thought about taking them off and going barefoot, but he figured that Anthony, his then boss, wouldn't be too thrilled with that. He still had his Gucci loafers. Every once in a while, he'd dust them off, give them a nice spit shine and wear them when he had to go to court. He was always careful of who his client was though. Showing up in $800 shoes to represent someone who was in trouble for having nothing seemed a bit cruel.

"You're right," Sylvio said, feeling like a child confessing a transgression to his trusted uncle. "I was pretty money driven back then.

Being a lawyer seemed to be the most lucrative profession for me at the time. But things change. People change."

"Yes, they do," Jessie agreed, nodding gently. "But what made you change?"

Sylvio honestly didn't know. He hadn't given it much thought until this day. But something had changed in him. There was a time not long before that he'd been embarrassed by his car, a tired Ford Focus, a 2000 model hatchback that would have died long ago in places like Colorado or Montana but thrived in the flat landscape of Texas. He remembered trying to hide the car behind venues at gigs, waiting for anyone present in the parking area to clear off before he got out, lest he be seen getting out of it. The car was all he could afford, but he knew once he got out of law school and passed the bar, he could get something fast, cool and expensive. But when his mechanic couldn't fix the brakes, couldn't get the air conditioning to work, couldn't fix the speedometer without tearing apart the dash and replacing everything behind it with expensive new parts that looked exactly the same as the old parts, he donated it to a local public radio station so they could get the money for the scrap. When he bought a new car, he got another Focus. With power windows this time. He was a full-fledged attorney by then, a public servant, but still, he could afford something sexier. He just didn't want it.

Was it Miriam who changed him? That was possible. Anytime a person brings someone that deeply into their lives, they both change. If everything goes right, senses of humor, tastes in TV shows, love of the same movies, politics, clean or dirty living rooms, the hatred or love of doing the laundry, all these things bouncing off of each other like a mad pinball machine, both parties are bound to change, aren't they? They must.

But had Miriam changed? If this principle applied to him, it must apply to her as well. But for the life of him he couldn't see how. She was sweet, pretty, conscious of others and herself, and loved to laugh. She told him early on in their dating that she bartended—because she liked it. Yes, the money was good, especially with her being petite, young and attractive. But she grew up in a reasonably well-off, middle-class home. Her childhood was happy. She wanted for few things growing up and didn't seem to think she deserved more. She'd expressed empathy for people who didn't have much, but it wasn't something she talked about often. Her social media accounts were mostly jokes, memes and funny stories. She wasn't really a crusader for anyone or any cause. He loved that she didn't let the dirt of living stick to her. She didn't bring it home. She smiled often.

"So, what made you change?" Jessie repeated, seemingly ignoring his non answer and the extended silence.

The One and True Son

Sylvio looked Jessie in the eyes. "I don't know really."

Jessie nodded.

"Do you still dream about your parents?" Jessie asked, looking back at Sylvio, deeply, but gently.

Sylvio felt a sensation come over him, one that he'd felt once before. It felt as though he'd stepped out of the moment, out of this cell floors below the city above. He was sitting in the chair across from Jessie Carpentero and yet he wasn't. He was somewhere in between. Jessie was there, in his chair, those loving, probing eyes, gazing back at him. And he was there too in the second place. Sylvio couldn't see Jessie there, but he could *feel* him.

Do you dream of them, Sylvio? Sylvio felt Jessie say. *Do you play in the streets of Coimbra? Do you climb the ruins with your father? Does your mother smile while you play? They're always happy to see you, Sylvio. They are visiting you. They are with my Father. They know you are with me. They know you will please them. They know you will please the Father.*

Yes, Sylvio said with his mind. *Yes, I see them. They come to me often. We play on the stones of structures left by Rome. They hug me and smile. They play with me. They love me. I see them.*

Do you remember the wine? Sylvio, Jessie asked. *Do you remember the wine made from the essence of all life, from the water?*

I do, Sylvio replied. *I remember the water I brought you. I remember the change that happened in front of me. How? How did this happen?*

The will of the Father, Jessie answered. *It is the will of the father. The will of the Father is what you remember, Sylvio. The will of the Father. You perceived it and it will be there for you. Do you believe me?*

Sylvio could see the whole scene again. The wedding in Cafracana. The clean water splashing into pitchers on a clear, hot Texas day. The finest wine. The finest.

Yes, I believe you.

When Sylvio opened his eyes, he was alone. He sprang from chair; his eyes whipped around the room. Sylvio spun in place. How?

A voice came from the corner of the room. "Mr. de Graca. It's good to see you awake. We were afraid that the suspect had done something to you."

It was a voice Sylvio didn't recognize. It almost hurt his ears.

"Where is he?" Sylvia shouted. "Did you take him?"

"We have him," the voice said. "He is being questioned. You can leave the cell now. The lights in the floor will lead you to the elevator."

"Where is he?" Sylvio shouted at the corner of the room. "Where did you take him?"

"We will be in contact," the voice said.

The bolt threw on the door.

"Where is he!?" Sylvio shouted again.

There was no reply.

The Mechanism

Richard Fondlen knew he had to get home. He felt as if he'd swallowed a good-sized rock as he flew to San Diego, a sensation he'd never felt on flights that would take him to the deadliest, most toxic places on the planet. In truth, he never feared death, his or anybody else's. The sight, or frankly the idea, of pain, of blood, of exposed brain tissue never caused him the slightest discomfort. He'd been known to enjoy a snack while performing what had been termed by his legal defenders in areas of power as enhanced interrogation techniques. He always brought a napkin to knock any errant crumbs from his chin.

But the conversation he'd had with Erica, the anger and disappointment in her voice shook him to his center. How this weakness occurred in him, he had no idea.

Richard had never sought a partner, a wife, even a girlfriend prior to Erica. The tone in her voice caused something in him to crumble.

"It will not end well for you."

That's what she said. He could interpret that in any number of ways. He could take it to mean that the operation he was on would go south. But how could she know about what he was up to? Really. How could she *know*? She could've meant that people would find out that the man was innocent, this man Jessie Carpentero. She could've meant that she knew that he'd set the man up from the beginning; that that was what he does, that he never worked for any insurance agency, at least one the type that she'd heard of. She could've meant that she knew that he hired the people who actually blew up the temple, that they work on his instructions. But that wasn't where this fear came from. The fear that sat in his belly like a tumor. It wasn't a type of fear he'd had any experience with, the fear of loss.

* * *

The One and True Son

Richard Fondlen was born in Chicago to the plain and drug addicted daughter of a wealthy lawyer whose downtown offices had a view of the Sears Tower, and the Lake Michigan locks, an engineering marvel that reversed the flow of the Chicago River in order to draw the filth of the then second largest city in the country downstate to the farmland bordering the mighty Mississippi. His mother's unplanned pregnancy was treated with Victorian sensibilities; she was removed from her exclusive private college and given a freshly built, four-bedroom ranch style house in suburban Hoffman Estates, a town sprouting from derelict soybean and corn fields about 30 miles northwest of the city. The streets, soon to be wide suburban roads, were still mostly dirt paths waiting to be paved when Stefanie Fondlen and her newborn son settled on Hassell Road in their brick front, one story, exile.

By the time Richard reached school age, a brand-new school had opened. Stephanie dropped him at his first day without going in the building. "I don't have to look at you," she said, smiling, as she handed him a paper bag with a peanut butter sandwich and a can of Coke and pushed him through the door. As a child, no one really enjoyed looking at Richard, especially the woman who gave birth to him. His unusual hair, teeth and eyes were the only remnants of his father's that Richard ever saw. His scalp was covered with patches of rusty wirelike hair, his scalp an arid desert unable to grow what should have been puffy auburn hair like his mother's. His teeth were as sharp as arrowheads. As his primary teeth awaited replacement, his overeager permanent set pierced his gums and grew over them at the age of three. The baby teeth eventually fell out, often with pain and blood, but his adult teeth never shifted.

And his eyes. His eyes were black pools of misty oil, soulless and deep. He was the only child who was not only allowed to wear sunglasses at school; he was encouraged to do so.

His mother bought him new clothes once a year at the beginning of each school year. He was a slow growing child and Stefanie Fondlen was grateful to be able to hold on to the money. She reported to her father, when he'd make his monthly phone call, that she was clean and sober and regularly attending meetings at Narcotics Anonymous and going to temple at least three times a week. Indeed, she attended the NA meetings regularly, often participating more vigorously than her fellow addicts. She spoke of Yahweh taking the wheel for her, cleansing her soul. She never left a meeting without feeling lifted up, purified. She attended temple regularly, but the three times a week turned to four, then five. Buoyed by her new-found addiction she found herself at temple daily, often for five or six hours at a time, pleading for a continued influx of grace and light. On

The One and True Son

those weekends and after school, Richard Fondlen stayed in their small house, alone, locked in by an inside/outside keyed deadbolt.

"Can I go to the temple with you?" a seven-year-old Richard asked, hoping to escape the bare white walls of the house, a house that stayed dark most nights except for the flickering of the old black and white TV, a curbside pickup his mother had obtained from a couple of streets away.

"No," his mother answered, blank faced, expressionless. "You look like a monster. Monsters are not allowed in the temple."

Stefanie Fondlen showered at least four times a day, sometimes five, depending on how much outside air she'd been subjected to on a particular day. Her skin was reptilian from the continuous stripping of her skin's oils; flakes of sloughed epidermis lay like sequins on every item of clothing she owned, not to mention on the TV and all the flat surfaces in the house, including the dishes in the cabinets and the toothbrushes on the bathroom vanity.

Unable to commune with the creator at temple, young Richard spoke to Yahweh with almost every thought he had. While making his way to school, walking the short few blocks to the school building, he would whisper praise to the one God, begging him for relief from his isolation. Outside the school, he observed his classmates, all congealed into squealing, playful groups.

In class, he'd speak to Yahweh in his head, begging to be passed over when a teacher solicited participation. Richard knew all the answers to the questions. He read at home almost obsessively, first his schoolbooks and then the Tanach. But attention meant eyes on him, and he could read the malice in those eyes, even if no mouths spoke of it. On the way home he prayed that no one would notice him making his way back to the dark, bare house with its unkempt lawn and already graying paint.

This was Richard Fondlen's childhood.

For his eighteenth birthday his mother threw him out. She put everything he owned, mostly clothes she'd picked up for him from Goodwill, out on the front porch with a note that read: Join the service. As a present to himself he left the clothes where they were and walked the couple miles to the nearest recruiter. It was an Air Force office located in a strip mall at the end of Hassell Road. He'd graduated from the local high school just a month before. Stefanie Fondlen went camping on his graduation day with a local temple group.

"Good afternoon," the man said, "I'm Staff Sergeant Gillette." He gave Richard's hand a hearty shake. Sergeant Gillette was a short, fit man with a thin military haircut and an impeccable blue Air Force uniform. It had to be custom fitted. His light blue dress shirt was ironed with a precision

The One and True Son

Richard guessed could only achieved by computer. The creases could cut someone. Unlike most people Richard encountered, the man, with four stripes stitched invisibly to his upper sleeve, neither winced or scowled when Richard entered the storefront office festooned with photos of attractive, impeccably uniformed young people performing their high tech duties in exotic locales all over the world.

"I'm so glad you caught me before I left. I haven't seen anyone all day. This is going to sound weird, but I'm starving. You want to go across to the Burger King with me and get something to eat? Your Uncle Sugar is paying."

"Uncle Sugar?"

"Uncle Sam," the sergeant nudged Richard. "Air Force speak. You're interested in joining, right? Let's go eat and talk. It's kinda cramped in here."

Richard just stood for a moment. He couldn't remember being invited to eat with anyone, let alone someone who he'd met maybe a minute prior. He nodded and followed the sergeant across the parking lot.

Sergeant Gillette ordered for them, two Whoppers, two large fries and a couple of chocolate shakes. Richard scarfed down the food like a man starving, which wasn't far from the truth. His mother rarely kept food in the house and when she did it was something *for her diet* that he wouldn't be allowed to touch. The sergeant watched him eat, taking small bites of his own food occasionally. Neither spoke until Richard finished.

"Man, you tore that up," Sergeant Gillette said offering a sympathetic smile. "I guess now that we've eaten, I can ask your name."

Richard blushed. "Oh, Richard. Thank you for the food. I was hungry."

"I know it was kinda weird pulling you over here, but I was going loco in that office. It's kinda small. If no one comes in for a while I get a little stir crazy, you know?"

Richard did know.

"So, I guess you're interested in serving your country," Gillette said smiling brightly. "How old are you? Sixteen? Seventeen?"

"I'm eighteen, sir," Richard said wiping special sauce from his chin.

Gillette took a swig from his milkshake. "You can call me Lyle. Are you still in school?"

"No," Richard answered. "I graduated last month." It occurred to Richard that this might be the longest conversation he'd had in years, outside of talking with his teachers about an assignment.

"Good!" Lyle Gillette exclaimed. "That was going to be my next question. If you were getting your GED, I'd have referred you to the Army."

Richard snickered.

"I'm serious," Lyle said, chuckling a little himself. "We only take the high school grads now. We're the high-tech branch. We want the smartest we can get. Are you smart, Richard?"

Richard shrugged. "I got good grades, mostly As and Bs. I never had many problems with schoolwork."

"That's what I wanted to hear. Any job you're looking for in particular? We've got the most high-tech jobs in the world."

Richard shrugged again. "I really hadn't thought about it. I suppose I'm open to just about anything."

"Again, that's good, Gillette said. "Leaves it wide open for you, although if was me I'd steer around being an SP."

"SP?" Richard said.

"Security Police. Maybe it's me, but it doesn't sound like a great time walking around a B-52 in the middle of a snowstorm in Minot, North Dakota."

Gillette straightened his back. "Mind if I ask you a a personal question?"

Richard shook his head.

The sergeant leaned in on his elbows. "Is your health okay? I mean, I'm not trying to be rude, but I don't see many bald eighteen-year-olds. You haven't had cancer or anything like that, have you?"

"No," Richard said in an even voice. "I was born with very little hair. It just never grew. What little I did have fell out after a while. I don't know why. It's just always been this way."

"And the eyes?" Gillette inquired. "You've been inside this whole time, and you haven't taken your shades off once. Any light sensitivity? Or vision troubles?"

"No, no trouble there,"answered Richard. "I wear them out of habit mostly. I've got weird looking eyes, I guess. People say they're weird anyway."

Gillette leaned back in his chair. "Let's see."

Richard hesitated. He hadn't remembered being this uncomfortable in a while. No one asked about his eyes. They mostly just looked away. He took off the sunglasses.

"I've seen worse," was all Gillette said. "They work, right?"

"20/20," Richard answered.

"Excellent. So, when do you want to come in?"

"Today would be good," said Richard.

"Whoa Nelly. You're eager. That's good, but unfortunately it doesn't work like that. We've got to do some paperwork, a background check, stuff like that. You've got to take the AVSVAB."

"What's that?"

"I guess we missed you when we were recruiting in schools. The ASVAB is a bunch of tests to see what you're good at. If you got As and Bs you should have no trouble. We give it at the processing center downtown. I can get you an appointment pretty quick, I'm sure. The whole process will probably take a couple of weeks. You can wait it out at home. Get some last-minute partying in before basic."

Richard looked at his empty Whopper wrapper.

Gillette watched Richard and sighed. "Problem, huh? No home or no parties?"

"Both," Richard said.

"You got parents? Cousins? Anybody like that?"

"I had a mother up until today. I'm eighteen. It's my birthday."

"You didn't have any trouble with the law, did you?" Gillette asked.

Richard shook his head. "Never. It's a long story. Let's just say we're both better off without each other."

The two sat at the table for several minutes, not speaking. Finally, Lyle Gillette spoke:

"Well, happy birthday, Richard. I'm just temporary duty here. I asked for it because I did a tour in a desert in California that had a woman behind every tree. Problem was, there were no trees. I wanted to come home. I'm from Palatine. Anyway, Uncle Sugar leases a townhouse in Barrington Square for me and my two colleagues. This is my idea. You can squat on our couch until we get this paperwork done. I hope you don't mind a less than comfortable sofa."

"No, that's fine." Richard said.

"Great. You can hang out and watch TV. It won't take very long. Just don't mention to anyone where you're staying. I'm pretty sure I'm not supposed to do this, but fuck it, right?"

For the first time, Richard smiled. "Right. Fuck it."

The townhouse was what one might expect for military personnel off base. Spartan with scuffed white walls, a few Holiday Inn starving artist paintings nailed up here and there, two plain bathrooms, one upstairs the other down, both with the same mauve colored sinks and tubs. The mirrors swung out, with medicine cabinets hidden behind them. The furniture, fairly new, but bereft of any discernible style provided seats where seats were required and table where things could be set. A bulky color television with a weak color palate sat on a faux wood microwave cart. A bulky VCR sat on the shelf underneath it. Lyle and the other two recruiters welcomed Richard into the house offering him cold Miller Lite and pizza at almost every meal, including and especially breakfast. Richard turned down the beer.

A few days later Lyle accompanied Richard on a Metra train from Roselle to the MEPS, the Military Entrance and Processing Center, to get his physical and to take the aptitude test. Richard had no qualms over taking the AVSAB but feared what the physical would find. He'd never been ill as a child, not to his memory anyway, but he'd always been treated as if he'd appeared diseased. Did that mean he had some underlying condition that he wasn't aware of? His mother never took him to a doctor, so he wasn't sure why people often had such a visceral reaction to the way he looked. He wasn't particularly strong, the opposite really, so rather than watch Phil Donahue all day, he did as many exercises as he could think of on the rusty orange carpet of the recruiters' townhouse. Lyle told him he'd have to lift 50 pounds over this head, something he was pretty sure he could do.

When they arrived at the processing center Lyle Gillette gave Richard a shake on the shoulders.

"You've got this," Gillette said, smiling. "Go in there. Let them do their thing. Just keep saying to yourself, 'I got this. There'll be no problems.'" With that Richard went into a cold locker room where other potential recruits were stripping down to their underwear and placing their things in scratched white lockers with keys they pinned to their t-shirts. No one looked at Richard. The others were as nervous as he was and didn't have time or the mind capacity for judgement.

An Army sergeant came into the room from a back door. He held the door open with his foot. "Stow your gear quickly. Physicals will commence in four minutes." He stood and watched the potential recruits, disinterested, glancing at his watch in 30 second intervals. When the four minutes were gone, he ordered them to line up at the door.

The recruits were weighed, their height noted, toes checked for fungus. The operation was cold and methodical. Surgery scars were only questioned if they seemed fresh or if they covered a large area of skin. Richard was placed in what looked to be a soundproofed room with four other men who sat in chairs provided. They were told to put on headphones and handed a button with a cable attached.

The One and True Son

A voice came through the headphones: *You are going to hear a series of tones. When you first hear a tone, press and hold the red button you're holding in your hand. Hold the button until you hear the sound fade away. When you hear the tone cease, release the button. Any questions?*

The recruits all looked at each other. One was an older looking black man, maybe in his late 20s with thick, ropey forearms. He looked annoyed. The other two looked to be latino and looked so much alike, Richard thought they had to be brothers.

As Richard listened, a high-pitched sound tickled his left ear. It was a distant squeal, barely auditable. He released the button when it faded from his hearing range. The sound snuck into his right ear next. A whole range of tones bounced from ear to ear for in the same manner for several minutes. When the headphones remained silent the sergeant came in to the room holding cards with a grid and squiggles on them. Richard became alarmed when he looked from his and the ones of his co-testers. His card had a series of scratched ink marks at regular intervals, building in height and tapering off again. His colleagues' cards looked as though a small child had gotten a hold of a black pen and scribbled all over them.

"Fondlen," the sergeant said. "You're done. Perfect hearing. You must not like Zeppelin." He turned to the others. "We're going to do this over for you three." He looked at the two who appeared to brothers. "You two speak English, right?" They nodded.

"Good," he smirked. "Try doing what I told you to do this time." He had no comment for the man with the ropey forearms. He looked at Richard. "Go to the next station."

To Richard's surprise, he passed the physical with no problems. They tested his eyes, but made no comment on their appearance, a rare event in his life. After being poked for nearly an hour, he returned to his locker and put back on his clothes. He was then escorted to the testing room. It seemed to Richard that the building had been a school or a recreation center at one time as the testing room had a gymnasium floor. High school style desks and chairs waited in clean perfect rows, spaced strategically apart to prevent cheating. The recruits were told they had to wait for the room to fill up before the testing would begin. The chairs filled with young men and women, most of whom were looking around as he was. They fidgeted with their pencils; one kid about Richard's age doodled on the desktop until he was surprised from behind by a sergeant with a face like a Boston Terrier who held out a sponge and a can of cleanser.

"Clean it off now, or you won't be taking no test," the sergeant hissed. "You ain't in detention class. Clean it off good." The boy, cowed by this immaculately uniformed person complied.

After 25 minutes, with the room sufficiently filled with nervous young people, the metal doors swung shut with sound like a small caliber pistol blast.

The dog faced sergeant stepped to the front of the room, his highly polished shoes clicking on the hard wooden floor.

"All right, listen up!" he said, projecting his voice from his chest without actually shouting. "I will be dispersing the Armed Services Vocational Aptitude Battery, also known as ASVAB. It is this test that will determine your job assignment in the armed service you are volunteering for. Do *not* look to anyone else's test or you will be immediately disqualified. Do *not* speak to anyone in the testing area. If you don't understand a question, skip that question and move on. If you complete the test section before the allotted time you may go back and address the question again. Do *not* go back to previous sections of the test. Anyone caught doing so will be immediately disqualified. Are there any questions?" From his expression, it was clear that the sergeant didn't want any.

Soon Richard had the test booklet on his desk along with an answer booklet and two dangerously sharpened pencils.

"You may begin."

At first, Richard thought there must be some other test. It had to be much harder than the one than this. He breezed through the general science questions with fifteen minutes to spare. When they got to mathematic reasoning section, he stole a glance around and noticed some recruits looking to the ceiling as if Yahweh would supply some kind of calculator up there. Richard never felt so confident in his life. Even the mechanical and electrical portions of the test, the part that worried Richard the most, seemed to come to him as if a stream of answers were pumped into his brain.

Before the test, the only part Richard knew he'd do well on was the language part. He'd read at least four hours a day since he could remember, mostly books he could get from the school library or the Tanach, but sometimes magazines that he smuggled in his room like *National Geographic* or *Newsweek*. He had a keen ear for listening to people as well. He'd watched TV sparingly, but when he did, he was more interested in *how* people spoke than what they said. He could spot a liar on the news long before they'd be exposed by normal events. Often, it took the media months or even years to finally discern any truth when Richard knew it when he heard it. Take the trial of the football player accused of brutally murdering his wife and her friend. Richard knew the first time he heard the man speak about the crime that not only had he done the bloody deed; he'd enjoyed it. It wasn't *what* he said. Richard couldn't even remember exactly what that was. He remembered the man's squint when he said certain words, how his voice stretched out words to make them sound convincing. Richard knew he'd get off too. He'd hired the most expensive and accomplished liars in the business.

And so the language portions of the test were a stroll through a very familiar park. When he approached the test monitor, his test and answer books in hand, he couldn't help but smile. The test monitor glanced up at him and winced. That was the only time that happened that day.

Another sergeant ran his exam through a computer that read the answers he'd dotted in. When the results printed out, she smiled. "Fondlen. These are the highest scores I've seen since I've been stationed here. Let's see what jobs are open to you." She typed a few clicks on her keyboard and her printer spit out a sheet on yellow paper.

"Congratulations," she said. "You've been offered everything short of full bird colonel."

He was offered Medical Service Specialist, otherwise known as a medic, Weapons Systems Analyst, Electronic Warfare Technician, even a Media Information Specialist, someone who'd go on the Armed Forces Network and do news shows. Obviously, the tests didn't include a photo or that would never have been offered. There were twenty other jobs, one involving being part of an air crew, flying on the eyes in the sky, the AWACS, a mutant aircraft with a large UFO-like antenna for directing air traffic in a war zone among other classified duties. The sergeant seemed keen on that one. "You'd get to fly which is what most people think you do when you join the Air Force. You'd actually be able to say you do."

Richard hadn't really thought about flying. He'd never been on a plane before. His mother flew a couple times a year to go on spiritual trips with her temple group, which usually meant Richard was left with a loaf of bread and peanut butter with streaks of jelly from jelly jars of the past. He certainly wanted to get as far from Hoffman Estates as he could get. A plane certainly was a way to get far away.

"That does sound interesting," Richard offered.

"If you don't mind flying, it's great," the sergeant replied. "Not only that, if you don't want to be a lifer, your skills will be highly marketable when you get out. I'd jump on it. It's pretty rarely offered."

"How soon can I leave?" Richard answered.

He joined Lyle Gillette at the Burger King across the street to tell him how things went. Gillette seemed almost giddy. "I knew that Whopper was a good investment."

The One and True Son

Gillette was the first person in Richard Fondlen's life that he could say he actually liked.

The next day Lyle Gillette drove him to the train station in Roselle. On Lyle's recommendation Richard took with him what could fit into a medium sized paper bag: a toothbrush and toothpaste, a change of underwear, some deodorant and a novel that he'd picked out from some old ones they'd had in the recruiting office. The book was *Marathon Man,* by William Goldman. "You'll like that one. It's got Nazis and a scared guy that doesn't know what he's stumbled into. You can't drink on the plane, so you might as well read."

They shook hands when the train pulled up at the station. "If you want to, after tech school, you can request helping me out in the recruiting office. But if you don't feel like doing that, at least send me a letter now and then to tell me how you're doing."

Richard only nodded his head. He really felt like smiling, but in his life up to that point, smiling at people didn't always result in reciprocation. He boarded the train and went to the upper deck of the train car where he could get a seat by itself. He watched Lyle Gillette as the train lurched toward Chicago. It struck Richard that the sergeant watched the train go. He wondered why.

The train made its way through the suburbs and neighborhoods of a city that he'd lived near his entire life, but never passed through, not even for school field trips. His mother refused to sign the permission slips, claiming she didn't have the meager three or four dollars required to pay for the bus. He often sat in the office stapling papers for the school's secretary while the other students went to the Field Museum or the Museum of Science and Industry, some for the third or fourth time. The secretary found busy work for him to do, but she wasn't much for conversation.

He stared out the dark green tinted windows at the older houses that made up the city neighborhoods, the brownstones and the abandon warehouses. It was a bit like looking through a zoo enclosure, glassed in, the animals hiding from those going by. There were thousands of people out there, hiding in their nooks, waiting for the noisy train to pass. That's how it felt, anyway.

An hour and fifteen minutes later, the train made its way through the maze of tracks outside Union Station, ducking from the gray light of the day to the dark underside of the city's primary train station. Richard waited for the other passengers, mostly business types, to stand and file out, many still reading from their newspapers or magazines. When the crowd cleared, Richard made his way down the narrow walkway to the even narrower stairs that would lead him off the train.

The One and True Son

At the Armed Forces Debarkation Center any hint of civility toward the services' inductees that may have taken the form of a *please* or a *thank you* at MEPS vanished, replaced by loudly spoken declarative statements, usually beginning with the words "You will".

You will report to room 7B.
You will remove that hat.
You will put out that cigarette.

Some of the recruits, like Richard, had expected terseness when they entered the doors at the center. Lyle gave him a taste of what he would expect, albeit with a smile on his face. No one was smiling here, but why would they? It was clear that not everyone had been so briefed, as one recruit who came in with an Army group from Gary, Indiana decided he didn't like the tone a sergeant used when addressing him.

"You will sit in this row of chairs," the sergeant in charge instructed, "and you will remain silent until spoken to."

"Fuck that," the recruit replied, sitting in the chair. "I ain't at no boot camp yet."

"What's that, P*rivate?"* the short, muscular sergeant hissed back, his face turning a deep violet.

"I said fuck that," the recruit shot back. He'd probably had similar conversations with teachers and police officers in his not so recent past. "You don't hear so good. Maybe you should have another physical." He laughed showing lots of clean white teeth. "And I ain't no fuckin' private. Not yet."

"You *will* listen to instructions," the sergeant said, lowering his voice, "and as soon as you signed that contract you became a private, P*rivate."*

*"*Bullshit,*"* the young man said, his smile dimming just a bit. "I didn't see that shit."

"Stand up, Private!" the sergeant growled. "You *will* come with me."

"Nah, I'm good." The recruit put his feet on the back of the chair in front of him.

The young man occupying the chair turned looking curiously at the feet that put a pair of dusty footprints on the back of his Cheap Trick concert shirt. He didn't appear to want to be drawn into the conflict.

The sergeant stormed off. For a moment, it looked like the defiant recruit had won the battle, but seconds later the sergeant returned with two burly, humorless Army MPs.

"On your feet," the largest of the two MPs, a man with scarred knuckles who looked like he could do a few rounds with Muhammad Ali.

337

"What?" the recruit replied, a little vinegar removed from his tone. "I wasn't doing nothing. I gotta go to bootcamp."

"On your feet," the MP repeated. "You're going home."

"Bullshit!" the recruit shouted. "I gotta a contract. I ain't going nowhere but bootcamp."

The MPs weren't debating. Moving faster than anyone of that size should be able to, the one doing the talking quickly seized the recruit by the ankles while the other got him in a full nelson and lifted him off the chair. The recruit protested continuously, his voice fading away as they carried him down a hallway. A door slammed behind them.

The sergeant returned minutes later telling them that they will be able to talk, but they *will* keep their voices low.

The recruit next to Richard leaned over. "I don't think that guy would've done too good in Basic."

Richard, somewhat stunned that the guy actually talked to him, nodded agreement. "Why would he want to go in the service if he wanted to act like that?"

"Beats me," the recruit shrugged. "He was on our bus coming in from Gary. He was giving everyone shit. Most of us here are just trying to get out of where we are."

Richard nodded again.

"So which branch did you join?" the recruit asked.

"Air Force. What about you?"

"Same," the recruit smiled. "What your name? We might as well get acquainted. Looks like we'll be in Basic together."

"I'm Richard."

"I'm Jerry. You go by Rich or Rick?"

"Richard. Just Richard."

The two recruits talked on and off for two hours as they waited for the sergeant to come back in. Jerry did most of the talking. He was from Munster, Indiana, a middle-class town about 30 miles from Gary. Jerry said he really wanted to get away from Indiana, but Richard couldn't see why from the way he talked of hang gliding at the Indiana Dunes and attending concerts at the Hammond Civic Center. "I saw this British band get booed off the stage there once. This was just before New Wave hit. They had weird colored hair, and their lighting was a bunch of white spotlights. They were opening for a bunch of long hair old school rock bands. They got two songs in before somebody in the front row threw a full beer can and hit the lead singer in the face." Jerry shrugged. "I didn't think they were that bad. They walked off the stage flipping off the crowd.

The One and True Son

The next two bands dropped out and we sat and smoked reefer for three hours until the headliners came on. The crowd was so stoned we barely noticed the band was playing. It kinda sucked. The band that got booed is real big in England now."

"Didn't they asked you if you smoked marijuana at your recruiter?" Richard asked.

"Yeah, they asked," Jerry smirked. "I told them it was *experimental*. Do you smoke?"

Richard shook his head.

"You're better off really. It makes you lazy as shit. Everything's funny though."

The conversation fascinated Richard. He had no music preferences; he'd barely heard much music at all. The idea of going to a concert where full cans of beer could be brought in, let alone thrown at a musician was the most ludicrous thing he'd ever heard.

When the sergeant reentered the room, most the recruits were pretty talked out. It didn't take long for the room to fall silent.

"All stand," the sergeant barked. The recruits did with a minimum of shuffling.

"Raise your right hand and repeat after me: I, state your name."

The recruits did as instructed, murmuring their names in an indecipherable din.

"Do solemnly affirm that I will support and defend…"

The words were virtually meaningless to Richard. He knew the dictionary definition to all the words, but he felt none of them. He just needed a place to go.

The recruits were packed in comfortable coach buses each going to different airlines according to which branch they'd committed to. The marines were headed to Parris Island in South Carolina, the army to Oklahoma, Missouri, Georgia or Fort Jackson, also in South Carolina. Richard and Jerry were headed to Travis City, Texas.

Their plane touched down at the Travis City International Airport at 2:15 am. Most of the recruits were groggy from a day that saw multiple modes of transportation over a single day. Apparently, some recruits didn't get the memo about no drinks on the flight as they nursed alcohol induced headaches and creeping nausea. More than one young man held back the urge to vomit. The recruits boarded school bus type buses painted dark Air Force blue. Some men talked softly, wondering aloud just what it is they'd signed up for. Jerry told a story about a time he'd opened the rear school bus door on the last day of school. He set the alarm off.

"I hopped off of that bus and, for no reason, turned around and punched in the rear taillight. I don't even know why I did it. I liked the bus driver. She was cool. I didn't even hate school. I just turned around and popped it and the thing broke. I guess that was kind of stupid."

Richard didn't know to agree or disagree. He'd never ridden in a school bus. This was the closest he'd ever come to it. He kept quiet, nodding in the dark.

Travis City seemed sleepy. It was definitely not a 2 am town. The traffic was light and the city, as they passed through it, seemed put to bed, resting. As they grew closer to the Air Force Base, a behemoth by Air Force standards, the sky ahead of them glowed sodium orange. The bus driver, a three striper, spoke over the PA:

"We are approaching the gate at Lackland Air Force Base. As soon as we cross through it you *will* shut your mouths and keep them shut. You will speak only when spoken to." The driver let go of the button sending an earsplitting crack through the bus speakers.

The driver/airman negotiated the streets of the base. A series of squat four story buildings waited for the new recruits. There appeared to be no one outside doing pushups, something Richard imagined happened all the time for some reason. The bus swung around into the circular driveway of one of the buildings.

The driver/airman spoke again, his voice taking on a new and threatening tone. "You *will* line up beside the bus. You *will not talk.* You *will not* do *anything* unless instructed to do so. You *will* wait until your gear has been unloaded from the bus. You *will not* touch *anything* until instructed to do so." The driver, a man with two stripes on his sleeve got out of the bus and stood outside the door.

"Now LINE UP!" he shouted.

The recruits, most of them quickly recovering from the early hour, stepped out of the bus and stood next to the bus.

"I said, *LINE UP!"* the airman bellowed. "Does that look like a line to you?" He pointed at the door on the lower part of the bus, behind which was their luggage. He pointed at a spot on the pavement. "I want one airman right here and the rest line up behind him. Now *move!"*

One recruit scrambled to be exactly where the airman was pointing while the others filed behind him, their faces blank.

The driver/airman reached down and swung the door to the luggage area open. He started pulling suitcases and athletic bags from the bus and thumping them down on the pavement. The first recruit in line saw his and went to grab it.

The driver/airman turned on him. *"DID I TELL YOU TO MOVE, AIRMAN?"*

The recruit, all eighteen years of him, stared at the man in uniform, his jaw flapping like a door with a loose hinge. "No." he finally said.

"THEN YOU DON'T MOVE!"

The driver/airman continued unloading the bus. He found Richard's paper bag. "Who brought their lunch?"

Richard saw his paper bag. He raised his hand.

The airman almost smiled. "Well, we've got a genius in the group." He tossed to Richard who almost dropped it.

"The rest of you will pick up your bags quickly, one airman at a time, and form a line of ten airman. When the line is full, form another." He pointed to a spot about 10 feet from the bus. "Females, line up over there." He turned and pointed at spot about thirty feet away. "Males over there."

The recruits stood frozen, obviously afraid to move.

"DIDN'T I SAY PICK UP YOUR BAGS!?" he screamed. "MOVE!"

Richard stayed put as the others lined up behind him. They were the first squad, grabbed their bags as fast as they could move. Two women had the same model suitcase, and both grabbed for it. Their eyes opened wide in the sodium light.

"Are you ladies here to dance?" the airman snapped. "Maybe we can get some music for you." One woman let go and picked up the other suitcase, not bothering to look at the identification tag. They both scrambled to get in line.

Once everyone had their things, the driver/airman turned to the two groups standing in four squads. "I have to say, this is about the sorriest looking bunch of clowns I've ever seen. I probably should've left you at the airport." He turned to two sergeants a man and a woman who appeared from nowhere. The man had four stripes, the woman five. They both wore Smokey the Bear hats tilted down just above their eyes.

"They're yours now," the driver/airman said. "Good luck." With that he got in the bus and drove away.

The Training Instructors moved with practiced precision to the front of the two groups.

The woman spoke first. "Listen up! You are now in squads. You should be *exactly* behind the person in front of you. The person at the front of the line, for now, is the squad leader. If I look down the squad, you *will* be exactly behind the person in front of you. Is that understood?"

No one said anything.

"I said, *is that understood?!"*

The One and True Son

A few of the recruits answered in a chorus of disjointed yeses.

"You are to address me as Tech Sergeant Stocker or ma'am. You are to address my colleague as Staff Sergeant Tonks or sir. Do you understand?"

This time the confused group answered with a combination of all three monikers.

The sergeant took off her hat, wiped her brow and replaced her hat. "That airman was right. This group may be the most hopeless pair of flights I've ever seen."

Sergeant Tonks nodded in unsmiling agreement.

"When we are addressing the group, you will respond with ma'am or sir," he said with a growl that seemed to come from a much larger man. His eyes were cold in the early Texas darkness. "Now pick up your gear."

Both groups bent over to retrieve their gear, once again, everyone but Richard Fondlen. He had to admit to himself he was enjoying this already.

"PUT EVERYTHING DOWN!" the male sergeant barked.

The stunned and highly fatigued recruits dropped everything at once with a conjoined thump.

"When I tell you to pick up your gear, you pick it up quickly. There will be no hesitation. You will hold your bags at your sides and stand at attention. You will stand straight with your head facing forward. Now, PICK UP YOUR GEAR"

This process repeated until the sergeants were convinced that the recruits were broken enough for the night.

"When we enter the dormitories the men will turn to the left, women to the right. Do you understand?"

"Yes sir," the miserable recruits mumbled.

"I said, DO YOU UNDERSTAND?"

"YES SIR!" The recruits replied with apparently the required volume.

They filed silently into the building, climbing the stairs to the second floor. As instructed the men turned to the left, the women to the right. No one entertained childish pranks or turning into the wrong dormitory which might happen in a school or college situation. It had been impressed upon the recruits in the early morning hours in Travis City, Texas that there was no time for such things.

Inside the dormitory, names were called, and bunks assigned. Richard found himself bunking next to Jerry Ronco. Jerry shot him a *wow, here we go, smile.* It had dawned on Richard that Jerry hadn't recoiled from him even though he wasn't wearing his sunglasses, a suggestion from Lyle. He thought back through the pervious 24 hours. No one had turned away from him or commented on his appearance. Not even the less-than-polite staff at

The One and True Son

the debarkation center. He was just another recruit. Part of a crowd. That had never happened to Richard Fondlen.

The recruits were told they had five minutes to shave every hair on their faces. When the sergeant asked if anyone had problems shaving, a kid from Oklahoma, a hulking football player type, thought it was a joke and barked a loud laugh.

"What's funny, airman?" Sergeant Tonks shot at the recruit.

"That's a joke, right?" the kid replied sheepishly. "Like someone here can't hold a razor."

The Training Instructor walked to just within an inch of the Oklahoma kids face.

"First of all, who are you talking to?"

"Uh, you." the kid said with a shrug.

"I didn't hear you?" the sergeant hissed. "Did you say, 'Uh, you?'"

The kid nodded.

"You just volunteered for latrine duty. Congratulations, you're the first. I want to tell you something first. Lean down so you can hear me."

The kid tilted his head.

"IF YOU CALL ME 'YOU' AGAIN I'LL SET YOU BACK IN TRAINING SO FAR, YOU'LL BE IN BASIC UNTIL YOU RETIRE!" And that was the threat they'd hang over all of the recruits for the duration of basic. It wasn't push-ups or running laps. It was being set back in training to be tortured all over again. Fondlen approved.

The sergeant turned those hard eyes up to ten.

"YOU WILL ADDRESS ME AS SIR OR I'LL HAVE YOU LICKING THIS FLOOR CLEAN TONIGHT! IS THAT UNDERSTOOD?!"

The hulk from Oklahoma suddenly looked like a little boy.

The Training Instructor turned back to the rest of the recruits. "Now, does anyone have problems shaving?" Nine recruits, all black, raised their hands. They had something called shaving bumps caused by the texture of their hair. Richard imagined that the kid from Oklahoma was going to have a rough time with some of the other recruits.

Within fifteen minutes they were in their bunks. Snoring commenced a few minutes later, another in the seemingly endless events that Richard had never experienced. He did not fall asleep like most everyone else. He wasn't tired. He was energized.

At 5 o'clock the next morning the recruits were awakened to the sound of a bugle, reveille, and the crashing of a cut off broomstick twirling in a steel garbage can.

The One and True Son

"Get up!" Sergeant Tonks bellowed. "Get your clothes on, shit, shower and shave. You have fifteen minutes to assemble downstairs in squads. Move!"

The groggy recruits jumped out of their bunks. They put on their civilian clothes they'd worn the day before. The rest of their belongings were locked in a large closet near the entrance to the dormitory. They scrambled into their clothes and rushed to get a place at the twenty sinks along the latrine wall. Figuring they didn't have time they all passed on the shower part of the instructions. Even though most of them had shaven just hours before, they did it again, just to be safe. Streams of blood ran down the faces of many of the recruits.

Fifteen minutes later they stood outside, in rows once again. Sergeant Tonks, again, seemed unamused by the disheveled group that stood before him.

"We will be moving to Supply to get your uniforms and cut your hair. You will not speak unless you are cleared to do so. You will march in formation. You will march *directly* behind the man in front of you. The men at the beginning of each squad will use their peripheral vision to stay aligned to the airmen next to him. Do you understand?"

"Yes sir!" the recruits responded.

"I didn't hear that," the sergeant said. "Sound off clearly."

"YES SIR!" the recruits shouted.

The new airmen marched off to be shed their civilian attire, have their heads shorn and be inoculated from diseases with high pressure injector guns that left bumps like bloody volcanoes on the men's deltoids.

Their hair was zipped off their heads with almost surgical precision. When Richard approached the barber, a man with a beergut and long sideburns, he didn't know whether or not to sit down.

"You tryin' to be a smart ass or somethin'. You think shavin' your hair would get you outta sittin' in my chair?" the man sneered. Sit your ass down."

Richard said nothing. He sat in the chair as instructed.

"Get your ass outta that chair. You ain't got nothin' to cut."

Confused, Richard, again, did as instructed and lined up to get the rest of his gear.

The uniforms smelled of moth balls and thick starch. The recruits were issued jackets, gloves, combat boots, running shoes, dress shoes, hats, both formal and fatigue, socks, underwear, and PT (physical training) shirts with their squadron number. With everything stuffed into their new duffle bags, the recruits returned to the dormitory.

The One and True Son

As Richard placed his gear in his locker, he discovered that he recognized no one. The colorful array of street clothes and hair lengths were replaced with a monochrome palate of drab green and clean scalps. Even Jerry Ronco blended into the others, indistinguishable from the men around them.

Ronco turned to Richard. "Man, you don't look nothing like you."

Richard, maybe for the first time in his life, told a joke:

"That's probably a good thing."

The six weeks started slowly, with synchronized marching, folding underwear into six-inch squares and running at 5am. Richard did all these things, surprising himself that he could improve with every week. Jerry wasn't so lucky. With his uniform and new hair style, he bore an amazing resemblance to Radar O'Reilly from the TV show MASH. Apparently, Sergeant Tonks was not a fan of the show, or at least Radar. Tonks rode Jerry hard, constantly correcting his marching missteps, pulling him from the squadron to dress him down in front of the flight.

At their first uniform inspection Ronco made a fatal error. The recruits were told in the first week of training that their boots, which endured the Travis City heat, Texas dust and many other indignities were required to be, in nearly all situations, shined to a chrome-like shimmer. Jerry had taken to buffing them up by rubbing the toes on the back of the opposite pant leg. The result was two black streaks along the calves of his trousers where there weren't even supposed to be wrinkles. Sergeant Tonks said nothing. He told Ronco to step out of formation and took his 341, a form recruits were required to carry at all times in the left breast pocket of their uniform shirts. The form was meant to be a carrot/stick device. Something well done would get the recruit a positive review on the form and much praise from the instructors, not to mention cushy duty like mowing the grass on base in the latter days of training. Something done wrong brought wrath, scorn and punishment. Latrine duty, washing the flight's laundry or crawling under bunks to collect dust bunnies while the rest of the flight enjoyed base liberty. Too many negative 341s brought the most feared punishment: Set Back. Those two streaks had been it for Jerry. His bunk remained empty for the rest of the training. Richard saw him once, toward the end of basic. Richard was in the base exchange, buying some toothpaste and other toiletry articles for his expected departure to tech school at the end of the week. He donned dress blues, complete with what the recruits referred to as the "bus driver hat". Richard spotted Jerry hauling huge loads of laundry at a nearby dormitory. He stood for a moment watching him. Ronco's big grin was gone. He looked exhausted and miserable. Richard watched him for a moment, expressionless. He wouldn't see Jerry Ronco again.

In the last week of Basic, Richard was pulled from classroom instruction. No one was yelling at him, so he figured he hadn't angered anyone unknowingly, but it struck him odd that he was the only one from the flight to be pulled from any sort of training. Sergeant Tonks handed him a base pass with a building number and a time on it.

"Do I have to march there, sir?" Richard asked the sergeant; for the first time he noticed the sergeant cracked a smile.

"You'd look pretty stupid marching across the base on your own, wouldn't you?"

Richard nodded, hoping it wasn't some kind of Basic Training last week trap. The sergeant handed him a base map.

"Look for the street signs. Follow the map to the building that's circled. Stay on the right side of the road, there and back. If anyone stops you, show them the pass. Any more intelligent questions?"

"No sir," Richard replied.

"Get moving and get your ass right back here when you're done. No stopping at the BX or anywhere else or I'll personally make sure you get set back to kindergarten."

Richard felt a freedom that he hadn't experienced before, not just since he started Basic, but, perhaps, ever. He was wearing his dress blues. The recruits had been wearing them to classroom lectures all week. He walked down Truemper Street, turned right on Barnes Avenue and left on Nellis to the Airman Training Complex. Along the way he saw formations of recruits, some fresh off the airport bus, others further along, the latter with slightly more defined hairlines and more confidence in their steps. No one bothered to stop him to ask him why he was wondering around without his flight. He felt that maybe, people thought he was past basic, past all the forced togetherness. He expected to find some kind of screening at the door but found none. He tracked down a sergeant, expecting to be berated for approaching her.

"Excuse me, ma'am. I have a pass to come to this building. Do you know where Room 42 is?"

The sergeant smiled at him. Actually, he smiled a real smile. It confused Richard. He thought that sergeant training included instruction in the high art of sneering. She pointed down a hallway. "Go down there to the end of the hall and turn right. It's on the left about three doors down."

Richard nodded.

The One and True Son

"Don't worry," the sergeant said. "You're almost done. Soon you'll be in the real Air Force. She patted him on the shoulder and went on her way. Richard was more confused than ever.

He followed her directions and just as she said, he was in front of Room 42.

He was met at the door by a two-striper who took his pass and checked Richard's name off a list and handed him back a small piece of paper.

"Go to seat C-14."

The room was a maze of connected cubicles each with its own set of headphones and a number and letter stenciled on the cubicle wall. A row of four different colored buttons were embedded in the desktops. Richard found his seat. Before he sat, he looked around the room. There were about 12 other recruits in a space that easily could've sat 50. Richard sat stiffly in the chair. Ten minutes later, a sergeant spoke loudly across the room.

"Put on the headphones now."

Richard did as he was instructed as did the other recruits. He could hear the cords shuffling in the other cubicles.

From that moment, the sergeant spoke through the headphones.

"You are here today to test your ability to differentiate language patterns. You will hear a phrase from a native speaker of a certain language. Following that you will hear four short phrases that may or may not be from the same language. Each phrase has a corresponding button. Using the buttons on the desktop, choose the one phrase that comes closest to the language you heard in the opening phrase. The opening phrase will be repeated twice as will each of the subsequent phrases. Press the button which most corresponds with the opening phrase"

Richard wasn't sure what they could be looking for with this test and he feared he might mess it up. He stared at the laminate wood of the cubicle, straight ahead, and concentrated. Once he heard what they were going to play for him, he might be able to figure it out. After a moment, a slight hiss filled the headphones followed by a sentence-worth of a language he'd never heard before. He heard the same phrase again. Then, as promised, he heard four more phrases, each sounding a bit different in inflection, some so different to English that he found himself contorting his face in ways he imagined he'd need to move his mouth to produce such sounds. When the four phrases finished, he was sure the second phrase he'd heard was related to the opening phrase and he confidently pressed the green button with the letter B stenciled above it. The test went like this for over an hour. When the last phrases were played, the voice in the headphones announced the end of the test. He stood and took his new pass from the two-striper there

The One and True Son

and left the building the same way he came in. Twenty minutes later he was back in the dormitory.

On day 30 of training, after parade, after distribution of awards and some stripes, Richard was preparing his gear to move to his tech school. Richard had received orders to transfer to Sheppard Air Force base, a smaller training base in Wichita Falls in the northern part of the state. It would be an all-day bus ride. Richard wasn't much for excitement; he truly didn't know if he understood the feeling or if he'd ever experienced it, but he was sure the strange feeling in his abdomen had something to do with it. According to his orders he'd be departing at 0600 the next morning. The orders didn't last long.

"Change of plans, Fondlen."

It was Sergeant Tonks.

"I don't understand, sir." Richard said.

"You can knock off the sir shit now," Tonks replied, now openly smiling. "That's really just for officers. Adds to the pressure when you're trying to scare the shit out of 50 newbies, but you made it through. You even got honor grad."

Richard looked down at the white, blue and yellow ribbon above his breast pocket.

"You still have to pack your gear. You'll be moving across base to permanent dorms."

"I thought I was going to take a bus?" Richard said, not really disappointed, but curious.

"Yeah, you still might. But they've got other plans for you first." Tonks handed him his orders. "There'll be a truck around to pick you and your gear up in about an hour. Congrats. You're done with basic, airman." Suddenly, the man who appeared to be cold and driven by rules and military discipline looked human, even kind. Richard wondered which was the real person, the sergeant or the guy who was talking to him.

The truck arrived as scheduled. Richard's colleagues seemed impressed that not only was he not leaving with the rest of them to learn how to fix airplanes, or to guard a post, or to put out a fire, or for a couple of them to learn how to feed 1000 people in a day. He was doing something important. Even though they'd been in the service for the same amount of time as Richard, they knew when something special was happening. Leave a day early from Basic Training. That was unheard of.

The permanent quarters were spartan, but clean, with furniture that looked like wood, but was made of glued together sawdust with a wood grain veneer slapped on it. There was no TV or radio. The airman that

The One and True Son

helped him lug his gear to his room on the second floor told him he'd have to provide that himself.

"If you go to the BX, you can get great stereo equipment and a TV super cheap. That's what most of us do who live on base. Until you get a couple stripes you can rent them. Maybe you shouldn't buy anything until you know where you're going."

"Is this your duty base or do you train here?" Richard asked.

The two-striper, or Airman First Class, was a string bean with light brown hair. He was tall with small tight muscles that clung to his rolled-up fatigue sleeves. There was an air of Alabama in his speech and a smile of genuine friendliness.

"I went to tech school too, to be a mechanic. I wasn't too good I guess because they made me a driver and sent me back here. It's cool though. I really like Travis City. A lot of pretty señoritas, you know? I still live on base though. An A1Cs check ain't so big and the rents here can be pretty steep, even for a shithole. You must be pretty smart though."

"Why do you say that?" asked Richard.

"'Cause you're in this dorm. They only put people in here for big jobs. Secret stuff from what I hear. You notice anything about your room?"

Richard shook his head.

"Look around. How many beds in here?"

Richard was puzzled. "One?"

"That's right," the A1C winked. "You won't find a single bedroom for an Airman Basic anywhere in the Air Force. Hell, I got two roomies. One's cool, but the other one's a holy roller. He's always trying to get me to go the base temple. He don't drink beer or nothing. He looks at us funny when we come in from partying. You're lucky. You don't have to deal with nothing like that."

With a promise to come by and show Richard all Travis City's night spots, the A1C took his leave.

Richard had no idea what he was doing or what his training would be. His orders only said that he would billet in this dormitory and some kind of numeral code to describe his training. Other than Richard, there seemed to be few people in the dorm. The halls were quiet. Richard listened for the murmurs of a television or maybe even a distant stereo playing Pink Floyd or Prince. No, no sign of other airman, male or female. That night, Richard sat in the dark and listened for signs of life: footsteps, a cough, a fart, anything. For the first time since he left the train station in Roselle, Richard was on his own. He thought about that for a long time that night. He discovered he was fine with it.

The One and True Son

He woke in the morning with a start. There was no reveille, no banging of garbage cans, no scrambling to the sink to brush his teeth. He gathered his toiletries and walked down to the lavatory. There were five shower stalls, all empty, all dry. Richard looked at himself in the mirror, really looked for the first time since training started. His face had narrowed, the pudginess that once looked back at him was gone, replaced by taut cords connecting his cheeks to his jaws His eyes, black as coal, stared back with interest for the first time he could remember. He stripped and stepped into one of the shower enclosures and soaped himself thoroughly, scrubbing himself almost raw, his body, naked of hair, was hard under the pressure of the soapy washcloth. His leg muscles were pulled tight, like a gazelle's. Richard had never felt so powerful. He stood in the water for a long time.

When he returned to his room, clad only in the white briefs he'd been issued the first day of Basic, he found a visitor waiting for him. He snapped to attention. For some reason there was a captain sitting on his bed.

"At ease, Airman," the captain said, obviously amused by Richard's attire. "Get some clothes on for fuck's sake."

Richard rummaged through his gear, pulling out a fresh uniform and hung it on a hook in the closet.

"Didn't you bring any civies with you to Basic?" the captain inquired.

"No sir," Richard answered clearly. "My recruiter told me I wouldn't need them."

The captain smirked and ran his hand through his brush cut hair. "Well, I guess that makes sense. Get your fatigues on then. We'll get you some clothes at the BX."

While Richard changed, the officer walked around the room. "Man, they spare no expense for our defenders of democracy."

"Its's probably the best room I've ever had, sir," Richard said, not looking for sympathy, just stating a fact.

"You've had some sorry rooms then," the captain replied as swiped a finger along the veneered, empty bookshelf. "And you can drop the sir shit with me. My name's Gene Gebhardt. You can call me by either one. I don't care. In uniform and outside you still have to salute and all that. But in civies and during training, I'm Gene or Gebhardt. Got it?"

Richard nodded.

"They said you were smart," the captain said.

Gebhardt's car was right outside the dorm, parked in a reserved space. The car, a Lincoln, still had the new car smell; the seats still had the factory firmness that comes from lack of rear ends in the passenger's seat. They

The One and True Son

drove to the BX, a much larger building than the one Richard was allowed to use during Basic. Once there, Richard headed to his preferred style, Khaki dress pants and shirts with button down collars.

Richard grabbed a pair of trousers with pleats and a checked sport shirt collar.

Gebhardt flipped through the clothing draped over Richard's forearm.

"How old are you? 70? Dump that shit and go get some jeans. And maybe a couple t-shirts that say something clever on them. You'll need some comfortable shoes. Don't get some old grandpa shoes either. They've got Nikes here. Good ones."

"But sir…" Richard stopped when he noticed the glare Gebhardt gave him. "I don't have that much money. I've only been paid twice, and I sent some of it back to my mother."

"Why did you send it to that bitch?" the captain said, as if in passing.

Richard shivered.

Gebhardt took no notice of Richard's distress. "Don't worry about it. It's in the budget. Now go get the fucking shoes. And while you're at it, pick up some sunglasses. You need to cover those eyes."

Richard had never shopped like that, not that he'd had much experience. Before the captain took him off base for lunch, he ordered Richard to put on his civilian clothes. Gebhardt drove them to one of Travis City's most popular Mexican places with a large outside patio and, according to the captain, the best fucking fajitas in the US.

"You want a margarita?" the captain asked talking through the menu.

"What's that?" Richard asked.

"It's tequila and sour mix. Kind of foo-foo if you ask me. If I'm going to drink tequila I want it in a shot glass, preferably served between a señorita's tits. You might like it though. They bring it in a glass about the size of a paint bucket. You might want some alcohol on board."

"I don't drink, sir," Richard said.

"Well, you might want to start," the captain said without a hint of a grin. "And what did I tell you about that *sir* shit? Especially out here."

Richard stared at the captain through his new Ray-Bans. "I'm sorry. It's just that I got out basic yesterday where I had to say sir and ma'am to everyone. It's going to be a hard habit to break."

"True that," the captain said. "Work on it."

The waitress came, a young woman, maybe a year or two older than Richard with long, sleek black hair and a ring pierced through her left eyebrow.

The One and True Son

"Dos fajitas de pollo por favor, y dos Coronas, mi corazon." the captain said looking up at her smiling with clean perfect teeth.

The waitress smiled a smile that Richard had never had thrown in his direction.

"Al mujeriego le encanta coquetear con las mujeres y dejarlas en el aire," responded the waitress. Richard didn't understand what she'd said but he knew she wasn't angry.

"Pronto estaremos juntos, mi vida." the captain purred to her.

The waitress kissed her fingertip, placed it on his lips and left to put in the order.

"She's very pretty," Richard said. "What's her name?"

"Haven't a clue," the captain said, again with that smile. "But you're right. She is pretty."

Captain Gebhardt turned his full attention to Richard.

"You know you're special, right?"

"Huh?" said Richard, off guard.

"You know that you're different than everyone you trained with. Different than the TIs. Hell, you're different than me for that matter."

That was one thing Richard had known for sure. He'd always known. He was different than everyone he'd ever seen. His mother had made sure he knew it. She told him that the only one like him was his father, and whoever he was, she didn't like him.

"How am I different from you? Except, of course, rank and an attractiveness to women."

Gene Gebhardt looked at Richard as if the sun was shining directly in his eyes. "You have no idea, do you? I guess that's not really shocking considering where you came from."

The waitress came back with their beers sweating in their clear bottles with a lime capping them off. She handed the two men napkins, but Gebhardt's had something written on it. "Llámame después de las ocho." she said opening her gorgeous brown eyes wide, then closed and opened them slowly.

"El tiempo esta quemado en mi corazón," Gebhardt answered in a low breathless register.

The waitress set down the beers and a basket of tortilla chips. She brushed the captain's shoulder delicately with her hand and left to attend to other customers.

"What did you say to her," Richard asked.

"She gave me her number and asked me to call her after eight. I told her I would."

"It sounded like you said more than that," Richard said, amazed."

"See," Gebhardt said. "That's you being different. You don't speak the language, but you knew that there was more to it than what I told you. That's one of your gifts.

"Gifts?" Richard said.

"Yep, gifts," Gebhardt replied. "Try the beer."

Richard looked at the bottle like it was a dangerous animal. "There's a lime jammed in it."

"Push it into the bottle," Gebhardt said. "It adds flavor."

Richard did what he was told. He picked up the bottle and took a swig.

"How do you like it?" Gebhardt asked.

Richard made a face. "It tastes like dishwater. Cold dishwater with lime."

"Drink up," Gebhardt said reaching over with his bottle and giving Richard's a clink. "We've got a lot to discuss."

"I have to be drunk to discuss it?" Richard asked.

"Not drunk but buzzed. This is serious shit."

The lunch came. Richard had never seen a better meal in his life. It was served on a thin metal box with holes in the sides, the top acting as a tray. A Sterno in the box heated the tray packed with spiced chicken, grilled onions and peppers, filling the air with a scent that only comes from the work of an expert chef. The tortillas were served in a round container with a lid; inside the tortillas waited, moist and warm. To Richard, it looked like a roomful of food. Bowls of Guacamole and salsa oozing with onion, chiles, cilantro, lime, and cubed tomatoes added to the palate of delicious smells. He had no idea where to begin.

"Take a tortilla and lay it your hand," Gebhardt explained. "Kind of cup it your palm. Then add what you like." He started filling the tortilla using a large spoon. "I like all of it. Then I top it off with the best homemade guac you'll ever have. I swear this stuff has cocaine in it."

Richard mimicked his instructor's actions, starting with the peppers and onions, adding a mound of chicken and a healthy dab of guacamole. The tortilla's sides strained from all the food. His tastebuds came alive, Richard believed, for the first time in his life. The two men sat in silence and savored their bounty.

After both men emptied their heated trays, Gebhardt ordered another round of beers.

The One and True Son

They sat silently drinking; Richard imagined that this is what it must be like to be a king.

"That beer still tastes like dishwater?" Gebhardt asked, smiling.

"Best dishwater I've ever had," Richard answered, almost smiling himself.

"You're learning already," the captain said looking satisfied.

"What exactly am I learning?" Richard asked.

Gebhardt sat back in his chair. "It's a long process, but I know we picked the right guy."

"How do you know?" Richard asked.

"I just do. That's all you have to know right now. But I suppose this is as good a time as any to get on to business. First off, you're going to college."

"College?" Richard nearly shouted. These were his first beers ever. "I haven't even applied."

Gebhardt threw him that smile of his. "Yes, you did. You're already accepted, and the university is proud to have you."

Richard looked around, his mind spinning. "But...why? How?"

Gebhardt ignored his questions. "You're going to study languages. Do you know that test you took? Listening to the different dialects? This is one of the things that is special about you. You answered them *all correctly*. That's never happened before."

Richard rubbed his forehead.

"Any idea how many different dialects you heard?" Gebhardt asked. "Just a guess?"

Richard shrugged. "I don't know. Five?"

"Nice guess, but you're wrong. There were five *languages*. There were seventeen dialects. You identified each one correctly. That's like catching a five-dollar bill in a tornado."

Richard sat back in his chair. "So, you want me to be in a listening post somewhere, right?"

"Something like that, but a bit more...intensive. We'll get to that in due time. What I do know is we've got the right guy. You have your ticket for the rest of your life. But I have to tell you, the training is going to be — let's say, unorthodox. It won't be like anything you might imagine. It's an unusual program."

That day Gebhardt taught Richard how to fold a quesadilla. Later he would teach Richard things that were previously unimaginable.

The One and True Son

Richard soon discovered he was the sole resident of the dormitory. He woke every morning at five a.m. He'd walk nude to the shower knowing no one would meet him in the hall. There would be no one taking up the shower stalls next to his. If he needed to defecate, he left the stall door open. With his jeans and pithy t shirt he would board an Air Force bus like the one that brought him to Lackland just as it did months before. The bus, of which he was the only passenger, would drop him at a VIA bus stop where he would take two buses to get to the Travis City campus of the University of Texas. He had introductory classes in Farsi, Arabic, and Hebrew in the morning. He'd have lunch, by himself, in the large dining facilities on campus. In the afternoon he'd attend classes in Spanish and Portuguese. Richard didn't have to worry about any of his classmates being in more than one of his classes. No other student had a schedule like his. No university would allow it. But there he was. And he breezed through the classes as if he were learning to breathe.

He spent most of his evenings on base, mostly at the base theater watching second run movies. Sometimes he'd go to the same movie three or four times, particularly comedies, trying to figure out why they were appealing to other people. Sometimes he'd identify some value. Others, by the fourth time seeing them, he'd give up.

He saw Gebhardt infrequently. Some weeks he'd visit him in the dorm once or twice. Other weeks, Richard was on his own, his only human contact was with his professors or his interaction with the Air Force dependent running the box office at the theater. Richard didn't miss mixing with people. It seemed normal to him. Just like home.

He didn't know it, but Richard wasn't going for a degree. He was registered only through the summer semester.

When his final grades came in, Gebhardt showed up at the door with a bottle of champagne and two long, thin glasses.

"Did I tell you we picked the right guy?" He beamed as he popped the cork. "I guarantee this won't taste like dishwater." As if to himself he muttered, "It better be good at $180 a bottle." He poured the glistening liquid into the skinny glasses, took one for himself and handed the other to Richard.

"Don't drink it yet," the captain ordered.

Richard had no plans to do so.

"First," Gebhardt continued, "hold your glass up to the light. Look at the clarity."

Richard did as ordered.

The One and True Son

"See the other side of the glass? Even though there's mist on the side of the glass, can you see your fingers? Not just the fingers, but the fingerprint?"

Richard looked through the glass. The drink, light golden and bubbling, was alive in the glass.

"That's purity," Gebhardt exalted. "That's refinement of purpose. That is what we strive for in our dealings. Refined, pure, purpose."

"I see them," Richard said.

Richard wanted to take a sip, but suspected Gebhardt wasn't done. He was right.

"Now bring the glass up to your nose," Gebhardt continued. "Breathe in the scent. Color your mind with it. That is the scent of someone who knows their cause. Someone who provides the perfect result of their labor. Remember that scent. Remember that color in your mind. That is what to strive for."

Richard, again, did as instructed. He closed his eyes. His mind filled with visions of French fields on pale dry, flinty soil. The tiny green grapes hung from their vines like small children climbing on a favorite uncle who'd been gone on a long journey. They sucked in the sweet sunshine around them, eagerly, wanting to please their absent uncle.

Gebhardt raised his glass to Richard's and plinked his glass.

"You can drink now, Richard."

They stood smiling at their glasses.

"I guess I did well on my exams," Richard said although he already knew he had.

"Fuck yeah, you did. You did *perfectly,*" Gebhardt gushed. "I knew you would. As a reward there's a plane waiting for you."

Richard stared at the captain.

"Yeah, a plane. You're going on a vacation. A real one."

"Where am I going?" Richard asked.

"Where do you want to go?" Gebhardt answered as if it were no big deal.

"Seriously?" Richard asked.

"Uh-huh," Gebhardt answered, stretching.

Richard looked confused. "But why?"

Gebhardt took a seat on Richard's bunk. "A reward. You did great. You did everything I expected of you. And you'll need some rest."

"For the next semester? I think I already speak better than some of the professors."

356

The One and True Son

Gebhardt laughed. " I don't doubt it. Yeah, you won't need it for the next semester. College is done. You've earned your degree as far as Uncle Sugar is concerned. You'll need rest for the next phase of your training."

"Next phase?" That sounded ominous to Richard.

"We'll talk about that later. Right now, you need to tell me where to point the plane."

Richard looked at his champagne glass.

"France," he said.

Richard and Gebhardt arrived at Paris's Charles De Gaulle Airport in early morning. They flew on a US Government jet, no security checks, no delays in claiming their bags. They hadn't been on the tarmac for five minutes before a rental car joined them at the base of the stairs, a blue Renault R5 turbo, a squat automobile, inconspicuous on the narrow streets of France, but peppy enough to get them around efficiently and quickly. Gebhardt climbed behind the wheel and took off into the insane labyrinth of the Paris streets.

"You've got to learn to drive," Gebhardt said over the whistling wind ripping through the open windows of the cramped car. "It's the most liberating feeling in the world to be able to do battle on any street. Even these fucked up French ones."

Richard knew that he never mentioned not learning to drive.

"I've always wanted to," Richard replied. "My mom…"

"I know," Gebhardt interrupted. "She's in the rearview mirror now. We'll get you trained so you can compete at Indy."

They quickly left the chaos of Paris and hopped on Autoroute A4 and headed northeast. Richard had read about the sites in Paris: the Arc de Triomphe, the Eiffel Tower, the Place de la Concord, and they were interesting in an old movie sort of way. But since the offer of unlimited travel, Richard had one interest. A little over an hour later they approached the ancient city of Reims. Richard could feel the chill in the air, even in August. He needed that crispness after the seemingly endless arid, punishing Travis City sun. The age and beauty around him nearly made Richard swoon.

"Is this where we're going?" Richard asked. "It's beautiful."

"We could stop here. They've got their own version of Notre Dame. Great breakfast places. Lots of tourists though. We're going a little further south, a place called Épernay. It 's the *real* capital of Champagne."

Gebhardt steered the car onto the N51. Soon they were passing chateaus with names that Richard had never heard, but most people his age assumed was very expensive champagne: Moët and Chandon, Perrier and Jouët, Magus Pérignon. Each chateau a palace for its own version of what early pioneer, Magus Pérignon himself, referred to as "drinking stars."

Richard sat in stunned silence. His world had been suburban ranch style houses and split levels. What he was seeing was beyond imagination, beyond belief.

"Beautiful place, isn't it?" Gebhardt said, noticing Richard's gawk. "We'll get to see those places. All of them, if you want. We have to check into our apartment first."

"Apartment?" Richard asked.

"Don't cream your Jockeys," said Gebhardt. "It's nice, but not that fancy. We don't want to be around too many people. It's right in the center of town. We're almost there."

As promised, Gebhardt whipped the car into a driveway and drove around the back of a large, nondescript building to park in front of an old looking, three story partial wood frame house.

"Stay here. I have to get the key." Gebhardt hopped out and in less than a minute, returned with an unusual cylindrical key. "We're on the top floor. Grab your gear."

Although the apartment was *nothing fancy* according to Gebhardt, the two-bedroom A-framed apartment was easily the fanciest place Richard would've seen, let alone slept in, up to this point in his life. The walls were framed in ancient old beams that reminded Richard of stories of pirate ships and traveling on the seven seas. There was a stiff European style sofa and two equally stiff, but highly colorful, easy chairs. A small kitchen with a microwave, toaster oven, and refrigerator took up a corner of the apartment.

"There's a bottle of Champagne in the fridge, but you'll have enough of that later," Gebhardt told Richard. "Pick your room."

There were two large bedrooms on opposite sides of the apartment, both raised from the living area by a short flight of stairs to doorless platforms. Richard looked at the closest one to him and set his gear there. Gebhardt went to the other.

"Where's the latrine?" Richard called across to the captain.

Gebhardt answered: "It's that door on the right. Though I wouldn't call it a latrine. It's got a hot tub."

"Hot tub? Don't all tubs in France have hot water?"

Gebhardt laughed. "Probably not. But this is a special tub you can sit in an ease your muscles. It kind of blows the water around. You've never heard of one?"

The One and True Son

"Honestly, no," Richard answered.

"Huh," Gebhardt derided him. "Some genius."

Richard took a shower, European style, standing in the middle of the tub and using the handheld shower nozzle. He found it far superior to the American way of showering and made sure he hit every nook and cranny. Both Richard and Gebhardt changed clothes and set out along the Avenue de Champagne, where they'd passed the chateaus of the champagne giants of the world.

"We can go to any of these you want," Gebhardt told Richard, "But we want to start off with the Big Kuhuna."

"Big what?" Richard asked.

"You did live under a rock. The Big Kuhuna. The biggest boy on the block. The Mag himself."

Richard stared, blankly.

"Magus Pérignon. He was one of the early wizards of bubbly. I guess there wasn't much for the old moreh to do but sit around and figure out tasty ways to get hammered. Moët and Chandon distribute Mag, but it's so famous that it gets its own chateau."

When they'd arrived, Richard had trouble believing what he was seeing. How could any building be this beautiful?

They passed through the wrought iron gates and crossed the stone courtyard to the front entrance. Next to the large elaborate glass entrance doors, a sign permanently mounted and engraved in polished brass read in both French and English: Tours and tasting, by appointment only.

Richard stopped. "Do we have an appointment?"

Gebhardt swung open the entrance door. "Don't need one." Gebhardt said and dramatically waved his arm beckoning Richard to go through it.

The lobby of this place was, again, beyond Richard's belief. The walls were all gilded in a polished platinum. Built-in wall shelves with dim lights shown on bottles of the special wine as if they were exhibits in a museum. Lights in the ceiling lit the room softly, pleasing to the eye. In the center of the room stood a stylized bar of the same polished platinum, wide at the top, smoothly narrowed and widened again at the floor. There were no barstools.

Behind the bar stood a serious looking man of about 40, as polished as the walls and the bar, clothed in an expertly tailored dark gray suit with a tasteful narrow skyblue tie.

"Bonjour, Michel," Richard said to the man, smiling.

"Ah bonjour, Monsieur Gebhardt," the man replied. "C'est si agréable de te revoir. Sommes-nous ici pour faire un achat aujourd'hui?"

The One and True Son

"Pas aujourd'hui, mon ami," Gebhardt replied. "Voici mon ami Richard." Gebhardt switched to English. "Perhaps we could have a tour?"

"Of course," Michel switched languages with him. "It would be our pleasure to have any friend of yours as our guest today. If you will give me a moment to prepare the staff."

Michel bowed and exited through a doorway Richard hadn't noticed before.

Gebhardt turned to Richard. "What do you think?"

"Amazing," Richard responded. It was the only word he could think of.

"This is one of the places you will have access to," Gebhardt said, looking at the room rather than Richard. "I want you to remember that. There's a whole new world open to you. It will come at a cost. Don't think it won't. But I know you. I know you probably better than anyone else you've ever met. You will be able to handle the cost. I promise you that."

When Michel returned, he brought two women with him. "Allow me to present Mademoiselles Eloise and Sabine. They will take you on a tour through the facility. Feel free to ask them anything you wish. They are most knowledgeable of all the workings of the winery and of the local culture and history. When you return, Mr. Richard, we have a very special gift for you. Until then, I leave you in their very capable hands." That said, Michel departed.

One of the women, the tallest of the two, stepped forward, offering her hand to shake. "I am Eloise. Let me say that Sabine and I are honored to show you our winemaking operation. You will notice when we go downstairs that the air is quite cool, about 11 degrees celsius. These temperatures remain year-round. If you are prone to feel chilled, may we offer you a thin jacket before we descend into the caverns?"

Richard and Gebhardt looked at each other. "I think we can handle the chill," Gebhardt replied. "We are anxious to learn."

With that, the small group headed through the door Michel had come through to a wide set of stairs. The contrast between the twentieth century operation and the less lit, ancient operation below was apparent from the top of the stairs. Thick, hand-hewn railings led the way down through the centuries, down to the barrel vaults and the trapped air of medieval France.

At the base of the long stairs, Sabine turned to the men. "Gentleman, if you look at the walls of the chambers you will notice a white, crumbly material. This is chalk. The same chalk that produces the most famous wines in the world." She smiled her perfect smile. She was a young woman, maybe 23 years old, at the most. Her raven dark hair was natural and framed her face perfectly. Her slim frame moved with elegance in her gray pants suit, the same gray as Michel's and Eloise's. Her eyes were ice blue.

"This is not to say that your California wines are not excellent," she looked slyly at the two men. "They are just not French."

Everyone laughed appropriately.

They stepped into what appeared to be an intersection of barrel vaults. At each wall stood inclined shelves, each filled to capacity with dusty, dark green bottles, all neck down.

Eloise spoke: "The bottles that you see here are quite young, perhaps 5 or 6 years old. Magus Pérignon is only sold at vintage. You will not find a bottle from this year in any establishment in the world. For some years you will find no wine as the grapes were deemed unsuitable for our prestigious blends."

Richard spoke up: "You said blends. I thought wines were made with one kind of grape for one kind of wine. You know, green grapes for whites. Red or purple grapes for reds."

Gebhardt and the two women looked to each other, acknowledging the naïveté of the newcomer.

"This is incorrect," Sabine answered, "although I understand why you would think this. Magus Pérignon is a combination of the grapes that make up the wines, pinot noir and chardonnay. It is special fermentation and added sugars that provide the carbonation."

Richard was fascinated. He and Gebhardt followed the two women further under the chalky soil. The air was moist and cool with the sweet musty, earthy odor that one finds when a stone is turned over to show the side that hasn't seen the sky for a long time. Richard looked at everything, the arched roof of ancient brick, the subtle downgrade of the concrete floor. They passed chambers carved out of the sweating walls, filled to capacity with thick glass bottles, each with its own share of dust, remnants of the years of waiting to be consumed.

"How many bottles would you say are down here?" Richard asked.

Sabine took the question. "It is said that if the bottles in these tunnels were distributed there would be enough to give every man, woman and child in France four bottles."

"And how far do these tunnels go?"

Eloise pushed her long slanted blonde bangs from her left eye. "It is not known exactly. Most of these tunnels are as old as civilization itself, at least in France. Some have collapsed, forgotten. Others are still in use with vintages that reach back a century, at least."

The small group emerged from the tunnels an hour later. Richard was energized. He had no idea that this existed in the world. He wanted desperately to see more. They found themselves back in the lobby where they were met by Michel, looking quite pleased with their return.

"I trust you found the tour to be an interesting one."

Richard stepped forward. "Michel, I can't tell you how honored I am that you and your colleagues took the time to show us this fantastic operation."

Gebhardt looked at Richard, beaming.

"I am so pleased," Michel responded. "Perhaps if you and Monsieur Gebhardt have the time tomorrow, you might enjoy to seeing the picking of the grapes. It is harvesting season and we are picking the grapes at the temple of Magus Pérignon himself. It is an exciting occasion for us here and these grapes are what make this sparkling wine unique from any other in the world."

"Would it be possible to pick them?" Richard asked. "At least for a little while?"

"It would be our honor if you wish to do so, monsieur," Michel said. "I will make arrangements for you to do so."

"I think I'll sit this one out," Gebhardt said, drawing a laugh from everyone else.

"Ah! Before I forget, we have something for you Mr. Richard. If you'll wait one moment, I will get it for you."

When Michel returned, he was carrying a bottle much larger than the bottles he saw in the tunnel.

"We would like to present you with a small gift to commemorate your visit." Michel handed the bottle to Richard. "It is a magnum of Magus Pérignon 1969 P3 Plentitude Brut. We hope you will enjoy this, and we hope you will return the next time you are in France."

Richard, touched, cuddled the bottle as if was a newborn. It is the first present he'd ever received as far as he could remember.

"Thank you, Michel," Richard said, bowing slightly. "I will treasure this."

As the two men headed out of the château, Gebhardt spoke. "Michel likes you."

"I love this place," Richard said. " I can't wait to get back to the apartment so we can have some of this."

"I think maybe we should drink the stuff that's in the fridge. That bottle you're holding costs about three grand."

The One and True Son

The next morning, at 5:30 the two men were awakened by the front doorbell. Gebhardt stuck his head out the window where he saw a dusty light blue Toyota pickup with a group of equally dusty workers, men and women, piled in the back. A small man in a blue work jacket who looked to be around 70 years old looked up to him from the front door.

"Bonjour monsieur. Nous sommes à la recherche de Monsieur Richard. Il voulait cueillir des raisins."

"Oui," Gebhardt called down to him, "Un instant. Il sera à terre."

Gebhardt turned to Richard who was pulling a sweatshirt over his head. "Looks like your ride's here, buddy."

Richard looked alarmed. "You're serious. You're not going?"

Gebhardt shook his head. "Nah. Picking grapes ain't my thing. Besides, it's your vacation. I'm going back to bed and maybe a little later go find a little petit-déjeuner."

Richard looked flummoxed.

"Breakfast," he explained. "Listen, I think this little activity will be good for you. Get you out in the open air, so to speak. You don't need a translator to pick grapes. They'll act it out for you. Besides, the way you pick things up I wouldn't be surprised if you come back reciting Victor Hugo in his native tongue. Now get your pants on and get down there." Gebhardt headed for his room but turned around. "Better wear jeans and sneakers. And put on a t-shirt on under that sweatshirt. You won't be cold long doing this kind of work."

After a few minutes Richard met the man by his truck. The older man reached out and shook Richards with a grip like a heavy clamp.

"Je suis Jean Pitout, S'il vous plaît monter à l'avant avec moi. Vous êtes notre invité." When the man saw Richard's confusion, he opened the passenger door for him and smiled. Richard climbed in the truck.

The ride to Le Temple d'Hautvillers took Richard through the most breathtaking bucolic scenes he'd seen in his life to that point. The vineyards along the way blanketed the hilly landscape like a finely knitted comforter. The narrow Roman roads were just wide enough to fit the small pickup truck with the workers arms dangling off the side which didn't seem to bother Jean one bit. His smile, a conglomeration of ground down yellow teeth and a set of gums that had far too much experience with tobacco and acidic wine, was easy and genuine. He rattled on in French pointing to this patch of vineyard and that ancient, broken structure and, as Gebhardt predicted, by the end of the journey, Richard was testing out words and easing them back at the old man. This seemed to please old Jean to no end.

The One and True Son

As they approached the blocky Temple d'Hautvillers, Richard was struck by the age of the temple, how dissimilar it seemed to modern temples with their stained glass and lighted exteriors, and how it paid homage to, or even duplicated pictures he'd seen of the Temple of Mount in Israel. Vineyards sprang from its grounds as far as the eye could see. If he hadn't been standing there himself, he'd almost swear he was looking at a painting.

The pickers piled out of the truck as soon as the truck was parked and moved quickly to stacks of black buckets and large plastic tubs that awaited them. There were other groups already in the field, moving through quickly, like a swarm of voracious insects. Richard joined his group and picked up one of the buckets. He saw a box of pruning shears and grabbed a pair as he'd seen the others do. He reached for a pair of work gloves, again, as he'd seen his co-workers do, but was stopped by Jean.

"Aucun sir," Jean said. "Monsieur Michel a dit que vous ne devez pas utiliser de gants. Il a dit que c'était des ordres de Monsieur Gebhardt."

Richard, confused behind his sunglasses, stood quietly, unsure of his infraction.

A picker from his group, a middle-aged woman with sun washed tied back hair stepped forward.

"John say, you must not use the…the glove. He say, um… Mr. Gebhardt say, no"

"Why?" Richard asked.

The woman shrugged. "John do not say."

Gloves or not, Richard experienced nirvana. He stood at the top of a row of vines and reveled in the perfection of the planting. The row ran directly downhill from him. There would be almost no shade from the rows that surround his chosen row as it was perfectly aligned, as he was sure that they all were, with a sundrenched path down both sides, the leaves lifting like hands, palms turned up, thanking the source of their energy, their food, and ultimately their flavor. Richard kneeled by the first vine and cupped a cluster of grapes weighing them in his hand. To Richard, they looked unearthly, like bundled green pearls. He caressed them as he lowered the blades of his shears to the stem that attached the grapes to their source and swiftly, cleanly, snipped the tender vine. He raised the green pearls to his nose and took in their fragrance, sweet and priceless. Richard tossed the grapes to the tub he'd set behind him.

He'd thought the work would be grueling, that he would experience some pain, some penalty for the bending, from the gripping of the shears. But he felt no soreness, no repercussion from his body for the labor he put it through. He moved quickly from vine to vine. In what seemed like minutes he'd stripped his row clear of its fruit. In what seemed like an hour, the sun began its descent below the horizon bathing the wounded vines in a healing warm orange light.

To say that his fellow harvesters were *impressed* with his zeal would be a gross understatement. The old and young among them chattered their praise in a language he was beginning to understand, patting him on the shoulders, each taking their turns to offer him a celebratory glass of wine. Richard felt free to smile among them. They could not see the details of his grin in sunless French night.

On the way back, Richard sat in the bed of the truck with his new comrades. The others slept, many snoring loudly. Richard was too exhilarated to sleep. He watched the late August stars mock the trucks movement by doing no movement of their own. He could still smell the grapes in the air.

Jean bid him farewell at the door to the apartment house with the traditional kiss to the cheeks and a brotherly handshake. It was after 1am.

Gebhardt was waiting for him in the living area of the apartment reading an old copy of *Paris Match*. He wore jeans and a t-shirt. It was the first time Richard had seen him so informally attired.

"Have fun Farmer Bob?" Gebhardt said after he lowered the magazine.

Richard looked to the old ceiling beams. "I can't describe it. It was…amazing."

"Well, you'd better take a shower before you hit your bunk. I could smell you when you pulled up in the truck."

Richard flipped on the lights and turned the water on in the basin.

He screamed.

Gebhardt raced into the bathroom. Richard stood at the wash basin. Under the harsh florescent light, he looked like a man who'd been shown his entrails just before having his head cut off. His hands were out in front of him, rigid, dripping with water. He looked as though he wanted to push the hands away, but they were attached.

"What? What's wrong?" Gebhardt asked looking around the room for the huge wild animal that must have entered through the lavatory window.

Richard couldn't speak. He held his hands out in front of him, his eyes gaped in horror. He sat on the closed toilet.

"Speak, airman!" Gebhardt ordered. "Get your shit together and speak!"

Richard held his hands out to the officer. "These aren't my hands!"

"What the fuck are you talking about? They're on your wrists, aren't they?"

The One and True Son

Richard stood, holding his hands in front of him. "Look at them! They're dry and scaly. They look like iguana's feet. I've seen these hands before! They're not mine!"

Gebhardt leaned back in the doorway of the bathroom. He took a deep breath and let the silence do its job. After a moment, he walked over to the younger man and placed an arm over his shoulder. "Richard," he said using a voice Richard hadn't heard before. It was sympathetic, calming. "Richard, of course they're your hands. You got them from your father and mother. They've been yours since birth. They've always been yours."

Gebhardt gave Richard's shoulder a shake and left the bathroom.

The two men spoke little on the plane ride home. Richard had mixed feelings about the trip. The chateau, the vineyard, they were beyond magic. Beyond anything he'd ever experienced in his life. It was beauty. It was beauty he'd never dreamed of. He never knew was there. But the shock of seeing his hands, her hands, his mother's hands, almost threw him off the cliff to insanity. The next morning, he begged Gebhardt to take him to a pharmacy where he bought every type of lotion he saw. He slathered it on thickly and waved his hands in air urging for the oils to soak in. But no matter how much he smeared on, there they were, his mother's hands. His mother's lizard hands.

Richard and Gebhardt sat in separate areas on the plane, Gebhardt forward, Richard in the rear. About an hour into the flight Gebhardt came down the center aisle holding two glasses and a bottle of champagne. Richard knew it wasn't just any bottle. It was his magnum of Mag Perignon. Gebhardt sat in the large leather upholstered seat next to Richard set the bottle and glasses on the highly polished wooden table in front of them.

"You okay?" He asked Richard.

Richard nodded.

"Well," Gebhardt said while reaching for the bottle, "I wanted to tell you what a great job you've done so far with your training, you've really met expectations. Exceeded them really." Gebhardt twisted the wire cage that had been holding in the cork for years. He gave the cork a twist, releasing it with a subtle burp. "I think we should celebrate. The next step in your training is the tough part. It is the reason you were chosen for the mission. Many missions really."

"I wonder if you picked the right person," Richard said, his voice distant. "I'm really no one. I'm just out of high school. I had no friends. I mean, I really kept to myself. Everything you've done for me is appreciated. Please, don't think it isn't. I might be smarter than I thought I was. But whatever you need of me sounds really important. It must be after

The One and True Son

all you've done." He looked around the cabin of the government owned private jet with its leather seats and polished woodwork. "But me? I just don't know."

Gebhardt poured the vintage champagne into a glass for Richard and one for himself. He raised up the glass for Richard, holding it up for him so he could see the delicate juice. "Richard. You see this wine. It has been pulled from the ground, crushed, and placed in thick dark glass. It was placed in a cool dark place, underground, isolated from the world. It was put there to perfect it, to truly ripen it. Its time has come. This wine is you, Richard. It's ready." He handed the glass to Richard.

"Take a sip." Gebhardt said.

Richard took the glass and drank.

"Is it ready? You tell me, Richard. Is that not the finest tasting drink you've ever had?"

Richard felt the grapes from the three different vineyards, with three different angles to the sun, dance on his tongue. It was an elixir. It was ambrosia. He had to agree that this was the finest flavor, of anything, of food, of dessert, of anything he'd ever placed in his mouth.

"This is you, Richard. This is you from now on. Even before you finish the training, I promise you, this is you. It will always be available to you. It's inside you now. You are the *mechanism*."

The two men arrived back at Travis City around 1am. There were airmen there to help with their gear. Gebhardt's car waited on the tarmac. They got in. Richard was tired.

"I can't wait to sleep in my own bunk," he said to Gebehardt. "There's nothing like a good old American bed.

"We won't be going back to Lackland tonight," Gebhardt said as they drove off. "As a matter of fact, your gear has been gathered and will be given to you later. We're going somewhere else. The last of your training starts tonight.

Richard remembered the first time traveling on the post-midnight streets of Travis City. He was on the recruit bus heading into basic training. He seemed to remember that he was more curious than nervous, wondering how bad the harassment from the TIs would be, wondering if he would sleep that night. This time, with Gebhardt, a person he trusted probably more than anyone he had in his entire life, something ate at him, twisting his gut to knots. Maybe it was the neighborhood, the buzz of the sodium street lamps, the peeling paint on the austere small houses and the vibrant, threatening graffiti that seemingly sprawled everywhere. Maybe it was the long stretch of cemetery they'd paralleled for what seemed to

The One and True Son

Richard to be beside them the entire ride with its old markers, tall unnatural shapes rising out the Texas dust. In the orange sodium lights, Richard swore he saw movement, shadows not thrown from the carved granite, but from something unseen that would not rest. He said nothing as they drove. Somehow, he knew any question would be left unanswered.

At the corner of Commerce and Pine, Gebhardt swung the car into a short drive-in front of what looked to be some sort of abandoned factory. Richard could see the open sky through the windows of the second and third floors.

Gebhardt turned to Richard. "You're not going to speak as we go in here. You're going to follow me. You're going to go where I go and you aren't going to ask any questions." With that he opened his door and walked over to what used to be the doors to loading dock and unlocked two padlocks one on each side and slid the metal door up. Gebhardt got back in the car and drove the car inside.

The car's headlights flooded into what years, maybe decades ago, was a work floor. An old forklift sat where it was abandoned, dead and dusty, in the cooling night air. Gebhardt grabbed a case from behind Richard's seat, killed the lights and turned the engine off. "Let's go," he ordered.

Richard followed Gebhardt across the floor riddled with broken glass and old food wrappers, to an old freight elevator. Gebbhardt set his case down. It was one of those brief cases that architects or salesman carry; it was much wider than a regular case. Gebhardt reached into his pocket and took out an old cylindrical key about 3 inches long and stuck it through an opening high on the door. He gave the key a twist and pried the doors apart with his hands. He opened the internal cage doors, picked up his case and entered the elevator. He motioned for Richard to follow. Richard stepped in and Gebhardt closed the cage behind him. Gebhardt threw a large switch on the control panel inside the elevator. They heard the engine engage with a large metallic clunk. Gebhardt pushed the lowest button on the panel and the elevator made a creaky descent into the basement of the old factory.

The car was parked on the street level. It surprised Richard that the elevator didn't stop on the next floor down but kept going three floors down. When the elevator finally stopped, and the doors squealed open their eyes were met with the glare of florescent lights.

"What is this?" Richard said.

"Did I tell you to speak?" Gebhardt hissed.

Richard shook his head.

"Then don't."

The room was large, maybe the size the apartment in France. The furniture looked odd to Richard, not utilitarian for say, sitting or working at

The One and True Son

a desk. Along the walls were several workbenches with different manner of unusual objects: a car battery, a baseball bat, wire brushes, mason jars filled with unknown liquids. In the center of the room stood what looked like an old-time exam table. The table, made of wood, and had no cushion. It was hinged in the center, a hole cut where someone's head might go. Richard's blood ran cold. There were straps.

Richard watched Gebhardt as he carried his case over to one of the work benches. Gebhardt opened the case and took out a red towel and spread it on the surface of the bench. He removed shiny chromed tools from the case; several appeared to be very sharp. One of the tools was the cleanest power drill Richard had ever seen. Gebhardt lined the tools neatly on the towel and turned to Richard.

"Richard," Gebhardt said, flatly, "you're about to meet your destiny. I picked you for this destiny and everything I know about you tells me you are uniquely qualified for it.You're…almost immune from its side effects."

"What…" Richard started to speak, but Gebhardt's shushed him with his hand.

"You still don't speak," Gebhardt said without menace. "You won't speak tonight. You won't speak until we're done here. It's your destiny. You don't understand it yet. You don't know its utility. It's—necessity. You need to experience what your subjects experience. The ones *you* will work on. You need to feel what *they* feel. Once you do, you'll understand why you're here. Why *you* are special. Are you ready?"

Richard nodded.

Gebhardt nodded back.

"Take off your shirt and lie on the table."

* * *

The room had similarities to the factory in Travis City where Fondlen had his first *experience.* This room, in the heart of the American government, deep under the swampland that gave birth to the most powerful nation on earth, was far more convenient for Fondlen and far more secure. There were no windows to peer through, no microphones to record the procedures that were Richard Fondlen's bread and butter. No news organization could leak his efforts to the press. There was only a workbench and an assortment of the tools of his trade. His assistants, people he used very sparingly, knew that they were involved in activities of which they could never speak. They would never get the opportunity.

The tall man was brought in through the one door. There was no reason to put a mask over his head. Carpentero was not a stupid man, Fondlen knew, and any attempt at a ruse to confuse him about location would be superfluous, a waste of precious time. Jessie's eyes locked on Fondlen's through the sunglasses as soon as he walked into the room. Neither man spoke. Fondlen's assistant, a nondescript bland man with a paunch and a haircut botched by some $15 stylist chain, stood waiting next to the tall man. Fondlen had to snicker. It struck him as he looked at the unlikely pair, who had the power here and who was helpless.

"Here we are, Mr. Carpentero," Fondlen said after a few minutes. "Do you have any idea what brings us here today?"

"I believe it has something to do with the Temple Bombing," the tall man replied.

Fondlen walked up close to the man. He could smell the man's odor, the smell of sweat, the musty smell of a man confined. Fondlen took off his sunglasses and looked in the man's dark eyes.

"No shower today?" Fondlen asked. "I would think a man of your *breeding* would consider his hygiene a bit more seriously." Fondlen stepped to the man, still in shackles and handcuffs, and sniffed. "You have a very *human* smell this morning. If your jailers aren't providing you the proper materials for you, soap and toothpaste and such, I'll speak to them in very harsh terms. Would you like that?"

Jessie didn't answer. He continued burrowing into the shark eyes of his captor.

Fondlen turned and walked over to a far wall and leaned his shoulders back against it.

"You said a moment ago that you're here for the temple bombing." Fondlen tilted his head. "That's correct I suppose, although superficially so. See, as it turns out, I think there is enough doubt that could be gathered, by an *excellent* lawyer mind you, in which this whole situation could be put behind us. Mr. Carpentero, there have been many people in your situation over the years. People who have been misunderstood, people who have been shoved in a spotlight not of their own making, that have paid dearly for that celebrity. Some have been great speakers, JFK comes to mind, who have stirred people; yes, I think *stirred* is a good word for this situation never realizing how severe the recrimination would be. Martin Luther King is another, a moreh like you. Ghandi—the list goes on. They had no one to warn them. They had no one to tell them of the dangerous path they were treading upon. I think you see that they all paid dearly for their belief in their own power. Don't you?"

Jessie continued staring through the lenses of Fondlen's sunglasses. Fondlen had to fight the urge to wipe his eyes, to try to ease the pain that began digging behind them.

The One and True Son

"Mr. Carpentero. May I call you Jessie?"

Jessie nodded.

"Good," Fondlen responded with his shark smile. "Very good. You see? Progress."

Again, Jessie remained silent.

"Jessie," Fondlen continued, "I'm not sure if you know this about me, but I'm a powerful man in this country. But why would you know that? I'm not on TV. I'm not on the internet." Fondlen giggled. "Like you, famous on the Internet and yet no one knew what you looked like until I found you. Bravo, my friend, for finding a new angle. That was very forward thinking for a...a carpenter. That's what you are, right? A carpenter?"

"Jessie looked away from Fondlen for a moment, then spoke: "Who would you say I am?"

Fondlen frowned. "I think I just told you. A carpenter, although I've never seen your work, but that's what the buzz is. So you answer a question with a question. Will you indulge me if I do the same?"

Jessie nodded.

"Do I look like a powerful man?" Fondlen asked.

Jessie thought for a moment. "You have the suit of a powerful man. You definitely enjoy the trappings of one. But what power do you think you have?"

Fondlen took off his sunglasses for the first time in Jessie's presence. He wanted to answer him with no barriers, show no fear. He could save his marriage if he played this right. "I have the power to end this. I do. I could make it all go away. I could identify the true bomber. I could clear you. I have that power."

Jessie held his gaze. "And what would I have to do?"

"Tell them that they're wrong," Fondlen said.

"Who would *they* be?" Jessie responded.

Fondlen tried the friendliest smile he had. "Your believers. The ones who believe you are the son of Yahweh. The billions of people on the internet. The ones who have no idea who you are yet claim you're divine."

Fondlen put his shades back on. "I'm sure it's a tremendous boost to the ego. All that attention and you can still go to the supermarket. You get the best of fame without the trappings. I understand that more than you know. But in the end, you're just a carpenter."

Jessie took a breath. "You say you have the power to take this all away. To free me. To make the charges go away. You seem to know who did the actual crime. And you call me the fraud."

The One and True Son

Fondlen went to speak but Jessie partially lifted his shackled hand.

"It doesn't matter what you think," Jessie said, almost in a whisper. "You say you have power, but you truly have none. You are only *allowed* the illusion of power. You can't stop what's going to happen anymore than I can."

Fondlen suddenly felt something he'd never felt before, not toward his mother, nor his father, whoever he may have been, nor his grandfather who wanted to pretend he'd never been born. He'd never known this emotion existed in him. But he felt it now: pure, blind rage. He looked to his assistant.

"Give this smelly house builder a bath."

Fondlen pulled up a chair and watched as the bland man strapped Carpentero to the special table. He watched as the assistant slipped a burlap sack over the carpenter's head and secured the straps across his chest, around his shoulders, over his ankles and wrists. He'd hoped he'd see the man who was taking the only thing, the only person he'd ever loved, away from him, show some sign of fear, some acknowledgment that he was about to begin paying for his crime. Yet he breathed normally. No clenching and unclenching his fists. He was accepting the punishment.

The assistant attached a simple garden hose to the utility sink and uncoiled it toward his subject. He then, while holding the table steady, pulled a pin that held it horizontal and tilted the carpenter's head toward the floor. Returning to the sink, the assistant opened the cold tap allowing the water to run to the drain in the floor. He picked up the hose and ran the water straight on to the burlap sack, exactly where the man's nose and mouth were. He ran it over the man's face for 15 seconds, then pulled it away, waiting for the man to clear enough of the water away to breathe. The assistant repeated this for 15 minutes, changing the amount of time he held the water over him by 10 or 20 seconds each time, making sure the subject couldn't predict how long it would take to drown.

Fondlen watched the carpenter's chest heave, saw the hands fight the straps trying to clear his airway of the threat of seemingly inevitable death. At 15 minutes, Fondlen said, "Stop." The assistant raised the head of the makeshift gurney. Fondlen smiled as he saw the burlap sack puff out and suck back in where his prisoner's mouth fought for air. He rose from his chair and walked over to the carpenter.

"Take off the sack," Fondlen ordered. The assistant did as instructed as if he'd been told to move a picture he was nailing on the wall a little to the left. "Tilt him up so we can talk."

The tall man's corkscrew hair dangled down over his eyes; eyes so swollen from the ordeal he'd been put through that they probably wouldn't open anyway. Fondlen positioned himself next to the carpenter and leaned in close. Intimately close.

"It seems that God needs air to breathe," He whispered directly into his ear. "Don't you find that odd? Hmm? I do?"

Fondlen straightened. "As I said before. This can all stop now. Just tell me you're a carpenter, just an ordinary man, and this all stops. No more pain. No more."

Jessie Carpentero turned his head, his waterlogged eyelids opened to slits.

"It doesn't matter anymore who you think I am," he gasped. "It's finished and there is nothing you can do about it. You can't stop it."

Fondlen clinched his razor teeth. He turned to his assistant.

"It seems our friend here is not yet clear in his mind. He seems to be quite wet. Perhaps the battery this time."

The assistant went to a corner and wheeled back a dolly with what looked like the battery to start a large truck. Instead of clamps there was cuff for an ankle and a cable to the water at the carpenter's feet.

Fondlen returned to his chair. *This isn't enough,* he thought. *If I'm going to lose everything, this isn't enough. I need something personal. Something small, but **very** personal.*

"Stop!" he shouted. "Unstrap him and walk him to the workbench."

The assistant did as he was told, efficiently and immediately.

At the workbench, Fondlen met Jessie holding a tool with which the carpenter definitely familiar: a hammer.

"If you would have cooperated, all this…this pain would've been avoided." Fondlen turned to the assistant. "Bring him to the corner or the bench. Hold his right hand flat on the surface. That's right, palm down. Good. Take a strong hold of his wrist."

Fondlen took off his sunglasses and set them on the bench. He stared at the tall man, opening his blank, black eyes as far as they would open. With his own relatively small hand he spread open Jessie's fingers.

"Mr. Carpentero. Jessie. I gave you your chance. It is out of my hands."

He brought the hammer down directly on Jessie's index finger, right on the nail. Blood spurted from under the nail as the end of the finger flattened. Jessie screamed.

"God feels pain," Fondlen said blandly. "Who'd have thought."

He brought down the hammer nine more times.

The Dissenter

As a child, Praise stopped believing in four leaf clovers. At four years old, she'd made it her mission to find one in the dry, sandy, Southern California dirt that her parents called a lawn. She crawled on her hands and knees, scraping them until they bled, dirtying up her best pairs of overalls or shorts or blue jeans or pastel t-shirts, much to the displeasure of her mother who greatly prized cleanliness. She crawled inspecting every patch of green she could find, getting her face down in the dirt, scrutinizing every serrated blade of crabgrass that might be hiding the illusive four appendaged plant.

Praise first read about four leaf clovers in a book her father had checked out at the library for her. Her dad always brought a book back from the library, back then, with large colorful pictures and simple stories of virtue and humor. When she was very young, maybe 3 or 4, he would read the books to her, showing her the words and how he sounded them out. Between her father and Sesame Street, Praise soon read the books to him, with the occasional bump from him if she got stuck on a word.

One evening he brought a book with strange little people, all dressed in green, wearing blocky buckled shoes and bursting green vests. Leprechauns, the book called them (the word was a real challenge to Praises' sounding out skills) and they were rich and cunning. The girl, a little white girl with red hair who looked to be about Praises' age, stumbled upon one while playing with her dog in a magical garden behind her house.

The girl, Erin was her name, saw the little man out of the corner of her eye and gave chase through the thick foliage, across a small brook with a bridge neither of which she'd seen before. There were talking fish in the water. Erin finally caught up to the leprechaun under a tall thick tree where he stood in front of a huge cauldron full of gold coins, his arms stretched around it.

"Please don't take my treasure, young lass," the leprechaun pleaded.

The One and True Son

"But I was told that if I find it you, you have to give it to me," Little Erin answered.

"Ah, that's true, lass, but that doesn't mean you have to take it." The leprechaun replied. "You see, this gold, while very pretty, is very heavy and difficult to carry."

"I see," said little Erin. "But you are no bigger than I am, yet you carry it wherever you go, don't you?"

"Yes, young lass!" said the leprechaun. "That's my point. The weight never goes away, and it only gets heavier and heavier. But…" the leprechaun shrugged, "it's all I have."

"I see," Erin responded. She really didn't want to take all the little man had. "Is there some other reward I can show my friends and family? To prove that I met you?"

The leprechaun thought on that a moment. He snapped his fingers and walked to the surrounding thicket. He reached into the dense bushes and pulled out a most unusual shamrock. The little man smiled and handed it over to the little girl.

"But it has four leaves!" Erin shrieked, delighted.

"It's much more special than that, young miss. You can press it in a book. It's very light. When you need a special wish, take it out and wish it." The Leprechaun snapped his fingers again. "Like that, you'll have it."

The little girl thanked the Leprechaun and went on her way.

From then on, whenever the girl needed something, really needed something, she would take out her pressed four-leaf shamrock and wish it to be so. The girl grew to be a happy adult for making the choice of leaving the treasure with the leprechaun and taking a smaller but a much more valuable treasure.

The closest Praise came to finding a four-leaf clover was some burclover growing in tall bundles in the corners bordering the property where her dad's weed whacker couldn't reach or growing tall through cracks in the pavement that ran parallel to the front of their house. Of course, she'd seen photos of four-leaf clovers. She even had a friend in grade school who had what she claimed to be a genuine four- leaf clover encased in a Lucite key chain. The friend said her father had gotten it from a car dealer who was handing them out while her father was waiting for service at the dealership. But Praise grew skeptical, not of the supposed magical powers of the plant many regarded as a weed, but of the entire existence of a four leaved variety. She looked everywhere she went; on picnics to wooded areas with her parents, on hikes with her mother when her father worked multiple long shifts. Not once, not ever did she find a four- leaf clover.

The One and True Son

* * *

Praise curled up in a ball clothed in her father's t-shirt on his living room sofa. It was a place she'd sought comfort all her life, speaking with her dad about school or the job or anything else that might've come up. It was her first move in weeks. Her days had been spent wrapped in the impotent warmth of her Spice Girl comforter surrounded by her multiple shelves of Beanie Babies. Not that it registered. Not that she saw the sassy grin on Scary Spice. Nor did she pick up Tracker, the cuddly stuffed hound or Smoochy, the stuffed frog splayed out as if he'd been run over by an 18-wheeler. She couldn't see anything in a room. She'd refused to turn on the light.

That morning, she finally made the call.

The journey to the sofa was epic, a trip she wasn't sure she could complete. Her father, devastated that he had to talk to her through her closed bedroom door, left to the public library. *It's the only place I can find peace,* he used to tell her when he'd disappear to its enforced silence during his years on the job. To the best of Praise's knowledge, it was a habit her father dropped at retirement.

"Fondlen told me the whole thing, baby," the former police sergeant pleaded through the door before he'd left. Praise was sure she could hear his whiskered chin rubbing against the wooden door. "You can go back. The force understands. You're a hero, really. You can go back. You're a good cop." He'd bought in. Praise understood. He was there when the whole thing unfolded, but he bought in for his own survival.

When he'd left for the library, she opened her door and made her way, naked, into his room, his and her mother's room, and opened the drawer in the tall dresser where he kept his neatly folded his t-shirts. As a child, her mother scolded her for eschewing her own soft pajamas for one of her daddy's oversized t-shirts, but it was scolding that never stuck. She loved pulling her knees into the thick white cotton, making a tent for herself. She was self-contained, like a cocoon. No matter how thoroughly the shirt had been washed, it still carried a wisp of her father's scent. Praise argued that she slept better in his shirts. Her mother gave up after a while. Praise believed that, after a while, her mother understood.

She found a shirt. She found the sofa.

LAPD had invited her back. They'd prepared a news conference where she would, in uniform, speak of the rule of law or some other vague notion and be presented with a medal for her "undercover" work in capturing the notorious temple bomber. They'd had her speech all written out for her; all she'd have to do was read it on a teleprompter. Praise hadn't actually

The One and True Son

refused. Her near catatonia was enough to convince them it was a bad idea. The PR office, the chief himself, all faded back to the shadows when they'd observed her mental state. Best to leave it alone, they thought.

The money came, as promised. It magically appeared, $300,000 dollars-worth, in an account that also magically appeared, somehow magically tax free. Her father told her of the existence of the account, apparently cued in by Fondlen. That was a couple of weeks before.

That morning, she called Fondlen at the number he'd given her.

"There's no one here by that name, ma'am," the FBI person said.

"Please," Praise begged. "I know he's there. Or somewhere. He's with the bureau. He—he arranged some funds to come to me. I want to give them back. It was all a misunderstanding. I don't want all this. I never did. Please. Please, get a message to him. I want to give it all back."

The phone was silent for a moment. Finally, the woman spoke: "No ma'am. I've had this line for years. There's no one here by that name. Perhaps I can put you through to another agent."

"I'm *telling* you he's *there!*" Praise bellowed into the phone.

The line went dead. Tears came fast and hot.

The phone rang. Praise picked up the receiver.

"Officer Johnson," a familiar voice said from the other end of the line. "I understand you need to talk. I'm quite busy, but I always have time for a colleague."

The hand holding the phone to her ear went cold.

"Fondlen!" Praise erupted. "I want to give back the money. I…I can't use it."

"Why would you do something silly like that?" There was an edge to Fondlen's voice, an edge she hadn't heard before.

"This is wrong!" Praise yelled. "I'm not a cop. I was. I'm not… I don't know. I can't take this money. Please take it back."

"Give it away," Fondlen said. "Wasn't that your mission? To help the powerless and the poor? Well, you should be happy. You can choose any charity you want. I hear the whales aren't out of the woods yet."

"Don't you get it?" Praise said and then she stopped herself from saying more. Of course, he *got it.* He'd known this was coming. She breathed heavily into the phone.

"Officer Johnson," said Fondlen. "Praise. We have a budget that far exceeds the pocket lint we gave to you. You provided a service. You didn't like where this Jessie character was going any more than I did."

"That's not true," Praise shot back.

The One and True Son

"Isn't it?" Fondlen said. "It wasn't hard to talk you into to giving him up. You are a cop after all. Maybe not by profession, anymore, but by blood. You followed your instincts and I think that history will treat you well for it."

Praise sat at the phone, mouth open, mute. She didn't know anything anymore. Her whole experience with Jessie, and by extension, Fondlen was muddled. Different scenarios flashed through her mind, conversations with Jessie and The Twelve, with people healed. Did those people heal themselves? Were they ever really sick? Was anything she'd experienced the last three years real? Was Fondlen right? Was Jessie? Was she?

"Well, Office Johnson," Fondlen said. "It appears I'm needed elsewhere. Thank you for the call. I always love to talk to the people I've worked with." It sounded like he was going to hang up but caught himself. He had one more thing to say.

"Oh! If you're missing your friend, Mr. Carpentero, you can probably catch him on CNN. I think the AG is arraigning him today. The networks love their perp walks."

The line went dead.

Praise slammed down the phone and raced to the television remote. Her family had never been TV watchers unless there was something on the news that had to do with the LAPD and for that they always watched local. She had no idea what channel was CNN, so she kept her finger pressed on the channel button, holding it down as the screen flipped through images of daily life. Cartoon cats chasing cartoon mice, celebrities with shiny white teeth doing cooking shows with clean, never used pots and pans, trash pickers paying hundreds of dollars for rusted out junk, ghost hunters stalking through old hospitals, football fans cheering at a 20 year old game, fake detectives solving scripted murders, real detectives solving real murders, drag queens doing fashion shows, stage mothers berating five-year-olds for missing a step, teen mothers with their own shows, male models flipping houses, billionaire families arguing over who started the most exciting make up line, middle aged models who finally found fashionable leak proof undergarments.

And finally, a familiar face.

It wasn't CNN, although he was probably on there too. Jessie was wearing an orange jumpsuit. Praise could tell they gave him and new one. She hardly ever saw one that looked freshly pressed. His chest was covered in a Kevlar jacket, his wrists and ankles shackled. Jessie's spongy hair hung down over his eyes, his beard, grown out from weeks in jail covered his mouth and neck. He walked bent over, like a bagful of broken branches. His gate was slow, painful.

The One and True Son

Fondlen wanted her to see this. He wanted her to see the results of her work. She'd never met a being so cruel. Jessie watched the floor as he walked. Praise knew this battered version of the man she once felt so close to would appear to the general public as a vagabond, a loner, a pathetic specimen, easy to despise for his weakness, easy to accuse due to his lowly stature, an inconsequential charlatan who, although he'd had a huge presence on social media, needed more attention and killed to get it. This was a sham. A lie. And she was part of it.

Jessie was led to a table in a crowded court room. Hateful flashes lit him up with multiple micro explosions. He had trouble sitting; court deputies held his elbows and eased him down onto the hard wooden chair. Once seated, Jessie rested his forearms on the table and spread his fingers.

Praise gagged. The ends of Jessies fingers were bruised black and as flat the table he rested them on.

The news commentators all had something to say about Jessie's appearance, but Praise heard none of it. The fingers were enough. She was done.

Praise left the TV on. She walked to her bedroom and went to the nightstand she'd had since she was five years old. The drawer opened with a plaintive shriek. She removed her service pistol. She'd placed it in the drawer when she'd left the force to follow Jessie. She hadn't given it much thought, putting the gun away with a full magazine. Her father carried a firearm most of his life. It wasn't a danger to him.

She sat on the edge of the bed and ran her free hand over her comforter. She was so thrilled when her mother brought it home for her. She kept it on her bed much longer than most teenagers would have. It kept her happy for so long. But Praise knew that she couldn't feel happiness again. That was finished.

She chambered a round and placed the barrel in her mouth, the front sight lightly touching her hard palate. She could taste the oil in the muzzle. She took her finger off the trigger guard and released the safety.

Why did you choose me for this? Praise thought.

She squeezed the trigger.

FIVE

The Defender

"The dogs miss you," Miriam lamented. "Do you think you can come home for the weekend?"

Sylvio rubbed his temples. He hadn't seen his wife in two months, his dogs in five. Sylvio had never imagined a case that could completely take over his life. He believed that he'd be able to control his work so that his personal life and more importantly, his family, wouldn't suffer. He didn't have to imagine such a case now. Everything he'd eaten, drank and slept for the past several months had some connection to Jessie Carpentero.

"I can't, Mir," he said swallowing his regret. "Especially now. The trial starts Monday. I've really got to focus. I feel so unprepared."

"I just thought a trip home might help you clear away the cobwebs," Miriam said. "You know, get you away from DC for a bit. It might help you think."

"If I come home, I'd probably never come back," Sylvio offered. "I've got to stay here. Once the trial gets going it'll be over before you know it. I'll be home before you notice I'm gone."

"Too late," said Miriam.

"Maybe, when I get back, we can start on that project we've been talking about."

Sylvio and Miriam referred to their quest to become parents as "the project". They'd held off having kids for the first couple of years of the marriage while Sylvio got comfortable in his position. They'd had a nice house in Austin for a while. His income allowed them to pay for a mortgage, his student loans and a reliable car while Miriam figured out what she wanted to do with the rest of her life. At this point in their marriage, she seemed content with maintaining the house, figuring out the bills and taking the dogs to the dog park. Just before he'd been assigned to the temple case, it looked like the project might become a reality.

The One and True Son

Wallowing in the sadness of this case, stirred a yearning in Sylvio for something positive, something creative, or more accurately, *pro*creative.

"I'm not sure I want to bring a child into this world," Miriam said, almost whispering. "Look at what you're dealing with this trial. People suck."

"Not all of them, sweetie," Sylvio countered, alarmed at Miriam's cynicism. "Good people bringing up good kids can change things, don't you think?"

"You're definitely in the right job," Miriam said. "You really think you can change the world."

"I try. Maybe I'm shouting at windmills. You've got a point though. Jessie thought he could change the world. Look what's happening to him."

"I miss you," Miriam said. They promised each other they'd spend more time together when the trial was over. Neither slept well when they got in their separate beds that evening.

At one time, Sylvio considered himself a pretty good lawyer. Inexperienced yes, but knowledgeable. But as the trial date crept up on him, self-doubt built in him to such a degree that he considered resigning from the case. He talked it over with Jenny Ruiz, but she was hearing none of it.

"You're not pussying out of this one," she scolded. "Somebody asked for you on this case and you're the best lawyer we've got."

"I'm recording this phone call," Sylvio teased. "I'll play it for the whole office."

"You do that, and I'll kick you squarely in the nuts. All kidding aside, you're up for this. You get this right and you'll be a superstar."

"Come on, Jen," Sylvio said. "I never asked for this. And the case against Carpentero is strong, if not airtight. And Jessie's popularity has taken a giant hit since his arrest. Some of the people who were calling him the messiah are now calling for the gas chamber. Public opinion was on our side when this case started. Now, at best, they think he's a deluded nut job, at worst, the next Gacy. I don't see how I get a jury on his side."

"If you ask me, you play up the messiah shit," Ruiz said. "They may convict him, but nobody really wants to execute someone who thinks he's a blood relative to Yahweh."

"He doesn't want me to," Sylvio said. "If it were left up to him, we'd just keep our mouths shut and wait for sentencing."

"Did he do it?" Ruiz asked. "Did he admit guilt? Maybe you can change your plea."

"No, he didn't. I mean I asked him straight out. He just looked at me, and I've got to tell you that when he looks at you, you can't see him killing anybody. Besides, the prosecution wants this trial. They know they can pin this on Jessie. They *want* to pin it on him."

"Big case like this. Who can blame them?" Ruiz said. "Everyone with a television or an internet connection has seen the security camera footage. The guy looks like him, but it never shows his face. I'd go after that."

"I am," Sylvio said. "I've got a video guy who's going to point out some discrepancies in the footage, but they've got a guy too. He's put a lot of people away with blurry footage."

"What about witnesses?" Ruiz asked. "Are you going to have any of his dojo on the stand?"

"By all accounts they didn't have anything to do with the attack. The prosecution will call them. They're saying they'll plead the fifth. They would've had the cop, if she didn't…"

Sylvio became profoundly sad.

"One less problem to deal with," Ruiz told him. "Don't worry. If Carpentero is the son of God he's bound to get a real classy rescue. Get your suits pressed and show them what you've got."

What he had were problems. The prosecutor was Julio Mastriani. It was Sylvio's first major case and he had to go up against a household name. Some thought of Mastriani as a bit long in the tooth. His breakthrough case came in the 70s when he was instrumental in putting away the upper tier of organized crime in Chicago, much to the embarrassment of the longtime mayor there. His face was plastered on the front pages of every newspaper in the country, not to mention the covers of such non-news publications as *People* and *National Enquirer*. For a while Mastriani had a shot at a decent political career, that was until he left his wife who'd been suffering MS for years for a paralegal at a prestigious New York law firm. The bad press ended those aspirations.

It was no secret that Mastriani wanted the temple bombing case. He'd actually gone on the political talk shows to advertise the fact. Apparently, his PR campaign worked because it was soon announced to great fanfare and hubris that he would indeed be handling the case. Sylvio didn't underestimate the old guy's media savvy. He was up against an aging but still dangerous adversary.

His second major problem was the judge, the Honorable Rosemary Strawberry-Huff. Strawberry-Huff came from a monied and politically entrenched family. By all accounts she had a brilliant legal mind. By those same accounts, she was a stickler for *by the book* trials. When she ordered that a trial convene at 9am, everyone involved had better be ready to go at

The One and True Son

9am, sharp. Any deviations from her parameters were met with strict discipline. She wasn't shy about sanctioning those who strayed. Sylvio had doubts as to his own trial prowess, especially when the person running the show had no problems using the whip of her position.

Sylvio slept little the weekend before the trial.

That Monday, Silvio mixed a cocktail of cold water and two trays of ice in the bathroom sink. He plunged his face into the water and kept it there until he had to breathe. He'd been hoping the cold would pull his face together, would make him look less like he'd been on a three-day bender and more like a sharp and aware advocate for his client. Instead, his face looked unnaturally red.

He picked out his most conservative, best fitting suit. Sylvio hated neckties. His mother struggled with him every time she'd taken him to temple, battling over how tight the tie was or how lopsided it was. The first morning of the trial he'd retied his full Windsor knot at least a dozen times, pulling it apart each time for perceived deficiencies. His hair, something he'd neglected lately, had been given an $80 haircut, an amount he'd not believed possible, even in DC. But it looked almost as good as the $20 cut he usually got in Austin. And his shoes, his wore his prized shoes that, in a way, first brought he and Jessie together. He'd polished them to mirrors. They still looked new.

The trial was set to begin at 9. Sylvio got to the courthouse at 6:30 and waited for Jessie's arrival to the court lockup. He'd hoped that the facility holding him allowed him to spruce up. Sylvio advised his client to take advantage of the jail barber and cut his hair to a more conservative style. The beard had to go too, in his opinion, but when Jessie arrived neither of his suggestions were heeded. The suit that Sylvio bought with his own money still hung on the fancy hanger it came with. As Jessie was shackled at wrist and ankle, a guard behind him carried it over his shoulder.

The guard unslung the suit and handed it to Sylvio. He smiled as he spoke to Jessie. "After the trial, can I have your suit? It's a nice one. I think it'll fit me. You won't be needing it."

"Maybe we should skip the trial," Sylvio said. "That way you could just take the suit."

"That'd be fine with me," the guard said, not smiling now. "But that's not the way this works, unfortunately. It shouldn't be a long trial so there won't be much wear on it. I can just iron out the wrinkles."

The guard opened the locked holding room and let them in. Once the door was closed the guard took off the shackles.

"Good luck, counselor," the guard told Sylvio as he locked them both in.

The One and True Son

What do I say to him? Sylvio thought. He didn't want to imagine what had happened to Jessie the night before or, for that matter, the last few months. Their conversations had been brief; Jessie had seemed taciturn and withdrawn, never issuing a complaint. But Sylvio felt deep within him that much had happened to his client on the way to trial this day.

"How are you feeling?" Sylvio said finally.

Jessie said nothing. He only stared at the corner of the room. Sylvio pulled a couple of chairs over and motioned Jessie to sit. He handed Jessie a legal pad and a couple of pencils.

"If you want me to ask something, use this to write down your question. Don't say anything. I know it sounds paranoid but there are a lot of ears out there and if you say something that might help the prosecution, it *will* make it back to them."

Jessie handed the items back.

"I don't think I need these." he said, softly.

Sylvio ran his hand through his hair. "I don't understand. You know this is a capital case, right? That they'll be seeking the death penalty if you're convicted. As your attorney I strongly advise you to pay close attention to what's going on here. If the jury gets any negative vibes from you, they won't hesitate to convict whatever you may be actually thinking."

Jessie lifted his gaze and looked Sylvio directly in the eye. "I know the ending of this story. I appreciate you trying to change it, but you can't. This is the way it's meant to be."

"Jessie, please. I'm trying everything I can to get you off of this. I don't for a minute believe that you had anything to do with that bombing. You wouldn't destroy the temple. You wouldn't kill anyone."

Jessie reached out his hand to Sylvio's and stroked it gently. "As soon as I was born in this body, I was meant to be guilty. So were you. I'm going to pay. I'm going to pay for all of us."

"That's insane!" Sylvio shrieked. "It makes *no* sense! How can *you* be *born* guilty?"

Jessie kept his hand resting on Sylvio's. "You are a good lawyer, Sylvio. You are. But the law I'm speaking of is my father's law, not yours. You may not understand it, but you cannot change it. But, if it will make you feel better, I'll take your paper and pencil."

Sylvio didn't feel better, but he handed them over.

The buzz from the gallery in the Federal Courtroom in Washington DC seemed more like the moments before a rock concert than the solemn proceeding it was intended to be, with reporters and other experts going over their notes and sharing speculation as if they were predicting what song the headlining band would lead with. A few lucky people were allowed to witness the spectacle as they had numbers that were picked in a lottery the week before. The dress code ranged from thousand-dollar suits to jeans and t-shirts. The noise only increased when Jessie and his attorney were brought into the room.

The courtroom itself was opulent in its appointments; the walls were adorned with dark hardwood panels, each panel exhibiting a featherlike grain that reached toward the arched white ceiling. The only interruptions to the wall panels were large flat TV screens on the two side walls and above the bench for evidential presentations. Jessie and Sylvio were shown to the defendant's table crafted of the same rich wood as the walls and covered with a heavy sheet of glass. Two flat screen monitors faced the two men so they could closely observe any presentations made over computer media. To their left sat the prosecution at an identical table. Julio Mastriani was an old hand in this courtroom. A younger associate sat with, a woman who'd assisted in other trials of note. She was a slim, tall brunette with an immaculate navy -blue suit and well quaffed but carefully not perfect hair. Mastriani glanced over at Sylvio and offered a pleasant, confident nod. Sylvio reciprocated.

The bench, again of this rich dark wood, perhaps mahogany, loomed high above the rest of the courtroom. Behind the judge's seat, four connected crosses of darker wood quadrisected the feathery patterned panels. In the center, just above the judge's head, the seal of the United States reminded everyone who was in charge here. A circular enclosure served as the witness stand, complete with its own flatscreen. A podium of matching woods faced the jury box.

The prosecutor and his assistant whispered to each other as they pointed to something in a manila folder. The gallery hushed slightly, hoping to catch a hint as to what they could be discussing. Sylvio and Jessie remained silent, Sylvio looking through notes he'd taken out of his briefcase, Jessie staring at the seal above the bench. At nine o'clock sharp a bailiff walked in from a door behind the bench.

"All rise," he ordered. The courtroom went instantly silent as everyone did as they were told. "Hear ye, hear ye. The United States Superior Court for the District of Columbia is now in session—the Honorable Judge Rosemary Strawberry-Huff presiding. All having business before this honorable court draw near, give attention and you shall be heard."

From the same door from which the bailiff came, entered a tall, broad-shouldered woman with stylish yet conservatively coiffed blonde hair, wrapped in an obviously custom-made judge's robe adorned at the cuffs with thick, black rope-like embroidery. Even without the elevation of the bench she would impose a formidable figure.

"You may now be seated," the bailiff finished as the judge took her seat.

Judge Rosemary Strawberry-Huff was born into a family of presiders, be it at a boardroom, a country club or, in her case the court. Her father was a well-known real estate developer on the West Coast, owning scores of apartment buildings, office skyscrapers, hotels and shopping centers all with the family name emblazoned ostentatiously in lights and metal meant to resemble diamonds. Her younger brother had run the business since the death of their father and has managed to keep the family name in the financial media, the front pages of national newspapers and the scandal rags almost constantly since taking over. The judge herself stayed out of the family business and was more than happy to sell out her share to her brother for a sum that is rumored to be somewhere north of eight figures. As she made her way up the chain of judgeships, she took great pains to avoid the spotlight, but was not above hyphenating the family name after her marriage some 25 years prior to her ascension to the federal bench.

Sylvio had seen her before, but only in a video for fledgling judges on how to run a courtroom. In the video she seemed pleasant, knowledgable and, if one could tell from a scripted video, reasonable.

"Good morning," the judge said as she looked over documents that'd been placed on the bench in front of her. With her papers shuffled sufficiently she looked up at the waiting courtroom. "We're gathered here to determine justice on case number DCC-13-17426, US versus Jessie Carpentero. Before we get started, I need to swear in the jury. Everyone in the courtroom please rise."

Sylvio watched the faces of the jury as they were told that *they* were the judges in this case, that they were judges of the fact and Judge Strawberry-Huff was the judge of the law. He looked at the eyes of the mix of jurors, male and female, blue eyes, brown eyes, eyes where the color wasn't easy to determine from the distance he was sitting. There was make up and preening on some eyelids, crow's feet and saggy bags on the perimeter of others. But all eyes were open wide. Sylvio thought the voir dire process had gone well considering the magnitude of the case. There were seven women, five men and one of each of the traditional genders as alternates. Sylvio didn't know whether he should be encouraged when two of the women flinched as they heard the charges that were issued on the defendant.

The One and True Son

"Mr. Carpentero is charged with three counts of capital murder and one count of terrorism," the judge said, gravely. "These are just charges at this point, and you must consider them as such. At this point in the trial Mr. Carpentero is considered innocent and will be considered as such until you bring a guilty verdict in this case. You are instructed not to discuss this case with *anyone,* not your wives, not your husbands, and not your fellow jurors. You will not discuss the case with the jury until you are released to the jury room to consider the evidence. Does anyone have any questions?"

A slim young man with a partially controlled explosion of acne on his face, seated in the back row, raised his hand.

"I was looking through the snacks in the jury room and most of them are expired. Can we get some new snacks?"

Snickers filled the courtroom. Sylvio wondered if the judge would see this as a cheeky slip of decorum, but the wisp of a smile that passed her lips told him that she wouldn't be sidetracked by a tiny issue.

"I'll get you some new snacks," she answered. "*I* won't. I'm a bit busy at the moment, but I'm sure someone here can get you some." She turned to the bailiff who disappeared out the door behind the judge.

More courtroom snickers.

"Let's get started. For the record, this is case number DCC-13-17426, the United States of America versus Jessie Carpentero. Prosecuting attorney, Mr. Julio Mastriani is present, defense counsel, Mr. Sylvio De…Graa Saa. Is that correct, counselor?"

"It is, Your Honor," Sylvio responded.

"New around here, aren't you?" The judge inquired.

"I'm from Austin, Your Honor. Austin, Texas." Sylvio blushed hoping the judge didn't take umbrage to his implying she didn't know where Austin was.

Sylvio let out his breath when the judge said: "Welcome to Washington, Mr. De Graca."

The judge continued. "The jury is present and on time. Thank you, everyone for that. Let's keep it that way, shall we. Shall we get started? Mr. Mastriani. Are you ready with your opening statement?"

"I am, judge," Mastriani flashing that well-known smile.

The judge smiled back. "I would expect nothing less. Please proceed."

Julio Mastriani strolled to the podium as a man would who has stood there many times before. His impeccable gray suit showed no evidence that he'd been sitting for some time. His shirt, stiff and absolutely white, fit perfectly at the cuffs and neck, his tie, a cool blue lay comfortably under his jacket. He wore stylish glasses, presumably from the same designer as

The One and True Son

the suit. Sylvio was surprised that he seemed to bring no notes, no paperwork of any kind. Mastriani poured himself a glass of water from the pitcher supplied on the podium, took a small sip and placed the glass back on the flat area of the podium.

"If it please the court," he said, facing the judge. "Counsel," he said, turning his gaze to Sylvio. "And, ladies and gentleman of the jury. We all know what this trial is about, don't we? We've seen wall to wall coverage on all the cable news shows, be they leaning right or left, since that tragic day, when one of our most sacred sights, in the very heart of this great city, the capital of this great country, was violently…" Mastriani paused as if he was seeking a word. "*Viciously* destroyed. We all remember that don't we?"

Sylvio was shook when he saw several of the jury's heads nod in agreement.

"And we all know from news accounts of the image of this man," Mastriani gestured with a flat hand toward Jessie. "This *man*, Jessie Carpentero. I have to emphasize the word *man*, because, ladies and gentleman, there are people in this world that think this *man*, born in Texas, the *man* before you is God. That's right ladies, and gentleman of the jury. There are people who are convinced, *convinced by this man*, that he is the son of Yahweh." Mastriani picked up the water glass on the podium and took a sip. "I'm sorry folks. I have a little cold." He took another sip from the glass. "Maybe if the defendant is correct in that he can cure me."

A few snickers filtered through the courtroom followed by a cold stare by the judge toward Mastriani.

"Sorry judge," he said with a slight smirk. "Couldn't resist. There have been many things we've been told in the media about Jessie Carpentero," Mastriani continued. "He never appeared in his videos. He is a conduit to Yahweh himself. That he heals people just by touching them. That he didn't even have to touch them. He could just say it was so, and miracles pop into existence. These *stories* drew millions, no billions of views on social media. Considering I have about 15 friends on Facebook, I have to admit, I'm impressed."

Mastriani sighed wearily and put both hands on the podium. "But on the holiest day of our calendar to many, may I say, most Americans, we finally saw the face of Jessie Capentero. Think back to that day. We all saw him. We saw the face of Jessie Carpentero on all our screens while we getting our oil changed, or our haircut, or at the pizza place that has TVs in every corner of the dining room. We saw the face of Jessie Carpentero." Mastriani stepped back from the podium.

The One and True Son

"Think back to that day, ladies and gentlemen of the jury. Think of that face you saw on every TV screen in the country. Was it the face of love? Was it the face of benevolent God? Was it the face of universal acceptance from our creator?

"Think of that face you saw that day. It was the face of an angry *man*. The prosecution will show that this angry man, Jessie Carpentero, was *tired* of his anonymity. He was famous, but not famous enough. He had conquered the internet and now he wanted to draw on that power to bring himself to the forefront. You will be reminded that the face that was supposed to be the face of God-made-man was filled with anger and hate as he assaulted legal, yes *legal* venders trying to earn money to feed their families. You'll be reminded of this man's violence as he flipped over tables and threw their wares, their means of feeding their families, onto the pavement."

Julio Mastriani returned behind the podium.

"But was that enough? Yes, Mr. Carpentero got his face out there. But we know the 24-hour news cycle. What's hot one day is beaten to death for a day or two and the media move on to the next atrocity, the next uprising, the next lottery winner. People go from overnight fame to overnight obscurity in the blink of an eye.

"Jessie Carpentero had sought this notoriety for some time, from at least his teenage years. We will show, ladies, and gentleman, that he had dreamed of being famous at as far back as that. And he saw first-hand how to get it.

"Ladies, and gentleman of the jury, you will hear from one of this man's followers. You will hear how they traveled from place to place to spread his message to wider audience, showing up at rock concerts, and mixing with drug dealers and others who market in practices that destroy children and adults alike. Again, I have to ask: benevolent savior or craven opportunist?

"Now you've been told, rightly so, that the defendant, Jessie Carpentero, is innocent until proven guilty. The judge told you that. I'm sure defense counsel will tell you that. Hell, I'll repeat it for you now. Jessie Carpentero is innocent until proven guilty."

Julio Mastriani gestured with two fingers toward the ceiling.

"Until ...*proven*... guilty. Ladies and gentlemen of the jury, that's what we are going to do in this trial. We are going to prove to you that the defendant, Jessie Carpentero is not a messenger of God or whatever he claims to be. He is *not* —*God.* He is a man, a vicious and calculating *man*. He is a master manipulator. And the evidence, the evidence ladies and gentlemen, will show that Jessie Carpentero is a murderer."

The One and True Son

The courtroom was so quiet one could hear the floor creak as the prosecutor returned to his seat.

Sylvio took a sip of water. Julio Mastriani did his job and true to his reputation made Sylvio's case just that more difficult.

"Mr. De Graca," the judge called. "Your opening statement."

Sylvio gathered up papers and tucked them in a folder, placed it under his arm and headed to the podium. He hated making statements with nothing in front of him. He would spread paperwork on the podium in front of him, but it was just for show. He hardly ever read what he brought up with him, but somehow having paper with what he considered facts comforted him, that the truth, as he saw it, on these papers would make its way into his statement and make its way into the thoughts of the jurors.

Sylvio took a long moment to look at the jury, to size them up. All eyes were on him. That was a good sign. There were no scowls, no signs of distaste. A woman in the front, a black woman in a conservative suit, nodded to him as if to tell him it was okay to begin. He remembered from voir dire that she had been a high school teacher. To Sylvio, her gaze said she'd like to have a conversation on the original meaning of that Latin derived term, an admonishment to the jury to tell the truth, to say what is subjectively honest and objectively accurate. The modern use is just the process of picking a jury. But the look in her eye said that she was looking to Sylvio to speak the truth, no matter what that truth would be. He wondered if he could do that. He wondered if she would believe him. He wondered what he himself believed.

He stepped to the podium, adjusted his papers on the wooden surface, and took one more sip of water.

"Your Honor, counsel, members of the jury and residents of the capital of this great country. I must say that I admire Washingtonians and their ability to navigate either by foot or automobile the labyrinth that Monseiur L'enfant designed for us and I humbly pledge to you that I will negotiate this maze every day of this trial to be here on time."

Sylvio was pleased to see the judge wasn't scowling; her eyes were locked on him.

"Here to this courtroom, in this city, to aid in justice being done. And justice is what we are all here for. Justice for the personal victims of that terrible crime. Justice for this wounded city, a city that has seen horrible crimes before, but never one this—spiritual, this—personal. We are all here for justice."

Sylvio looked from one juror to another. He was making personal contact. He wanted them to feel they were listening to a friend explaining a touchy subject.

The One and True Son

"But what is justice?" he continued. "In this beautiful courtroom the judge will tell you, the prosecution will tell you, I, I will tell you that justice is a thorough and truthful look at the evidence to determine if the man seated at the table with me is responsible for that heinous crime that brings us here. But justice is not looking for your opinion. Opinions are for judges like Judge Strawberry-Huff. Judges offer opinions on what a law means. They offer interpretations. That's not what we're looking for from you today. But that doesn't take the weight off of you. Sorry folks.

"No, members of the jury, we are not looking for an opinion from you. What we are looking for answers the question: does the evidence in this case show *beyond a reasonable doubt*, that Mr. Carpentero indeed was the one who committed this awful crime? This is not an opinion. It either shows that he did it or it doesn't show it. There isn't any, *well, it kind of shows that he did it*. The evidence either shows that he did it or it doesn't. That's what you're here to determine."

Sylvio shuffled through his papers for a moment. He needed a pause to allow what he just said to sink in.

"So, what does this mean? The prosecution will show you images, videos, photographs that will show you the suspect in this case preparing to do damage to the National Temple. They will tell you that the man in these images is actually Jessie Carpentero. This is part of the evidence they will show you. You've probably seen some of the images yourself, on the front pages of the newspaper, on 24-hour news. As a matter of fact, I'd say that it's virtually certain that you *have* seen them. These images are so widely disseminated, viewed by so many people, so many times, that they will probably be familiar to you. And when you'd seen them previously there was probably a headline or a voice telling you that these images are of the Temple Bomber, and they would be correct in saying so. But somewhere deeper in the story they mention the name of Jessie Carpentero. They mention his name right below the security footage of a tall man with a similar build and a beard preparing to bomb a national treasure.

"But does this footage show *Mr. Carpentero* preparing to bomb the temple? Is there a single clear image that shows, clearly, a face? And does that image show you that that face belongs to Mr. Carpentero? It is our contention, a contention we intend to prove, that there isn't a single image that shows the face of the bomber. And without that face, members of the jury, there is no way to determine if the man on that video is this man seated with me. There are no fingerprints, no shoe prints. There is no forensic evidence that Jessie Carpentero was even at the temple that horrible morning.

"But we have seen Jessie Carpentero's face at the temple, haven't we? We have all seen it, again, in the newspapers, on magazine covers, on the 24-hour news. The persecution…"

Sylvio stopped and addressed the judge. "I'm sorry, Your Honor. I misspoke."

The judge nodded. "The jury will disregard counsel's last remark. Continue counselor."

Sylvio took a breath.

"Thank you, Your Honor. *The prosecution* has even used the episode in his opening remarks. But please, be clear, members of the jury, that Mr. Carpentero is *not* on trial for his actions at the temple on Passover. You will hear Mr. Mastriani attempt to tie the two incidents together, but we must keep in mind that these are two separate events. Whether his actions on Passover were justified or not is irrelevant here today. The only question that is relevant is whether or not the evidence, *the evidence,* proves that Jessie Carpentero was the man on the news with evil intent. *That* is the question.

"We intend to show that *through the* evidence, that it is impossible to identify the bomber in that footage. Remember, members of the jury, that that is your duty here today. To answer the question: Was the bomber identified? If your answer is no, as we are confident that it will be, you must move to find Jessie Carpentero not guilty in this case.

"Thank you."

Jessie gathered up his papers and made his way back to the defendant's table.

"Thank you, counselor," said the judge, looking somewhat pleased with how the trial was moving along. "We will recess until 1pm. Everyone have a nice lunch and be back here promptly.

Jessie and Sylvio were escorted back to the defendant's lock up.

Sylvio took off his jacket and placed it on the back of a chair. "It may seem like the tough stuff is over, but really, it's just beginning. How did it look to you?"

Jessie loosened his tie. "I think you really are a good lawyer. I don't know having never seen one in action, but you seem to know what you're doing. Everyone listened very closely; I can tell you that. I know what you did though."

"What do you mean?"

"I know that you said 'persecution' on purpose. It wasn't an accident. Is that what they teach you in law school?"

The One and True Son

Sylvio smiled. "A slip of the tongue really."

Jessie sat in one the chairs. "No, it wasn't. You knew exactly what you were doing. You apologized very quickly. The judge admonished the jury to forget it, but you knew they won't. When someone tells you *not* to think of something, it's almost impossible *not* to do it. I imagine that can be a very effective strategy."

"Let's say I did it on purpose. We need all the help we can get."

"Not that kind of help."

Sylvio sat in the chair with his coat on the back. "Look, Jessie. This is a tough situation you're in. As well as we interviewed the jury, they all came from a pool of news consumers, and I have to say that you're a news cycle's dream. They get more money the worse they make you look. We need to use every tool I can come up with."

Jessie reached over and placed his large hand on Sylvio's .

"Do it again and you're fired."

Sylvio ordered in some sandwiches. Jessie said he wasn't hungry and sat quietly in a corner of the lockup. Sylvio thought he'd be relieved when the trial had actually begun, but he was filled with more anxiety than ever. He was thoroughly convinced that his client hadn't done what he was accused of, but Jessie wasn't really helping anything with his reticence to defend himself vigorously. But Sylvio wondered why he, himself, was so convinced that Jessie didn't blow up the temple? Did it have anything to do with what happened at the wedding in Cafracana? With the incident in Jessie's cell? It still kept Sylvio up at night wondering just what had happened to him at those two events. Was Jessie a hypnotist? Was his charisma such that he could dig into a man's consciousness?

Sylvio picked at a turkey sandwich. It was dry and rather tasteless. The bread tasted like some sort of byproduct of the paper making process. Still, it would be a long day.

"Jessie, I know you don't feel like eating but we might not get out of here until it's pretty late. Why don't you have a sandwich?"

Jessie adjusted in his chair. "Do you realize that years ago, though not too many, this trial probably would've been an hour at most? Go a little further back and it might have lasted five minutes."

"Yes," Sylvio nodded lightly. "Often, especially in the South, a trial was about the length of time it took to tie a noose and sling it over a tree limb."

"So now it takes weeks," said Jessie. "Do you think people have gotten closer to truth or have they just gotten fancier and more long winded?"

The One and True Son

"I'm really not sure," Sylvio answered. "We're imperfect beings. I think we're trying to do things correctly. Sometimes it just hard to know. Where are you going with this?"

"I'm just trying to see the plan," Jessie said.

At precisely 1pm Judge Strawberry-Huff banged her gavel and called the trial back into session. "Mr. Mastriani? Are you ready to proceed?"

"We are, judge. The prosecution calls Mr. Pierre Donadieu to the witness stand."

A man in his fifties wearing an ill-fitting suit stood and walked to the witness stand.

The bailiff swore him in.

The judge spoke. "Mr Donadieu, please spell your name for the record."

"My name is Pierre Donadieu. D O N A D I E U."

"Thank you," the judge said. "Mr. Mastriani. You may continue."

"Thank you, judge. Mr. Donadieu. Can you please tell the court your profession?

"Sure," the witness answered with a gravelly voice, which he cleared with dry cough. "I run an aviary and bird breeding business."

"For those of us without experience in this business could you please explain exactly what it is that you do."

"I breed and house birds. Sometimes I nurse birds that have been injured back to health, so they can return to the wild. And we breed birds for racing."

Mastriani faced the jury. "I didn't know they could even drive." Some of the jury got the joke and smiled slightly. Others got the joke and ignored it. Sylvio was happy to see that it annoyed one or two of them.

"I'm sorry," Mastriani blushed. "I couldn't help myself. What birds would you breed for racing?" Mastriani made air quotes around "racing".

"Pigeons sir. It's actually quite popular among some folks. They'll pay several hundred dollars for a thoroughbred."

This time there were more snickers from the court.

The judge whacked her gavel. "Order."

"I'm sure it's a great business," Mastriani said. "But you were in a different business until not too long ago. Is that correct?"

"It is. Well, I was doing the aviary and the rescue work, but I had another part of the business."

"And what part of the business was that?"

"I sold doves at the temple."

"You sold doves? Why would you sell doves at the temple?"

The witness loosened his tie slightly. "It goes back to an old tradition. A long time ago poor people didn't have anything of value to sacrifice at the temple, so the dover, that's what I am... or was... a dover, the dover would provide birds to sacrifice."

"But you didn't have people actually kill the doves, did you?"
"Oh no, I loved the birds. See, they weren't actually doves. They were pigeons. It was more of a symbolical sacrifice. The birds would fly around a little, find their bearings and fly back to the aviary."

"So really, you were renting the birds rather than selling them," Mastriani said, smiling.

"Yeah, I guess so. They always came home. These pigeons are like that. They like their home roost."

Mastriani took off his glasses and set them on the podium.

"Mr. Donadieu. The morning of the Passover attack, what were you doing?"

"Objection, Your Honor," Sylvio said. "The witness is giving testimony about an incident that occurred at the National Temple at Passover. The bombing didn't occur until several weeks after that event. Just because Mr. Carpentero was present at the first incident, it doesn't follow that he was present at the second."

The judge looked to Mastriani.

"It goes to motive, judge. The defendant had deep seated animosity toward the temple and those who have been there for years selling their goods."

The judge nodded. All right. I'll allow it. The witness may continue."

"I had finished setting up and was waiting for customers. I was talking to Parker. He's one of the venders. He sells t-shirts. I've known him for a couple of years."

"And what did you and this vender talk about?" Mastriani asked.

"He asked me if I thought that that Jessie guy from the internet would show up. He was afraid because of the attack on the Lincoln Memorial..."

"Objection!" Sylvio called. "There was no *attack* at the Lincoln Memorial. Mr. Carpentero gave a talk at the memorial, but it was peaceful by all accounts, even the police. There were no charges levied. It was an internet rumor that there was *any* trouble there."

"So noted," the judge said. "The jury will disregard the witness's use of the word 'attack' at the Lincoln Memorial. The witness will continue."

The witness cleared his throat. The objection had unnerved him. Sylvio could tell.

"Anyways, he was scared because he'd heard that the moreh's people were violent."

"Can you tell the court what stopped the conversation?" Mastriani asked.

"Yeah," the witness answered. "We heard a couple people screaming. Then we heard what sounded like tables flipping over."

"Did you see who was causing the disturbance?"

"Yes sir, I did."

"Is he here in this courtroom?"

"Yes sir," the witness answered. "He's seated right over there."

"Your Honor," Mastriani said. "Let the record show that the witness has pointed to the defendant, Jessie Carpentero."

"So noted," Judge Strawberry-Huff responded.

Sylvio looked over to Jessie for his reaction. There wasn't one. Jessie looked at the man as if he'd just said he was going to the store to pick up some milk.

"You stated before that this business, this dove business, was something you had done for years," Mastriani continued. "Your father had the business before you did. I understand from this testimony that you no longer have this business. Is this true?"

The witness shifted in his seat. "That's true, yes sir."

"Can you explain to the court why that is?"

"He let my birds loose," he answered lowering his eyes.

"Who let your birds loose?"

"Well, I mean, I did."

"Was it your idea to let your birds go, the heart of your business?"

The witness didn't look up. "No, it was Jessie's. The defendant. He told me to."

"That was a big blow to you, wasn't it? A family tradition, gone. Income that you counted on every year, gone. Isn't that true?"

The witness didn't speak.

"Mr. Donadieu? Isn't that true?"

The witness nodded.

"Mr. Donadieu," the judge interrupted. "You must answer the question verbally."

The witness looked at the judge, then at Jessie. He then looked to the prosecutor.

"Yes sir, that's true."

Mastriani slapped the podium, an action that he'd been known for, that he'd practically trademarked.

"No further questions, Judge."

Mastriani strolled back to the prosecution table and immediately picked up some papers and pretended to read them. Sylvio stood and took his place at the podium, again, notes in hand.

"Mr. Donadieu. First, how are you holding up?"

"Fine, I guess," the witness answered, looking at Sylvio for the first time.

"That's good. That's good."

"Objection," Mastriani interjected. "Is there a question here? The court's time is valuable."

Sylvio turned to Mastriani. "I'm sorry, Mr. Mastriani. I'm from Texas. Perhaps we're overly cordial on occasion. I apologize, Your Honor."

The judge nodded.

"Mr. Donadieu. You testified that you were discussing whether or not Mr. Carpentero would show up at the temple on Passover. Had you heard of Mr. Carpentero before this conversation?"

"I might've seen something about him on the Net. I'm not on it very much though. I got better things to do with my time."

"I'm glad to hear that. So would you say that you weren't afraid that Mr. Carpentero might show up?"

"No. I don't think I was that afraid."

"Would you say that the man you were talking to was more afraid than you were?"

Mastriani looked up from his paperwork. "Objection, Judge. Counsel is asking the witness to speculate how another person felt."

"I'll rephrase, Your Honor. Did the other vender express fear that Mr. Carpentero might show up on Passover?"

The witness tilted his head. "Yeah. Parker said he and his group were crazy. That they beat people up at the Memorial."

"So when Mr. Carpentero *did* show up, what did the other vender do?"

"He skedaddled," the witness said. "Left his t-shirts and everything."

"But you didn't run?"

"No sir. I had to protect my birds."

Sylvio turned and faced the jury.

"Yes, your birds. You had to protect them. Did you talk to Mr. Carpentero?"

"Yes sir, I did."

"Did he destroy your cages? Did he tip over your table? What did he do first?"

Sylvio looked at the witness. His eyes went up to the ceiling and to the left.

"He kinda talked to me first."

"Talked to you. Did he scream?"

"No sir. Just talked."

"So, at this point did you fear for your life?"

"No. No, I wasn't sure what he was going to do. But he seemed calm enough. I mean, for what he was doing."

Sylvio walked away from the podium.

"So, you talked. What did he talk to you about?"

The witness looked at his hand. He sat for a moment.

"Do you need me to repeat the question?"

The witness shifted in his seat.

"No, I heard it." He still didn't answer.

"The question seems to upset you," Sylvio said. "Did he threaten you? Did he say he would hurt the birds? Is there some problem with what he talked about?"

More shifting from the witness.

"Nah, he didn't threaten me or anything. He told me to take off my gloves."

"You were wearing gloves at Passover?" Sylvio asked. "Was it cold? I know it was early spring, but I don't remember anyone noting that it was especially cold."

The witness's eyes searched the inside of the witness stand.

"I always wore them," he said.

Sylvio went back to the podium.

"Do you have some kind of condition that may cause low circulation in your extremities?"

"No sir," the witness answered. I have a tattoo. I got it when I was mad at my father. It was a tough time."

Sylvio left the podium and approached the witness stand.

"So, he told you to take off your gloves. Why did he want you to take them off?"

The One and True Son

"Objection!" cried Mastriani. "Counsel is asking the witness to speculate as to what the defendant was thinking."

"Your Honor," said Sylvio. "I believe that the witness knows why Mr. Carpentero told him to take off the gloves."

"I'll allow it," the judge said. "Continue."

Sylvio locked eyes with the witness.

"Do you need me to repeat the question?"

The witness shook his head. "No, I remember it. He told me his father's name was written on my hand,"

"Had you ever met Mr. Carpentero before? Spoke to him in any way?"

"No sir. Not 'til that day."

"And you did what he said? You took off the gloves?"

"Yes, I did."

"Why?"

The witness's face flushed. "I…I don't know really."

"Were you afraid?"

"No, not…not exactly."

Sylvio moved closer to the witness stand. He spoke gently to the witness.

"Can I ask you to show us your hand?"

The witness grew even redder, almost purple. Slowly he held his hand up. The word LOVE had faded over the years.

"Let the court show that the defendant has the word 'love' tattooed on his fingers."

"So noted," said the judge.

"Do you know why Mr. Carpentero wanted to see your hand?"

The witness nodded. He appeared on the edge of tears.

"I know what he told me."

"What was that?"

The witness took a deep breath.

"He said that his father's name was written on my hand."

Sylvio went back behind the podium.

"Did he say that before or after you took off the gloves?"

"Before," the witness said. "Before."

"Why don't you wear the gloves now?" Sylvio asked, again kindly.

The witness spoke clearly. As clearly as he'd ever spoken.

"Because I don't need to."

The One and True Son

A small rumble shook the court.

Julio Mastriani stood.

"Judge, I object to this line of questioning. The defendant is not on trial for his *divinity.*" The attorney made finger quotes around the emphasized word. "This line of questioning has nothing to do with this case."

I'm beginning to wonder, Sylvio thought.

"Your Honor, it goes to whether the witness truly felt threatened by Mr. Carpentero. It was the prosecution who brought this witness to establish the malice of Mr. Carpentero toward the temple and those in it. If Mr. Carpentero was such a threat, why did he take the time to discuss a tattoo?"

The judge took a moment to think.

"Mr. Mastriani, you brought this witness. I will allow it. Any more questions, Counselor?"

"A couple more, Your Honor."

"Proceed," the judge said.

Sylvio turned to the witness.

"Mr. Donadieu. You stated earlier that Mr. Carpentero told you to release your birds. Did he release all of them?"

"No sir."

"Can you explain to the court what happened?"

"Jessie had me take one out," the witness said, his voice gravelly "He said it represented him. He let it go."

"And do you still have the bird?"

"Yes sir."

"Can you explain how the birds return to you? They never really are sacrificed, are they?"

"Well, they usually fly up and circle around until they get their bearings. Then they fly home. Scientists don't even know how it works."

"Have you ever lost a bird after it was released?"

"Yeah. I usually lose one or two. A hawk gets them or something."

"How many birds returned to you after that Passover?"

"Just the one," the witness answered.

"Mr. Carpentero told you that would happen, didn't he?"

The witness looked to Jessie. His expression shifted. He almost smiled.

"He did."

Sylvio took his place back behind the podium.

"One more question. There are places to buy new birds. They aren't outrageously expensive. Why didn't you just buy new birds and start

The One and True Son

over?"

This time the witness did smile.

"He told me not too."

"That went well," Jessie said as he and Sylvio entered the defendant lockup. The deputy locked Jessie in a cell that Sylvio was surprised they even had. It looked like something out on old movie where the authorities would lock up dangerous psychopaths clad in tight fitting straight-jackets. The deputy didn't say a word to either man. He locked the cell and exited.

"I'm not sure," Sylvio said. "The whole God's son thing. It might work on the internet; I'm not sure how it works on a jury."

Jessie loosened his tie, unslung it from around his neck and draped over one of the horizontal bars of the cell. He sat on the bunk that was bolted to cement floor of the cell.

"Is that what you think is going on here?" Jessie asked. "Am I some scammer that started this whole thing so I could get something from people?"

Sylvio sat hard on the wooden chair outside the cell. He loosened his own tie and rubbed his temples with the end of his fingers.

"I didn't mean…No, you're not that. This is a difficult case. I don't for a minute believe you did what you're accused of. I want the jury to see you the way I do?"

"And how is that, Sylvio? How do you see me?"

How do I see him? Sylvio thought. *He is certainly extraordinary. But so is Labron James. So was Mahatma Gandhi. Did they have the same effect on that Jessie has on me?"*

Sylvio sighed. "I was at the wedding. I know what I saw. I don't know how that water changed. I…I know that doesn't just happen. I know. I know that I've never met anyone like you. Does that make you God?"

"You've never asked *me*," Jessie said.

Sylvio sighed again. "I don't intend to. Not during the trial."

"Why not?" Jessie asked.

"Because I might believe you," Syvio answered.

Sylvio knew the next day of the trial would be a tough one. The witness was one of The Twelve. Sylvio fully expected that the witness's testimony would be short as she was expected to plead the Fifth Amendment as she and the other members of the group had done to this point

After the pleasantries extolled by Judge Strawberry-Huff on both the prosecution and the defense's promptness and the smoothness of the trial so far, Julio Mastriani stood.

"The prosecution calls Miss Debra Wilson to the stand."

The entire courtroom turned their heads when a small woman, looking much younger than her actual age strolled to the witness stand wearing an ankle length peasant dress and spartan sandals. Her arms and shoulders were uncovered showcasing the vibrant scarab tattoo on her right arm.

"Please state your name and spell your last name for the record," the judge instructed.

"My name is…" the witness said slightly above a whisper.

The judge interrupted. "I need you to speak up, Miss."

"My name is Debra Wilson," the witness said, this time with more vigor. "W…I…L…S…O…N."

"Thank you," the judge said. "The prosecution can proceed."

Julio Mastriani went to the podium.

"Good morning, Miss Wilson. Are you comfortable with me calling you that?"

The witness looked puzzled.

"Why?"

"According to the information I have, you usually go by a different name. Is that true?"

The witness nodded. One of her blonde dreadlocks fell across her eyes.

"Yeah, that's true. No one has called me by the name I was given at birth for a long time."

"And what do they call you?"

"Dimple."

Snickers in the courtroom were followed by the thumping of the judge's gavel.

"Why do people call you that?"

The witness pulled her cheek muscles up showing the deep impressions in the young woman's face.

More snickers.

"If the court needs to be cleared, I will do it in an instant," Judge Strawberry-Huff warned. "This is court of law, and it *will be treated as such.*"

"Did the defendant give you that name?" Mastriani asked.

Sylvia was on his feet. "Objection, Your Honor. What does this line of questioning have to do with the temple attack?"

"Judge, I'm trying to establish how close the witness is to the defendant," Mastriani explained.

Trying to establish that my client is a cult leader, Syvio thought.

"I'll allow it," the judge said. "Continue Mr. Mastriani."

"Miss Wilson?"

"No, I had the name long before I met Jessie. I don't like my real name. Dimple suits me fine."

"And how long have you known the defendant?"

"Three years. A little more."

"So, tell me, Miss Wilson," Mastriani said. Were you with the defendant and his followers that whole time?"

Here goes, Sylvio thought. *He's asking questions directly related to the temple attack. Fifth Amendment time. If she's going to plead it she'll do it now.*

"More or less," she answered. "I met him in the homeless camp."

"The one run by Dzon Adekunle?"

"Yes."

"Were you there at the time of Adekunle's killing?"

The witness's eyes flooded. She shook her head.

The judge spoke: "You must answer the question verbally."

"Can I have a tissue?" the witness asked.

The judged motioned to the bailiff who handed her a box.

"No," she said. "No, I wasn't there then."

"Was the defendant?"

"Objection, Your Honor," Sylvio said, standing. "Are we on a fishing expedition here?"

"I'll withdraw the question, judge. Prior to the temple bombing, how would you describe the mood of the defendant's group?"

Dimple looked to Jessie. She tilted her head and bunched her lips.

"Jessie was to himself a lot. He was very tense. Kinda quiet, which wasn't like him. He and Praise argued."

"You're speaking of Praise Johnson? One of the followers?"

"Yeah."

"What did they argue about?"

"Sometimes little things. Spending money and stuff. Praise didn't like the direction the group was taking."

"And what direction was that?"

"Objection. The prosecution is asking for the witness to speculate as to what another person in the group was thinking."

"I'll restate, judge," Mastriani said. "Did Ms. Johnson voice her grievance to you or the defendant?"

The witness nodded.

"She felt that the group was becoming more about Jessie and less about helping the poor."

Mastriani walked from behind the podium. "Miss Wilson were you with the group when the defendant left for a period of time previous to the temple bombing?"

"Yeah, I was there."

"Were any of you aware of the defendant's whereabouts?"

The witness shook her head. "No. We were all wondering. Especially Praise."

"Did you at any time go looking for him?"

The witness didn't speak for a moment.

"Do you need me to repeat the question?"

"No, I heard it. I did look for him. I didn't find him."

Mastriani came closer to the witness stand.

"Where did you look?"

Again, the witness didn't speak right away.

"Miss Wilson?" Mastriani prodded.

The witness shifted in her chair.

"There was a big old steel shed behind the house where we were staying. I thought maybe he needed to pray alone and went back there."

"Was he there?"

"No."

"Was there anything that indicated that he had been there?"

Again, the witness hesitated.

"Miss Wilson," the judge interjected. "We'd like to finish this case sometime this year. This is stressful. That's understood. But the court insists that you answer these questions promptly."

The witness nodded to the judge.

"Miss Wilson?" Mastriani prodded again.

"Can you repeat the question?"

Mastriani smiled. "Sure. Was there any indication that the defendant, Mr. Carpentero, had been in the shed?"

The One and True Son

The witness took a breath. "I opened the door. It had a padlock, but I pulled on it and it opened. It was a big shed. There were no windows, but light came in through holes in the roof, so I could see in."

"What did you see in the shed that made you think that the defendant had been there?"

The witness looked downward. "There wasn't a floor in there. Just dirt. The dirt was pushed around. There were tools all over the place. Like, hand tools. And a couple of plastic bags?"

"Can you describe the bags?"

The witness shrugged. "They were white. Plastic."

"Was there anything written on the bags?"

"Yeah. They said plant fertilizer. Or something like that."

Mastriani turned to the judge. "No further questions at this time, judge."

Sylvio dreaded this witness. She was one of Jessie's Twelve. He remembered her from the wedding at Cafracana. Sylvio had her investigated and found out a lot about Debra Wilson. A runaway at 14, she had a rap sheet as long as his arm before she was 20. Mostly prostitution. Some drug possession. Nothing after she'd joined the homeless guru's camp. He'd brought this all up to Jessie, hoping to persuade him to let him use it to impeach her testimony. Jessie wasn't happy. He told Sylvio in no uncertain terms that if he brought up one instance from Wilson's past, he would create the biggest scene in courtroom history. This was the guy that turned water into champagne right before his eyes. He figured he'd listen to him.

Syvio stood behind the podium putting it between him and the witness.

"Miss Wilson, you testified that there was discord between members of the group. Were you part of those arguments?"

The witness took a breath. "No, It was mostly Praise and Jessie. I didn't take sides. I'm a listener more than a talker."

"Did you have an opinion one way or the other?" Sylvio asked.

Dimple tugged on a dreadlock.

"I understood both sides, really," she responded. "Praise really wanted to help the poor. I get that. But, Jessie. He's…well…Jessie. He's special. He was…He is…

Her voice trailed off.

"Were you aware that Praise Johnson was a police officer?"

The witness looked down toward her sandals.

"I knew that she *was* one. I was there when she first joined Dzon's community. I saw how the cops looked at her when she'd quit and joined us. They hated her."

"She never told you she was still on duty?"

The witness looked Sylvio squarely in the eye.

"I don't believe she was."

Sylvio stepped out from behind the podium.

"I assume that you've seen news coverage on the group. Do you believe the police are lying that she was undercover?"

The witness crossed her arms.

"I'm sure of it."

"How can you be so sure that the police are lying, that all that news coverage is false?"

"I *knew* her," the witness said. Tears flowed. "I talked with her every day. I was around her almost constantly. She knew my story and I know hers. We were like sisters."

"Did she ever tell you that she was really undercover? Did you catch her contacting people? How can you possibly say that she wasn't lying to you and the whole group?"

The witness's face blushed.

"Because she killed herself!" she shouted. "Because she put a gun in her mouth and pulled the trigger."

A moan, like a wolf who'd lost its mate, echoed through the court. Sylvio turned around. It was Jessie.

"No Father!," he yelled."No! She couldn't! WHY FATHER?! WHY?!"

"Oh my God!" Dimple screamed. "You didn't know!"

She turned on Sylvio.

"You didn't tell him?!" she yelled. "You bastard! Why didn't you tell him?!"

The judge slapped down her hammer.

"There *will* be order in this court. Counselor, control your client!"

Sylvio turned to the bench.

"Your Honor, I request a ten-minute recess so my client can compose himself. He was unaware of the woman in question's death."

"I don't know how that could be, but I will grant a fifteen- minute recess. This *will not* happen again, counselor. Is that understood?"

"Absolutely, Your Honor."

The gavel came down again.

The One and True Son

"I'm sorry, Jessie," Sylvio whispered. "I...I should've told you. I *should* have. I couldn't bring myself to do it. I'm so... sorry. I don't know what else to say."

They had been removed to a locked chamber just outside the courtroom. Tears flowed in streams from Jessie's eyes. For the first time, Sylvio saw pain there, agony.

Jessie reached out and took Sylvio's hand.

"She had to forgive herself. That's all she had to do. Do you understand? Her part was written for her. She had no choice in what she did. All she had to do was forgive *herself*."

Sylvio didn't understand. There was a lot he didn't understand. And he couldn't lie about that. He couldn't lie to Jessie. So, he stayed quiet.

When court resumed, he vowed to himself to make short work of the witness.

"Miss Wilson. How far would you say the shed was from the house where you were staying?"

"I'm not real good with measuring and stuff like that."

"Estimate for us. Was it as far as I am to you standing at this podium?"

"Yeah, I guess," the witness said, twisting her face. "Maybe a little closer."

"Was the house you were staying in a solid house?"

"Solid?" the witness asked.

"Yes, solid. Well built. Did it have thick walls? Did it have windows?"

"Well, the house was just regular. You know, kinda thin walls. It had all the windows if I remember right. But most of them were boarded up"

"So you could hear in the house if someone was working on a large project in that shed?

"Yeah, I suppose I could." The witness smiled.

"Did you ever see or hear *anyone*, let alone Mr. Carpentero, enter or leave the shed?

"No, I didn't."

Sylvio turned and faced the jury.

"Miss Wilson, what do you think was stored in that shed before your group took up residence there?"

Dimples' eyebrow went up.

"I guess lawn mowing stuff. It's a big shed but I think that's probably what was in there."

"Would you call fertilizer 'lawn mowing stuff?"

"Yeah, I believe I would," the witness answered.

Sylvio turned to the judge.

"No further questions, Your Honor."

"I'm worried," Sylvio said to Miriam on the phone that night.

"Why?" his wife asked. "The news says you're doing a good job. Better than expected, some of them said."

"High praise indeed. I haven't screwed up my first major case in the first week. I'm sure there are law firms all over the country putting me on speed dial."

Miriam laughed. "You could have, you know. The trial could've been blown open by something you missed in the first day. But you handled it. The talking heads' scorecards have you ahead."

"That's what bothers me. This has been too easy. Mastriani must have known there were ways to pick those witnesses apart. He must've seen that I could make their testimony at least moot, if not helpful to our side. Right?"

"Maybe. Maybe not," his wife answered. "Sometimes there's hype around someone where there shouldn't be. Maybe this Mastriani guy is a marketer's dream, but a mediocre lawyer."

"His case histories don't bear that out. I can't help but wonder if he's got something he's holding back for the right moment."

"Isn't that illegal?" Miraim asked.

"Yeah, but so is running a stop sign and I've done that three times this week."

"They added a witness to the prosecutions' witness list. This is total bullshit. I asked for a conference with the judge. She'll see me Monday morning at 8."

Jessie took this news with little more than a shake of his shoulders. He was stretched out on his stiff bunk looking indifferent to the news. It was as if he were told that it would rain that afternoon.

"Sylvio. You're doing the best you can. It will turn out the way my father planned."

"And how is that?" Sylvio snapped. "Did he tell you how this will end? Because if this is a lost cause, maybe you'd do better with someone who doesn't care if you are convicted on a *capital terrorism charge*. This all can go much faster."

Jessie sat up. "No, it has to be you, Sylvio."

"Why? What is this plan you keep telling me about? Details Jessie. Details."

"Please. Sit down," Jessie said.

Sylvio sat in the chair.

"We are going to lose, Sylvio."

Sylvio jumped to his feet.

"Why? What plan *from Yahweh* could possibly include the death of *his son*?"

Jessie rubbed his temples. "*His* plan," Jessie said and took a deep breath. Since the creation, or nearly so, humanity has been out of balance from the Father's will."

"The Garden of Eden." Sylvio said.

"Right," Jessie nodded.

"But that's a metaphor!" Sylvio brought down his tone. "Isn't it?"

Jessie raised an eyebrow.

"The only way to correct this imbalance is what we are doing now."

"That's insane!" Sylvio cried. "The only way to save humanity is to kill you! To kill Yahweh's son? And you *know* this and accept it?"

Jessie's eyes were edged in tears. "I do."

Sylvio sat back in the chair. He took a couple of deep breaths and closed his eyes.

"I could file an insanity defense. If they talked to you for five minutes, they'd believe me."

Jessie smiled a tired smile. "It wouldn't work. This trial will end with a conviction."

"So why do you need me?" Sylvio said in a scratchy voice.

Jessie stood and put his hands on the bars.

"Because you know who I am."

The meeting with Judge Strawberry-Huff went much as Sylvio expected. Julio Mastriani said that the information had just come to light and the witness had solid credentials. Sylvio argued that he hasn't had time to interview the witness and questioned what a retired newspaper photographer had to do with this trial. At the very least, Sylvio argued, the trial should be put on hold until he can review this so-called information and interview the witness.

"I've seen the evidence," the judge said. "I think this could be ironed out in court."

Sylvio sniffed. "I haven't seen it, Your Honor. The rules of evidence in this trial mandate that I can review all evidence *before* it goes to trial."

"Mr. De Graca," the judge said, not looking Sylvio in the eye. *"I determine the rules of evidence in this trial. It is my determination that this will go forward in front of the jury. I'm sure that if this is an error, you can use it very efficiently on appeal. Now, we belong in court at 9am. It would be in everyone's best interest if we are not late. Any more questions?"*

Was she hinting at something? Sylvio thought. *Did she already know that he would be filing an appeal even before this trial ended?*

"No judge," Mastriani said, smiling.

"Mr. De Graca?"

"No judge," Sylvio answered. "No more questions."

"My name is Dale Green. G...R...E...E...N."

"Thank you, sir." The judge looked to Julio Mastriani. "You may proceed.

Mastriani took to the podium.

"Mr. Green. Could you please tell the court what you do for a living?"

The witness, a wiry man, maybe in his late 50s, with salt and pepper hair and crooked glasses, smiled. His mustache, which appeared to be something he'd been working on since adolescence, but never quite grew in, tilted with the incline of his lips.

"Nothing much," he said. "I retired in 2012."

"My apologies sir," said Mastriani. "What was you profession before you retired?"

"No problem. I was a photographer. A photojournalist."

"Is it likely that we've seen your work?"

The witness pursed his lips. "You probably have. I've covered presidential campaigns, tsunamis, terrorist attacks, riots, coups. It all depends on which newspaper you read I guess."

"Which papers have published your photos?"

"Oh, all of them at one time or another."
"I need you to be more specific."

"Sorry. Yeah. New York Times, Washington Post, Chicago Tribune, Hartford Courant, AP, Reuters. Probably others I've forgotten. I haven't put together a resume in a while."

"That's a lot of big names. Did you start with the cream of the crop?" The witness smiled showing a cracked front tooth. "No. I was freelance at the beginning. I had a police scanner in my car and I'd drive to wherever something was going on and try to get some shots of it. I had some friends at the local papers there. Some of the papers would buy my shots. Others not. Depends."

"It depends on what?"

"Depends on whether the shot was any good."

"Where was this?"

"Where I'm from. Oklahoma, City, Oklahoma."

Mastriani came out from behind the podium.

"You won some journalism awards there."

"Yeah, I entered a few shots a year. Even an honorable mention would help me out.

Eventually, I had enough good ones where some people noticed and I moved up north to the big boys, the Times and such.

Mastriani turned to the bench. "Judge, I'd like to present some of the witness's photos."

"Proceed, Mr, Mastriani."

The large TV screens lit up and the lights were dimmed in the courtroom. An image appeared, one familiar to most in the audience. On it was a black man, an immigrant, who had crawled and scaled balconies of a New York apartment building to save a small child who was trapped on a burning floor of the building.

"I imagine this is one of your more popular shots," Mastriani told the witness.

"Yeah," the witness agreed. "Got nominated for a Pulitzer for that one."

"The one that beat it must have been some shot," Mastriani said.

"Yeah, but like I said, honorable mention always helps," said the photographer.

The next image showed the twisted wreckage from an event that changed the world instantaneously.

"I don't think anyone in the courtroom has to ask where this is from," Mastriani told the court.

"I got down there just after the second plane hit. There were already people jumping from the windows. I can barely look at that. The image from the viewfinder is burned into my head."

The photo was from the base of Building Two on that horrible day. The camera was peering up the side of the building. Smoke poured from the jets' impact site and debris, some on fire, some charred black, rained down around the camera.

The One and True Son

There were lighter photos in the witness's portfolio. There was a photo of a president who'd just attempted to exit through a fake door in China, a boyish shrug rippled across his shoulders. And another president's family waving and smiling to the camera from the Truman balcony at the White House. The youngest daughter had a gap from missing baby teeth almost as big as her smile.

Mastriani switched to another slide.

"Mr Green. Can you tell me when and where this photo is from?"

The witness looked for a long time at the photo. He seemed pained when he spoke. In the photo was a boy, a teenager, looking at carnage that was just across the street from him.

"That shot was taken on April 19th, 1995. It was in Oklahoma City. It was minutes after the bombing of the Murrah Federal Building."

Mastriani stood looking at the boy in the shot, letting the courtroom take it in as well.

"Mr. Green. This seems to be an unusual shot. The bombing was across the street and yet you took a picture of a young person looking at it from the corner."

"Yeah, that's just what the city editor said," the witness responded.

"So," Martini shrugged, "Why? Why did you take this shot?"

"I took it because I was struck how the kid was looking at the bombing site. It was like he was taking it in. I couldn't for the life of me figure out what this kid was thinking. The expression. I'd never seen it before. At first, I wondered if he was involved somehow. I don't know why. I just couldn't read that expression. It drew me. To this day, I don't know why."

Mastriani faced the jury.

"Mr. Green, have you identified the boy, well young man, in this photo?"

The witness nodded.

"It took me a while, but I ran it through facial identification software. Once I got a name, I verified that the young man was living in the area at the time."

"And who was this young man?"

"Jessie Carpentero." said the witness.

Sylvio was on his feet. "Objection, Your Honor! Is this witness here to connect Jessie Carpentero to the Oklahoma City bombing when he was 15 years old?"

The judge sighed.

"Overruled, Mr. DeGraca. Sit down."

The Witness

"Is that his lawyer?" a guard asked his partner between sips of coffee and glances at the other screens in the front sector security room. They gaped at the man from the foyer camera that surveilled the public entrance to FloMax.

"Yeah, I think so," the other guard, Anvil, answered. The nickname, both with colleagues and the inmates, referred to his unusually flat head. "I saw a *60-Minutes* thing on him last night. Poor fucker. The trial killed his career. Damned near killed him too, from the looks of him. Would you believe that guy isn't even 40 yet? He looks like he forgot what a razor looks like."

A voice from behind them shut down the conversation.

"Why don't you boys change the channel? Maybe *Maury* is on."

"Sorry, Maggie," the first guard said with due deference.

"Don't be," said the AW-C, Associate Warden-Custody. "Just do your job. I know this is a big day, for the press, for the Justice Department, even the internet. But not for us. This is every day for us. We've got everybody watching today, but we have to keep everyone in here who's supposed to be. That's our job. Spend any more than a glance at the foyer and I'll throw you in with the cannibals."

Margaret "Maggie" Stokes left the room.

Anvil reached over and slapped his partner on the shoulder. "Man, why didn't you remind me she was in here?"

"You didn't remind me neither," the other replied.

Maggie Stokes left the control center and walked down the hall to her office and shut the door. She'd been in this same spartan office, devoid of photographs, awards and personal achievements since she came on the ADX team in the late summer of 1994. She came into the Federal Prison system from the Naval Consolidated Brig in Chesapeake, Virginia where she was the commanding officer for eight years, a long time at one assignment for Naval officer. And she was good: strict, by the book, and as fair as her job would allow. She was known at the brig for her habit of handing a personal Tanach to every new inmate and staff member she encountered. That chapped some asses of some constitutional purists she'd run into over the years, but she felt that Yahweh would protect her from harassment. So far, she was correct.

She plunked down behind her immaculate desk and turned in her swivel chair to face the large window, the only source of natural light and beauty in the whole facility as far as she was concerned. She knew that, to most people, the dry, rocky moonscape she faced nearly every day was anything but beautiful, but it was a sight she'd reserved for her. It was the way out if she ever wanted to take it, a privilege her inmates would never get to see. Not through their four-inch wide by four feet long cell windows. The Federal prison system designed the cell windows to *not* see the mountains, to *not* see the tufts of dried grass in the mountain desert.

She wondered if she'd take the way out now. Maggie made it a rule to not follow the cases that might end up within the walls of ADX. But how could she not follow this one? It was on every news channel every day. Every talk show host had a joke or two in their monologues: *The President had the Temple Bomber to the White House today hoping he'd cure his sagging approval ratings...*

He was on the front page of what was left of every newspaper in the country. Turn on the radio, Jessie Carpentero. Look at your phone, "Son of Yahweh Still Silent on Bombing." He was all over the internet before the bombing. That was doubly so now.

But she had to be honest with herself. She was interested in Jessie Carpentero. She read every story attached to every headline. She turned the volume up on the TV whenever his name was mentioned. And if she were honest with herself, she would admit that she knew who he was *before* the bombing. The YouTube algorithm picked up on her interest in all things Yahweh and plugged her in early. Maggie was immediately intrigued. One skill she'd picked up, first running the brig and later at ADX is the ability to determine sincerity from fraud. She knew when her inmates were telling her what they thought she wanted to hear or when something had profoundly changed in their hearts. She'd heard thousands of excuses and an equal number of confessions, and she could predict without fault, the ones meant to sway her and the one's coming from grief and contrition. And the people on those Carpentero videos were genuine. She knew it. She felt it. Something had moved in them that, to Maggie, had to be the Creator himself.

The One and True Son

And then the bombing. Maggie cried. Maggie *never* cried. She couldn't believe that the man that she'd followed on the internet would blow up a temple of Yahweh. The day the press identified Jessie as a suspect, she called in sick for work for the first time in decades.

After that day, Maggie knew she had to get her head and heart screwed together. She abandoned her television during the trial. She dug into her job in a way she hadn't in years, looking at the paperwork, talking to her assistants about their interactions with the inmates, most of the latter deemed too damaged, too brutal to participate in society. She knew what her job was here, but she still tried to make it so as many inmates as possible would be able to leave this place of ultimate isolation, be it to another prison or released to the world and be better for the experience.

When the trial ended, when Carpentero was sentenced to die, she knew he'd be coming to her. All the major offenders came here: the Shoe Bomber, the Underwear Bomber, the mastermind of 9/11, McVeigh. Most of them had an unimaginable sentence, a life inside what one of the former wardens called "the clean version of hell." McVeigh got a reprieve. He was executed.

Jessie Carpentero would also get a reprieve.

The day Jessie arrived she stood in the control room as she had this day. She faced the screen overlooking the underground in-processing center and looked for the man she'd only heard about on the internet. What would she see? A man of power? A king? Would the cameras be able to record him? It turned out they could because there, getting out of a windowless, unmarked van came a tall, yet beaten man. The air of majesty that she'd imagined would surround him like an electric fence, evaporated. He stood, shaky, broken. Maggie left the control room and ran to her office. She cried again.

The object of her fascination was now a daily presence in her place of employment. Maggie Stokes made no effort to speak to him. When she had business in H Unit, the area reserved for the worst refuse of humankind, she steered clear of his seven by twelve-foot cell with its concrete bed and stool, its faucetless sink, its unblockable toilet and its timed shower. If she knew she'd be in the vicinity of his cell, she'd send an underling in to do her talking and her listening. Carpentero had been inside with her for years and the only time she laid eyes on him was through the cameras in the in-processing area.

Someone knocked on her office door. Her administrative assistant was running somewhere around the complex, preparing for the day's event. Maggie stood and approached the door. She opened it deliberately, quickly. This was *not* the way an Associate Warden took visitors. She intended to blister the offender's ears.

"Margaret Stokes," a man in a ragged suit said; the suit felt almost accusatory. "My name is Sylvio De Grace. I'm the attorney for inmate Jessie Carpentero. I know you're busy today considering today's…event. Can I speak with you a moment? I just have a couple of questions."

The acid drained out of the Associate Warden. She didn't answer. She couldn't. She returned to her desk leaving the door open so the unkempt man could enter. He shut the door behind him.

"Everything has already been decided," Maggie said as the man took a seat in the chair across from her. "The appeals process has run its course. The president has said there will be no reprieve. Tonight at 8pm the sentence for Jessie Carpentero will be exacted as prescribed by federal law."

The attorney ran his hand through his longish hair. The streaks of gray that ran through it seemed incongruous to the head they were attached to, as were the dark circles under his eyes.

"Yes ma'am. He's to be killed at 8 o'clock. Exacted is an appropriate word. I understand this."

"Please, Mr. De Graca. Tell me you didn't knock on my door to debate the pros and cons of capital punishment. I don't have time for such a discussion, so if you'll please excuse me. You can close the door on your way out."

"No, Ms. Stokes. That wasn't my intention although you mentioning it does bring to mind the barbarity of the practice."

"Mr. De Graca. How many capital cases have you tried?"

"This is the one and only."

"As I suspected. Capital punishment makes you uncomfortable. If Mr. Carpentero was a Roman, he would be nailed up on two pieces of wood through the wrists and die over a period of days so the whole town could watch. If he was unfortunate enough to be born during the Renaissance, he might be burned at the stake. If he was born after that, the government may have sliced him in the groin and armpits and have his limbs tied to some nervous horses who'd be slapped on the hind quarters in opposite directions. Or perhaps just beheaded. Even a few short years ago, Mr. Carpentero could expect to be hanged, or suffocated with cyanide gas. Or have enough electrical current run through him to light up this whole county. Barbarity has a long history. But we are trying to be less so."

"I believe you use the three-drug method in these federal cases," said Sylvio.

"That's correct, although I have nothing to do with the actual execution," Maggie answered. "I couldn't even tell you what drugs they are."

"That would be sodium thiopental. It's a short acting barbiturate that knocks the prisoner out. That's followed by pancuronium bromide to paralyze the prisoner and stop his breathing. Finally, potassium chloride is given to stop the heart."

"Yes, Mr. De Graca. That is unpleasant, but all that takes place after the prisoner is unconscious."

Sylvio raised his eyebrows. "Does it? Are you sure? He looks unconscious and can't move, but how can you be sure he doesn't know what's happening? That he can't feel it? People have told stories of being patients under anesthesia in surgery and experiencing the pain of dissection, but they're unable to tell anyone due to the paralysis caused by the drugs. The executed can't come back and tell us if they felt it."

Maggie sighed. "I'd love to argue with you about this Mr. De Graca, but I have a rather busy schedule today. Have you expressed your opinions sufficiently so I may go about my day?"

"One question," Syvlio said.

"If you get one, I get one," Maggie responded.

"That seems fair."

"Go ahead then."

"When McVeigh was to be executed you sent him to Terre Haute. Why is Jessie Carpentero being executed here?"

"Mr. De Graca. May I call you Sylvio?"

"I don't see why not."

"Sylvio," Maggie said. "I don't know. It came down from the Justice Department that they didn't want Carpentero moved. We had to set up the facilities here. Perhaps they thought there was a security risk in transporting him. That's the honest truth."

"I accept that," Sylvio said, shrugging. "Your turn."

"I understand that you have taken this case personally. That your career, which was quite promising no matter which way the case turned out, was definitely more than promising. Some were saying you were the next F. Lee Bailey or Clarence Darrow, if you like."

"And the question?"

"Why? How did this all go so bad for you? You handled the case well by all accounts."

Sylvio pursed his lips and sighed. "Because those accounts were wrong. I made a major error."

The One and True Son

"How so?"

"I didn't tell Jessie about Praise Johnson's death. I actually wanted his shock to be expressed in court. I wanted them to see how attached he was to people, how much he cared. That he wasn't some psycho who killed people. That he *loved* them. Even those who may have betrayed him. When it all played out in court all people saw was a man who was not in control of his emotions. The trial went downhill from there.

"There was that and…" Sylvio trailed off.

"And what? And what, Sylvio?"

"I believe him."

There's one access road that services the prison in Florence, Colorado. It shoots off to the left if you're traveling south from the town of Florence which at its founding made its name by having three railroads, including one to move coal from neighboring towns. In 1862, oil was discovered making it the first oil center west of the Mississippi. There are two cemeteries, five temples, an elementary school and a middle/junior high school. Super 8 has a hotel there and there's a Carl's Jr, and it's as dry as a poor man's throat.

The access road is the only way in or out of the prison; it runs by the prison's three sections: Florence, Florence High security and the ADX or Supermax. The locals started calling it FloMax a few years ago when a pharmaceutical company marketed a new drug said to relieve a swollen prostate. The workers, the guards and others who served the prison, didn't like the new moniker at first, but like everything else from the outside world, it slipped in with a guard and spread like a virus. One had to be careful *not* to use it around anyone with "warden" in their job title.

Driving on Route 67 one couldn't help but notice the presence of the ominous facility jutting up from the flat dust approaching some stubby old mountains. There's nothing else there, not a tree or fire plug, and even if there were, the prison can't be missed. The glow from high intensity lighting can be seen 50 miles away on a clear night, which most nights are, and the buzz from the fixtures can be heard from the town if you listen carefully. The prison builders were kind enough to put the coiled layers of razor wire far enough from the road so tourists wouldn't be able to photograph it.

The press, TV and cable news and what's left of major newspapers, were well acquainted with Route 67. It's all they'd get to see when anything happens at the prison. The architects not only designed windows that didn't show prisoners the outside; they designed a one way in/one way out access road so no one could see in. Anyone unwelcome turning onto

The One and True Son

this access road is immediately met by a well-armed, well-trained cadre, some, veterans of the wars in Iraq and Afghanistan. Any deviation from the directive to return to Route 67 and request permission onto the grounds will be met with a strong response, a lethal one if need be. The press has had to film many a news story from the desert floor at least two miles from the facility.

An execution, especially of the Temple Bomber, was no exception to this directive. News agencies tried, as they do with every new high-profile story, but their pleas went unanswered. Subsequently, trucks from ABC (both the American and Australian version), NBC, CBS, CNN, MSNBC, FOX, NPR, Telemundo, TVP (Poland), RT (Russia) and other plain white trucks from less identifiable organizations cooled their brakes waiting for the story to come to them. Even the Weather Channel parked a van on the dusty road to observe the weather at a place where the average humidity hovered around 20 percent. Every truck had a reporter, and every reporter had a camera, a satellite uplink and a microphone. They all sat, waiting for some word of the would-be prophet's demise. At best, they'd get a statement by the warden on a makeshift podium on the side of Route 67. At worst, an administrative assistant from Media Affairs will hand out statements with the time of death in standard bureaucratic jargon about justice and the rule of law. But still the media sat, like it had in every high-profile case, like dogs waiting on a treat.

The press was the least of Maggie Stokes' problems.

She had her own issues with capital punishment. Maggie knew through her private studies of the Tanach that Yahweh sanctioned execution by a government, yet she still winced at the practice. The Creator would know if an executed person was indeed guilty of their crime. But could lowly humans *absolutely know* that a person sent to the executioner actually committed the crime of which they'd been accused? Wouldn't the fallibility of the human mind be prone to error? She'd read of a case in Texas. A man, a black man, convicted by a nearly all white jury decades before his scheduled execution. In the years after his conviction, new evidence was uncovered, new witnesses came forward. One witness, a damning one even recanted his testimony. And yet the needs of the criminal justice system demanded the action prescribed by law. He'd had his appeals. He'd had his say. His life was ended with crowds of protesters screaming outside.

Being black herself, Maggie understood the pain her community felt, that this was visited disproportionately on people like her. But she was a prison official. She'd sworn, under Yahweh, to uphold the law whether she agreed with it or not. She hoped the cloud that hovered over her in these last few days would lift when the deed was done.

The logistics of this execution were a nightmare. She told Sylvio the truth when she said she'd had no input on the change in venue for the event. The sentence for McVeigh was carried out at the Terra Haute facility. It was one of two execution centers left in the Federal system.

One day the warden showed up in *her* office, something that had never happened before. He surprised her when he said that Carpentero would not be moved, and the sentence would be carried out here. Her surprise doubled when he told her that he'd gotten a personal call from the Attorney General himself.

"We don't have a facility here, Jim," Maggie told the warden. "How are we going to do this?"

Jim Russo, the ADX warden for the previous eight years, answered her, fatigued. "We have to build one, Maggie. Guess who's the lucky person who'll oversee that?"

Maggie didn't have to guess. She was the associate warden in charge of custody.

"We're going to have to clear some cells," she told Russo. 'We don't have time to build an annex. I'll have to bring in architects. Security is going to have to be revamped for the new setup. This is going to be really disruptive."

"You don't have to worry about any of that," Russo answered. "Federal Prisons already has the plans. Some walls are coming down next week. The contractors are booked. The facility will be just like Terre Haute right down to the green wall tiles from what I understand. They even have an identical execution table. All you have to do is make sure no inmates get a good look at the outside."

"This is nuts," said Maggie Stokes. "You know that, don't you? He could be taken to a military airfield in a parade of Bradleys if they wanted. He could have a fighter escort."

The warden rubbed his forehead. The fuzzy remnants of what used to be a full head of curly blond hair looked more sparse than usual. "I know, Maggie. I know."

"So, I guess they're going to use this new room for other prisoners, right? They're going to ramp up executions? Is that what they're doing?"

"No, they're not," the warden said. "I'm sure they're not."

"How can you be so sure?" Maggie said, her trademarked *Doubtful Eyebrow* employed.

"Because I asked them, Maggie. I asked them. I'm as upset about this as you are, believe it or not."

She did.

The One and True Son

"There's got to me more to it than that," Maggie said, nevertheless. "Political people make promises all the time."

The warden nodded. "They don't schedule a wrecking crew for the next day, if they don't mean it."

Maggie Stokes supervised the shuffling of prisoners, in shackles and cuffs, out of their cells and into others that hadn't been used in years. Some time back, it'd been determined that more suicides occurred in that wing of the building as the sunlight found it very difficult to make its way into the narrow long windows. The lack of *any* sunshine along with 23 hours of solitary confinement had broken the spirits of even the most hardened murderers. Eighth Amendment lawsuits from families and civil rights groups poured in. News crews lined up on Route 67. After negotiation, the census was lowered at ADX with some prisoners, the less evil ones, transferred away.

And now they were putting inmates back in the lightless cells.

The reinforced walls that had to be torn down to make room for the death theater were no joke. Not only were they designed to keep prisoners within the ADX walls, but also to keep them as separate as possible. The walls were soundproofed so they couldn't communicate through them, and impenetrable so the inmates couldn't join rooms clandestinely. Special concrete was used as was solid steel, embedded in the center of each wall. The builders of the facility never dreamed the walls would be torn out in the near or even distant future.

The new construction team brought in jack hammers that failed embarrassingly often, with bent and broken hammers and failing hydraulic seals. At one point, explosives were considered to clear the undesired concrete, but were deemed too dangerous to bring into the facility. After thousands of dollars of failed equipment and more than one resignation on the team, the required area was cleared, and the building of the death theater began.

The chamber took six weeks to complete. To Maggie Stokes, the finished product looked like a hospital kitchen. The walls were tiled an anemic green, a color Maggie likened in her mind to an infection. The floor had scattered browns and grays tiles mixed in. Not quite in the center of the room, the team bolted the death table through to the cement. At first, the table looked like regular medical equipment, but with the panels swung out where the arms would be strapped, its true purpose became clear. The whole table could be tilted so the prisoner could speak his last words to the audience.

A large tempered glass window would provide the viewing gallery with a view of the event. Four rows of seats were set up for the most macabre theater imaginable. The audience would include witnesses, both of whom would be state officials, the warden, representatives of the Attorney General, and the families of the victims. These people would witness the extinguishing of a human life from comfortable seats ordered from a company that designs seats for movie theaters, complete, for some reason, with cup holders. A sound system was installed so the prisoner could express remorse. Or not.

The day Jessie Carpentero would draw his final breath, Maggie stood alone in the chamber, trying very hard to breathe herself. This was insanity. She was sure of it. She was equally sure that she couldn't stop it. Since his arrival, she'd avoided passing Carpentero's cell, but she would not be spared the horror of his execution. As Associate Warden in Charge of Custody, Maggie was obligated to witness the execution. She practically begged Warden Russo to do this for her, but he denied her request.

"I have my own problems with this, Maggie," he told her. "I can't tell you about them, but I do."

"Aren't you the head honcho around here?" She came off more terrified than insubordinate.

"I am," he said. "And Yahweh knows it. I'm not getting out of anything."

"Like Tim McVeigh, Jessie Carpentero's execution was scheduled in early June. McVeigh was put to death at 7am whereas Jessie would be killed at 8pm. Maggie wondered who in power decided the time. It was at the height of the daily news cycle. Someone wanted everybody to know this was being carried out. Carpentero had been transferred to a special holding cell the previous evening and offered his choice for his last meal. He requested only water. The guards, two men she knew well, tried to talk him into having something more. Maggie knew these men to be unshakable, but when their time with the prisoner ended, they both requested the next day off.

Two hours prior to the execution, the witnesses were led into viewing theater. Maggie stood to the left of the door. There were no smiles in this room. No one looked at each other. They filled in the seats from the farthest to the closest. There were family of those killed at the temple, easy to identify from the wads of tissue clutched in their hands. They wore suits and dresses and skirts and blouses. There were no protest t-shirts, no dirty shoes. No one wanted to be there as far as Maggie could tell.

The One and True Son

The lawyer she'd spoken to earlier in the day passed her as if she wasn't there and took a seat in the first aisle at the center of the window. He appeared nearly catatonic. Was it possible for a man to age in just a few hours?

Maggie waited with the rest. She stood looking over the witnesses who sat looking anywhere they could but in front of them, avoiding the thick glass. With fifteen minutes left in the life of Jessie Carpentero, another viewer entered the room. He wore an expertly tailored suit, brightly shined shoes and a pair of sunglasses. He was the type of person that one would swear they'd seen before but had no idea where that would've been. His bald head absorbed the subdued lighting of the room. This man was the first person to look at Maggie. She could feel his dead eyes behind the Ray-Bans. He looked at her past the time that anyone would be comfortable. He nodded and smiled. His teeth made her shiver.

Suddenly, Maggie wasn't sure she could breathe. She left the viewing theater, walking quickly, almost running, past confused guards, past the doors that contained the condemned man. Her electronic key shook in her hand as she swiped it on the lock pad. She rushed the door as soon as she'd heard it click.

The two guards seated there, the same ones from the morning, looked at her wide eyed.

"You okay, Maggie?" one guard asked.

At first, she couldn't speak. She nodded.

"You want some water?"

"Yes, please," she finally said, her voice cracking.

The guard stood and grabbed her a small cup from the cooler in the corner.

Maggie's took the cup.

"You sure you're okay?" the guard asked, putting a big paw on her shoulder. "I can get the doc down here in a second. You don't look so good."

"No, I'm fine," Maggie said, finally sounding somewhat like herself. "I don't like small rooms with lots of people in them. That's all."

The guard smiled. "Don't get a room here then." He was hoping to lighten the mood.

Maggie smiled back. It was a weak smile. "I'll do my best. Now get back to your screens. I'm fine."

The warden had said that Maggie had to witness the sentence being carried out. He didn't say she had to do it from the viewing theater. Maggie sat hard in a chair and turned a flat screen to face her. She paged through

The One and True Son

the different views until the found those of the death chamber. The cell door holding Carpentero opened. There were two guards on the outside of the door, and Maggie knew, two more in with the condemned man. This would be Maggie's first look at the prisoner since he'd arrived. Maggie gasped.

"You okay, Maggie, the same guard asked. "I can still get the doc up here."

"Just watch your screen, please," Maggie answered. "I'm fine."

Maggie wasn't fine. The man who emerged from the holding cell looked as if he'd been beaten daily since his arrival. She knew that couldn't be the case and blamed it on the monitor. Anyone seeing this man on the street would've assumed he'd not eaten in months. His face was gaunt, his lips shriveled around his mouth; the natural hue of his brown skin looked washed out. He looked like a man in his sixties, one in ill health. Shackled and handcuffed, the man shuffled, bent over. His face twisted with strain as he made his way down the corridor; he appeared to be not just dragging himself to the death chamber, but other things, unseen and unheard, with him. Maggie wanted to turn away, but she had no power to do so. Her body seemed locked.

Maggie switched cameras as the man negotiated the corner to adjoining corridor. She leaned forward to look closer at the guard to Carpentero's right. Was he smiling? Was that possible? She'd seen this particular guard for years without a thought one way or another about him. He was meaty, like most the guards and had a thick, close-cropped beard. Maggie turned the sound up.

"When you get to your daddy, say hello for me. Could you tell him I'd like a new Porsche? He'll know who you're talking about. I pray for it nearly every night. Tell 'em if he just gives me that, I'll stop bugging him."

Maggie made a note to fire that clown as soon as this was over.

The guards and the condemned man entered the death chamber. A lugubrious looking man waited inside dressed in an ill-fitting gray suit, a starched white shirt and beat up, but polished, shoes. A man and a woman in nurses' scrubs stood stiffly along the back wall both looking like they didn't know what to do with their hands. Carpentero entered first. His shackle chains got caught on the corner of the metal door frame and nearly sent him sprawling. The guards steadied him and moved him toward the man in the suit.

That must be the doctor, Maggie thought. She knew the Feds had trouble finding one who would participate in any execution let alone on a prisoner who claimed to be the son of God. But this being Colorado, they found a retired doctor in Pueblo, a nearby town, who said he could use the money. In his interview, he said that he had no feelings one way or the other about capital punishment and even less interest in the Temple Bombing. As long as he wasn't photographed, he'd be fine with administering the toxic cocktail.

The guards guided the prisoner to the death table. Each guard took a key out of their pockets and unlocked the shackles and handcuffs. With the hardware in hand, they walked back to the door. One guard rapped on it and handed the restraints out to another guard waiting outside. The door closed again and locked. The two guards took their places on either side of the door.

Carpentero made no moves on his own. The man and the woman in the scrubs boosted him on the table by his armpits. The woman rolled up Carpentero's sleeve, checked his pulse at his wrist and wrapped a blood pressure cuff around his upper arm. This horrified Maggie. *Why bother with that? To see if he's healthy enough to die. And what would they do if his blood pressure was too high? Give him a pill and have him rest until he was well enough to kill?*

With a grim nod, the woman indicated to the doctor that his vital signs were acceptable. The male nurse eased him back on the table and strapped him down; one strap across the chest, one around the waist, a strap across the upper thighs, and another holding down the condemned's calves.

Maggie switched screens to the one showing the viewing theater. Everyone was still. All eyes were on the events through the thick glass window. Tears streaked Carpentero's lawyer's face. The odd man with the shark's teeth leaned forward as if he were watching a close football game.

In the death chamber, the nurses started IVs in both arms. Maggie guessed they did that in case one failed. *The state must be thorough with its executions.* The condemned's arms were now extended out from each side on padded platforms that'd been folded out from the death table. The nurses nodded to each other. The man pushed a pedal with his foot and together with the other nurse tilted the table so Jessie Carpentero could face the viewers.

The door opened to the chamber and in stepped the warden, Jim Russo. Maggie knew Jim Russo. She knew him as well as she'd known anyone. He took his place, preordained no doubt, next to the table. Jim didn't want to be there. His eyes moved from the window in front of him, to the floor, to the table where Carpentero was strapped and back to the floor again. Maggie had never seen him like this.

She remembered first meeting Russo almost 20 years prior. She'd applied for the position the year before hoping that she might transition directly to ADX after her Navy retirement went through. She hadn't heard

The One and True Son

anything, even after the discharge paperwork went through, and she traded in her green active-duty ID for the light blue one for retirees.

She putted around Virginia for a while wondering if she'd have to volunteer at a hospital or buy a boat and sit in it until something came up, when she got a call from Colorado. The secretary who called, she'd assumed it was a secretary, asked how soon she could come to ADX and meet with the warden. Maggie asked how fast they could get her a ticket and pick her up at the airport. It turns out the next day was how fast.

She read up on ADX on the plane. The brig was tough. ADX was brutal. In the Navy the biggest problem for most of the inmates was lack of discipline, and, in many cases, lack of intelligence. Like other areas of American life, drugs screwed up a lot of lives in the Navy, but the Navy had a lot less tolerance for it. There were inmates in for assault, rape, even murder, but for the most part the sailors were doing time until they could receive their dishonorable discharges for doing or selling drugs. On every ship, at every station, there was always someone who thought it'd be a good idea to have ridiculous quantities of illicit drugs: marijuana, oxycodone, cocaine, even some of the old school stuff like LSD. The stupid druggies made up a large share of residents in the brig.

ADX was hardcore. Rapists who'd killed guards or other inmates. Mass murderers. Cannibals who preferred the taste of children. Think of a heinous crime and you'll find at least ten offenders at ADX. This place would be tough. Maggie knew it. Maggie was tough.

Her driver picked her up outside the small, but clean and modern Colorado Springs Airport. Her driver was a very young-looking man with a thick five o'clock shadow, black framed glasses and plugs the size of quarters in each ear. He expertly swung the white Silverado with small federal seals on the front doors under the entrance portico, the wheels screeching in front of her. Maggie reached for her bag. The driver leapt from the truck.

"Let me get that, ma'am," he said and flung the heavy bag in the back as if it'd been filled with packing peanuts. He opened the back door so she could climb in.

"How far is it to ADX?" Maggie asked.

"About 35 miles. Maybe 36 depending on how fast I go."

Maggie looked at him sideways.

"Little joke, ma'am."

Maggie shook it off.

"I'm Matt. Matt Hart. Everybody knows me at FloMax. I get things done when nobody else has the time for it. Like get you."

The One and True Son

"Important things then," Maggie added.

"Uh, yeah," Matt agreed. "Like that."

As he drove, Matt regaled Maggie with stories of the Old West that'd occurred in the area.

"We ain't too far from Cripple Creek. You know that old song?" He sang, "*Up on Cripple Creek, she sends me."*

"I don't know it," Maggie said.

"They still play it around here in some of the bars. I think it was from the 60s or something"

"I don't know it," Maggie said.

"Well, anyway, Cripple Creek started in the Gold Rush. Not the California one. The Colorado one. At first, they kinda tricked people to go here. They salted gold. You know what that is?" He looked at her in the rearview mirror.

Maggie shook her head.

"That's when someone puts gold that they already have in worthless rock and pretend that they have a strike. Thing was, someone really did find gold. Real gold. After that it was a boomtown. Brought all kinds of people here. Homesteaders, outlaws. All kinds."

"You grew up here, then?" Maggie asked.

"How'd you know?"

"I imagine there aren't many homesteaders nowadays."

"No," Matt laughed. "Just you, I guess."

"I haven't made up my mind on that yet," Maggie said. "Neither has your boss."

"Oh, I think they'll want you." Matt assured her.
"Really? Why is that?"

"Cause they ain't had me pick anyone up before." Matt said.

The distance bothered Maggie. The distance from any major city. The distance from the life she'd known. The kid yammered on in the front seat about Butch Cassidy, a man Maggie thought bore little resemblance to Paul Newman. And Jack Slade, a gentleman most of the time unless he got a hold of some whiskey; he tended to kill people after that. And a woman named Jane Kirkham who took to robbing stagecoaches, who, legend had it, was shot and killed by the local sheriff, her husband. The latter was so embarrassed by his spouse's lawlessness that he buried her in an unmarked grave.

The One and True Son

As the kid talked Maggie looked for signs of life in the dry landscape whooshing by her window. There were frightfully few trees and none of them deciduous. There was no green. Only brown sticks, rocks and dust.

"There it is," the kid called from the front seat.

"All I see is a gate," Maggie said, suddenly needing a glass of water.

"That's all anybody gets to see from the road," Matt Hart said. "You get to see the whole enchilada. Not many people get to."

Maggie breathed out. "Lucky me."

Matt hopped out of the truck at the front entrance portico and grabbed Maggie's bag from the bed of the truck. A tall man, probably 6 foot 6, stood just outside the glass doors of the visitor's entrance. *No suit.* Maggie thought. He wore unfaded jeans and a button-down sport shirt. He topped that off with a well fitted tweed jacket. The obligatory cowboy boots adorned his feet. At one time, the man must have had a formidable mop of blond curls, most of which had crept down the sides of his head abandoning a few soft bundles on top. *This couldn't be the warden.*

It could.

He approached Maggie. "Jim Russo. I'm the warden." He offered a big paw. "Glad you could come out and meet with me."

"It's my pleasure, Mr. Russo." She felt a pang, as if she might be lying.

"Please, call me Jim. Everybody calls me Warden or Mr. Russo. It's kinda stiff, you know?"

"Call me Maggie," Maggie said. He was the first thing she liked about this place.

"Let me show you around," Jim offered as he opened the door and grabbed Maggie's bag.

The warden gave Maggie the deluxe 50 cent tour, explaining about the windows and the extreme conditions the inmates were subject to. After that he took her to his office.

The warden's office was one might expect from a lawman in Colorado with lithographs of cowboys on the range and rather expensive looking porcelain figurines of horses in various poses of rebellion. The most impressive figure, a dark brown stallion about a foot and a half tall, stood reared up under a large glass case, its eyes wide in fury and fear, its teeth, white and sharp.

"You like horses." Maggie observed.

"Love 'em." Jim responded. "I started riding when I was six years old."

"So, you're a local?"

"No, I'm from Maryland actually. Baltimore County. Right outside of Baltimore City."

The One and True Son

"I didn't know they had horses in Baltimore."

"Like I said," Jim said. "Right outside. The city and the county are totally different."

They went silent for a moment.

"So, what did you think of the tour? Is this someplace you could work?" Jim asked.

"This is the interview?" Maggie asked. "Don't you want to ask me any questions?"

The warden smiled. "I just did."

Maggie shook her head. "No. About me. About my experience."

"I know all about that," Jim said. "I have some buddies in DC and they told me all I need to know. You're the best most of them have ever seen. They said, 'What you see is what you get.' That's what I want."

"This is a very important position," Maggie said, doubtfully. "There has to be more to the hiring process than a walk around the facilities and a look at your horse collection."

"Trust me. There is," the warden answered. "I've run background checks through five different agencies. They don't make 'em as clean as you are. But just the fact that you're questioning me, shows me my instincts are right. I need someone who's going to call me out when she thinks I'm wrong. The inmates here are considered the scum of the earth by most people. But they are *still* people. And every once is a while the system makes a mistake. I need a second opinion that's real, not what someone thinks I want to hear."

The warden smiled. "Do you want the job or not? I'll get you a horse for your office."

Jim Russo never did buy her a horse figurine. It was the only thing on which he'd ever let her down.

Were they letting each other down now?

"I'M SORRY, JESSIE!"

The scream came from the viewing theater. Sylvio De Graca plastered himself against the thick viewing glass. Two guards rushed and in tried to subdue the lawyer, but he tossed them off like stuffed dolls.

"I'M SORRY I FAILED YOU!" Sylvio bellowed. "I KNOW WHO YOU ARE! YOU ARE THE SON OF YAHWEH! YOU ARE THE ONE! I'LL TELL THEM! I'LL ASSEMBLE THE TWELVE! THE WORLD WILL KNOW WHO YOU ARE!"

The guards, men used to physically managing the unruly, lay on the floor for a moment, stunned. By the time they'd gotten themselves

The One and True Son

together, the lawyer looked deflated. Torrents of tears burst from his eyes. He turned to the guards who stood, unmoving.

"I'm sorry," the lawyer nearly whispered. "You won't hear any more from me today." He sat quietly and stared at the window. The two guards looked to the warden through the glass. The warden made a stand down motion with his hands. The guards retreated to the back of the room.

All eyes were now on the warden, a position Maggie knew he never wanted to be in. That was what he meant when he said he wasn't free of this. Maggie scrambled out the security room door and ran, full tilt, to the viewing theater. She *was* letting Jim down. He needed her to be there. She nodded to the guards outside and they let her in.

The look on Jim's face told her she was right. The creases at the corners of his eyes eased. He didn't smile. There was nothing to smile about. He nodded just slightly. She returned the gesture.

Jim Russo cleared his throat. "Jessie Carpentero. Today, sentence will be imposed on you by legal statute of the Federal Government after a lawful trial and subsequent legal hearings that have found you guilty of a capital offense under 18 U.S.C. 3596 (a) which provides for the sentence of death for the offenses for which you have been convicted. Do you have any last words you would like to say before sentence is performed on this day?"

Jessie looked to the glass. For a moment he looked to his lawyer, Sylvio De Graca. The pity in his eyes, the sadness for what the man was going through, was plain to most everyone in the room. He tilted his head as he gazed at the man broken by his situation. He closed his eyes slowly and reopened them. It seemed to be a conversation between just the two of them.

Jessie looked through the glass. His arms, strapped to supports, his bulging veins perfect for the day's activity, pierced in each arm, the tubes of death attached, ready to perform their task. The condemned man's eyes scanned the viewing theater, looking from face to face. Then, for a moment he appeared to look beyond the walls, beyond the razor wire and the arid mountains. He seemed to look to faces beyond the room, beyond the state, beyond the country, beyond the oceans. And finally, tears fill those dark eyes. Tears flowed over his cheeks, down his jumpsuit's chest, to splashing on the newly tiled floor. Later, those in the viewing area agreed that it seemed hours before he spoke.

"I love you all. Without exception. I love you all."

He closed his eyes.

Jim Russo moved to the back of the room.

The One and True Son

The female nurse moved to the left side of Jessie with a rolling stainless steel tray. She unzipped his jumpsuit down, nearly to his navel. Taking a razor she shaved three small areas, two on his upper chest and one on the lower on his abdomen. She opened three sticky patches and stuck one to each shaved area. She reached for three wires attached to the side of the death table and attached one wire to each patch. She lightly tugged on the wires ensuring good contact. With that, she withdrew to the back of the room and flipped the switch on what appeared to be an EKG machine. The machine showed a normal rhythm.

The male nurse moved forward with his own stainless-steel tray. On it were three large syringes with tags on them, one tag green, the second yellow and the final red. The doctor joined the nurse at his side and picked up the first syringe, the one with the green label. Gingerly, the doctor took the protective cap from the syringe's needle and squirted a quick stream into the air. He reached for the clear tubing in the IV and found an injection port midway down the tubing. He poked the two-inch needle into the small rubber cap and slowly pumped the barbiturate into the saline solution flowing through the tube.

Jessie Carpentero's eyelids fluttered. They didn't close. His body seemed to settle into the thick padding of the death table. His breathing slowed and deepened, rhythmically moving air in and out. The female nurse approached Carpentero. She took the stethoscope from around her neck and placed the ear tips in her ears. With her left hand she placed the flat surface of the bell on the Jessie's chest. She listened for about a minute, nodded to the doctor and returned to her place at the back of the room.

The doctor took the second syringe from the tray, the one with a yellow label. This was the pancuronium bromide, a paralyzing agent. The doctor repeated the procedure he'd used for the first injection, careful to clean the injection port with an alcohol swab before inserting the needle. He injected the entire contents of the syringe and withdrew the needle.

Jessie's rhythmic breathing halted. His complexion changed from a slightly malnourished brown to bluish purple. There were gasps in the viewing theater; a few turned their eyes.

Again, the female nurse approached the prisoner and listened to his chest. And again, with a nod, she signaled the doctor to continue.

The doctor picked up the syringe with the red label. This was the potassium chloride, a lifesaving salt, essential to the human body, but lethal if given in high doses, depolarizing the heart and sending it into a deadly arrhythmia.

The One and True Son

For the third time, the doctor cleaned the injection port and drove a two-inch needle into the cap. He emptied the syringe slowly. For the first time, a slight strain appeared on the old doctor's face, as if the liquid put up some resistance. After what seemed a long time, he withdrew the needle and backed away from the condemned man.

The rhythm on the EKG screen modulated frantically. Soon it turned to a line of rapid jagged saw teeth, hundreds, one after the other. After a few moments the teeth slowed to an irregular wiggle. Moments after that, it went flat.

Again, for the third time, the nurse approached the body of Jessie Carpentero. Her hand shook slightly as she placed the flat side of the stethoscope bell on his chest. The nurse moved the stethoscope to the prisoner's side and listened. After a few minutes she withdrew the listening instrument and backed away from the body. She nodded to the doctor.

The viewing theater sat in silence. The guards in the death chamber and viewing theater all looked to the body laid flat on the padded table. The straps slackened. Jim Russo watched the body too, standing near the door, his face blank. The doctor, the nurses, all stood motionless.

Jessie Carpentero breathed no more.

And then he spoke. The chest did not move. The eyes which had remained open since the first injection stared at the ceiling. His mouth opened and he spoke.

"Forgive them, Father," his breathless mouth uttered. "I'm coming to you."

And then there was a sound. Anyone who's had a mosquito hovering outside their ear would know this sound. It's a weak, hungry sound, relentless and distracting. A few members of the audience massaged a canal of one ear or the other with a fingertip.

The sound grew stronger. High pitched and painful; a pain that dug at the lower jaw, the sinus cavities, the teeth.

And the sound grew. Its pitch strengthened, refined, tightened in oscillation. Unheard, painful screams filled both the viewing and the death chambers. Everyone, the powerful and the anonymous fell to the concrete floor. Once there, prone or supine they felt the very ground beneath them shiver. The electricity went out.

And then they saw the light. It emanated from the walls, the floors, the body on the table. The thick glass separating the two rooms glowed greenish white, a nonconductor overloaded. Cracks formed in the corners of the chambers. The air filled with the dust of pulverized cement and iron.

In the foyer a member of the prison staff watched through the large lobby glass as clouds, dark and threatening, formed in a dry clear sky, quickly, removing the sunlight from the area around the prison. The staff stood, silent. The ground rattled under their feet.

And then, it was finished. Everything stopped. The clouds broke and cleared as fast as they'd formed. Alarms sounded throughout the building. No one moved.

Back in the viewing theater Maggie Smith stirred on the floor. She ran her hand along the side of her face and found blood there. She looked around her. Everyone was bleeding from their ears, some from their noses. Maggie knew where she had to go. She tried to stand but was slapped back to the ground with vertigo.

And so she crawled. She crawled to the lawyer who lay flat on his back, his blood running into the hair on the back of his head. When she could reach him, she grabbed for his arm and shook it.

"Sylvio," she cried. "Can you hear me?"

The lawyer stirred. With a great effort, he rolled to his side.

"Sylvio," she cried again. "Sylvio, I know."

The lawyer reached over and wiped the blood off her cheek. And then the tear.

The End